NUWORLD:

CLAIMING TARA

book 1

Laurie Fitzgerald

NUWORLD: Claiming Tara, book 1

ISBN: 978-0989987707
Cover by Fantasia Frog Design

Electronic Book Publication August 2013
Trade Paperback Publication 2013

For questions or comments about the quality of this book, or to contact the author directly please send an e-mail to nuworldwriter@aol.com.

Nuworld: Claiming Tara is a work of fiction. Names, characters, places and incidents are products of the author's imagination. Any resemblance to actual events, locales, or persons, living or dead, is entirely coincidental.

To my mother, who believed in this book from the beginning. She listened to me brain-storm, rant, whine and cry through all the trials and tribulations of re-writes, edits, and the decision to self-publish. She was also the first to teach me about Crator. I love you, Mom.

FOREWARD

THERE ARE SO MANY WORDS...

WHILE WRITING *Nuworld: Claiming Tara*, which takes place on our planet roughly 900 years in the future, it crossed my mind that their language would be different. Words change over time. 900 years ago people spoke a lot differently than we do now. Even in our lifetime we have seen changes in our language. I know I'm always trying to keep up with new expressions and slang that my boys use. It only makes sense that in the future people will speak differently than we do now.

I decided—and you're very welcome for this—not to create a new language for my characters to speak. It was continually on my mind, however, that living so far into our future; the characters in *Nuworld: Claiming Tara* would very likely be impossible for us to understand. I wanted this to be on your mind when you read this story, as it was on mine.

My son, Jonathan, helped me research. We also used our imagination, which means we made words up. For the sake of making this a good read, or at least I hope you will think it is, many words in this book are the same as those we use today. However, to help give the feel of a different society, others are not.

I've included a glossary, which follows this foreward.

THERE IS SOMETHING YOU NEED TO KNOW...

I ORIGINALLY wrote this book twenty years ago. I escaped into this world, into the future with these characters, and wrote the entire series in a couple of years.

There are nine books, however only six are published. I originally published them as Lorie O'Clare. If you're curious, or wish to compare the old with the new, *Nuworld: Claiming Tara* was previously published as *Nuworld: The Saga Begins*. You might be able to find some copies on eBay, or I'm sure someone is selling downloads of it on Amazon. I decided to change the title and publish these books as Laurie Fitzgerald when I began making so many changes in the story.

AND FINALLY, FROM THE FUTURE IN THE FUTURE...

THERE ARE so many side notes involved with this series: notes going into further details in certain scenes, autobiographies of many of the characters, and writings from a few of the characters. If these books reach any level of success, or if you simply ask nicely, I might publish some of them on my website for you to read.

I am going to share a short piece of Lord Andru's writing, even though by the end of this book he is only three. I think it makes for the perfect **INTRODUCTION** into this book. He wrote it approximately forty winters after *Nuworld: Claiming Tara*.

I invite you to visit my website at www.lauriefitzgerald.net. Join my newsletter, befriend me on facebook, or simply send an e-mail and let me know what you think of this book. I'd love to hear your thoughts.

Laurie

GLOSSARY:

Activate – Sign on/log on to a computer.

Age Of Searching – this is a Runner tradition. Young Runners between 18 and usually no older than 23 leave their clan and travel (almost always alone) to learn more about Nuworld and experience different cultures. They return to their clan afterward and are considered an adult.

Bangstick – Looks very similar to our rifles or a large pistol. They vary in size and use bullets.

Beam – Flashlight.

Caller – a telephone. It's a Gothman term. A caller is attached to the wall and has a receiver (mouth and ear piece) that lifts off the box so a person can speak to someone else at a different location. Visualize a wall house phone from the 1970's. It buzzes to announce a call.

Claim/Claimed – a Gothman term. A claim is a spouse, either man or woman. Claimed means a person is married.

Clicker – same thing as a computer mouse, although embedded into a landlink the way a mouse would be on a laptop.

Cold box – refrigerator.

Comm – a Runner communication device. It is a thin wire that wraps around the ear and comes down to the mouth. The person using it taps the mouth piece and speaks at the receiving end hears a beep letting them know someone wishes to speak with them.

Crator – An entity that Neurians believe created Nuworld and everything that lives on it. He is their God and becomes the Runner and Gothman God as well.

Cycle – one month. (Half-cycle is two weeks and a quarter-cycle is one week.)

Day-afters – a hangover.

Eating Knife – similar to a metal skewer but thicker. Not quite as wide as a knife. Runners and Gothman only use this one eating utensil.

Eliminator – Runner weapon. It is best to hold it from the shoulder. It can take out the side of a large building or quite a few people at once.

Evening Of Settling – A Runner tradition. When a Runner clan quits travelling and settles in for a period of time they have a celebration. It's held the first night and there is a lot of food and alcohol.

Funerals – Gothman bury their dead. Runners burn their dead because clans are nomadic and they don't own land.

Guardian – Began as a Neurian belief that people who turned into animals travelled around Nuworld and kept an eye out to make sure Crator's people were always safe. The Dog Woman is a guardian. Most can't see Guardians. Tara can see the Dog Woman, who appears to Tara and advises her.

Groundmobile – a car. (Looks like an old Jeep.) Runner women drive them when they are pregnant and can no longer ride their motorcycles, or when hauling babies or children. They are also used to haul supplies. Claimed Gothman women seldom drive and most don't know how. A widowed claim or older unclaimed Gothman woman might learn to drive one if she doesn't have anyone to do it for her.

Groundmobile covered with artillery – looks like a tank.

Headscarf – Runners wear these over their heads to protect their head in battle. Pulls over head with openings for eyes, nose and mouth. They are made of the same black material that Runner clothing is made—bullet proof material that would appear to us as something between silk and leather.

Image – a picture, whether hanging on a wall or seen on a landlink screen.

Landlink – Runner computers that Gothman incorporate into their society.

Merchant's Lane – Gothman term. An alley, usually between two buildings.

Network – same thing as our World Wide Web/Internet

Oldworld – the civilization that existed before Nuworld. (This would be our civilization.) An Oldworlder is a derogatory term, which would be the same as us calling someone a barbarian.

Open room – a porch attached to either the front, back or side of a house.

Sound Transmitters – speakers/microphone

Test Of Wills – A Runner tradition. Instigated when a Runner leader dies and has no heir. Runners enter a competition. They must pass a written test of their history. The second stage is simple elimination fighting in a ring. All clans may participate and watch the fights.

Transmission – e-mail.

Viewers – binoculars.

Walkntalk – very much like a walkie talkie. Gothman used them in their military prior to Runners introducing the comm into Gothman society.

Watermobile – a boat, barge or anything that moves over the water. It is a generic term. There are different types of watermobiles.

Warrior's death – an honor given to a Runner or Gothman who died in battle. In Gothman, the claim of a warrior given this honor has higher rank.

Winter – one year

INTRODUCTION:

(Taken from the writings of Lord Andru, son of Lord Darius, roughly forty-four winters after the events in this story take place.)

AS GUIDED by Crator, and with aid from the Dog Woman, in spite of her riddles, I will share the history of Nuworld as I have come to understand it. I am the tenth Lord of Gothman and share this information, not because I wish to document my heritage, but because it is important that we see that what has happened before it is proclaimed to happen again. As I understand Crator, He has given me the power to change it, and to break the cycle.

Oldworld ended with Greene Day, right before the new winter of 2082. I quote from the Books of Crator.

"And Greene, not a color, nor a time before winter, but a man, brought the world to an end." Books of Crator, Story 15.

The sixteenth through twenty-fifth Stories in the Books of Crator tell us how war broke out among nations in Oldworld and destroyed their planet. Although misguided by greed and power, there were intelligent leaders during those days. They saw the insanity festering among other leaders and prepared for it. The Books of Crator say the warriors of Oldworld were very powerful, but they weren't able to stop a bomb so great that it destroyed the entire planet. During Oldworld time the planet was called earth. Since Oldworlders destroyed that planet it is fitting that today the planet is called Nuworld.

Crator makes it clear in the thirtieth Story, *"And before two thousand one hundred winters shall pass, men, women, children and all that they own, shall move to live in the levels of cities beneath the ground."*

We know from our documented history that this did happen. All that Crator says in His great stories came true. I'm aware that our teachers again argue as to whether these stories were written before, or after Greene Day. I know of the argument that the Books of Crator wouldn't have survived the devastation of our planet so long ago. But I stress, this does not matter.

Our descendents rose up from where they'd lived for hundreds of winters beneath Nuworld and established our nations that we know today. This is a very important line from His stories.

"*It was then that man rose from the ground. As he did before so shall he do again.*" Books of Crator, Story 43.

If we are not careful, once again insanity will erupt on Nuworld. I take credit for making Nuworld greater than it ever was during the winters of Oldworld. I know, however, that I am not perfect. We stand strong with the Runners ready to fight by our side. Crator has blessed us. We are very powerful warriors. It is therefore my wish, and what I hope to pass on to my son when he becomes Lord, that we never allow this insanity to return, fester and destroy us. No man or woman will ever be permitted to develop a weapon so powerful that it would destroy all that Nuworld is today.

So it is decreed: *Andru Bryton, Lord of Gothman*

CHAPTER ONE

TARA CURSED her foolishness. Patha had warned her about taking the Gothman for granted. When would she ever learn?

The flat plains gave way to more jagged hills, and she knew without a doubt that she was surrounded. She saw no one, but they were there, keeping their distance. The Gothman—the other warrior race on Nuworld—hid themselves well. But her skills were better. Much better.

Tara took a deep breath and reflected on the information she'd recently learned. The plains, known as the Freelands, lay behind her now. And good riddance. Although the land there thrived and the wildlife plentiful, the people were boring.

Bred from the feared and respected warrior race known as the Runners, she struggled in understanding the Freelanders. Tara knew from the stories told by her people that Freelanders welcomed her people more than other races. But that didn't mean she felt comfortable around them. She had a hard time understanding a race who worked their land and made no effort to develop a military. Their weapons were primitive and used mainly to hunt.

"What are they going to use? A gardening tool to defend themselves?" she mumbled.

Tara grinned but the smile faded as she assessed her surroundings. This is what she loved about the *Age of Searching*. It was the time in her life she would have to explore different people, learn about them, and learn from them. The Freelanders were definitely too dull for her liking.

Since growing out of adolescence and arriving at the *Age of Searching*, Tara had begun to crave knowledge of the world, as did all Runners. The stories told by clan elders around the fires about other races no longer satisfied her; she needed to see these people and their lands for herself.

Until reaching the *Age Of Searching*, Tara traveled with her clan, moving according to the seasons, learning the skills of the warrior, and racing on her motorcycle with other teenagers. She'd helped to care for the younger Runners, cooked for Patha, who had raised her since she was a small child, and cleaned their trailer. Once that life had been enough, but now it wasn't.

Of all the stories told around the fires, Patha's stories of the Gothman intrigued her the most. Runners and Gothman had a hatred for each other that transcended the winters. She had asked why over and over again, but no answer ever satisfied her. For many winters she'd thought about the causes. The only reason she could see for Runners and Gothman despising one another was that each race thought the other inferior.

Tara meant to find out for herself which race was correct.

After traveling this far, Tara now had the perfect opportunity to see what kind of warriors the Gothman actually were. Of course entering Gothman wasn't what most Runners would view as an opportunity. *More like a suicide journey.*

She shivered as adrenaline kicked in. Chills started down her spine and spread. Hills grew larger around her. The rugged countryside was a sure indication she had entered Gothman territory. She ran her fingers over smooth metal. Her laser rested, secure, on her belt. Tara hoped her plan would work and not end up instigating her demise.

She navigated her motorcycle around protruding rocks half-buried in the ground, keeping most of her attention on the surrounding area. What was up until now a leisurely jaunt suddenly became much more than a drive through a new country—it became a strategy course unlike any she'd driven as a teenager learning to be a warrior.

An explosion vibrated the air. Tara nearly crashed her motorcycle into a tree.

"Ahhh!" Tara, daughter and heir to the leader of the Blood Circle Clan, didn't scream because something exploded!

She'd heard stories about the weapon that exploded when shot, leaving a foul smell in the air, but she'd always thought them fictional. But now...now she realized it was true. It was actually true. Tara's heart pounded in her chest. She'd just heard her first bang stick.

"Stay focused, warrior," she whispered under her breath. "Don't get distracted."

Another shot flew through the air, and a large branch crashed to the ground.

She screamed again and leaned closer to the body of her cycle.

Where were the Gothman? Behind the rocks? Somewhere in the approaching forest? How far could they shoot?

Primitive or not, these Gothman weapons can do damage.

Tara licked her dry lips. She'd looked forward to meeting the Gothman, but she hadn't expected to encounter them this soon, or under such deadly conditions.

She drove into the cool, sweet-smelling forest, and stopped her bike once the woods surrounded her. After hiding her motorcycle between two giant boulders, and confident it wouldn't be found, Tara pulled her landlink off the handlebars and slipped it in her pocket. The Gothman would find great pride in retrieving a Runner's bike. No other race in the world had achieved the level of technology her machine represented.

As she searched her surroundings, some of the stories of the Gothman she'd heard around the fires came to mind. Gothman only taught their men to fight. Gothman women weren't educated.

"It's a waste!" she muttered under her breath. "Imagine! Half of a race needing protection!" It made no sense. Runner men and women were taught the same skills. Gender had nothing to do with what a person might excel at doing.

More bang sticks created explosions all around her. Tara broke into a run.

"You men want to play with this woman? Then come get me!" She moved easily over rocks and around trees, adrenaline flowing from the thrill of being the hunted.

Two Gothman approached on foot, moving stealthily from protruding rocks to a large tree. Tara stopped walking, her breathing loud in her ears. They were a fair distance away but also stopped walking. She'd been spotted.

As she squatted, one of the men raised a long brown, thick stick to his shoulder. It was a slightly darker shade than the brown leather pants and jackets both men wore. Even at this distance it was easy to see how large both men were. They would be formidable opponents in hand to hand combat, something she hoped not to put to the test.

Slowly, Tara pressed herself against the forest floor. Stretching out, she gripped her laser and brought it forward, taking aim.

This time, when the bang stick exploded, she didn't scream. A large branch cracked overhead. She rolled to the side, banging up another trunk just as the branch fell to the ground. It made a loud thudding sound and sticky needles sprayed toward her. If she hadn't laid down they would have hit her.

She smelled the explosives and her heart raced as she watched part of the tree next to her disappear as another shot fired. Tara aimed her laser and pressed the trigger. She shot once, twice. Two Gothman fell dead on the forest ground.

Not waiting for their friends to discover her location, Tara ran through a cluster of pines as fast as the dense foliage would allow. She then slid to a stop—and stared face to face with the largest, and most definitely, ugliest man she'd ever seen. If it weren't for the smell of the brown leather covering most of him, his body odor would have been unbearable.

"Runner," the grotesque man grunted. His face was covered with scars, one of them causing his lip to curl unnaturally.

"Gothman," she replied, kept her laser at her side and fired. Then barely managed to leap to the side to avoid the giant of a man from tumbling forward on top of her.

Within minutes she'd eliminated three more Gothman. Patha was right; these people loved to fight but hadn't mastered the art of being true warriors. They were loud and easy to spot. They fired without having true aim and their weapons' explosions and putrid odor gave their location away every time.

She slowed to a trot and listened as the breeze carried the scent of the pines through the air. Trees stood far enough apart to allow wide sunbeams to graze the ground. Grass and patches of moss glowed an emerald green, offering a bright contrast against the patches of sky. It was a deep blue, indication that the sun would set soon. With twilight, the long shadows would make it more difficult to spot a person hiding, especially one clothed the color of tree trunks. The stories said Gothman warriors always wore brown.

Tara studied every bush, tree, and rock. She stopped at each sound, wondering if more Gothman waited to attack. The Gothman had successfully controlled these lands for hundreds of winters. She found it hard to believe there weren't more lying in wait for her. Did they think a woman might do no harm?

She continued walking at a slow pace, getting her bearings by studying the sun shining through the trees. The silence grew eerie in its stillness. Tara sensed something was very wrong.

Her skin prickled. They were watching her. Why didn't they try and kill her? Instinct told her to run. Run like hell. Return to her motorcycle and safety. But those same senses also urged her to go on. After all, the Gothman had seen and fired at her, yet now kept their distance. She'd even taken out a handful of their men, yet they didn't retaliate.

What were they waiting for her to do?

The smell of the pine invaded her senses, telling her she was now deep in Gothman territory. Her chances of walking into another ambush were growing higher. The Gothman people were said to be well protected by rocky hills and thick pine forests.

Tara used the rocks to her advantage as natural shields and held her laser as she scanned for life-signs. The Gothman controlled large amounts of land. They certainly couldn't do so if it weren't well guarded.

The smell of wood burning caught her attention.

She started through the pines looking for its source.

A small wooden house with a stone foundation appeared through the trees.

"I don't believe it. It really does exist." Tara stopped and stared at the house, which was permanently attached to the ground.

Before her stood the small, wooden house Patha had described over and over again when he talked about Gothman. Patha was known for embellishing on many of his stories. She'd heard them numerous times, and noted the changes as he shared past adventures with any new Runner visiting their clan. But he'd always described this hidden, tidy looking home just as she saw it now.

Tara approached cautiously, making sure to stay hidden by the trees until she was sure of its occupants. Light flowery, faded curtains were closed on the inside of glass windows, preventing Tara from seeing inside. Voices trailed through the night air, and the front door of the house opened. She moved nimbly through the natural camouflage until she was able to see inside the house.

"It will go well for you to notify us immediately if you notice anyone." The deep grumbling man's voice broke through the still night air.

While the Gothman accent had been mimicked for Tara before, it still sounded strange hearing it for the first time.

"Of course, I'll call immediately if there be any disturbances. I daresay you're too kind to protect an old lady."

Tara watched two large men leave the small home and move toward motorcycles. A petite woman stepped outside her door and stood on the open room of the house and wrapped a knit shawl tightly around her shoulders. The tilted roof of the open room extended from the secluded house and wooden posts supported it. A swing, wide enough for two to sit on it, hung on chains from the open room's ceiling and to the side of the woman. She didn't move toward it but remained planted where she was, holding her shawl tightly around her as she watched the men leave.

"Tell his Lord that I'll be sure to have a warm pie to his house in time for lunch. I look forward to seeing his mama. Is she well?" the woman called after the men.

The two men grunted in answer and started they're noisy bikes. They took off down a gravel road, raising dust into the night air.

Tara studied the woman who remained on the open room watching the Gothman warriors until the sound of their motorcycles was barely audible. She continued to stand there, glancing up at the sky, apparently surveying the first of the stars as twilight faded to darkness.

The woman tightened her grip on her shawl and finally looked toward the trees where Tara remained hidden. "You can come out now. I'm a simple woman and I'm no threat to you. I know about Runners, and you didn't come to my house by accident, so come out and allow me to be hospitable."

Tara didn't move.

Patha had talked about the Gothman woman, Reena, many times. This lady definitely fit the description. She was a small woman, petite but in nice proportion. Dark gray hair was twisted around her head in a wide bun. Her skin didn't look wrinkled although laugh lines created creases by her eyes and mouth. The lone light hanging from the open room roof accented the rest of the woman's features with graceful shadows.

Tara needed to be cautious. She could defend herself if this woman tried calling the Gothman warriors back, but there was no way of knowing if there were more in the house. The Gothman had any number of places to hide their motorcycles in the surrounding trees.

The old woman must have read her mind. "Now, I know you're there, Runner. I can smell your leather. I know you're armed, and I daresay I don't have a gun. I don't feel like going back into my house, wondering who is outside watching me. That much is certain. So, come out now!" she ended, her voice shrill.

She had thought her Runner attire would aid in hiding her, but the old lady's comment made her rethink that decision. Tara glanced down at her clothing. The thick leather protected her skin in battle. The black Runner material, known throughout Nuworld as being virtually bulletproof, was woven with a thread made from crushed glass. Her boots laced to her knees and thin black gloves fit like a second skin, adding to the practicality of clothes worn by all Runners. Ridding herself of her Runner clothing would be smart. Maybe the old lady would prove useful.

Tara moved out of the trees and toward the open room. She didn't watch the woman, but instead focused beyond her through the open door, looking for movement. She needed to make sure she wasn't walking into a trap.

"Well now, there you are. That black leather hides you well in the shadows. Come on in. I promise I'm quite alone. So tell me your stories. How do you know of me?" The old woman spoke without taking a single breath even as she turned and walked back in to her home.

Tara followed her.

Reena stepped to the side, allowing Tara to see the inside of the home before she shut the door behind them. The kitchen was merely a wall along the side of a small living room. She put a tall thin pot on the stove and lit a match to start the fire underneath it. A pie was produced out of a cold box and the old woman pulled a plate out of the freestanding cupboard. Reena placed a large slice of the pie on it.

"It's apple. I reckon I'll make another one in the morning for the Lord's family. It helps to show my loyalty, you know. Lord Darius knows I've entertained Runners before, but I like to keep peace in the family, so to speak." She placed her hand over the pot, then reached for a rag hanging on the cold box and removed the container from the stove. "Do you like your coffee hot?"

"That'll be fine. Thank you." Tara couldn't believe it. The woman had coffee. That was a coveted treat. The plants making the rare drink didn't grow in their nation and were only obtained with very good connections. How would an old Gothman woman have such connections?

Reena picked up a wooden knitting needle and gathered together a project she'd obviously been working on for some time. It looked like a sweater. Tara wondered at the patience required to take on such a task.

Crow's feet appeared next to the old lady's eyes as she smiled, then used one of the knitting needles to point to a lumpy couch with a multi-colored quilt thrown over the back of it. "Sit. I'll be curious to see how you plan on eating that pie with your Runner headscarf over your face, and I'll be mighty offended if you refuse my food. My pies are known throughout Gothman and if you travelled through the trees with the usual Gothman hospitality to greet you, I daresay you should be hungry."

Tara pulled the black scarf from her face and stroked the red circle around the embroidered red drop of blood—the symbol of the Blood Circle Clan, to which she proudly belonged. Although she missed her clan, if she lived through her adventure in Gothman she would have the best stories to tell around the fires. Tara folded and set the headsgroundmobilef on the couch next to her.

She placed the mug of coffee on the wooden table in front of the couch and eagerly tasted the sweet dessert. It was as good as promised.

"I'm thinking if the Gothman guards knew they were chasing such a beautiful wench as you, they'd have fought a bit harder to capture you."

The woman's laugh made it hard not to smile.

If a person was judged by their home, then Reena was a warm, caring person with patience and a solid foundation in her culture. The small wooden house permanently attached to the ground offered several different aromas that Tara easily distinguished.

The wooden walls and floors smelled of the spicy scent of the forest. The pungent smell of brewed coffee mixed with the sweet bouquet of baked apples. Other aromas floated through the air as well, not as easily defined—the pungent tang of spices and herbs used either for cooking or medicinal purposes, and a sterile smell, possibly soap used for laundry or bathing also hung in the air.

There were a variety of handcrafted items in addition to the faded patchwork quilt on the sofa: a knitted blanket hung over the back of the rocker where Reena sat, and several stitched wall hangings framed the walls. These items offered pieces of a story about the woman sitting across from her, smiling peacefully and glancing at her occasionally with gentle blue eyes.

Reena tried hard not to stare at the beautiful young woman sitting on her couch. Tara's light brown hair fell past her shoulders and was as supple and shiny as silk. Her complexion was fair. That Runner garb would prevent her from being tanned by the sun. Her skin was smooth, at least what Reena could see of it, with no battle scars, which was a relief to see. The girl's sapphire eyes took in everything around her. They glowed with intelligence and a bit too much cockiness for her own good.

Not that she should be surprised, Reena thought with silent resignation. It was what got Tara this far, and was what would keep her going. She'd waited so impatiently, knowing Tara was on the *Age of Searching* and would eventually show up. But now that she was here, all Reena wanted to do was insist Tara remain with her and not go further into Gothman. That wouldn't work though. Tara would continue her adventure and nothing Reena would say or do would change that. She knew Runners all too well. If only that glow would stay there, these next few cycles might be tolerable for all of them.

"My goodness, you're so beautiful. The men of these parts won't be leaving you alone. Now you know Gothman women don't know the skills you've learned. It will be hard shielding yourself. And a Runner found inside Gothman will be killed."

"So I've heard."

Reena had to try, although Tara's unconcerned answer wasn't surprising. "Well now, that's good then. What's your name, and whose stories bring you here?"

"I'm Tara of the Blood Circle Clan."

"Ah, Patha's stories sent you here." Reena nodded and started to rock in her chair. It wasn't as if she had doubted who this Runner was, but now she knew for sure. She would never have the skills of a Runner woman. But it was her own adventures and stories that kept her calm and quiet at the moment. Those were the skills Reena had mastered over the winters, wearing a mask indifference. "I'm Reena and you may call me that. Now, are you Patha's daughter?"

"I gained that honor at the age of four, but not by birth." Tara chewed as she spoke. "I'm on the *Age of Searching* and have heard the stories about you. Those stories also told me that Gothman don't like women."

Reena laughed, but then worried she'd insulted Tara. It was hard not to get up and move closer to this young Runner.

"Gothman like their women just fine," she said, and smiled when Tara looked confused. "They like them in the kitchen and in the bedroom. An unclaimed woman such as you will be plenty liked in Gothman."

Reena stopped laughing and asked what she needed to know. "So, Tara of the Blood Circle Clan and daughter of the leader of all Runners, I would think you've come here with your head full of stories of Gothman. I know a Runner doesn't enter new land without a plan. So let's hear it."

"I—"

"You're an excellent warrior," Reena continued on. "You got past the men protecting Gothman's borders. But if you display your skills you'll be put in jail. Gothman women don't fight. You're young and unclaimed. I daresay you'll be raped until you're claimed. Although as pretty as you are, I bet you're claimed the first day you're in Gothman."

"I've been attacked before. Don't worry about me. No one is going to rape me. I promise. I know how to handle myself." Tara gestured with her fork. "Possibly you have some clothing I could borrow. If I could mingle among the Gothman, I'd learn so much."

"I'm sure your skills are outstanding, but ten men against one woman aren't good odds…even if that woman is a Runner."

"I thought—" Tara began.

Reena shook her head but already saw the inevitable happening. Why Patha hadn't put a stop to this, Reena had no clue. She might not be able to change Tara's mind, but she would protect her the best she could. "I might be able to find some clothes that will fit you. You're small, like me."

"Would you be willing—" Tara's rush of words were cut off once more.

"I daresay in my youth I had much of your beauty. We can't hide yours. The more you change to fit in to our culture, the more trouble you'll bring on yourself."

"I would never cause trouble." Tara's expression brightened. "I will dress plain. I won't bring trouble to you, or to me. All I want is to walk the streets of Gothman. There are many great stories about your people, Reena. I want to witness for myself a culture so different from mine. Will you help me?"

Reena's warnings had been ignored. She also saw if she didn't agree, Tara would find another way into Gothman. Reena didn't like it. But if she helped Tara at least she would know where she was. "Yes, I will help you," Reena relented. Patha had sent Tara to her. There was no way she would let Tara out of her home without knowing her better first. "I've known a Runner or two in my day. You want to know about us, and if I don't help you I'm sure you'll resort to another plan,. You'll stay the night here. I'm sure Lord Darius' men will be keeping an eye on the woods for a Runner through the rest of the night."

Tara watched the old lady get up from her rocking chair and open a door leading to a bedroom. Tara didn't move, but listened as the woman continued to talk to her about Gothman. From what Patha had told her about these people, Tara wondered why Reena didn't have a man around. Gothman women didn't have a say over who claimed them.

"I'm sure I've an extra nightgown for you. We need to get you out of those Runner clothes immediately. I've many visitors and to be certain we'll have to come up with a story to explain your presence. The women around here use me for a midwife and the Gothman like to reproduce. I stay quite busy." Reena retreated down a hall and into a dark room, her voice trailing off as she moved.

"Let's see." She returned a minute later holding up a long paisley nightgown with white ruffles around the collar. "This is modest enough, and I think it might fit. I'm thinking I'll have to wash some clothes for you to wear during the day. Not to worry, I'll provide you with a decent wardrobe. Go change into this. We'll figure out the rest in the morning."

Tara took the nightgown to the bathroom and slowly disrobed. She felt as if she were shedding her Runner heritage as she changed. Along with her clothes she was leaving behind the ways of the Runner. So far on her *Age Of Searching*, when she came across a different culture they knew her as a Runner. People kept their distances. They knew and respected who she was. It wouldn't be that way in Gothman. Runners were shot on site here. From this point forward she would be a Gothman woman, outwardly void of any rights, passive and submissive. Somehow she had to pull off the role, or be killed.

Her thoughts drifted back to her first encounter with the Gothman in the forest. She hadn't planned on making such close contact with the brutal race so soon. They knew a Runner was here. It didn't make sense that she'd managed to get this far without more Gothman warriors looking for her. Considering the close range when they used the bang sticks, she should be wounded or captured, if not killed. Gothman warriors had to have better skills than what she saw on her way here. Someone knocked on Reena's door. Tara shoved her worries away, grabbed her laser, and hurried out of the bathroom.

CHAPTER TWO

TARA HURRIED down the hallway but then stopped in her tracks. What happened to being submissive? Here she was, ready to protect the old lady who had been so hospitable toward her by barging in to the living room with her laser. And giving herself away in the process.

Passive, she warned herself, *be passive*. Forcing herself to slow down, she tiptoed to the end of the hallway.

"Joli, my dear, you're not here for a social call at this hour…am I right?" There was sincere concern in Reena's tone.

From her post at the end of the hallway, Tara caught a glimpse of a very pregnant young woman standing in the middle of the living room, her gaze focused on the ground. She heard the thud of boots moving with slow determination, making floorboards creak. She pressed her body flat against the wall. She would rather observe than be seen at this point.

Someone else hurried into the small house. The pitter-patter of small feet sounded everywhere. A young boy, with strawberry-colored curls that bounced ridiculously around his face, almost ran into her.

Tara didn't move. Luckily the boy didn't look her way but paid attention to another person who'd entered Reena's cabin.

A booming male voice echoed off living room walls. "She's got the pain, Reena. And I daresay it's not her time yet."

Tara knew if she peeked around the corner, she would chance being seen. She gripped her laser in her hand. It was weird not having her Runner attire for added protection. In the flowing nightgown she was vulnerable, exposed. Although the evening air felt cool against her skin, small beads of perspiration formed between her breasts and down her spine.

"I know it isn't her time yet," Reena snapped, showing no fear of the burly man who stood almost twice her size. "Togin, you're wound tight. This is woman's work. Be gone with you. I'll call for you when I need you."

"I know you can help, Reena. She isn't taking it easy like you said."

A shadow spread across the carpet, and floorboards moved beneath a heavy burden. From the sounds, Tara guessed the man was moving toward the door.

"I'll be at the tavern in town when you need me. Some of Lord Darius' men are hovering down that way, I hear. Figured I'd see what's about in the town."

"Then I shall call for you there should I need you." Reena's tone gave no indication that warriors in town bothered her in the least.

The door closed soundly. Tara heard a loud sigh escape the young Gothman woman and the chattering questions of the small boy and another youngster. A girl. The tension in the room had disappeared with the hollow thud of the door.

"Likely you can't be taking it easy when he has you waiting on him hand and foot. Not to mention you've got the young ones to care for. My now, look how the three of you are growing." Reena's words sounded full of laughter.

Tara glanced around the corner and saw a teenage girl hovering over the pregnant woman.

Reena ran her fingers through the girl's pale red hair. "Most likely, you'll be getting claimed before you're much older as pretty as you're getting to be."

The young girl giggled and blushed.

"Reena, the pains are steady. I fear I've thrown myself into labor."

Joli looked down the hallway and spotted Tara. "Oh my goodness, you're already with someone. Togin should have noticed before he left."

"Nonsense. This is my niece, Tara. My brother sent her to me just today. One of the Barg brothers wants to claim her, and my brother will have no doings with the likes of them. He sent her to me to see if I could get her claimed here in Bryton." Reena gestured for Tara to come to her. "Help me get Joli into my bed, will you? I'll get my herbs to brewing. They should stop that child from coming before his time."

Tara and Reena walked Joli into a large bedroom, which was no small feat, given that Joli was close to full term and quite heavy. Tara literally carried her to the bed, taking as much weight onto her shoulders as she could. Reena never would have been able to handle the situation on her own. Tara welcomed the distraction of making sure Joli was comfortable, or as comfortable as possible.

Having a fair bit of birthing knowledge through the winters with the women in the clan, Tara noticed Joli's baby was low. Although Tara had never had a baby, she knew cramping was common when the baby was positioned in the womb to be born.

Tara remembered helping a clan member thrown into labor. Only a child at the time, Tara still remembered pounding Wild Yam root into powder to help soothe the pain. She watched Reena use the same root now.

"Joli dear, I save this bedroom for all my special ladies who visit me," Reena cooed as she pulled an old, but clean, blanket to the end of the bed once she was done with the roots.

Tara half placed, half dropped Joli onto the sheet. The woman struggled in her arms, making it hard to place her gently.

"Grab some more blankets from that shelf in the closet." Reena pointed to a closed door and Tara turned. "I'll put the kettle on to boil." The older woman scurried from the room.

"If we can get you to lie on your left side, it should stop some of the stomach discomfort," Tara said quietly, trying to match the dialect of the Gothman. She helped the woman but didn't think she looked too comfortable when Tara finally left her alone to find Reena.

Reena was digging through one of the cupboards when Tara entered the living room. She saw the three children standing awkwardly in the middle of the room, their large brown eyes showing fear and worry for their mama.

"Ah, not to worry, little ones." Tara knelt in front of the three children and reached her arms out to hug them. "We'll take good care of her now."

"I'm thinking you'll have to give up the back room tonight, my dear," Reena said to Tara. "Let's give the children some of my pie, and then we can put them down in the bed back there. We have a long night ahead of us, I fear."

After a quick check of her herbs on the stove, Reena set out plates on the counter and began slicing pie. "Seems more nights than not, my house will fill with family members. I get accustomed to having the bodies around. I daresay there's plenty of blankets."

Tara sat the three children around Reena's kitchen table and fed them each a slice of the pie she'd so recently enjoyed. The children eagerly took in the sweetness and had it gone in no time. Tara grabbed a cloth and started applying it to the fingers of the youngest before he could damage Reena's house. The boy, who couldn't be school-age, Tara decided, as she looked at his soft baby skin, immediately fought his restraints.

"My mama always sends me out to the water buckets," the boy complained.

Tara kept a firm grip on the sticky hand until all remnants of pie were gone. "It's dark outside."

"Being afraid of the dark is for women." The child stood in defiance and forgot to run when Tara released him.

She ruffled his curls, bringing him back to reality, and smiled at the older daughter who was clearing dishes.

"Reena?" Joli called out, then groaned.

The old lady patted Tara's shoulder as she passed on her way to Joli. Joli's grunts grew louder, and the children stared at the closed door.

"Let's check out the sleeping arrangement, shall we?" Tara herded the children toward the hallway.

"I want to say goodnight to my Mama." It was the first time the middle child, a skinny girl with a shapeless dress hanging on her bony figure, had spoken.

"As soon as your mama's cramping has eased, I'm sure she'll come gather the lot of you." Tara smiled at the child, who didn't smile back.

She nestled the three under thick quilts covering the bed. A small lamp on a tall narrow dresser provided the only light for the room and sent long shadows up the wall. Tara sat with them and hummed quietly. After a few minutes, it dawned on her that she hummed a Runner lullaby. The children stared glassy-eyed at the ceiling and didn't comment so she continued until she noticed eyelids bobbing.

"Does it hurt terribly to have a babe?" the oldest asked, continuing to stare at the ceiling.

"I've never had a baby, so I don't know," Tara whispered the half-truth, watching as the youngest curled into his sister and plugged his thumb into his mouth.

"When the claim to the man who lives next to us had her last baby, she screamed through the whole thing. Couldn't talk more than a whisper for almost a cycle after that. Her claim says he is gonna keep her with child just to keep her quiet." The brief tale was said without inflection, and Tara couldn't guess from the young girl's expression how she felt about such an atrocity. Tara wanted to tell her the brute should have his balls cut. "I should be with Mama."

"I'm thinking your Mama would appreciate you keeping an eye on your brother and sister for her. They will be frightened if they wake in a strange bed." Tara hoped she didn't exaggerate the Gothman accent, but the young girl seemed relaxed speaking with her, so she guessed she was speaking the inflection right.

Tara remained with the children until all three were asleep. She crept over the wooden floor into the kitchen. Reena's house was quiet and she didn't want to disturb the pregnant mama.

"You've a way with the young ones," Reena said as she stirred something over the stove. She reached beside her and picked up a bottle containing a green powder, then began sprinkling it into her concoction.

"I've had a fair bit of experience in that area." Tara thought of all the children who were often left in her charge when the clan travelled. More times than not, she had wanted part in the adventures of the adults, instead of playing with kids. But she wouldn't deny she had learned from the experience of babysitting.

"I daresay your knowing that will come in quite handy in these parts. As my niece, you're now officially my apprentice. Come here and sift the root from the brew."

It was a long night. Tara stared at the almost empty pot on the stove, thinking there was no way Joli could possibly consume more of the liquid. She knew if she helped Joli to the bathroom one more time, her muscles would be too sore to defend herself against Gothman warriors if the need arose.

Other than the sound of branches brushing the roof, it remained quiet. Later in the evening, however, Tara thought she heard something else. Someone was moving around outside the small wooden cottage. No one else in the house heard the boots crunching out front. Tara guessed the branches scraping the roof were loud enough to conceal any other sound outside, at least to an untrained ear. Tara knew what she heard, once even aware that someone stepped onto the open room. The squeaking of wooden floorboards gave away their position.

The curtains were drawn, and she had no light from outside to aid in seeing into the darkness. That put her at a disadvantage she didn't like. She knew whoever was outside would be able to see through the thin curtains and into the cottage. With two lamps in the living room and the overhead light burning in the kitchen, Tara was on display to anyone who cared to look. No one ever came to the door, though. Tara ached to go outside and investigate but knew Gothman women wouldn't do such a thing.

A short time later, Reena plopped down on the couch in the living room. "Well, the pains have stopped, and I am not afraid to say I don't know as I could have helped her without you." She smiled at Tara. "You were a smart one to stay out of sight when Togin was here."

Tara glanced again at the curtains that hid the window. She didn't hear anything else, and Reena didn't act as if she had heard sounds outside. It was pointless to say anything. Instead she watched Reena make hot tea and joined the older woman when she relaxed on her couch.

Reena continued her quiet musings. "I couldn't speak on this when his claim was still awake. She'd be loyal to him. He's one of Lord Darius' men, and I'm a thinking he slipped his wife some powder to bring the baby just so he might get another look in here."

Tara shook her head. Gothman women had less say than Tara had imagined, even over their bodies. She took in the information and but didn't know what to say.

Reena was thrilled Tara had made herself at home. She took her time with her tea, enjoying its warm rich taste and Tara's company nearby. But she was exhausted from the night and finally rose and moved into the kitchen to dump the tea leaves.

She watched Tara's sapphire eyes that took in everything around her without comment. Reena wondered if she'd looked that wise when she was Tara's age. She seriously doubted it.

"We'll do the dishes tomorrow. I'll call Togin and let him know he can fetch his family come morning."

In spite of being exhausted, Reena had a hard time falling asleep. Patha had always made good on his promises. He had said Tara would come to her. So much time had passed that she'd started to have doubts. She should have known better than to ever have doubted Patha.

In the quiet hours of the night, Reena fought the urge to get up and make sure Tara slept comfortably. Tara wasn't a child though. And Reena didn't want to wake the children. As a Runner, Tara would have spent countless nights sleeping in different locations. It sounded like a terrible life, always on the move. Not to mention, Runners were feared by everyone and tolerated more than accepted, anywhere they went. But Tara seemed happy. That was all that mattered. Reena had told herself that enough times over the winters to make it a mantra.

Her heart ached. Reena knew it wasn't from the bit of wild boar soup that she'd had earlier. Her life had been happy too. She had to admit. There were choices. Everyone had to make them. Reena had made the right one. In spite of the pain, she saw now it was true. The young woman sitting in her living room was beautiful, intelligent, and a warrior. She controlled her life and answered to no one. Tara was as powerful an heir to lead all the clans someday. It was more of a life than Reena would ever have been able to offer.

Tara had heard stories of Gothman communication devices and was curious to see one. She knew their use was limited—only one person could be heard at a time. Tara thought they must not be very reliable since she also knew the person speaking couldn't always be heard that well. She wanted Reena to call Togin now, just so she could watch it operate. It was obvious the old woman was worn out, though. Unfortunately, Tara had to wait until morning to learn more about these people.

As she struggled to remember what the devices were called, her eyes grew heavy. Maybe finally she would fall asleep.

Morning came sooner than Tara would have wished. The homemade blanket, which she had pulled over her sometime during the night, had kept her very warm. Tara inhaled the many smells from the cottage the blanket had absorbed, and experienced a strange sensation of peace fill her. The irony of it all brought a smile to her face and she stood and folded the blanket. She was in enemy land, being hunted. If discovered she'd be killed without question. Peace was the last thing she should be experiencing.

Tara entered the bathroom to shower and found a plain peach-colored dress hanging on a hook. The streaming hot water felt good after her long journey and late night. The soap Tara used didn't smell like Reena, and she wondered if the lady had put it in the bath just for her. She would have savoured the hot water longer, but knew the day would be full of adventures. It was time to experience them.

The dress fit surprisingly well. The thin material was light on Tara's skin. After a lifetime of wearing thick leather Runner clothing, she felt almost naked. She adjusted a matching belt, which accented her narrow waist and displayed her figure nicely. A pair of plain tan cloth shoes finished the picture. Looking in the mirror, Tara stared at her Gothman appearance.

"Tara-girl? Do ya know what you're getting yourself into?" she whispered, imitating how Patha would talk to her. Tara stared at her reflection and nodded. "I'll be careful, Patha," she told her reflection.

Tara adjusted a garter holster up her thigh. After tightening it so it wouldn't slip, she slid her laser into the holster. As long no one groped her, her weapon wouldn't be noticed. There was no way she was entering the heart of the enemy territory unarmed.

"All you have to do is keep those Gothman men from touching you and you might live through the day," she told her reflection. Twisting to see herself at all angles, she finally forced herself from the mirror. It would be smart to spend as much time as possible with the other Gothman in the house instead of alone in the bathroom. She needed to get used to being dressed like this around other people. If she let herself be distracted by how exposed she felt while in town, it would cost her life.

Tara entered the living room just in time to say goodbye to Joli and the children.

Togin stopped in mid-conversation with Reena to stare at Tara when she entered the room. He didn't look like a warrior asked to go to any measure to find out if there was a Runner in Reena's home. He looked like a sex-slaved pig who'd just forgotten his pregnant wife stood next to him. Tara scowled at him before looking away in disgust. She looked at Reena in time for the older woman to frown at her.

"This would be my niece, Tara." Reena walked over and wrapped her cool fingers around her niece's arm and gave it a hard squeeze. "She was a great help last night in saving your unborn child."

"Mighty fine-looking lass you are." Togin put his burly hand around his claim's arm and pulled her out the door.

"You're welcome," Tara muttered sarcastically after Togin and his family walked off the open room. "And apparently now I have to learn to smile at pigs like him as well as pull off being submissive?"

"There's nothing wrong with Togin." Reena waved Tara's concern with a chuckle.

"He just undressed me with his eyes with his pregnant claim right next to him."

"That's just a man for you. But Togin is good to his claim. I've never seen a bruise on her or the children. Joli has a nice home and nice clothes." Reena scowled and put her hands on her small hips. It was the first time she'd looked this upset. "Togin would never leave Joli or his children. He is there, every day, taking care of them."

"I wasn't suggesting," Tara began, confused by Reena's sudden outburst.

"No, no, of course you weren't." Reena sighed and looked defeated. "I need to get my bath."

Tara stared after her until Reena closed herself in her bedroom. Turning into the living room, she began straightening the room as two things dawned on her. Reena was Gothman. This was her home and these her people. Tara would be smart not to insult their ways. But also, Reena had struck out on a more personal level. Was it a broken heart? Had some man not stuck around to give her a nice home and children? Had it been so bad that no other man would claim her?

Tara washed the dishes and made the beds. As she straightened the rooms, it dawned on her that she really liked the mundane tasks. She also wanted to cheer Reena up. She was Tara's only Gothman connection. Tara hadn't meant to strike a nerve.

Reena was surprised when she came out of the bathroom and saw the condition of her house. "Goodness me, child. You're mighty full of hidden talents for a Runner. And just look at you in that dress? You're more stunning than any lass I've seen in this town. It will be his Lord himself taking a notice in you."

"His Lord?" Tara frowned as she studied the pattern of the quilt folded over the couch.

The stories around the fires about the Lord of Gothman were not good. He was a monster, cruel to the bone with no heart or soul. He didn't fight with honor but instead trained his men to kill and destroy. He had no desire to learn from others, and as a result, kept his people in the dark about the rest of Nuworld. And women! Don't even get her started on the stories she'd heard of how he treated women. Tara kept her thoughts to herself and waited to hear what Reena would say.

"Oh yes, my dear. The Bryton house has ruled Gothman since the winters of my grandmama. They've always been quite powerful, and each generation has added land to our nation. Lord Jovis Bryton ruled for over forty winters. He passed on last spring and his son, Darius, is now lord."

Tara followed Reena to the small bedroom Joli had occupied and listened as she continued. It was smart to learn all she could before going into town.

"Lord Jovis' eldest son, Juro, was to rule next, but shortly after his papa's death Juro drowned in the river to the east. Darius was next in line, and so now he rules." Reena pulled the sheet from the bed, and paused, lowering her voice to a whisper as she met Tara's gaze. "It was murder, were the rumors, although just rumors, mind you. Not one would stand up to Darius and challenge him, I know that much. He's a ruthless warrior they say, although he keeps Gothman peaceful and happy. The stories from the old warriors say he still has much to learn, however."

Tara didn't try to hide her smile. If last night's attempt to capture her was any indication of the man's abilities, then he definitely had a lot to learn.

"This is quiet talk, child hear me, not to be muttered outside this home, even as gossip. Lord Darius will not hear a word spoken about his dead brother. He's powerful, and many stand behind him."

Reena hurried out of the room without another word.

Tara followed with her arms full of the used sheets and blankets, dropping them in the basket that Reena indicated.

"Oh to think, an old lady's memory should always be checked." She chuckled to herself. "I put the apple pie for the Lord's family in the oven while you were showering. I'll be struck down if it's cooked a moment beyond perfection."

Reena pulled the pie out of the oven. It filled the room with a wonderfully enticing smell. Tara felt a twinge of hunger when she breathed in the scent of the sweet apples.

"Some fat added to those bones will make you look more Gothman." Reena pulled a plate of sweet rolls from the overlarge breadbox on the counter.

Tara and Reena enjoyed honey rolls for breakfast, washed down with fresh cool milk. Then Reena washed the sheets used the night before. Tara marvelled at the antiquated machine that vibrated to an off-rhythm beat as it spun the sheets around and around. Most things in Reena's household consisted of basic domestic items; the type of things Tara had heard were used in Gothman. But then there were mysteries like the coffee, and no man when all females were given claims. The main thing Tara had learned was that Gothman women relied on their men to provide for them, yet Reena was somehow providing for herself.

Tara made herself useful and went out to chop firewood while Reena worked on laundry. Extra fuel would be needed to help keep the house warm as the nights grew cooler. She stacked the logs in a pile alongside the house, then sat on the front open room to nurse some scrapes. "It'll take some time to get accustomed to this light material you have me wearing," Tara admitted as Reena applied a salve to one of her scratches.

"It'll be easier for you if you accept the women's chores and leave the men's chores to the men. But I have a feeling you will do what you want." Reena smiled. "You might as well make me aware of the other talents you possess before we go to town. Do you sew? Have you done any quilting? The Gothman do not take well to strangers, but they welcome family with open arms. Announcing you as my niece will help you in town."

"Well, I've—"

"You can obviously keep a house and you're good with the children, but the women socialize over their chores. We'll go to town and stop at the market to pick up a few necessaries. The women folk'll be there doing the same after they've taken their sons to school. It's a social time for us, and the gossip's usually good and plenty. You do like gossip, don't you?"

"I'm not much—" Tara gave up trying to talk when it appeared pointless. Reena didn't seem interested in her answers.

"On Saturday mornings we meet for a quilting session. If you can partake, I'll announce your presence for this Saturday. It will send quite the talk through the town." Reena was more intent on Tara being the way Reena wanted her to be. "I enjoy good gossip, I do. And you, my dear, will put a mark on Gothman that won't soon be forgotten. I can feel it in my bones." Reena paused and looked at Tara. "So, what is it we shall say you can do?"

"Well," Tara began, then waited for the interruption. When none came, she continued. "If you're talking about the blanket thrown over the back of your couch, I've never seen one like it before. I'm a quick learner, though."

"Hmm, it won't do for you to be a novice quilter. Not at your advanced age. The gossip'll fly on that one faster than the news of your being here. You'll offer to watch the young ones while the rest of us quilt. I dare say that'll work. I'll try to teach you on the side, ah, that will do, yes it will."

Tara wrapped the pie in a cloth and placed it in a wooden basket. Reena scurried from room to room preparing for their trip to town. The old woman chatted the entire time, obviously excited about introducing Tara to the women of the town. Slowly the couch filled with items to take into town—the pie for his Lord, stacks of quilting patterns, some clothes left behind by a previous pregnant lady that Reena had washed and needed to return. And last of all, a sweater made from a rough yarn Tara didn't recognize, which Reena packed for Tara in case she got cold. Tara found herself leaning against the counter in an effort to stay out of the way.

Her laser had slipped while chopping wood. Tara hoped she wouldn't be doing anything that strenuous in town. But she needed to be prepared. Besides, hiking her dress up to get her laser, now that she thought about it, would bring her even more trouble around Gothman men. She took advantage of Reena being busy and slipped it into her dress pocket.

They placed the basket containing the pie in the backseat of Reena's groundmobile—an old rusty two door with black interior. Tara had never been in one before, and grinned like a child when, unable to resist, she reached inside and turned the steering wheel one way then the other.

"Stop that," Reena scolded her when she came out of the house.

"Sorry." But Tara continued grinning.

When the groundmobile hesitated to start, Tara volunteered to check under the hood and hurried to get her black gloves from her Runner clothing inside before checking the motor.

Reena yelled from the driver's seat. "The cable to the battery is more than likely loose."

Tara stared at the motor in disbelief. If only Patha could see this! Once, he had shown her sketches of an ancient motor. But to think Gothman had recreated them and used them daily. Maybe this race had a bit more intelligence than she gave them credit for having. Although if they did, they wouldn't be using such relics.

"Okay, try it now." Tara grinned again when the groundmobile lit to life, sputtering and shaking enough to send birds flying from the trees.

The gravel road leading away from Reena's house was uneven and tree branches overhead made it feel as if they drove through a tunnel. Tara noticed when they reached a stone paved road that one would have to know specifically where the road to Reena's house was, or they would never find it.

The morning air was crisp, and Tara appreciated the knitted sweater Reena had given her before they left. She enjoyed the sweet smell of the pines and the variety of birds singing their morning songs. The road caught her attention as well. Flattened rocks, more than likely from the surrounding hills, varied in color, making it as unique as the people who had created it.

It didn't take long to reach Bryton. Reena told Tara that once it was known as Smithton, in honor of the Smith lords who had ruled for winters. Now Bryon's ruled Gothman. As long as Reena had lived the town had been called Bryton.

Merchants' stores soon appeared on either side of the street. The town itself was surrounded by rocky hills providing natural protection. Most of the buildings were made of the same white stone as the hills around it.

Tara noticed a large residence on a hillside. Built at the opposite end of town from where she was riding, it was high enough to be visible above Bryton. Even from a distance, Tara could tell that it was very large. The thought of a stationary house, one that never moved and remained in the same place for the lifetime of a person, would be hard to believe if she weren't staring at it. She'd go crazy staying in the same place all of her life.

"Lord Darius lives there with his mama and youngest brother, who is still a child. The lord has another brother, Mikel, who is Lord Darius' advisor. Mikel and his claim live in Bryton with their children," Reena explained.

Reena stopped her groundmobile alongside other groundmobiles at the edge of the street. Mamas and their daughters were everywhere. The women stood in small groups, chatting, while small children ran up and down a hard stone path in front of the stores.

Tara slowly opened the door and stood, taking in her surroundings. Reena seemed oblivious to the reaction Tara caused. But Tara tensed when women and children whispered and stared at her with obvious curiosity. Reena held her head high, as if proud, and gestured for Tara to follow.

"We'll go into the grocery store first. It's run by the Olgoods, an old family. Once we introduce you to them, I daresay the whole community will get word of your being here. They'll all know who Reena's niece is before the day is out." Reena walked with purpose toward double doors propped open with polished tree stumps.

A plump older woman standing behind the counter looked up and smiled when the two women entered. "Ah, Reena, it's nice to see you."

A short man with gray whiskers and a potbelly remained sitting on his stool next to where the woman stood. "And who might this young lass be?" He looked Tara over as if she were a side of beef he might purchase.

"Thelga, it's good to see you. And Garg, you're looking well." Reena nodded her head to the couple. "I'd like you to meet my niece, Tara. She's come to stay with me just this other day. I daresay she's quite a bit of help to an old lady."

"What a comfort for a woman with no children, yes" Thelga said, clasping her hands over her large girth. "I daresay you'll have her claimed before the week is out. She's quite the looker."

Garg grunted and got up. He walked toward the back of the store without saying goodbye.

"I know she is." Reena winked, apparently not daunted by Garg's departure. "Her Papa's a mite bit picky though, if you ask me. But who asks an old lady? Turned down a claim already. She's his only daughter, you see. So, now she's with me." Reena clucked to herself and moved toward the fresh produce. She took a basket from a stack by the door and handed it to Tara.

Tara wandered past barrels of produce as she followed Reena, and watched with curiosity as the older woman poked and sniffed, pinched and shook each vegetable before selecting what she wanted. Evidently, it was quite a task for Reena to find food items that suited her needs, but finally she seemed satisfied with her choices, paid for the items, and nodded as she led them out the door.

"Well now, that's done," Reena said as she chuckled to herself. "Thelga'll be quite busy letting the town folk know of your arrival. I swear to you now that half the town will come down with some ailment or another just to come see old Reena's niece." She laughed out loud and wrapped her arm around Tara's. "You did mighty fine in the store. Now I need to pick up some more yarn. Sirlah Maken's shop is just up the street. I'll be going in alone. It won't do to have them noticing your lack of seamstress skills. It'll be there that I tell them you'll help with the young ones at the quilting. I'll point out we have enough quilters and too many wee ones. It will make sense. You wander around, if you like."

Reena left Tara on the sidewalk and hurried down the street.

Tara was amused by how much Reena was enjoying herself. Left alone, she walked the opposite direction looking into each store window. She hoped she appeared shy and submissive when she glanced tentatively at anyone who looked her way.

These were the women she'd wondered so much about. They lived a life of domesticity, completely oblivious to anything outside their daily routine. They grew up, anxiously waiting to be claimed, then fell into a role of servitude and inconsequential gossip. So far, she wasn't too impressed. How did these women go through life with no say in matters that involved them? How were they complete inside when they needed a man simply to exist?

Tara passed a gap between two of the stores. It was wide enough for a groundmobile to move between them. The tall buildings cast shadows, and she guessed this wasn't a place where the townsfolk walked. It was full of trash in barrels and the smell reflected that fact, along with flying insects hovering over the bins.

Several kids were at the other end of the alley, and she stopped to watch them. Young boys, appearing to be hiding, clung to the shadows. Tara guessed they had sneaked out of school. A smile played on her face when she spotted several more children enter the dark road behind the first group.

"There they are!" one of the boys yelled.

She slipped easily enough behind a large trashcan and squatted unnoticed as she continued to watch the boys.

"You'll be dealing with me now." A large boy of thirteen or fourteen winters walked with confidence toward the group Tara had first noticed. "Let's see if you can fight, Torgo." He was almost twice the size of the younger boy he had singled out.

The younger boy didn't seem to have any fighting skills. He backed awkwardly down the alley. The other kids spread away from him, hope of escape obvious in their faces.

"Don't be telling me we have a coward here?" The large boy laughed, lunging at the younger one as he feigned a punch. "It couldn't be."

Torgo turned and made an attempt to run, but he was easily overtaken and thrown to the ground. He tried yelling but the older boy sat on him and put one hand over Torgo's mouth. Then he started hitting Torgo. "Not only can you not fight, you would cry like a baby for help?" The large boy laughed again while the other boys stood around watching.

Tara removed the small laser from her dress pocket and shot at a trashcan next to the group of boys. The metal can sliced in two. Pieces flew down the alley in opposite directions. Its lid slammed against the wall. It made a horrific sound, the noise echoing off the buildings, which intensified the clatter.

The frightened boys jumped and scattered down the side street. Torgo tried to get up and run, but fell back to the ground. Tara stood from where she had hid and walked over to the scared and bruised boy.

"You know, boy, often if you act like you're willing to take a challenge, a bully will back down," Tara said, doing her best to sound Gothman. "Let me see you now." She held up his face and looked at the scratches that were starting to bleed. "It'll be hard to explain how you got those while studying in school." She smiled at the child.

He smiled back cautiously. "How did you do that?" Torgo sputtered.

"I'm not rightly sure. I threw a rock. I was trying to hit the boy that was pounding you. That trash can had to be rotted clear through." Tara rolled her eyes and the young boy laughed. She hoped no one inspected the destroyed can too closely.

His laughter stopped suddenly as he looked past Tara toward the sidewalk.

Tara turned and saw a man sitting on a motorcycle, watching. Blond curls fell to his shirt. His expression was impossible to read. Dark, penetrating gray eyes stared at her, and he didn't blink once. He looked rugged, distracting, but more than that. He was captivating. The man shifted his attention to the boy, then looked at Tara again with a bit more interest.

By the size of the motorcycle he was straddling, the man was fairly tall. He wore a dark plaid shirt with a brown leather jacket over it. The jacket was unbuttoned and stretched across a broad, muscular chest. There was a crest embroidered on the sleeve of his jacket and another matching crest on his bike.

"They challenged me. What was I to do?" Torgo leapt away from Tara and stood as tall as his young body would allow. He didn't have any problem getting to his feet this time.

"Back to school with you. We'll talk about this later." The words were barely out of the man's mouth before the boy took off running as fast as his legs would take him.

Tara stood silently, continuing to watch the man when he studied her. The boy was his son, and she would never allow herself to show interest in a married man, or claimed man as the Gothman called it, but it was hard to look away. After so long, she was finally standing face to face with a Gothman warrior, and a gorgeous one at that.

"Who might you be, lass?" The man's voice was softer now. He studied her, as if memorizing her features, or perhaps trying to remember if he had seen her before.

"I'm Reena's niece. My name's Tara." A bit too late, she remembered to lower her eyes. For some reason, she didn't want to act submissive toward this man.

"Come here."

Tara's gaze shot to his. She bit her lip to stop herself from telling him no. Slowly, she walked the distance between the two of them. If she'd researched the crests of the different Gothman families she might have an idea of whom she was dealing with. Instead, she stared into the most unique shade of charcoal gray eyes she'd ever seen. There was a hardness there. This man gave orders and seldom took them. She saw it in the calm, sure way he sat, straddled on his bike, and watched her approach him.

"Reena's niece, Tara, what are you doing here?" He had a beautiful Gothman accent. Which was odd because the mixture of slur and guttural in the dialogue wasn't something she'd normally call beautiful.

"Waiting on my aunt."

"In the merchants' lane?"

Since she didn't have an answer Tara decided it was a good time to appear submissive. But the moment she lowered her gaze, the man grabbed her chin. She flinched. At least she prayed that was how this trained warrior read her body language. In truth, it took tightening every muscle in her body not to knock the pompous man off his bike.

"I haven't seen you before."

"I've just arrived and came into town with her today for the first time."

"I see. Well, Tara, Reena's niece, I'll be thanking you for breaking up the fight for my younger brother's sake."

Tara looked him in the eye, forgetting about submission. *Younger brother, not claimed?*

"You're welcome," she said and focused on how the loose fitting off-white shirt under his brown leather jacket didn't prevent her from seeing how well built he was.

His expression didn't change nor did he bother to say who he was. He also gave no indication if he thought it odd that a Gothman woman prevented a fight. Maybe the women here stopped boys from fighting. They spent their lives raising children, after all. Tara tried relaxing but the overwhelming urge to back away from his grip prevented her from doing so.

"You're quite beautiful." He turned her head, his grip tightening along her chin and neck. "You've been brought here to be claimed."

The man didn't make it a question. Tara quit looking at his chest and shot her attention to his face. He wasn't looking at her but tilted her head to the side so that her hair fell over his hand. His gaze was directed lower on her body. The man took his time, moving her head as he gave her a serious once over.

There was only a moment but Tara saw it as an opportunity to learn about male Gothman. Her initial reaction wasn't good. Never in her life had she been man-handled as if she were a product that might be purchased at will. It unnerved her. Her gut told her to fight back, force his release, demand he treat her with respect.

"That should be a successful endeavour," he murmured and released her.

Tara stepped back involuntarily and caught herself adjusting her clothes. It seemed he still gripped her neck and her fingers fluttered to where he'd held her before looking at him.

"I'm not sure that—" She broke off, hesitating on how to respond without giving herself away. How was she supposed to answer him? Although, it dawned on her, he hadn't asked a question so maybe silence was best.

He looked at her a minute longer, then left her standing there and drove down the street.

Tara exhaled slowly, willing her heart to stop pounding as she walked to the sidewalk and stared after him. Her skin tingled where he'd held her chin and neck and she didn't like the sensation. It shouldn't matter what he said about a claiming. That wouldn't happen. She was here to observe and that was it. But had he said *thank you for breaking up the fight*? Had he seen her shoot the trashcan?

Reena hurried toward Tara, the older woman's attention moving from the departing man to her niece. "Well child, your first day in town, and you've the honor of meeting Lord Darius himself." Reena sounded absolutely delighted.

"That was Lord Darius?" Tara stole another glance at the gorgeous man disappearing down the stone road.

"Yes, my dear. What did he say to you?" Reena handed the bags of yarn to Tara and started walking to the groundmobile.

"Come now, tell an old lady everything. He hasn't claimed anyone yet, although I daresay the rumors are that he's been with every girl in town. Now he's seen you. Maybe that will change. It's plain to see you are prettier than any other girl this town has to offer."

"He said, 'thank you'." There was no way she was sharing the entire conversation she'd had with the man—with the Lord of Gothman. *Hell be doomed!* Did he figure out she was a Runner?

Reena turned to Tara, a puzzled look on her face. "A bit strange, but then he always has been odd from the gossip I hear."

Reena didn't ask anymore questions, apparently content simply that Tara had met Lord Darius. Which was fine with her. She mulled over the encounter, replaying every moment while rubbing where he'd held her and trying to understand what he might have seen in her.

The two reached the groundmobile, and Tara put the bags on the floor behind the two seats. Her mind raced. What should she do if the ruler of this land had seen her with a laser more sophisticated than any Gothman had ever created? Lord Darius would have instigated the search for a Runner the night before. He might put two and two together and realize where the Runner was hiding, which was in plain sight. Tara had better make sure her next move in this community was carefully thought out if she were to stay alive.

CHAPTER THREE

"THERE WERE some children fighting in the alley. One of them was hurt and I was helping the child when Lord Darius showed up and told him to go back to school," Tara explained when Reena started questioning her while they drove through the remainder of downtown. "I didn't know it was Lord Darius."

"Well, now you know who he is and he most certainly knows who you are." Reena seemed quite pleased. "Imagine the lord taking a fancy to you. And I might add, I saw the way you were looking at him." She nudged Tara with her elbow and let out a low chuckle.

"You act as if you want me married, or claimed, as you call it."

"Well my dear, you can't very well experience our culture as a female if you're not claimed. There'd be nothing else to do with you at your age but to show you off for a claiming." Reena smiled at Tara. "I'm an old lady, my dear. I daresay you've brought excitement to my life."

"I don't want to be claimed."

"You better keep thoughts like that to yourself. You'd be suspected as odd for sure if you say something like that out loud." Reena clucked her tongue but glowed when she glanced at Tara.

The two were silent as Reena drove slowly through the town. Tara looked out the window at the community, watching the people on the streets. Young women worked in gardens with children running around them. The houses were clean and well kept. It was odd that people would want to raise children in the same place their entire life.

Tara had spent many cycles in one location before, but there was always a sense of excitement when it was time for her clan to move to a new location. These people would never experience that. The thought wasn't too appealing.

"I daresay this must all seem so strange to you." Reena seemed as if she'd been reading Tara's thoughts.

"I was just imagining what it must be like to live in one spot all your life."

"You'll probably never know that feeling, sweet child. You're a Runner. I can dress you like a Gothman and teach you how to act like a Gothman, but the Runner is in your blood. You must forgive an old lady. I've spent the morning going on about my niece come to stay with me. It's a pleasant thought, and you're quite the young lady to be showing off. I guess I got a bit carried away. I wouldn't know what to say if I weren't talking about getting you claimed. That's what we do with our young ladies."

Reena had now driven through the town and was turning onto a paved road winding up a hill. Their next stop would be Lord Darius' house.

Tara wondered if he would be there. The man was strong, not only physically, but he'd appeared more intelligent than she'd originally given him credit. He ruled all of Gothman and hadn't been the designated heir. He had taken the right to rule. Tara guessed he would also be manipulative and shrewd.

There were also the facts that he believed women didn't have the intelligence to do anything other than birth babies and raise them. He was not a fair man. And hadn't she already determined that the warrior skills of his men were inferior to her own? Tara frowned and scolded herself for finding him appealing. Obviously he had a lot to learn.

The road ran past beautifully landscaped scenery. The grass on the ground was cut short and tall pine trees were scattered through the yard.

As they approached the house, Reena watched Tara. Tara had grown up living in trailers, never having a piece of land to call her own. Reena knew that Runners were proud of their nomadic existence. She wondered if the home they were about to visit might alter Tara's perspective.

Perfectly nestled among the foliage, a large stone house stood proudly before them. A wide front open room wrapped around both sides of the front of the house. Wooden swings on chains hung from the flat roof on each end, and sharply carved stone stairs led down to a pebbled walkway that travelled out to greet the road. There were thick, square pillars made of stacked stones on either side of the stairs that led to the door. More pillars held the extended roof that covered the open room. It was the same kind of roof that was over the entire home. The house itself was several stories high with a large veranda off the third floor.

Tara studied the vantage point offered by the veranda, guessing that it enabled Lord Darius to survey his land and ensure its safety. Standing watch on that ledge probably gave him a great vantage point to see all of his town.

Two large men wearing brown leather pants and jackets stood in the front yard and walked to the groundmobile. Reena slowed to a stop.

"My apple pie as promised." She smiled at the large man leaning over, peering through the groundmobile window.

Tara remembered seeing him at Reena's home the night before. He had been one of the Lord Darius' warriors looking for her.

"Who do you have here?" The man tossed a toothless smile at Tara. "I daresay his lord will like this much more than your apple pie."

The other man stepped forward and leaned down to see in the groundmobile as well. He didn't look familiar. He was younger, with an unshaved, round face. Both men were particularly ugly.

"She is my niece," Reena said coolly. "Will you announce us? Or are you going to stand there with your jaws hanging?"

"How you've lived to be an old lady with that mouth of yours is a mystery to me," the man Tara recognized snarled, and straightened. He spoke into a black box that he pulled from his waist.

Reena knew how she'd lived to be an old lady. She was protected. Her one and only love had seen to that. She wasn't sure if Lord Darius knew the history behind why his papa had declared her unavailable for a claim. He'd upheld his papa's wishes though, and for that she was grateful.

She looked at the beautiful young woman sitting next to her in the groundmobile, whose sapphire eyes made her appear too wise for her winters. Tara was watching the guard speak to the lord through his walkntalk. Reena doubted Tara had ever seen the Gothman communication device before. This was a young lady who digested and analyzed everything she saw, and Reena saw the qualities of a natural-born leader in Tara. Nothing she did to make her Gothman would hide that quality in the lass. Reena knew how strong it ran in Tara's blood.

Lord Darius would claim Tara instantly. In fact, he might already have done so. A man didn't always tell a woman immediately when he claimed her. She would find out soon enough. Tara would fight it, but Reena knew it had to happen. They were meant to be together. Tara would help Lord Darius realize his potential. The lord would teach Tara a thing or two as well. Even as her heart tightened, Reena knew Patha had been right.

Tara struggled to hear what the guard said into his black box, wondering to whom he might be speaking, but the groundmobile's motor made it impossible to hear. She watched with fascination as the man held the black box to his mouth, and his thumb moved to press a button on the side when he spoke.

A minute or two passed before the man returned to the groundmobile window. "Pull over to the side." The guard pointed to an area off to the left of the large stone home.

"Of all things, I know where to park." Reena waved the guard away and drove her groundmobile to the side of the house.

"Grab the basket out of the backseat, child," Reena instructed Tara as she looked toward the door up those stairs in the open room. "You ever seen anything so magnificent?"

Tara reached for the basket then turned. "It looks so permanent."

The front door opened and a lady about the same age as Reena walked out onto the open room. "Reena, I'll be, it's so good to see you again, my friend." The woman reached out and hugged Reena. "I daresay it takes the scare of a Runner to bring you to my doors these days. What to think, I wonder."

"I stay quite busy with the way this town is populating itself," Reena said, and the two women laughed together and hugged again.

"Ah, so here she is." The woman took Tara's chin in her hand and turned her head from side to side. She glanced sideways at Reena and wrinkled her brow. "She's the spitting image of you at her age. And she's your niece, you say? Well now, you're definitely related, that much is true."

Tara smiled politely and glanced at Reena. She stared at the smooth, crushed pebble floor and no longer smiled. Tara wondered how a friend of Reena's who'd apparently known her most of her life, wouldn't know how sensitive she was about never having children.

"I'm Hilda Bryton."

The lady didn't notice the look on Reena's face but focused on Tara. Hilda was a large woman, taller than Reena. She wore a long loose frock flowing below her knees. Her silver-gray hair was wrapped in a bun behind her head.

Tara pictured Hilda raising Darius, and Torgo, the young boy from the alley, and she had two more sons, one of which was dead. She wondered how much influence the Gothman woman had in their upbringing. Or had their papa controlled the way in which they were raised?

"My Lady," Tara said quietly with her eyes lowered. She offered a slight curtsy.

"You know how the gossip flies through this town. I heard she was quite the beauty, but the words do her no justice. You'll be mighty proud of this one, won't you?" Hilda patted Reena's arm.

"I hadn't seen her myself since she was a baby. Until just last night. She is beautiful."

"Ah, my manners, to entertain you in my open room. What am I thinking?" Hilda laughed and opened the front door wide. "Please, do come in for a visit. Reena, when have we last sat and had a good talk of the goings on. I'm sure I don't remember."

Tara followed the two old women into the house. She gasped when they walked through the door and she caught her first look at the magnificent home. At that moment, if someone were looking for a Runner in disguise they would have immediately suspected her. She had never been inside such a structure. The most shelter she'd had from the elements throughout her life were the trailers Runners lived in while with their clan. How could anyone ever be safe, or comfortable, when they had no way of hearing the sounds outside? They would never know if the weather changed, or if someone were approaching.

Tara wanted to run her hands along the walls. They looked so solid. This house had been built to stay right here on this land, never moving. Runners moved when the weather changed, when trade agreements improved in a different area, or when news of a dispute or challenge in another area came forth.

But not the people of Gothman. They ignored Nuworld and focused only on themselves. This house would be an excellent place to ignore the outside world. The arched ceilings allowed for a wide stairway to show all of its glory as it climbed in front of them to a second floor. Tara remembered seeing windows outside indicating more rooms on a third floor. She wondered where another staircase might be. Glancing at the ceiling gave no indication.

As they left the entryway and walked through two glass doors, Tara found herself in a large room with glossy wooden floors and a large area rug so thick that her feet sunk in it. She felt how soft it was through her thin cotton material shoes.

This room was as large as her entire trailer.

Beautifully carved wooden chairs had forest green cushions resting on them. There was a long sofa made out of the same dark green material. The wood on the tables on either side of the couch, as well as the oval one in front of it, were polished to the point that Tara saw her reflection in them. She almost did a double take at the strange-looking woman staring back. It wasn't often she gazed at her own reflection, let alone without her headscarf.

"So, sit down and tell me all the goings on," Hilda directed.

Reena made herself comfortable on the well-padded couch. "Be a dear, Tara, and set the pie on the dining room table." Reena pointed to the room adjoining the one they were in.

Tara placed the pie on a long wooden table and walked over to one of the long glass windows. She stared out at a sprawling, well-groomed yard with gardens, and heard the muffled voices of two men working in the yard. They were pulling something off a trailer attached to a sturdy-looking, much more modern groundmobile than what Reena was driving. There was mud splattered on the sides, as well as caked to the wheels of the groundmobile and trailer, as if it had just come a distance to get here.

Lord Darius walked across the yard toward the groundmobile. Her gaze followed his every move. His long stride and tall features sent a warm sensation through Tara's body. It had been a long time since she'd seen a man so sexually appealing.

Her attention shifted from him to the truck.

The men struggled to lift something from the bed and set it on the ground—her motorcycle!

Tara groaned. They wouldn't be able to start it, since it was coded, but they'd found it and brought it here. A lot of good it was going to do her if it was stuck up here! She watched the men lift the bike and carry it to a shed before she turned to join the women. Those solid stone walls seemed to close in around her, trapping her and preventing her escape.

"Enjoying the scenery of my backyard, are you girl?" Reena grinned as if she knew Tara's thoughts.

The old woman would never know how wrong she was in guessing what was in Tara's mind.

"I daresay it's my son you'd be admiring." Hilda looked at Tara but then turned to Reena. "They would make the most handsome claim in all of Gothman. Can you imagine? We would be sisters for real."

"Just think of those gorgeous grand babies to show off." Reena clasped her hands together as if it had just been finalized.

Tara glared at the two women as she joined them in the living room and sat on the end of the couch. Her future was ready and waiting for her. She had worked hard to deserve the title of heir to rule all Runner clans, and no one would take that from her. Especially two scheming old women with nothing better to do than play claim-maker with two people who were strangers to each other. Learning all there was to know about Gothman, and Lord Darius, would make her that much better of a leader.

The two women continued to chatter endlessly, talking about whatever came to their minds and laughing at each comment that was made. Tara blocked out their conversation and dwelt on her own predicament. For the time being, she was stranded. She hadn't given any thought to leaving in the near future, but now she couldn't if she wanted to, unless she stole a Gothman motorcycle or pulled off the near impossible and rescued her bike.

Tara didn't want to leave, she wanted to stay and learn about these people. But having the option of departing taken from her was annoying. An image of Darius appeared in her mind. She imagined how smug he must have felt to have found her bike. Tara knew at that moment she would get it back. She would not let Lord Darius best her.

Tara stood, too restless to sit, and worked her way back to the windows. The men sounded like they were arguing outside, but try as she might she couldn't hear what they were saying over the women's voices, or through the blasted thick Gothman glass. She finally gave up and turned her attention back to the women.

"So, you'll be staying for lunch then." Hilda smiled and got up. "I've some cold ham for sandwiches, boiled new potatoes and cheese rolls. That pie will go along famously."

Reena and Hilda walked through the dining room and back toward the kitchen. Tara followed, but none of the windows in the kitchen offered a better view of the men, or her bike.

"I had a girl to help with the house for a time. But Lord Darius didn't take a liking to her and sent her back to her parents. I will say this big house is too much for an old lady to manage." Hilda winked at Reena.

"I know what you're saying, I do at that," Reena sympathized. "My hands wear out long before the housework does these days. I've a liniment you might try. It does take the sting out."

"Tara, be a dear and go cut some of those flowers out back in the garden, will you?" Hilda opened a drawer and pulled out gloves and clippers. "Take these...ah...there you are. Use caution, girl. The thorns can bring blood faster than you may think."

Hilda watched Tara leave out the back door then close it so it didn't make a sound. Never had she seen anyone move as Reena's niece did. It was as if the girl were one with the ground she walked across. Quite captivating, and it was more than outer beauty. There was something in the girl's eyes. Hilda wasn't able to quite place it, but the girl seemed to put everything she saw and heard to memory. And Tara didn't look like one to forget.

Hilda looked at Reena, who was still looking at the back door. Tara was already out of sight.

"Your niece, you say?" she asked.

"Isn't she beautiful?"

"That she is." Hilda didn't think Reena had a brother.

To call her friend out on a lie would be a serious offense if she didn't have proof. Hilda held her tongue, which was really hard to do.

"Do you think Darius will claim her?"

Hilda didn't try speculating what her son might do. "Is that what you want?" she asked instead of answering.

Reena hesitated, and for a moment seemed to look sad. When she looked at Hilda, her expression was serious.

"I want her to be happy," Reena said and sounded too serious.

This time it was easier for Hilda to hold her tongue. She wasn't sure any young lady would be happy as the lord's claim. He was way too driven. She supposed that was good for Gothman but she doubted he'd ever be happy with any one woman.

Gloves and clippers in hand, Tara entered the backyard. There was no sign of the men, so she turned her attention to the different rose varieties growing bountifully along the side yard. As she knelt at the flowerbeds, she inhaled their strong fragrance. There were yellow and white roses and she began to clip a few of them. She jerked at the sound of footsteps and spun around as she stood.

"Ah, lass, no reason to be so jumpy. I won't hurt you." A tall man with thick curly blond hair stood before her. He smiled but focused on her body, not her face. "I'm wondering why a lass as pretty as you hasn't been claimed. You're too pretty to be keeping to yourself." He reached for her breasts.

Tara pointed the clippers at him. "Stay back," she warned him.

"Now that ain't fair. I just said I wasn't going to hurt you, and here you are ready to hurt me. I daresay you're a wild one." The man laughed and started to grab the clippers from Tara.

Submissive be damned. She wasn't about to let this brute maul her. That wasn't how she planned to experience Gothman. "I said stay back," she repeated and pulled the clippers back, then punched the man hard in the stomach with her other hand.

The man was packed with muscle. He doubled over for just a second but then stood again, the grin still on his face.

"Ah, nothing like a frisky one." The man lunged forward, sending Tara to the ground.

He was heavy and the ground was hard beneath her.

Tara moved faster than he anticipated, managing to avoid his full bulk on top of her. When he pushed to his knees, she brought her knee up hard in his groin and he howled loudly.

Tara rushed to put distance between them when he grabbed her foot and pulled hard enough for her to fall flat. The garden gloves protected her hands as they slapped the ground, but she groaned, knowing her rear end would be bruised later.

He crawled toward her and she turned around, nailing her fist against his jaw. The stunned man didn't move as she jumped up.

"You leave me alone," she growled through clenched teeth.

The man sat staring at her as she walked away. Tara was satisfied with his dumbfounded expression, although she hoped no one saw her act out of character. If she was lucky, the man had been so humiliated he wouldn't comment on her ability to fight.

Tara headed toward to the house, then paused. She turned and grabbed the cut flowers lying on the ground where she'd dropped them. The women would question if she returned without the roses. And if they hadn't seen her escapade, she didn't want to have to tell them about it.

As she walked back to the house, she noticed Lord Darius staring through an opened upstairs window on the second floor. Adrenaline already pumped through her, but sudden panic made her heart race painfully. Her mouth went dry. The lord wasn't stupid, like she'd originally thought. She didn't regret putting the jerk in his place, but if she didn't watch herself around Lord Darius, it would cost her life.

He was definitely watching her, and Tara wouldn't pretend not to notice his appraisal of her. She stopped and studied him in return, wondering what he thought. Tara was sure she saw him grin when she finally looked away to return to the women.

Lord Darius turned from his bedroom window. A sudden thought hit him like a punch to the gut, but he had to be wrong. His walkntalk chirped and he turned to grab it.

"Your Runner bike is secure, my lord," one of his guards said.

Darius growled his response and tossed the black box on his bed. It chirped again. He ignored it. Someone tapped on his door. Darius stalked across the room to open it.

"Darius, would you like your guests to join you for lunch today?"

His mama stood in the doorway, and he forced a blank expression so as not to unnerve her. "You need to hire more help." He tried to sound calm. It wouldn't do to upset his mama. The last thing he needed right now was one of her fits. "You don't need to be climbing those stairs to find out how many people you'll serve."

His mama beamed. "Funny you should mention that. We were just talking about some more help."

Darius waited for the woman to continue.

"Reena has brought her niece today for a visit."

"You want Reena's niece to help you around the house?"

"We had talked about it."

"Have her start tomorrow." Darius thought about the scene he had just witnessed in the yard. Reena's niece, Tara, needed some serious training. And damn if the thought of doing it himself didn't have its strong appeal. "And it'll be just the guards and me that will be eating."

His mama looked very pleased with herself as she left the doorway and shuffled toward the steps. The woman was obviously plotting. It's what women did and their actions didn't much matter to him. Their submission mattered to him. The way a lady honored her claim by obeying him and presenting herself properly in public mattered to him. What would it be like to have a woman who obeyed him in all areas, yet held on to enough of her wild nature to satisfy him in bed?

Darius turned back to the window. He would have that woman under his roof. In fact, he would have that woman. What better way to learn how she had learned to fight like a man. He had his strong suspicions as to where she'd learn to fight. The why was a strong mystery. Darius scowled at the shed where his men had put the Runner bike. His scowl deepened. Once he understood this formidable race, he'd have answers to many questions. He'd also better understand that sensuous little brown-haired woman who dared play as if she were a Gothman female. But if she liked games, Darius had no problem showing her the rules.

Tara was quiet when they drove through town and back up the hill to Reena's home. She entered the small house and started a fire while Reena sat and wiggled her feet.

"Hand me that bag of potatoes along the kitchen wall, child, and I will get started on a salad for our meal later."

Tara brought the bag, then helped peel and slice the potatoes.

"Well, child, what do you think of Gothman now that you've had good exposure to us?"

Tara stared at the flames while the peeler dangled from her hand.

"I saw Lord Darius and two other men with my motorcycle. They put it in a shed behind the Bryton home."

"No! That's not good."

"I'm stranded for the time being." Tara turned and looked at Reena. Once again she felt the sensation of claustrophobia, and the feeling didn't settle well at all. "Not that I was planning on leaving any time soon, but now I can't. It'll be rather difficult to get it back without being noticed."

"Well, I don't know now." Reena was quiet for a moment. "Hilda mentioned something very interesting before we left. She'd like you to come live at her house, to help out with things."

Tara pondered at the thought of living under the same roof with Lord Darius. She imagined sparring with the virile lord, and wondered if she would be able to fight with his hands on her. She looked up at Reena in time to see the older woman smile.

"What are you scheming? I'm not interested in marriage, Reena. Not to mention Lord Darius is not the most talkative man, and the men who work for him have no manners."

"I've no doubt you'll put them in their place. Did one of the guards get a bit fresh with you, child?"

"I had to fight one off when I went to cut the flowers for Hilda," Tara said.

Reena glared at Tara and made a chuckling sound. "It's not like a lady to fight off a man."

"I'm not just going to lay there and play dumb so some brute can do what he will with me." Tara stressed, trying to make Reena understand. "No one should have to do that."

"You know you remind me a lot of myself when I was your age." Reena smiled. "Granted, I was no trained warrior. But, I was loyal to one man. When he left, I'd have no other. So today, I am alone."

Tara studied Reena, wondering what she would have been like as a young lady. She imagined her to have been quite beautiful. Tara wondered where that man was today who had captured the older woman's heart.

For some reason, Tara couldn't see Reena falling hard for any man unless he proved himself better than the rest. Reena had a quiet dignity about her. Not for the first time, Tara saw why Patha had included the older woman in his stories.

"And you, you will be loyal to one man too, someday. It's in your nature." She chuckled and reached for her knitting. "So, you'll live in the Bryton home?" She paused and then added, "You'll be close to your motorcycle."

"I'll give it some thought."

Later that evening, Darius stood in his bedroom. Maps lay strewn on the bed next to him, and additional charts were scattered across the long wooden table to his side. It had been a long day. Hell be doomed! It had been a long night.

His men weren't pleased when he ordered that the Runner not be brought down. But they were loyal and obeyed his command. He had warred with his own decision but was sure he'd made the right one. His papa had never made any qualms over Runners. If seen, they were killed. No questions asked.

The Runners were skilled warriors. They would kill a man on sight. No one had ever questioned that knowledge about them. Runners didn't associate with Gothman people. They weren't allowed in Bryton at all. Only once in Darius' lifetime had he ever known an exception to that rule.

That was with Reena. His papa had never shared the details. Darius knew from time to time a Runner visited Reena. His men kept him informed. Reena had been the one to bring her *niece* into Bryton to introduce to his people. He'd just happen to be in the right place, at the right time, to watch Tara use a weapon he'd never seen before to shoot a trash can and scare a bunch of young boys who were bullying Darius' younger brother. He'd inched back to the edge of the building and continued watching when she consoled Torgo. This same woman, armed with an incredibly dangerous weapon, had then attempted to appear docile and willing when he'd spoken to her. The way her pretty blue eyes had glowed with emotion when he'd purposely handled her got his dick so hard he'd barely been able to think of anything since.

Darius paced to his open bedroom door, filling the doorway as he stared down the wide, dark and quiet hallway. Her behavior in his garden remained imprinted in his thoughts as well, even more of a distraction. No. He would be honest. The woman more than distracted him. It took all he had not to send for her right now. No Gothman lady, unclaimed or claimed, behaved like Tara.

It was as if she believed she had a right to refuse him. If he didn't know better, Darius might think the woman had been raised believing she would choose her claim. For some reason that turned him on. This was proof that he needed to sleep.

Not only did the lass not act like other Gothman woman, she didn't move like any woman he'd ever met. There was a confidence about her. She seemed trained. Not once did she panic, or hesitate, when she'd stood from clipping roses and attacked Judo, one of his well-trained warriors, in Darius' back yard. She'd known what she was doing.

Returning to where his maps were sprawled, Darius rested his fists at the edge of his table and stared down at them. He'd planned to spend his evening going over the revised borders of Gothman. Over the past quarter-cycle he'd travelled along those borders, confirming for himself the extent of land he ruled. It had been just over a handful of nights that he'd slept on the hard ground with his men while surveying Gothman. Tonight he was to validate the new maps drawn up to show all of Gothman. Once he gave his approval, Darius planned to have more maps made and sold in Bryton. His people knew they were strong. They knew he protected them. It wouldn't hurt to show Gothman all the land that was theirs and hopefully encourage some to move on to undeveloped land.

These maps in front of him had consumed his thoughts until a blue eyed, brown haired woman had strolled into his life.

"She hardly strolled," he grumbled to himself.

His vision blurred. "Get some sleep," he ordered himself.

The beautiful young woman who had come to call on his mama had been trained to fight. Like she was a warrior—like she was his Runner. But it would be seriously frowned on if the Lord of Gothman took a Runner to his bed.

He turned and moved back to the open window, running his fingers absently through tangled curls. The signs were there, damn it. His men were in an outrage, and Darius was confused. Not that he would admit his confusion to a soul. The Lord of Gothman offered no weaknesses. But hell be doomed! He would understand Tara.

His papa, Lord Jovis, had never enlightened Darius on any of the thinking behind his decision making. The reasons for not doing that weren't a secret. Darius had not been the intended heir. That didn't bother him. He didn't need his papa's knowledge to rule Gothman. Darius knew he possessed a strength his papa never had, nor his older brother. Dwelling on either of the two was wasted thought. The only thing Darius wanted to know right now was why were Runners such a deadly enemy?

"Maybe those Runners are wondering the same thing." Darius immediately dismissed that possibility. They wouldn't send one young lady into Gothman, where he most definitely had the most deadly warriors in all of Nuworld, if they wanted answers about his people.

Darius knew next to nothing about their race. And he didn't like not having all the facts. He pushed away from the table and maps. It was now his top priority to learn about these people.

He would learn how to operate that strange bike he had housed in his shed as well. He would learn what Runners had done to Gothman to earn such harsh laws implemented against them. And above all his other questions, he would learn why one incredibly beautiful Runner had entered Gothman without an escort...

...and what that Runner was doing in his house.

CHAPTER FOUR

TARA WAS thoroughly exhausted when she left the house where the quilting session had been held. Reena had arranged for her to care for at least fifteen children. Tara had never obtained an accurate count of the kids running around the backyard, for she had spent the entire morning changing diapers, nursing scratches and pulling children out of trees when they cried for help. Although fun at first, after several hours she had been ready for Reena to rescue her.

It was hard to conceal her relief when Reena finally came out the back door of the house with several other women and announced they were through with yet another quilt.

"Help me load everything, my girl," Reena said, as she dumped the contents from her arms into Tara's.

"What is all of this?" Tara adjusted the folded piles of material, trying not to drop anything as she followed Reena to the groundmobile.

Reena laughed and glanced over her shoulder as several of the women gathered children in the yard. She leaned in to Tara when she spoke again.

"It's the makings for the next quilt. I'm thinking anyone could see that." Reena didn't speak loud enough for anyone else to hear, and Tara got her point.

A typical Gothman woman would grow up in this domestic life. Tara fought not to feel sorry for their suppressed existence. Oddly enough, these women didn't look unhappy. Maybe it was because they didn't know what they were missing. It dawned on Tara that most likely was why the leaders of Gothman had made a point to not allow outsiders in, or why their people never travelled beyond Gothman borders. If these women knew how much different their lives might be, certainly they'd never be happy living like this any longer.

Tara managed to put all the materials in the back of the groundmobile in a somewhat orderly fashion. She watched Reena mingle with the other women, who now were chattering outside the white stone house. It was so permanent the walls of the house actually disappeared into the rocky ground it was built on. From what Tara heard, their conversation wasn't about anything important. They discussed what someone had worn the other day, and a pregnancy that didn't appear to be normal. Tara knew she should listen and learn the ways of these women. After all, that is what a Runner did when entering a new community. But her thoughts continually strayed.

The image of a tall, powerful-looking lord kept distracting her thoughts. Although she knew the Gothman lord maintained a society where all women were docile and simple, a woman like that would be boring. She'd offer him more excitement than any of these women ever would. Maybe like these women, Lord Darius simply didn't know what he was missing.

"Are you about ready?"

Tara snapped out of her thoughts, and chastised herself for the direction her thoughts were heading.

"Our next stop is the Bryton home," Reena announced cheerfully.

The woman around them began whispering and studied Tara.

When Tara had agreed to stay at the Bryon home, Reena had decided it was imperative that she teach Tara more about being Gothman. Tara wasn't sure if it was because she'd told Reena about attacking the guard or because Reena liked the company. Tara doubted it had anything to do with Reena worrying about Tara's life being in danger under Lord Darius' roof.

She looked down when she climbed into the groundmobile. This time she wasn't trying to appear submissive. Tara heard the women whispering loudly. Her cheeks flamed. Tara tried hiding her embarrassment at the realization that she would soon be all the Gothman women talked about.

"You aren't having second thoughts now, are you?" Reena asked once she sat in the groundmobile next to Tara. "We agreed to take you after the quilting was over."

Tara noticed worry in the older lady's tone. "No, of course not." Tara tried to reassure Reena with a smile. "We talked about this last night. Moving into the Bryton home and helping Hilda with the housework will be an ideal way to learn more about Gothman."

"Not to mention you will see much of Lord Darius," Reena added, giving Tara a side look as she started the groundmobile.

"True." Tara wouldn't deny an attraction to the man. But there was a lot about him she didn't like. "He has my bike, Reena. I need to keep an eye on him."

The two guards on duty in front of the Lord's house didn't pay any attention to Tara and Reena this time as they parked and ascended the open room stairs. Hilda greeted the two of them with open arms and laughter.

"Reena, you are too good to an old woman to share such a fine young lady with me." There were tears in Hilda's eyes. "You'll be treated quite fine, Tara. Don't worry. Do come inside, both of you. Reena, come see Tara's room. It's ready for her."

Hilda and Reena entered the house. Tara followed them carrying the cloth bag Reena had given her, with her Runner outfit under all her new Gothman dresses. Her laser was in the bag, too. She had decided not to wear it while watching all the children. Now in Lord Darius' home, she felt exceptionally naked without it. They climbed the wide staircase and walked to the end of the hallway where Hilda inserted a key into a door.

"This is my wing of the house." Hilda led the two women through the door. She pointed to a closed door. "This is my room. You'll be next to me. As safe as can be. Don't you think, Reena?"

Tara was amused about their concern with her safety. Hilda seemed to be emphasizing this to Reena as there was a problem. She smiled to herself at the thought of two old women worrying about her well-being. She had a bit of trepidation over agreeing to live in Lord Darius' home, but for very different reasons than Reena and Hilda.

Hilda opened the farthest door at the end of the hallway. It was a beautifully arranged bedroom. The carpet was as thick as the carpet in the living room. A single bed had several comforters spread over the top, and a knitted blanket was folded at its foot. A bureau and dresser were on one wall and a small couch against the other. Two glass doors led to a balcony that looked over the backyard and provided an excellent view of the rocky hills spreading for miles beyond the yard. The room was glorious. But for all its fancy furniture and niceties, Tara liked the fact that part of it opened to the outside the best.

"You consider this your home," Hilda said. "Arrange the room as you please. You unpack your bag, and I'll see Reena to the door. Come down when you're ready, and I'll show you what chores you'll be doing. It's a true pleasure to have you here, child. I just know you'll be happy."

"She'll bring life back to this house if she does anything, that much is certain." Hilda told Reena when they started down the hallway.

"I know she was only with me a quarter-cycle, but I'm going to miss her." Reena replied.

"You're the one that brought her into town and went all about showing her off. You knew you'd lose her by doing that." It was the last Tara heard as the door at the end of the hallway closed.

Tara set down her bag on the bed and looked around the room once again. She walked to the glass doors, opened them, and stepped onto the balcony.

Patha, guess where I am now. Here she was, a Runner, inside the home of the Lord of Gothman. She smiled, rather satisfied with her *Age Of Searching.*

Gothman were actually tolerable people. Both genders needed a lesson in equality, though. Gothman women needed to stand up to their men. If the women here had a clue about how their lives might be, they would give up this submissive lifestyle in a second.

What kind of thinking was this? She wasn't here to change this culture, just observe it, *right?* It would be wrong to allow some type of attachment or loyalty to these people. No Runner ever did that on their *Age Of Searching.*

Maybe it was time to leave. It wouldn't be hard to get her motorcycle now. She'd seen the men move it out of the shed and put it out in the backyard, unattended and unguarded. Maybe if she sneaked out after dark. She would be out of Gothman territory within no time.

Tara mulled this over as she stared at the beautiful hills rolling farther than the eye could see. The rocks jutting up from the earth added to the glory of the view.

Far in the distance, someone raced over the hills on a motorcycle. The rider dodged rocks that sprang up from the earth with a skill equal to her own. The rider was familiar with the terrain. She imagined the thrill of the ride.

Tara wanted to be on her bike and take the same path. She wasn't familiar with the terrain, yet it called out to accept its challenge. Her hands itched with the temptation, and she rubbed them on the soft material of her dress. But for now, she was expected downstairs. Tara turned from the tantalizing scene. At least until nightfall she would continue with her role. Then she'd make a decision about staying or leaving.

The bureau held ample space for the dresses Reena had given her. The older woman had spent a great deal of time over the past quarter-cycle creating this wardrobe. Tara gazed at her Runner clothing at the bottom of her bag. The black leather looked so appealing compared to the Gothman dresses. If anyone found her Runner clothing, however, it would mean her death. Leaving them at Reena's would endanger the woman's life. Too many people moved through that house for Tara's liking.

Tara stroked the silky headscarf and fingered the bright red symbol of her clan. She wrapped her Runner clothing around the landlink from her bike. Tara searched for an appropriate hiding place when she heard voices coming up the stairs. She stuffed her Runner clothes and landlink back into her bag and shoved it under the bed.

Hilda and the young boy Tara had met in the alley were climbing the stairs when Tara reached them.

"So, you're coming to live with me now?" The boy grinned from ear to ear. "Do you want to see my room?"

"Ah, all in good time, my child." Hilda patted the boy on the head. "Tara, have you met Torgo?"

"Only for a moment." Tara almost caught herself clasping her hands behind her back, the pose of a warrior. Instead, she relaxed her features and stared at innocent gray eyes. "We've not been properly introduced, though."

"Well, this is my youngest son, Torgo. He is quite the handful." She hugged the boy and ruffled his hair. "Go play, child. Tara and I have work to do now."

"Will you spend time with me later?" Torgo asked Tara.

"I look forward to it." Tara winked at the boy and his face lit up before he took off running down the hallway.

"It's too bad for the boy. He has no papa to teach him how to be a man. His mama might as well be his grandmama, and Darius is so busy he's no time for him, that's for certain." Hilda walked down the stairs with Tara. "He's a good boy, high-spirited like they all were at that age."

"Maybe I could spend some time with him," Tara offered.

"Ah, that would be nice. It's the training of a man he needs though." Hilda led Tara to the kitchen and opened up a back pantry. "Well now, here are all the supplies. You'll be cleaning the house for now. Over time, I'll teach you how to prepare Lord Darius' favorite dishes. Until then, I'll keep doing the cooking. I like to cook." She laughed and patted her stomach. "I like to eat my cooking too. It wouldn't hurt you to eat my cooking either." She laughed again, then turned as the back door opened.

Lord Darius entered the room, his hair wind-blown. Had he been the rider in the hills?

"Good. Your help has arrived." Darius studied the young woman standing in his kitchen.

The light material of her dress made it easy for him to see how toned her body was. This woman hadn't birthed a child. She sure didn't look like she spent a lot of time sitting and chatting the day away like so many other Gothman women either. She was fit and trim, her breasts perky, and her body toned. She wasn't soft and round like so many Gothman girls her age. Although a bit on the thin side, every inch of her appealed to him. He imagined her full of energy, a bit on the defiant side, and possibly even bordering on insubordinate. Darius never considered those attributes in a woman before. But this woman, who was sizing him up as he did the same to her, might be a nice diversion to the overly submissive ladies he'd been presented with so far.

He noticed the intelligence in blue eyes fighting not to return his stare. She might even be able to hold a conversation. From the spark in those sapphire eyes—that dared him to end his mental evaluation—he imagined she might even be somewhat of a challenge.

That thought damn near made his blood boil. The last thing he needed was to get hard while standing in his mama's kitchen. Darius tried focusing on Tara's faults.

Whoever had taught her how to be a lady had failed. She didn't appear shy or humble in his presence, like every other lass he'd known since boyhood. Unfortunately, he found her demeanor refreshing. Darius smiled, and decided an untrained woman might prove a welcome distraction.

For the first time, Tara saw a genuine smile light up Darius' face. It transformed his already distracting good looks. Darius was incredibly sexy. Her insides melted from her toes upward, and a recognizable warmth started between her legs and spread too fast to stop. With the sudden onslaught of awakening desires, it seemed the very air around her sparked with lustful currents that spiked the tiny hairs on her skin to attention. She licked her lips and met his gaze.

"Reena just brought Tara to me," Hilda was saying and shut the pantry door, then faced her son. "And where have you been? Traipsing around the countryside alone again, I see."

"The hills called out to me. And, I needed to rest my brain." He glanced from his mama to Tara. "Have you ever been on a motorcycle, Tara, niece of Reena?"

His direct question took Tara by surprise. The wrong answer might give her away. Gothman women didn't ride motorcycles. So why would he ask? The fact that she'd been on a motorcycle for as long as she could remember, probably longer if she knew Patha, didn't matter. To admit that would raise suspicion. There was no way he should be suspicious right now. Although, his question suggested he might have doubts about who she really was. Tara started to smile while working up a satisfactory denial to redirect what he might think of her.

Hilda spoke first. "For Gothman's sake, Darius. Of course she hasn't been on a motorcycle before. Look at her. She wouldn't know the first thing."

Darius didn't have to look. He'd already memorized her face, her figure, and the rest of her, even though the parts he ached to see the most were tantalizingly beneath her loose fitting dress. Tara was unlike any woman he'd ever seen. He was a trained warrior, the leader of all Gothman, skilled at controlling his feelings, his emotions. What he saw before him was a challenge. Tara hadn't answered when he asked if she'd been on a motorcycle. Instead those sapphire eyes had looked amused. This had to be the Runner he allowed to escape in the forest—he felt it in his gut—and would prove it with time.

"I'm looking at her." Darius said, giving Tara his full attention. He decided it was time to start proving his theory as to who this woman really was. "Come with me, lass. I'll take you for a ride on a motorcycle."

"Darius!" Hilda protested. "I would think…we were just starting—"

"Ah, your housework can wait." Darius grabbed Tara's arm and turned to the door leading outside.

Tara almost yanked free when Darius grabbed her arm. Winters of training made it instinctive to defend against such a touch. Her body tightened before she thought. She made the effort to relax. Taking a deep breath, she didn't pull away. When he opened the door he glanced at her. Powerful gray eyes devoured her, and she didn't look away.

Tara worried she heightened suspicion by almost pulling free when the lord took her arm. As she met his gaze, however, identity wasn't what was going through the lord's thoughts at all. Instead, Tara saw unbridled passion. She stepped through the door and gulped in fresh air. She would definitely need to keep a clear head.

It also helped when Lord Darius let go of her arm. She walked alongside him but gave herself space, which allowed a better view of the man and his actions. He was tall, very tall, with large, solid muscles through the shoulders. His golden hair hung in curls well past his ears. But it was those intense gray eyes that sealed the package. Darius was probably a formidable warrior to rule Gothman. He was also a sexual predator who would likely welcome a fight before fucking her. Knowledge she'd be smart to keep in mind.

"I've something to show you." Darius walked in the direction of his bike, which was parked next to the shed. The shed that harbored her bike!

Tara ached to throw open the doors and make sure her motorcycle was alright. Instead, she appraised his motorcycle. It was much larger than her bike, and was of Gothman style with its long narrow seat that came up in the back. It wasn't designed for speed. Instead it was large and sturdy—designed to handle the rough terrain it travelled each day.

It was hard to stay calm and not rush forward, when Darius walked around his bike and opened the shed door.

"Look at this, if you will, my lady." He walked into the shed and pointed. "Have you ever seen anything like it?"

"Both are very nice. Are they yours?" Tara was incredibly relieved to see the shed wasn't locked. Nor did the door squeak when he opened it.

"It's a Runner's bike."

Darius sounded proud as he ran his hand over her bike that she'd owned and taken very good care of for almost ten winters.

"Are we going to ride it?"

"I wish we were." Darius looked at her. "It has some kind of lock on it. Once I break the code on it, I will. You can believe me on that one."

"I do believe you." Tara stroked her bike. She was glad to see it wasn't damaged. It didn't appear tampered with either. She did a visual inspection and fought the urge to squat next to it and reassure herself that all was still in working order.

"Let's go." Darius walked out of the shed and shut the door after her.

Reluctantly she followed to his bike. Tara stifled a gasp when large hands encircled her waist and lifted her onto it.

"You're heavier than you look, lass. You're quite the thin one. I would think you'd be light as a feather, but every muscle of yours is built up as if you did man's work."

He looked at her with those deep gray eyes, so unlike any shade she'd ever seen before. They held her captive when she tried to look away. When he dropped his hands to his sides, she almost wished he would put them back on her.

"I've worked hard all my life." Tara forced herself to look at the ground.

"I'd like to hear about that life sometime," he said and eased on the long seat in front of her.

Tara stifled a groan when the smooth leather of his pants rubbed her inner thighs. The man didn't offer her a lot of room behind him, and her body was forced up against his backside. Her legs spread wide to accommodate him, which caused her dress to slide up, exposing a fair amount of leg. The position left her feeling incredible vulnerable, a feeling she didn't like. At the same time, being smashed up against this virile man's backside sent a rush of heat through her too strong to ignore. There wasn't time to sit and evaluate her conflicting emotions however.

"Hold on tight, my lady." Lord Darius started the bike and took off quickly…very quickly.

Tara's inner thighs locked against his legs. She grabbed him and pressed herself against his back.

Darius would enjoy the mission of exposing this Runner. And yes, she had to be the Runner. Any Gothman woman would have fallen off the bike and landed flat on her back from his quick take off. Yet Tara had remained glued to him as his bike left the ground to fly over the uneven, rocky ground.

If Tara hadn't been an expert rider, he would have killed her right there on the spot. Maybe that was what he had in mind. He raced over the first hill too fast for their ride to be a casual view of the countryside. She hugged his body, moving as he did, keeping her head down. Taut muscles rippled underneath her hands, and she fought not to move her fingers over them.

They rode faster than she expected, almost as if racing into battle. The wind slapped her hair against her face and, when she tried to look up, made her eyes water. Lord Darius' motorcycle rumbled loudly as he went flying over hills and around rocks. If it weren't for the many winters she'd been on a bike, she would have flown off to her death.

After some distance, Darius slowed his bike and stopped. They were at the base of a very rocky hill, and a gutted path disappeared into the pines leading up it.

Tara allowed her hands to move slowly down Darius' chest until she rested them on either side of his waist. His body was as fine tuned as the machine they sat on. He would make an incredible adversary, or an incredible lover. Now wasn't the time to decide which. She was being tested here, and she planned to do her fair share of testing in return.

"You've been on a bike before. Don't deny it. I wouldn't be surprised if you rode rather well, too."

Lord Darius turned his head, but his expression wasn't readable. She might hide the truth about who she was but a Runner would never lie about her warrior skills.

"Good thing then," he said as if she'd answered him. "Are you ready for a climb?"

"I think so," Tara said, trying to sound unsure, but she was thoroughly excited about the fact that they were not through with the ride.

"Wrap those arms around tight now."

Darius didn't go as fast this time. He used caution on the rocky path and the bike groaned under their weight as he revved the motor and pushed the large motorcycle up the dangerous path. He enjoyed Tara's body pressed against him. When she did as she was told, and wrapped her arms around his waist once again, he grinned, knowing she couldn't see his expression. No woman had stirred him like this before. Not only did he want her body, for some reason he had a desire to know her thoughts. The reason came to him too quickly for him to process. It was simply there. Gothman women all thought the same thing. They wanted a good claim, a nice home, and children. They would raise those children and spend the rest of their lives talking endlessly about the goings on—the gossip in Bryton, who was doing what, how they were doing it, and who they were doing it with. If Runner women wanted the same thing as Gothman women, what was this woman doing on his land?

"I'm going to show you a very private place. I've been coming here since I was a boy. I hope you won't think less of me if I say I like to escape from ruling this land once in a while."

"No, my lord, I won't think that." Tara also watched the road, if the jagged path was actually that. She didn't have to press against him now and was able to focus more on her surroundings.

He skilfully navigated the bike around each rock and protrusion without any instruction from her, although she did have to bite her tongue a time or two to keep from pointing out large rocks. Eventually, the path led them to a clearing at the top of the rugged hill.

It was a small shady area of grass, completely surrounded by pine trees and hidden from the world. "Oh, it's beautiful," she said without thinking.

Tara again ran her hands down the side of his chest, and adjusted her legs, feeling him all the way from her inner thighs to her crotch. This man over stimulated every inch of her.

He would not make a good enemy. Not only was his physical strength twice that of hers, his body tormented her beyond what it should. Heat scorched her skin wherever they touched. It was a noticeable distraction. Beyond that, the natural warrior blood running through him, his ability to connect with what was around him really appealed to her. One fact made all of this very unpleasant. It was impossible to make Darius a lover. The simple truth was that he was already her enemy.

Darius cut the engine. This time, Tara slid off from behind him before he was able to put those confident hands on her and help her off the bike. She twisted and shook her hips to adjust her dress, and knew Darius watched. Tara made quick work of it instead of arching her body, or pressing her hands to the curves of her hips the way her mind suggested she might. Flirting with danger might lead to an attack. She turned to see his eyes on her rear end and knew a sense of power, one she needed to use very carefully.

"So, when did you first ride on a motorcycle?"

Those powerful gray eyes never left her while she walked across the small patch of thick, wet grass to a large rock and sat down on it. The cloth shoes she wore were useless. Tara wrapped her arms around her legs, pulling the material of her dress so that she felt less exposed and watched him as he climbed off his bike. He suspected her, of that there was no doubt. Or did he know her true identify and simply toyed with her? There had to be a way to find out.

Tara thought of the best way to answer. If Darius killed her, Patha would have his revenge. If she killed him, it would also start a war. Her instincts usually didn't fail her when caution was called for. This man was a threat, but she didn't sense hostility, nor had she since she met him.

By the look in his eyes it didn't appear that he had murder on his mind. His gaze was incredibly seductive yet guarded. She smiled and decided to take his comment as a joke.

"You really don't think I can drive your big motorcycle." Tara liked her response. It was time to change the subject, though. "Why did you bring me up here?"

"I want to know you better. I've seen your response to my men's advances, and I sure don't want to be made the fool in front of them."

Tara looked down at the ground fighting a grin. He walked over and sat down on the rock next to her. He didn't hesitate but put one arm around her back and rested his hand on her shoulder.

Tara's entire body tightened from his forwardness, and the urge to elbow him in the gut was almost as strong as the urge to turn and kiss him before he kissed her. These warring emotions were clouding her ability to think.

He pointed at the hill across from them with his other hand. "There's a cliff up that way. You have to climb to get to it, but you can see all of Gothman from up there. That, my lady, is my favorite place of all." Darius pointed to some rocks further up the hill. "Are you up for the climb?"

"I don't think I could do that, my lord." He was trying to test her. She wouldn't allow him to fail her. "I would tear my dress for sure."

"Of course." Lord Darius leaned against the wall of rock behind them and stared at her. His hand moved from her shoulder to rub the center of her back. "You're very beautiful, Tara. I know for a fact there's not a lady in all of Gothman that comes close to your looks."

He smiled and reached to stroke her hair. "I can't help but wonder if you'd attack me if I tried to kiss you." Darius looked at her, seeming amused at the thought. "And the way that body of yours is fine-tuned, I wouldn't be surprised if you'd have some luck at it."

Tara turned to look at him, but didn't answer. The thought of attacking him if he tried to kiss her created a rush of warmth between her legs. His face was inches from hers and those gray eyes seemed capable of owning her every thought. She fought a grin as she imagined challenging him.

He must have noticed her slight change in expression because his eyebrows rose, as if sincerely surprised that she might be considering attacking him. He really didn't know anything about Runners.

But he did suspect her. She was certain at that moment that she'd betrayed every secret she had by meeting his gaze. He would own her every thought if she didn't pull her eyes from his. He was reaching deep toward her very soul.

She fought for control of her thoughts with every ounce of power she possessed. Just because he suggested sensuality didn't mean she had to submit. He was accustomed to passive women but at that moment she didn't like the role she was supposed to be playing. Her defiance might prove an ugly taste for him. Then what? The lord might throw her on the ground and have his way with her, unless she took charge of the situation. If she did, though, it might mean a death sentence.

Passive, be passive. And if you are he will definitely fuck you.

It became clear if she fought him, or remained submissive and allowed him control, the end result would be the same. If she fought his advances and refused to fuck him he would have his answer about her true identity. No matter the end result, she had to play the part of a Gothman woman, or risk a possible war.

Tara studied Lord Darius and those beautiful gray eyes. The sunlight added color to his blond curls, some of them pale as corn silk, while others were darker than gold. His hair bordered a smooth face, shy of a small scar that interrupted an otherwise perfect jaw line. She curled her hands into fists to prevent herself from reaching up to touch that scar and trace it just to see if it would alter his expression. He had no wrinkles, no worry lines, nothing to indicate he was consumed or tortured with hard decisions. His features were perfect.

"Would you have me fight you, my lord?" she whispered.

His lips parted, and he dropped his gaze to her mouth. "No woman has ever tried to stop me before."

"And you think I would have some success at it?"

His chuckle forced his Adam's apple up and down, and sent chills through her heated body. "I'm thinking you are like no other woman."

The laughter in his eyes was almost her undoing. She wanted to pounce on him, to slap him for his pompous attitude, and to kiss him just to show him she had what it took to overpower his supposed omnipotence.

"But no, my lady, you won't be successful at stopping me."

Tara jumped to her feet. She stood over him with her hands still balled in fists at her sides. Every bit of sense she had, along with winters of training to understand all types of attacks, prepared her to take the offensive. She towered over Darius, planting her feet firmly on the ground, and inhaled deeply to clear her thoughts.

"You think you can have me as you please, simply because you desire it?" Tara barely remembered at the last moment to speak with a Gothman accent.

"There is no doubt, my lady."

"And if I don't wish it?"

"My lady," Lord Darius whispered, almost growled. "You do wish it."

Tara had never met a man more sexually sure of himself. He excited her and filled her with outrage. She stared at him.

Darius relaxed, then crossed his arms across that broad chest. Rope-like muscles twitched under his tanned forearms. He seemed at ease, as if allowing her time to accept the inevitable.

Tara narrowed her eyes. "You will not rape me," she hissed.

Darius laughed, and she took a step backward. "My lady, I'm thinking that won't be necessary."

He straightened his legs, stretching them so that long corded muscles rippled underneath his brown leather pants. Every inch of him was perfect. Tara found her gaze travelling over the bulge at his crotch and forced her attention to keep moving. He might need a slight attitude adjustment, but she imagined him well-endowed. There wasn't anything wrong with fucking a man who was more than a bit sure of himself. Once that thought entered her mind, it was hard picturing leaving this secluded place before finding out.

She found herself standing between those long, powerful legs but then saw he had needed to rearrange his position to allow room for his growing erection. This time Tara didn't look away from the hardened length now visible under the material below his belt. Beyond a doubt, she had never met a more pompous, self-righteous, and incredibly sexy man as the one who now seemed to surround her with his aura.

Tara turned to create distance, and Darius bent one leg, blocking her path. She didn't jump around him, or stumble over him, but merely stopped. "Is this how you take every lady who catches your eye, my lord?"

"I've never waited this long before." Darius sounded amused. "But then any other lass would have submitted by now."

Tara almost said she wasn't any other lass. Those would have been her exact words to any other man, but Lord Darius wasn't any other man. No man had ever stimulated her emotions like this before, much less one who kept her guessing at the same time. She might enjoy this man, and it would be a long time before she grew bored.

"Do they fall at your feet? Or do they simply strip in front of you?" Tara asked as she continued to stare at the leg blocking her path.

"Has it crossed your mind to do either?"

Tara sensed Darius' movement and turned as he leaned forward. "No," she stated, unable to do more as one large hand interlocked fingers with her smaller hand. Tara didn't oppose the touch, but studied his hand, which now held hers. The rough heat from his grasp sent warmth up her arm at an amazing speed.

"I'll teach you to submit." Darius didn't make the statement as a threat, but spoke the words gently, as a papa willing to show a child a new lesson.

When he pulled her to him, the only thing crossing Tara's mind was that likewise, she would teach him manners. The intensity of his gaze, those gray eyes, so unique in color, watching her while he drew her closer, gave her the impression teaching him anything would be quite the chore. Stubborn and powerful, ruthless and aggressive, she saw the bad and the good in him with defined clarity.

She wanted to look away, anything to distract her. But damn it if she didn't want to taste him and know the source of the heat that flooded through her with just his touch.

His arms wrapped her into him, almost crushing her in their grip. And then he kissed her.

Tara didn't try stopping him. Placing her arms on his shoulders, then grabbing hair on either side of his head, she returned the kiss with an aggression she'd never used on a man before.

He slid her off the rock and onto the ground. His strength made her wild. All attempts to conceal her identity were forgotten. A thick fog of lust consumed her senses. His body was strong, powerful, and dangerous. It excited her more than anything had before. She fought to strip the pants away from the treasure that would be hers.

He was huge, hardened to stone. She felt, more than saw, his erection. His hands were rough on her as he used confident expertise in removing her dress. It was tossed to the side and instantly forgotten. Then Darius' hand was between her legs, testing her for moistness. Not that she wanted foreplay. This wasn't about romance. It wasn't as if the two of them would ever have a relationship.

"Let's see if you fuck as well as you defy a man, my lady," he growled.

Tara was up to the challenge. "On your back," she insisted, pushing against him as he spoke.

Darius pushed his finger inside her instead of obeying. He did lift himself off of her partially, but only to grab her hair with his free hand and pull.

"The first lesson in submission is not telling me what to do," he whispered, lowering his mouth to hers as he spoke.

She wasn't able to answer. His finger impaled her. Her scalp burned where he pulled her hair. The mixture of pleasure and pain damn near sent her flailing into her first orgasm.

But the kiss ended and his finger slid free before she peaked. Tara blinked, taking a moment to gather her wits. Before she did, Darius rolled to his back and pulled her on top of him.

"Fuck me, my lady."

Clarity returned and she found herself amused instead of frustrated that she hadn't just come. If Lord Darius needed to feel that edge of superiority over her, she'd allow him to entertain the notion, for a moment or two.

She straddled him and forced the penetration herself as he grabbed her breasts. Darius slid so deeply inside her that she fought to control the moment.

He pulled back as she rocked forward. Then he lunged, almost choking her with the depth he reached.

Tara collapsed on him. But before she recovered and regained her strength, his powerful arms wrapped around her body and he lunged again. Fighting to gain control was the hardest thing she'd ever done. She dug her fingers into his chest and pushed—hard—forcing herself up. As his grip around her intensified, she took advantage of the preoccupation and thrust her hips down, consuming every inch of him inside of her, tightening around him, suffocating all life out of him. She was, most definitely, the victor.

A muffled grunt, deep within him, rose to a howl as she forced his orgasm. Then, not willing to let him have his pleasure without her, she thrust again and leaped to meet the intensity with her own climax. She held him inside her, while he stretched and filled her. Closing her eyes, she rode the waves of satisfaction that rushed through her. Where she had tried to show the upper hand, she had instead received the privilege of being fucked good and hard, allowing her one orgasm and leaving her wanting more.

This was not lovemaking. There had been no foreplay. Pure and simply, it was a struggle of powers. A ruthless, dominating nation taking on another, equally powerful and equally dangerous. Through the act of sex, they'd tried to conquer each other—and failed. If they'd attempted to keep the act purely physical, playing the part of the skilled warrior, and not allowing emotions to interfere—again, they both failed. The pleasure had been too great and the power struggle too intoxicating. Tara saw all of this as true and knew she'd have to give further thought to it later.

Darius eased his grip on Tara. He sat up, still inside her, and stared deeply into that place he'd just experienced. There couldn't possibly be another woman like her on Nuworld. Sex had always been an act of pleasure, sometimes necessary, sometimes simply to amuse himself. It had never occurred to him how the pleasure might intensify with a willing, enthused partner. Darius enjoyed sex as a predatory act. Sometimes the look of fear, or submissive anticipation, excited him enough to pursue a lady who caught his eye. Tara had offered him neither, yet she had brought him to a hardened boil like none had before.

What was it about this woman?

Intelligence mixed with her beauty in a way Darius hadn't thought possible. She wore the two qualities in a way that drew him. He wanted to know her. It dawned on him that he had never really cared to know any woman before Tara. Women served a purpose, but one of them wasn't companionship. With Tara, he wanted to know why she thought the way she did, what ticked behind those blue eyes.

But there was something else. Darius wanted to make Tara his. This woman was no Gothman, but she was on his land, acting the part of a Gothman. There was mystery behind her, but that didn't bother him. All knowledge of her would be his in time.

What fascinated him was his desire to possess her, and all that she was.

"How do you feel about the fact that with one word I could have you rule this land at my side?" Darius whispered into her ear.

"You know nothing about me. I may make a lousy ruler." She returned his gaze, snagging her fingers in his hair, then pulling them free. "I would think something like that should be a mutual decision, my lord." She pushed herself off of him and looked around until she spotted her dress.

"I'm not surprised you'd answer like that, my lady." He wasn't daunted by her boldness. "You're not like any lass I've met and I've known a few. They're always polite and submissive, of course, and they say only what they think I want to hear. You think for yourself. I like that. Why are you like that, Tara?"

"I guess I don't see why women have to be less than men." She looked at him, as if checking for his immediate reaction.

There was no need to respond. She was in his world and he didn't doubt she knew his laws. Instead, he got up and picked up the pants Tara had managed to pull off him. Showing this woman how to submit would be more pleasure than he originally thought.

Tara noticed Darius could go another round. She liked that quality in a man. She had to admit, more than his sexuality impressed her. Darius acted interested in her. Tara didn't fool herself into believing his curiosity was drawn by affection.

She knew better.

Darius questioned her nature because he needed confirmation she was a Runner. His tactics were far more impressive than capture and torture. Tara also considered that he might think she wasn't an enemy.

Gothman and Runners might have a bad history, but that history didn't affect her. In fact, Tara wasn't sure if there was reason for the two nations of people to despise each other. Ignorance had made them enemies. Tara wondered if knowledge might make them allies.

Tara got dressed and walked to his motorcycle, guessing he wasn't pleased by her last comment and would probably take her back to the house. The man wanted her compliance.

She was sure she knew his thoughts. Any Gothman woman would do well to be claimed by the Lord of Gothman.

But Tara wasn't Gothman, and he there was nothing he had to offer that she wasn't able to obtain on her own. She guessed that since she didn't dance in appreciation to his suggestion, she had offended him, and possibly bruised that mighty ego.

"The Gothman culture has been the way it is for hundreds of winters," Darius finally said, and buttoned his pants.

She turned and walked back to him. "Cultures can change, don't you think?"

Darius wasn't looking at her face.

She wondered if he even heard her question. He seemed more intent on studying her breasts. "And who better to start a change but the leader of the land? I've never known a man like you." Tara ran her hands up his chest, feeling the pounding of his heart under muscles that tightened against her touch. "Gothman is powerful, and that power comes from you. You alone can alter the state of women, and no one would stop you."

She watched her hands caress his chest, feeling the ironclad strength as well as his heat. The scent of their sex lingered. Her insides swelled, pulsed and ached for him to be inside her again.

Darius lifted her chin with one finger. Those gray eyes captivated her. Did she see amusement?

"Now, why would I change what already works so well?" Darius tapped her chin with his finger, then started toward his bike, leaving her standing there.

She forced her thoughts to clear, knowing a point should be made here.

"I've heard you're a great leader, Lord Darius. I'm sure you can do anything if you set your mind to it."

He got onto his bike and his expression turned hard. She smiled at him and easily slid on behind him.

Snuggling behind him increased her desire to have him again. But her brain was in pure turmoil. She feared that she'd allowed him to learn more about her than she'd wanted to share.

He'd openly admitted that she was different from any woman he had been with. Tara had to acknowledge that his ability to keep her from knowing whether or not he knew she was a

Runner was excellent strategy. It kept her alert and guessing. Instead of responding, he started the bike and turned it around with those thick, muscular legs of his.

Darius took his time returning to the house. His emotions were absolutely contorted beyond recognition. Tara was no Gothman. He had his Runner. Of that much, he was certain. The woman stirred something inside him, though. She'd also appealed to him physically. He would have her again, and soon. It was more than physical lust though. She'd just challenged him and she'd done it on purpose.

No one questioned the laws and traditions of Gothman. Nor would anyone dream of questioning him. Yet this female didn't hesitate to do so. Darius didn't need to explain to her why women had the role that they did. Conversation like that would have been a waste of his time. And really, it wasn't the issue itself, but the fact that this female had enough spunk to speak to him in such a way. No woman, no person, had done that before.

He thought about the past few winters and how he'd taken whatever he'd wanted, and how no one, absolutely no one, had stood in his way. If they'd tried, they'd been killed. He felt no remorse. He'd not been heir to Gothman, but had known since he was a child that he was the one meant to rule. His older brother hadn't had the backbone. His papa had known that, but was too preoccupied by tradition to allow the middle son to rule. So, Darius had taken matters into his own hands.

Once becoming Lord of Gothman he had continued taking what he wanted. And that had included practically every available lass in Bryton. Not that any had objected. His mama had brought every young Gothman woman she found into the household. He'd slept with each one of them; at least he was pretty sure he had. But then, he'd lost interest. Each one had taken the edge off, fucking him when he went to them. But beyond that, they bored him. The Lord of Gothman needed a claim. He would push on thirty winters before long, and he knew the town anticipated he claim one of their available women. More than once he'd told himself to just claim one of them and be done with it. But the thought of having any of those women under his roof for the rest of his winters rubbed him to the point of irritation.

His younger brother, Mikel, frowned upon his promiscuity. Mikel was too much like their papa, Lord Jovis.

Darius knew what his papa would have said if he'd learned Darius just had sex with a Runner—something he definitely planned on doing again.

In Darius' tenth or twelfth winter, his papa had engaged in a heated argument about Runners *with* a Runner. Darius hadn't witnessed the event, but he remembered his papa's tirade over it afterward. What had stuck in Darius' mind over the winters was that his papa relented to the Runner's wishes. He remembered thinking his papa was weak not to stand up to the Runner. It had also put a kind of awe in his young mind as to the type of man who would argue with the Lord of Gothman and survive to have his way.

It dawned on him suddenly that the argument had involved Reena. And it was Reena who'd brought Tara to them.

Darius knew Reena associated with Runners from time to time. She allowed a lone Runner to spend the night in her secluded cabin before continuing on his way. Darius hadn't seen reason for concern. The woman lived outside the town. She didn't gossip about her occasional visitor, and his guards never reported that the Runner caused problems.

But with Tara's coming, something had changed. She was the first Runner to enter Gothman and venture further into the community. Maybe he'd get his answers faster if he interrogated Reena. Although that definitely wouldn't be as much fun as seducing them out of Tara.

As he pulled into the backyard and parked behind his shed, he already plotted how he would know why Tara was here, and what she wanted. He already knew what *he* wanted. Tara hopped off the bike and started walking toward the house without saying anything.

Darius grabbed her arm and spun her around. "Your second lesson in submitting is to leave my side when I say it's okay to do so."

To his surprise, Tara leaned into him, going up on her tiptoes. "Does the Lord of Gothman wish to fuck me right here for all his guards to see?" she whispered.

Before he answered, because honestly, he'd never seen such boldness out of a woman, Tara ignored his instruction and once again started toward the house. Darius grabbed her and almost knocked her off her feet with the aggressiveness he used to spin her back around.

"I'll say it again, my lady. You're different from any woman I've known. I'm curious why you'd like to see Gothman culture change. Changing to be like whom, I'm wondering." He looked at her hard, but Tara remained silent, staring back with an expression so calm he knew it had taken winters of training to master it.

Darius studied her tanned complexion, her brown hair that fell past her shoulders and was soft as silk. Her lips were full, and he ached with a sudden urgency to kiss them again. He focused on her eyes, a blue that darkened with her emotions, as he was discovering. Right now they were a rich, pure, rare dark sapphire, challenging him.

He moved his attention to her breasts, perky and full, with nipples hardened to a tempting peak under her dress. He released her arm and ran a finger over one nipple. She didn't flinch, which pleased him for a reason he couldn't identify. Darius pulled her close. "We are going to do this again, soon. Now you may go."

CHAPTER FIVE

DARIUS DIDN'T spend much time at home. Tara ached to see him more, to touch him, and to experience his touch again. But the leader of Gothman was awake and gone often before sunrise, and seldom returned before late in the evening. Many nights after she had retired for the day, Tara sat in her bedroom with the door open and listened for when he would climb the stairs.

Tara itched to know what politics distracted him. No Gothman woman would think of asking the lord about his business. She wanted to join him in his office, ask about his day, and exchange stories. She wanted to share experiences with him and learn more about how the man ticked. But to do any of that would spread suspicion. She'd already done enough of that. As much as she ached for Darius to know her better, that would be a fool's mission. So she sat alone in the dark of her bedroom every night, wondering what Darius thought of her, and if he would ever act on that knowledge.

Tonight she had fallen asleep before he'd come home. It had surprised her how much a permanent home needed cleaning, and how exhausting that work was. Her eyes fluttered open at the sound of his boots on the stairs. Slow and steady, her heart raced with anticipation. With every breath, her breasts swelled, pressing against the covers while she listened to him move down the hallway.

A door opened, but didn't close. He had gone to his room.

She ran her hands down her body, imagining Lord Darius touching her. A fever burned inside her, an ache for him grew with every moment that she lay in the dark, straining to hear what he might be doing. Her frustration peaked when his door finally closed, the house growing quiet once again. Embers smoldered while a fever she couldn't control made her insides throb for a man she knew she could never truly have.

"What will we do today?" Torgo asked, as he sat on the stool in the kitchen watching Tara clean breakfast dishes.

"Well now, I will have to check with your mama and see if there are any extra chores she has in mind for me. I have to earn my keep, you know." She smiled at his forlorn look.

"Mama will have you busy forever," he complained, looking disappointed.

"I don't know about forever, child." Hilda stood in the doorway. "I'll have you clean the first floor today. It won't take long, as long as Darius doesn't take you away again."

Tara blushed.

Hilda grinned and chuckled as she walked out of the room.

"Has my brother claimed you yet?" Torgo asked.

Tara was surprised at the question, but the look of innocence on his face reminded her that this was his culture. "No, child, he hasn't."

"When I get older, I'm going to claim a girl as pretty as you."

Torgo followed Tara around the house, talking to her as she dusted the rooms and cleaned the floors until she'd finished the first floor. The late morning air was brisk and a cool south breeze floated down from the hills as the young boy led Tara to the grassy meadow beyond the backyard.

"To be a strong warrior like your brother, you must start your lessons at a young age." She squatted to collect several small rocks.

"And what do you know about being a strong warrior?" Torgo laughed.

Tara squinted at the boy who stood next to her, silhouetted by the sun. "I grew up with brothers who all worked to be great warriors."

Torgo accepted the explanation with a quick nod. Every Gothman boy dreamed of being a great warrior.

"Darius said he would teach me to ride a motorcycle when I was a little older." The boy put his hands on his hips and stood a little taller.

"Ah, that's good. I think we should see how your aim is today. Do you see that tree over that way? Hit it with these rocks." She handed him the rocks.

Torgo hesitated. "It's too far away."

Tara took the rocks from him and threw them one at a time, hitting the trunk of the tree each time. She bent down and gathered more rocks. "Now, you try."

Amazed, the boy took the rocks and threw them, missing the tree each time.

Tara agreed they could move closer.

After many attempts, Torgo finally started to hit the tree. His excitement showed through his young eyes and he hugged Tara joyfully. "They won't pick on me at school anymore." He attempted a jig as he jumped around in a circle.

"This is just the beginning of many things a great warrior will need to know." They walked slowly back to the house together.

"Throwing rocks?" Torgo looked confused. "Is this something you did with your brothers?"

"Did you just learn to throw rocks today?" Tara eyed the young boy whose face showed his eagerness to learn.

"Yes. All I did *was* throw rocks." Torgo sounded confused.

"Ah, I think you learned several things today. Give it some thought. Meanwhile, practice on different targets. Maybe tomorrow we can get outside again. It sure is a nice break from my chores." To Tara's surprise, the young boy jumped at her and gave her a tight hug.

"Why are we sitting out here?" Reena faced her lifelong friend across the table and pulled her shawl tighter around her shoulders as she shivered against the morning chill.

Hilda waved her hand to the servant girl to refill both of their coffees. "I thought it would be more private."

"Private?" Reena picked up her cup of coffee and held it in both hands. "Old woman, what are you up to? And why do you keep glancing at the house?"

"Tara is in there."

"Are you afraid she'll blow the place up?"

"No." Hilda laughed, leaned back in her chair, and dismissed the servant with a wave of her hand. "You are my good friend, Reena."

"Over forty winters." Reena nodded and sipped her coffee. "You spiked this with Gothman wine."

"Just to take the edge off."

"You thought it would get me blabbing."

"You have secrets?"

Reena laughed. "At my age? We have plenty of secrets."

"I guess that's true. I'm thinking of Tara."

"Is there a problem? Lord Darius hasn't sent her packing."

Hilda nodded. "She has been here longer than any other girl I've brought to him. But Reena, she'd rather play in the hills with Torgo than sew, or clean. She can't cook. And you won't believe it, but my son took her riding on his motorcycle, of all things. That girl was glowing when she came back."

Reena went white as a ghost and almost dropped her cup on the table between them. Hilda was finally getting through to her friend. Maybe now she'd get some answers.

"When did he take her on his motorcycle?"

"A good half-cycle ago. Ah, yes. It was her first day here. Reena, no Gothman girl would enjoy such a thing. It's not proper," Hilda stressed. "Tell me why is she like this?"

"A half cycle? Yet she's inside cleaning. Why are you complaining?"

"It's the only thing she does know how to do," Hilda muttered.

Reena pushed away from the table. "I'm going to go see my niece," she said, and hurried toward the house.

"Reena!" Hilda called after her, but her old friend just moved faster.

Hilda huffed, more convinced than ever that something wasn't quite right.

"Remember you said we would hike along the creek today." Torgo leaned against the doorway, watching Tara put fresh sheets on his brother's bed.

"I remember." Tara grabbed the large comforter from the floor and threw it on to the bed. She wondered how many women the lord had brought to this bed. Her stomach tightened at the thought and she turned her attention to Torgo. "If I suggest something, promise you'll keep it a secret?"

Torgo's gray eyes—eyes just like his brothers- grew wide and he grinned. "Of course I can keep a secret. What is it?"

Tara glanced into the hallway. No one else was upstairs.

"It would be a lot easier to take a hike along the creek if I had some pants. Your mama is resting, and your brother isn't here. If you have a pair I could borrow, it would also keep my dress from getting dirty."

Torgo almost leapt for the hallway. He stopped in the doorway and turned to face Tara. "I'm sure I have pants for you," he whispered. "And you're right about your dress. Mama would have a fit if you got all messy. We can't have that."

"No, we can't." Tara grinned as the boy hurried to his bedroom.

The pants Torgo offered fit her well enough with a belt. She observed herself for only a moment in the mirror in her bedroom before joining Torgo in the hall. Halfway down the stairs however, Tara stopped and Torgo ran into her backside. Darius stood talking to two of his guards in the living room.

Tara mentally chastised herself for not hearing them enter the house. She motioned with her hand and the two of them backed up the stairs. Tara cringed with every noisy footstep Torgo made. "Let's try the other staircase," Tara whispered and pointed toward the back of the house where the servant's staircase led to the kitchen.

They made it to the kitchen, and Tara reached for the doorknob on the back door, when a sound alerted her already heightened senses. She pushed Torgo behind her, as she turned and faced one of Lord Darius' guards.

"My lord," the guard called, and at the same time pulled his oversized Gothman bang stick on Tara.

"What are you doing, man?" Darius frowned as he pushed past the guard and spotted Tara and Torgo. "Put that away. Now!"

"But my lord, we have her in pants now. I daresay that says a lot."

"It tells me nothing," Darius' voice boomed. "Out with you and your man. I will meet with you in a moment."

Tara heard the front door open and close, but kept her gaze pinned on Darius' large backside. Muscles twitched under his shirt, which stretched against his broad shoulders. Large and dangerous. Her heart fluttered, missing a beat while she worked to keep her expression relaxed.

Darius turned and cocked his head as he studied Tara. "I do believe I like you better in dresses."

"The pants are mine, Darius." Torgo stepped around Tara. "She didn't want to upset mama by messing up her dress."

Tara rested a hand on Torgo's shoulder and smiled. She felt him tremble but he stood tall and faced his brother. Tara was proud of him. "It's okay, Torgo. We've done nothing wrong."

"I'm thinking I will be the judge of that," Darius scolded. "Where is it that you are going dressed like this?"

"Torgo and I are going hiking along the creek." Tara worked to focus her thoughts on something other than the virile man studying her. She risked suspicion and needed to put any questions to rest. "I thought it would be nice to give Hilda some peace and quiet while she rested."

"I see." Darius sighed and waved a hand.

Torgo took that as a dismissal and pulled the door open before his plans were cancelled. Tara turned to follow the boy who already ran across the backyard.

Darius grabbed her jaw before she turned from him. He cupped the top of her neck and turned her to face him. Without a word, his mouth covered hers.

She gasped at the heat from his lips as her mouth opened to return the kiss. Her fingers eagerly slid under his leather jacket and traced the strong chest muscles under his shirt. Pressure mounted between her legs and made her knees wobbly. She felt herself getting wet. Tara grabbed his shirt and held on.

"Be back within the hour, or I will be looking for you myself," Darius whispered. "And, my lady, no one else will see you dressed like that. Cross me on this and I'll see to your punishment myself."

Tara wanted to make him hunt for her, but she would be with Torgo so she pushed that fantasy to the side. As for anyone seeing her teach Torgo how to be a warrior—well she was in full agreement they not be spotted. He released her jaw, and let his hand slide to the nape of her neck. She let go of his shirt and let out a jagged sigh.

Darius turned her toward the door, let go of her, but then gave her a quick swat on her rear end. "Be careful now, my lady."

"I'm always careful, my lord," she said, managing to keep her voice steady. She hurried to catch up with Torgo, but turned to give Darius a delighted smile. The kiss was awesome. The slight sting on her ass made her crave him even more. And she was so much more comfortable in pants. "You have nothing to worry about. We will be fine."

Tara scrubbed windows the following morning and watched Darius secure a leather bag to the side of his bike. She still ached from waiting for him to seek her out the day before. But apparently the Lord of Gothman had many other responsibilities besides hunting her down. He was gone when she and Torgo returned to the house and hadn't returned until the early morning hours.

Finally, she had all the cleaning she could take and threw her rag to the floor. Tara marched through the house to the back door. After their kiss the day before, she knew he was still interested. She saw no problem with saying hello. Unfortunately, Hilda came down the stairs at that moment.

"I must say, you do make my old house sparkle." She smiled at Tara. "Have you cleaned most of the windows?"

"No, my lady, I've gotten as far as the living room and dining room." Tara stopped and leaned back to inspect her work. She hadn't cleaned many windows in her life, but this was the second time in almost a cycle that she'd wiped down these windows. They didn't look like they needed any more cleaning to her. "I'm glad my work pleases you."

"You're still here and that pleases me more than your work. But, I'll be needing you to take a break for now. I have a list of things I need from the grocery. The windows can wait 'til you get back." Hilda handed the list to Tara along with the keys to her groundmobile. "I'd go myself but my head hurts this morning. Be sure and get all the news from Thelga."

Tara returned the cleaning supplies to the pantry and paused to look longingly out the back door at Lord Darius. Several of his guards joined him and she watched them for a moment. They seemed to be in a rather serious discussion, and she was curious what they were saying. Hilda's groundmobile was parked out front, and Tara had no reason to leave through the back door in order to hear their conversation.

Their voices grew louder, and the guard who had attacked Tara was telling the rest of them something. Whatever he said upset Lord Darius, and he lunged at the man. The man backed down but continued to grumble. Tara simply couldn't make out what they were arguing about, even when she went to the back door and put her ear to it. She finally turned and headed out the front door to the groundmobile.

The argument between Darius and his guards proved a good distraction, so no one noticed Tara teach herself how to drive Hilda's vehicle. It was newer looking than Reena's. The exterior was a puffy blue and the interior seats were overstuffed and covered with smooth, highly polished seats. It had very large windows and wouldn't suit at all to ride into battle. Granted, with it being Hilda's groundmobile, that wasn't likely to ever happen.

Tara had read about groundmobiles on her landlink, and she knew the mechanics of them, but driving one proved a slight challenge. The groundmobile lunged forward, and the engine lurched to a stop. Tara killed the motor several more times before she was able to make the small contraption move slowly along the road.

Bryton was lively with people going in and out of different shops. Children and dogs ran up and down the sidewalk, and women and older girls gathered here and there catching up on the latest gossip. Tara parked the groundmobile in front of the grocery store and smiled politely at four women standing outside. They smiled back but then returned to their conversation with more excitement than ever. She heard them say her name but didn't bother trying to overhear what they said. She was sure gossip would spread about her living in Lord Darius' house.

"Ah, good morning to you, girl." Thelga smiled broadly as Tara entered the store.

"And a good morning to you." Tara smiled in return and picked up a basket from the door.

"It's quite an honor you have done your old aunt, being claimed by his lordship, and all." Thelga clucked. "And you only being in our town for such a short time."

Tara grabbed her basket again to keep from dropping it. She looked at the old lady, stunned. "What are you saying?" Tara couldn't do more than whisper. "I have not been claimed by anyone."

"Oh, do you say, maybe you haven't been told. I'm sure I'm right. It was my claim who told me. He heard from the lord's guards." Thelga leaned on the counter and her eyes twinkled, knowing she got to be the first to share the news. "It happened this way to my granddaughter, too. She was claimed, and the men folk had such a merry party over it they forgot to tell her." Thelga laughed at the thought. "I know for a fact there isn't a prettier girl in town than you. I'm not the least bit surprised, to be honest." Thelga saw the look of shock on Tara's face and was trying to be reassuring. She reached over the counter and squeezed Tara's arm with her rough fingers. "There isn't a life a girl could ask for as nice as the one you'll have. Your sons'll be lords."

Tara was so surprised by what she'd just heard that she turned to walk back out of the store.

"Ah, my lady, your list?"

"Oh, yes…here it is." Tara handed the list to Thelga, then just stood there. She wanted to give Thelga the third degree and find out every bit of information she knew about this claiming. A guard had told her claim? When had Thelga heard this? How long had she known? Tara kept her mouth closed however and stood awkwardly in the middle of the store while a young errand boy took the list and ran through the store gathering the items.

Two young women not much older than Tara entered the store and smiled politely at her. They moved over to the produce, and Tara heard their conversation easily.

"My mama took a pie to her aunt the other day. The old lady said it was what they'd planned all along."

"I daresay she wasn't in town but a day when the lord claimed her. Imagine the likes, all of us having our hopes so high for so long. She comes along so merrily like, and he claims her right off."

"Yeah, and I heard she can't cook. She apparently is only good at one thing." The two girls laughed, then noticing Tara overheard them, started whispering.

Tara's blood boiled. This was too much. Hearing that Reena had planned her claiming all along put Tara into a rage. Was it true Darius had claimed her before she'd even gone to live in the house? The only time he'd seen her prior to that was in the alley when she'd kept Torgo out of that fight. Did Reena know at that point and Hilda, too? The entire town seemed to know this casual bit of information and somehow had overlooked sharing it with her.

The young errand boy brought the basket to the counter with the items from the list. Thelga arranged the items in a brown box with no lid and smiled at Tara.

"Don't you worry yourself none about the comments of girls such as those." Thelga didn't move her lips when she whispered. "They've all tried for the lord and failed. They're jealous of you. You hold your head high. You should be proud. You are a lady."

"You're right and thank you." Tara left the store and walked to the groundmobile.

Her eyes burned with angry tears as she drove back to Lord Darius' house. Her hands shook and Hilda's vehicle died so many times that Tara wanted to pull the circular handlebar off the dash and hurl it out the oversized window. She remembered Reena calling it a steering wheel but at that moment she didn't care.

Darius had asked her about being claimed when they'd driven into the hills together. Had he already claimed her by then? Was that why she was sent to his home to live?

Tara remembered watching him from her bedroom window her first day there. Darius had raced over the hills to get home. Now she knew why he had hurried home that morning almost a cycle ago. She had been made to believe she was hired help. Apparently the joke was on her.

She drove the groundmobile up the hill to the house with enough force that the tires skidded on the gravel road. Grabbing the box of groceries, Tara ran into the house. A piece of fruit fell out of the box and rolled across the floor. Tara didn't care. She tried not to sneeze when an array of fragrances from the spices Hilda had asked for drifted to her nose. Darius was in the living room with his guards, and she stormed past them into the kitchen.

"I don't see why you don't listen to reason, my lord," the large guard who'd attacked her growled loud enough for her to hear.

"Judo, the reasoning isn't sound. Not another word." Darius' growl chilled her blood. "And Mikel, my mind is made up."

"What's wrong with you? Why won't you listen when it comes to that lass?" Mikel, Lord Darius' younger brother, shouted.

"I said I was done discussing this." Darius used a tone Tara hadn't heard before. He spoke softly but there was a cold edge clipping each word.

"Your brain isn't doing your thinking for you, my lord. We found the bike, and you yourself have commented on her abilities. Her thighs are wrapped around you so tight you can't see the truth. She's your Runner! You've let her into this house, and now she'll bring down Gothman." Mikel sounded just as pissed. "Our papa would be disgraced if he knew what you were doing."

"That's enough!" Darius roared.

Tara shook with anger. She wasn't going to do anything to Gothman and she sure wasn't going to be anyone's claim.

Tara fought to clear her head. Right now she needed to think and not worry about a claim that had no bearing on her anyway. It was foolish being upset by it when she had bigger problems on her hands. Darius' men knew her true identity. And from the sound of it, wanted her taken down. Yet Darius hesitated. She only pondered for a moment that he hesitated because of a mutual attraction. Darius ruled a very powerful nation. His hesitation might be for other reasons. Tara needed to think straight if she were going to second guess his thinking.

How many men were in the living room? Three or four? Her first course of action needed to be how to take them all on and escape the house to her bike.

The front door slammed, and the house grew quiet.

Had they all left? Where was Hilda and the other servants? Tara needed time to think. In the past, when her temper threatened to get the best of her she'd take off on her motorcycle and drive until she calmed down. When that wasn't possible, she'd pick a fight with someone in her clan until she'd released all her anger on her poor victim.

The house was still quiet. Tara wandered out of the kitchen.

The living room was empty. She headed upstairs. Hilda must have been asleep in her room, or at least resting. Tara wasn't sure how anyone might sleep through the yelling match that had just occurred in the living room. If Hilda had overheard, she might now be fearful that she had a Runner in her home.

There wasn't time to worry about that right now.

She stepped quietly past the closed doors to her bedroom. The balcony seemed the only likely spot to sort through all her thoughts and make a plan of action.

Her smartest move was to leave Gothman and put as much distance between her and this nation as possible. Oddly enough, it also sounded wise to stay. "Why would he hesitate?" she murmured to herself. Maybe the Lord of Gothman saw that Runners weren't his enemy. If that were the case, she might ruin potential communication between her people and his.

"Tara, you're back. Will you come down? I've waited for you forever." Torgo stood in the yard looking up to her. He smiled and waved. "Hurry, I have a surprise. Put on a pair of my pants if you want. But hurry."

"Alright, boy. Calm down. I'll come down." Tara went to Torgo's room and found a pair of his pants. If she needed to hurry to her bike for any reason, it would be easier to escape wearing pants instead of the impractical dresses she wore every day.

She didn't care if any of the guards saw her. After overhearing Darius arguing with his brother and guards, she wasn't as angry as she had been hearing about the claiming. It would serve Darius right. If he had indeed gone and claimed her after she said she thought any claim should be mutual, then he could suffer the consequences. Or, worse, if he had claimed her before and then mentioned that he *could* claim her just to tease her, he had insulted her intelligence. In the end, none of it mattered. He couldn't force her to be his claim. And if he knew she was a Runner, he must also know announcing a claim on her would only make him appear the fool if the truth ever came out.

The blue pullover shirt and dark pants she borrowed from Torgo fit snugly. Tara guessed she probably showed a bit more of her figure through the clinging material than she planned. But she moved easily in the outfit and that mattered more than her appearance.

"You won't believe what I got." The boy danced around her when she entered the yard. "Look!"

Next to the shed was a motorcycle about the same size as Tara's.

Torgo ran to it and patted the seat. "It's mine." He glowed with pride. "Darius gave it to me just this morning." Torgo looked around them then whispered, "You can ride. I know you can. I heard my brother talking with his men. Will you teach me? My brother isn't in a very good mood today. He gave it to me and said we would ride, but then he got some kind of news and left."

"What kind of news did he get?" Tara asked.

"I don't know. What I do know is I want to learn to ride. Darius learned to ride when he had twelve winters. He told me so. I have fourteen, and I don't know how yet. You'll teach me, won't you?" he begged, with gray eyes a softer version of his older brother's. "I know some of my brother's men think it's odd that you know how to fight. But I don't think it's strange at all. Your papa was smart to teach you all he did."

Tara wondered how the boy was so open-minded when his older brother seemed so closed to new ideas. "Of course I will." Tara ran her hands over the small bike.

It was well designed, painted a clean metallic red, with the word *Bryton* written in gold. The seat curving up in the back was of the familiar Gothman style. It was an impressive motorcycle. Tara was just about to straddle it but hesitated at the surprised look on Torgo's face.

She turned her head to see Darius walking around the shed coming toward them.

Torgo looked as if he just got caught with his hands in the cookie jar. "I was just letting her look at my new motorcycle." Torgo blushed and leaned on one foot then the other.

Darius stopped next to Tara. He stared down at her.

She noticed the undeniable lust in his eyes. Her insides quickened in response, but it was the hard edge around them that had her pay heed. She looked up at him and pretended not to notice the warring emotions so visible on his face, then looked back at the boy. "Torgo, a true warrior never lies." She looked directly into the youngster's eyes. "My papa said that to my brothers again and again."

Torgo took a slow deep breath and squared his shoulders. "Tara was going to teach me how to ride because you're too busy."

Tara immediately felt very proud of him.

"Torgo, you'll make an incredible warrior some day." Darius gave away his feelings on the matter when a small, crooked smile appeared on his face. He was proud of his younger brother, too. "You'll have that lesson, but first I want to speak to Tara. Run on along now, boy."

Torgo looked at both of them before slowly walking away from his bike.

Tara faced Darius. His shoulders were broad enough to block the sun. He towered over her—emphasizing his domination. And that's when all the anger inside of Tara raced through her blood once again. If Darius noticed, he hid it well.

"Come here." He walked back toward the shed and opened it, pointed to the bike inside, then stared back at Tara. "A true warrior never lies. Those are your words."

She stared at her motorcycle before looking at Darius. Then clasping her hands behind her back—the stance of a warrior—she waited for what he would say.

"Can you start this motorcycle?"

Tara met his gaze. She wouldn't be caught that easily. Not to be outdone, she issued a challenge. "And you?" She would turn this around on him. "I've heard people say you're a true warrior."

Darius walked to the other side of her bike. "Ask me anything. I've no reason to lie." He leaned on her handlebars, his legs on either side of her front tire, and stared into her eyes.

"You've already lied to me." She glared back at him, wanting to pounce on his pompous ass and wipe the smug look from his face.

Darius raised his eyebrows, looking surprised. Then his gaze narrowed and grew serious.

Her words affected him, her accusations a serious charge. But she was the enemy here, on his land. She knew, as he did, that there was no way she could beat him in hand-to-hand combat, yet she'd still take him on if need be. Her anger was genuine. She'd become involved with this culture and this family. If she were to become a part of this family, it would be her decision, not his. She would never take a man who didn't know her mind and simply decided he liked her body. They had experienced wonderful sex together, but sexual compatibility wasn't enough to build a relationship.

"You think you know what you need to about me, but you haven't asked me anything. You don't even talk to me." She grabbed on to the back of her bike with clenched fists, growing more outraged at the thought that he would claim her with so little prior knowledge of who she really was.

"I know that you're even more beautiful when you're mad." He smiled and reached for her face.

Tara smacked his hand, knocking it away with a good amount of force. "I'm not unclaimed land to be taken without asking."

Darius pulled back his hand slowly and straightened. When he spoke, it almost sounded like a reprimand. "If you're referring to the claiming, I've broken no laws. I've a right to any unclaimed lady in Gothman. There's no discussion required. That's been the law of the land since before my papa was born, or his papa before him. Are you trying to tell me you think you're not affected by the laws of this land?"

Tara watched his muscles twitch. He stepped to the side of her bike until his face was close to hers. Enough emotions moved around inside him it was hard to see which dominated by simply studying him. She didn't care if he were amused or mad as hell."It's a bad law," she whispered. "I'll not be claimed unless I say I'm claimed."

Darius slowly moved his gaze from her face down to her breasts. The tip of his finger stroked the fuel tank on her bike. "Can you start it?" he whispered.

He challenged and seduced her simultaneously. Tara took a step backward.

Darius grabbed her. He pulled her against him, holding her arm and lifting her to her toes and against his virile body.

His touch sizzled her skin, and the smell of man and leather consumed her senses. But outrage overpowered her.

He must have surmised that his touch wouldn't cause her to swoon because his expression became serious. "This is your bike…" He lifted her higher. "…And you are a Runner. Start this bike, and I'll never tell a soul. I'll say I started it. At this point your only threat here is me. And my dear lady, right now I'm no threat at all."

He let go of her arm and placed his knuckle under her chin, then tilted her head back so his lips brushed over hers. Touching her mouth with his, he growled, demanding a response when she did nothing.

Tara pushed away and gasped for air, trying to get her bearings. She studied his face and hoped she wasn't making a mistake.

"A warrior doesn't lie," she said.

"True," Darius agreed. "I won't lie to you." Tara broke away and walked around him. He didn't stop her. Touching the bike, she ran her fingers over the handlebars for a moment, then grabbed it without looking up and rolled it into the sunlight.

Darius followed with all the eagerness his younger brother had displayed a short time ago. "I'd love to ride it. It must possess a speed not known in Gothman." He watched her every move as she climbed aboard.

Tara looked around to ensure the yard was empty from any of Darius' guards. Immediately she took off with a jump, causing the bike to literally leave the ground.

"You can ride it if you can catch me," she yelled over her shoulder.

"Ah, yet again you believe you can tell me what to do?"

Darius ran to his motorcycle, which was parked along the side of the shed. He was laughing when he reached it.

Tara made it to the edge of the backyard, then spun around and stopped. She would make her challenge a fair one. It would not do to beat him and have him say she had some kind of edge.

He brought his bike up alongside hers and stopped. His bike rumbled a lot louder than hers did. "We both know your bike is designed to be faster than this one." There was fire in his eyes.

Darius was indeed a true warrior. He was thrilled by her challenge and excited to take her on in a physical activity other than having sex. She saw it in his eyes. Tara smiled wickedly. "This bike may be faster, but you know the land like you know the gloves on your hands. It'll be a fair race. Just name the destination."

"We'll race to the cliff I wanted you to climb. You're not in a dress today." He grinned as his gaze raked down her pant-clad body. "And, my lady, the claim stands."

Tara didn't respond but instead took off across the meadow with all the skills of her Runner heritage. Darius was right at her side, dodging the rocks and ruts in the ground that opposed both of them. The two sped fast, pushing their limits and skills to the edge.

Although Tara didn't know the terrain, she'd travelled at high speeds across a lot of countryside she hadn't known. She didn't look next to her to watch her competitor but instead kept her eyes ahead of her, soaring over the gullies in the land. She climbed and descended hill after hill, and when she spotted the crag with the rocky road outlining it, she added to her speed and easily left Darius behind.

The rock-strewn road was steep, and her bike was not designed for such travel. Tara decelerated, fearing the bike would literally slip out from under her. She crept up the hill aware of Darius approaching from behind. She knew the dust from the gravel impaired his vision and intentionally spun her tires on the road to further slow him down. A large rock came up on her before she noticed, and Tara slid off the side of the road, scraping her leg. The sting from the scrape intensified when she put her weight on it, but she wouldn't let an abrasion cause her defeat.

She glanced down at Torgo's torn trousers and the scratched skin underneath.

Darius came up behind her and slowed his bike. "Are you okay?" He looked concerned.

Tara righted her bike and took off, yelling, "Gothman have never cared about Runners. Why start now?" She grinned as she reached the patchy area surrounded by the pine trees where they'd had sex.

She looked at the rocks Darius suggested they climb and drove over to them, then parked. Knowing there was no way she would be able to ride up the jagged rocks to Darius' cliff, Tara jumped off her bike and lunged for the first group of rocks.

She'd rock climbed for sport as a child and from what she saw, the jutting wall offered little challenge. Nonetheless, her heart pounded as she grabbed the first tier of rocks and pulled herself up. When she anchored her foot on the next level up, the sting from her scrape raced up her side, letting her know how bad she'd cut her leg. More than anything, she wanted to beat Darius. He would see that she would never submit.

Darius easily matched her skills. Reaching the first ledge of rocks, Tara turned and looked to see where he was. The tree-covered hillside, hiding a rocky ground strewn with protruding roots, hadn't slowed him down a bit.

Darius had parked his bike next to hers and also jumped for the rocks. He was impressive on the rocks and appeared to crawl up the side of the cliff with little effort. She remembered that he'd told her he'd come up here since he was a boy.

The second set of rocks was more jagged, and she was forced to move around them since she had no gloves. Ahead of her, a good fifteen feet above, she saw what appeared to be a flat ledge. Ignoring the sharp jabs from the rough boulders, Tara hurried to reach the top. As she crested the rise, she looked out across the grass and was overwhelmed by the view beyond.

No wonder he'd chosen this place as his sanctuary. A leader would easily be reminded why he was willing to fight for his land when it was laid out before him in such a panoramic fashion. Tara pulled herself up on to a large rock and sucked in her breath as she witnessed the glory around her.

The countryside was beautiful, providing a view to the north as far as the eye could see. The rolling hills went on for miles, and although not visible, Tara knew mountains lay beyond. She had spent her life travelling the land that she now looked at from a distance.

It seemed as if the sky was higher, spreading out farther than usual. It looked bigger to Tara than she knew it should. Very few clouds prevented the aqua color above from almost overwhelming the vast shades of green below. For a moment, its beauty transfixed her.

But she had a man to whom she needed to prove herself. With a quick glance around her, she reached for the next ledge and pulled herself up to lean on her elbows. That's when she saw the grassy flat area at the top of the rocks. It was a small secluded section of Nuworld secluded from all around it. Tara relaxed her sore leg for a moment, before putting her weight back on it, and took a deep breath so she could judge the depth of her injuries. As she did, she noticed Darius pulling himself up from the other side of the plateau. Hell be doomed! He'd been behind her. How had he ended up over there?

He pulled his body over the ledge with ease and sat on the ground, catching his breath for just a brief second. Then he moved over to her and reached to help her up.

"Get back, you!" she said through clenched teeth and pulled herself up. Tara didn't take defeat well. She cursed the time she'd wasted enjoying the view, knowing the victory would have been hers otherwise.

The smug grin on his face showed that he would enjoy gloating. "I won. You have to let me ride your bike now." Darius sat back on the ground and smiled broadly.

Tara sat next to him and pounded the ground with her fist as she scowled.

Darius leaned forward and brushed her hair away from her face.

She glanced at him out of the corner of her eye and broke out laughing. She knew herself well. Back at the house she had been fuming with anger. The ride and the intensity of the rock climbing had freed her of all hostilities. Physical activity cleared her head every time. "You're lord of all this great land." Tara swung out her hand, gesturing to the magnificent view in front of them. "How can an invader of your country possibly stop you from riding that motorcycle?" She pointed to her bike next to his, parked beneath them against the rock wall.

"You've done a good job of stopping me so far." He laughed with her.

"So how long have you known I was a Runner?" She looked at him, serious now.

"Ever since you shot that trash can to prevent my little brother from getting the tar beat out of him. Although, for skipping school, he should have had worse than that."

"I don't understand. Why didn't you capture me right then?"

"You had me curious. We were scouting the town, looking for a Runner, an enemy in our land. I didn't find an enemy. I found a woman acting differently than other women. I saw a lady, beautiful beyond all measure, who made my blood race in my veins. You were out of place, but not a threat." Darius blew out a breath and stared down at the grass between them.

Tara sensed he chose his next words carefully and watched while he thought. Finally, he looked at her.

"Runners don't enter Gothman. It's an automatic death sentence. Why are you here?"

"The need to explore is in a Runner's blood, my lord. I've heard the stories of Gothman. They fascinated me. I needed to see how a nation was so powerful when half of its race had no clue how to fight or defend itself."

"And what have you concluded?"

"Why do you care what I think?" she answered sarcastically. "I didn't think it was my mind that impressed you."

Darius smiled and put his arm around her. He took her chin and lifted her face to his. "At first, that was true. You are so beautiful. There is more to you than that, though. I didn't know women like you existed. I've yet to find a man that is my match, much less a woman. But you may be that exception. You stand up to me, and challenge me. I'm not sure how I feel about that yet."

Darius looked so focused, yet his expression remained gentle. Something released inside her, like a dam breaking—something she'd never experienced before. He had made her so angry yet she also knew a longing to be right here by his side indefinitely. Patha described love to her once. He told her that love was when you were content to be with one person no matter what you were doing. He had said that when you weren't with this person they were somewhere in your thoughts always. He had also told her that no matter how mad you may get at that person, true love never allowed you to stay angry for too long. Had it been the motorcycle race and rock climbing that soothed her anger, or was it something else?

"Not to mention, my lady, you've made it quite clear I can't do anything with you unless you say it's okay." He brushed his lips gently across hers. In one quick motion, he stood and pulled her with him then held her in his arms. He pointed to the countryside that lay magnificently in front of them. "Look at it, Tara. We can rule this together, you and I. You must say that has some appeal to you."

"Darius, we're enemies," she pointed out, although made no effort to be released from his arms.

He captured her lips with his and passion ignited that sizzled through her clear to her toes. This man had abilities that were off the chart. Instantly he untucked the shirt from Torgo's pants, which hung low on her hips. His hand glided over her flesh, moving up underneath the loose shirt until he cupped her breast. Darius tweaked her nipple and the need that had already been stirred to life inside her suddenly reached dangerous levels.

Tara wrapped her arms around his neck and pulled him closer. Heat from his lips, his flesh, his hands, set her blood to boil. Tara arched into him, pressing the length of her body against his. Every inch of him was so hard with warrior packed muscle and touching him sent rushes of energized chills throughout her body.

Darius grabbed her rear end with his free hand, pressing her against him.

When his mouth left hers, she gasped for air. He began a trail of kisses down her neck. She let her head fall back giving him full access.

Darius maintained a tight grip, his touch fueling a fever rising within her. She began sensing, through fogged thinking, that he interpreted her reaction to his passion as submission. He wanted to control her. Tara would have to show him how Runner women expected to be treated. She pushed to put distance between them. It took more effort than she thought. The moment she tried freeing herself from his embrace, all that packed muscle surrounding her tightened, holding her prisoner.

"You're not my enemy," Darius informed her. "You're my match in every way. I don't want the likes of you as an enemy."

She smiled at him and then went up on tiptoe to brush her lips against his again. "So, do you want to ride that motorcycle?"

"Soon," he said and pulled her to him. Both hands were under her clothes now, down into her pants, and clutched her bare ass. He pressed her against him and set her on fire.

Tara collapsed to the ground pulling him onto her. She needed skin against skin, wanted to explore this virile body that had grown to be more than a distraction. She yanked at his shirt.

He assisted by putting enough distance between them to take off the offending material. He reached for his pants.

But she stopped him. "I want to do it." His grin gave her a rush, and goose bumps danced over her skin.

Tara pulled free the belt and squatted. She then tugged off his boots, looking up at him. "Does a powerful woman threaten you, my lord?" she whispered, taking one boot, then the other, off.

"Nothing about you threatens me, my lady." His blond curls bordered his face as he looked down at her with such intense gray eyes.

Tara pulled down his pants. She placed kisses around the thick mass of hair that did nothing to hide his rock-hard arousal. It might threaten him once he learned she was heir to lead all Runner clans. Her title equalled his if not surpassed it.

She offered his erection no attention, but kissed her way down his legs as she pulled his pants off of him. "I might say the same of you," she murmured, glancing up at him although her vision blurred as she breathed in his heady scent.

"Now it's my turn, my lady." Darius reached under her arms and dragged her over his naked and aroused body. He shocked her wherever he touched her, and the moisture between her legs soaked through her clothes.

Darius didn't take as long to undress her. She was naked within seconds. He held her as he rolled to his side, then placed her on her back. Darius took her hands and laid them above her head. Then, slowly, he kissed her. And slowly, so slowly, he moved down her body, kissing every inch along the way.

"Submitting to me, trusting me, in no way makes you less of who you are." His hands caressed and stroked as he continued his exploration. And his voice was a sultry rumble against her flesh when he continued speaking. "Our ways are new to you, my lady, but I'm a patient man."

When Tara wondered how much truth there actually was in that statement, Darius drove his point home. There was no rush this time. She let her head back and surrendered to his perfect torture.

Darius wanted to explore and get to know, very well, every inch of her. He spread her legs, and she didn't fight him. Instead she lifted her hips off the ground, moaning her eagerness for him to continue. Darius chuckled as he blew soft air onto the downy hair between her legs. Tara gasped, and he enjoyed watching the rush over her body. He saw her glistening moistness surrounding her entrance and proving how aroused she was. He kissed the moist area first, then tasted her. Tara yelped and arched her hips further, grabbing the back of his head as she fought her release.

It was her way. Apparently this was how Runners raised their women. Tara wanted to control every aspect of her life, including her orgasm. This might as well be one of her first lessons.

Darius smiled, knowing she was exactly where he wanted her to be. He licked his lips as he sat up, enjoying her taste on him. Tara groaned and reached to pull him back to her. He searched her fogged-over blue eyes as he situated himself above her, resting his erection against her swollen opening. Tara arched again, trying to enclose herself around him.

He was engorged, and he needed to slam into that heat. But he teased her for a moment, until her blue eyes widened, and her mouth opened in a silent protest. The moment he knew her explosion was eminent, he entered her. He moved with a steady pace, pushing into her heat until he felt intoxicated, then pulling back until his body shook with need to return to the center of her heat.

Tara reached for him, her face flushed and beyond beautiful. Her blue eyes were wild when she succeeded only in scratching his chest before he grabbed her hands. He held them over her head with one hand and pressed his other palm against her hip.

"Still," he grumbled.

Darius stroked her inner satiny walls with his cock. She was so hot. So incredibly wet. And when she shook her head from side to side, refusing his command in spite of him having her pinned and her apparent inability to speak, her hair streamed across her face and around her shoulders. If he stared at her for the rest of his life it wouldn't be enough. No one would have ever made him believe a woman would get to him like this.

"Darius!" she cried out.

Her pussy pulsated against his dick. The heat surrounding his shaft was almost unbearable. Darius thrust harder, impaling her with more force than he had with her so far.

"Yes. Yes!" Once again her feverish gaze pinned his. "Like that," she said, breathless. "Don't stop."

He didn't want to. Hell be doomed! It was the last thing he ever wanted to do. Telling Tara to obey him wouldn't work.

Her nature was too structured. And his guess was that she'd been allowed to run wild doing what she wished. He had to show her how to submit.

Darius slowed his pace.

The look Tara gave him might have been comical when she suddenly looked outraged. She struggled against his grip on her wrists.

"I said don't stop," she hissed through clenched teeth.

"I'm not stopping, my lady," he promised her. "But you will consent to my lead."

Tara relaxed noticeably and quit struggling against his grip on her hands. She let out a loud sigh. "Don't make me hurt you," she said, her voice low and threatening.

This time he did chuckle. Tara suddenly asserted all her strength against him. Darius let go of her hands and she came to a sitting position, pushing against his chest.

"I'm taking over," she informed him.

Darius pushed her to the ground, grabbed her legs, spread them then let her heels rest against his shoulders when he leaned over her. "That won't be happening any time soon, my lady."

He crushed his mouth to hers when she opened it, likely to cry out her insistence that she wouldn't submit. Tara's fingers glided up his arms and to the back of his neck. She clasped them there and moaned into his mouth.

It was his undoing. If she ever learned he might do whatever she wanted just to hear that sound, to feel her suffocating heat around him, all would be lost. Darius drove deep inside her. He thrust, feeling the friction create a fire between them too hot to extinguish. He rode her until she knew he planned on never letting her go. When the pressure building inside that heat became too much, he thrust hard, aggressively, and brought them to climax simultaneously.

Tara stared at him, fighting for her breath.

He'd controlled her, and he knew it.

Tara dressed in silence, almost disbelieving of the sex she had just experienced. No man had ever done to her body what Darius had just done. She was numb, more than satisfied, and almost in awe. Her thoughts still floated in a fog of aftermath.

Darius dressed without saying anything then pulled her close as they faced the breath-taking view that stretched endlessly beyond the edge of the cliff. It felt right being in his arms. He was strong, powerful, and still very dangerous. But then, she noted and grinned, so was she. All of it excited her.

"I'll ride that bike of yours now." He returned behind them to the edge of the ledge they were on and shimmied down to the first set of rocks. Darius reached for her to help her down as well.

Tara laughed. "I'm your match in every way. I believe those were your words." She sat and scooted down the rocks without his assistance.

They leapt down the remaining rocks together and within seconds were back at the motorcycles. Darius eagerly climbed onto her bike.

"Are all Runner bikes this small?" he asked.

Tara made a face at him. "That's my bike and you'll take care of it."

She showed him the order in which to push the buttons on her handlebar to start the bike. His satisfied smile turned to a frown when she climbed onto his bike.

"Are you sure it's not too big for you, my lady?"

"My papa's bike is at least this big, and I have ridden it a time or two, *my lord*." She stressed his title, sarcastically implying his superiority over her.

Side by side, they rode down the rocky road and back out to the meadow.

Tara enjoyed riding the big, noisy, cumbersome motorcycle. There was something raw and untamed about it, although it would be difficult to use in battle, she thought. However, the nature of the Gothman wasn't to sneak up and attack their opponent but to roar into battle with screams and confidence of victory. This bike suited Darius's nature just fine. If anything, she understood Lord Darius and his people just a little bit better after riding on the large bike that took each rut in the earth with a roll of superiority. She wondered what Darius concluded of her nature after riding her bike. When they'd passed the first group of hills, he slowed her bike to a stop. She pulled up next to him.

"Park my bike here and climb on behind me. I'll come get it shortly. It'll make it a bit easier to justify the story I'm planning to tell if we are seen. When we're back, you may take Torgo out to the field and give him his lesson. I know he's quite eager, and there's no reason to disappoint the boy."

Tara climbed on behind him. Her bike wasn't designed to carry two easily, but she enjoyed being as close to him as was required for them to ride together. She wrapped her hands around his waist and locked her fingers together. He held her two hands in his and skillfully drove her bike back to the shed with his free hand.

CHAPTER SIX

A HALF-CYCLE of riding lessons proved enough for Torgo. Tara awoke one morning to the sound of his bike cruising over the hills. She lay in her bed for a while listening to the rumble of the teenager's motorcycle and remembering her first experiences on one. She'd felt so mature and independent riding by herself, free to go wherever she pleased. Tara knew what Torgo must be experiencing without getting up to go to the balcony and watch.

Tara showered, dressed, and was absolutely ravenous as she hurried down the stairs to help prepare breakfast. Hilda and Darius were in the kitchen talking. Hilda didn't sound pleased.

"I just don't understand. It was you yourself that said it was final." Hilda wrung her hands as Tara entered.

"It is final. However, I have matters of ruling my people, mama. Now isn't a good time."

"You're people need this. There'll be talk, otherwise." Hilda reached for her son.

"Oh blast it all with your talk, woman," Darius barked. "I said it's final and that's the way of it. Nothing more need be done. If there's talk, I'll rely on you to silence it."

"Good morning." Tara looked at the two of them ready with questions.

"Tara, certainly you want…" Hilda looked at Tara as if relieved that she would side with her on whatever issue she and her son were talking about.

"Mama!" Darius interrupted her with a firm tone in his voice. "Tara, walk with me to my bike."

Tara watched Hilda grab a dishtowel and twist it in her hands. She was clearly upset. When the two women made eye contact, Hilda waved after her son, who already was out the back door.

"Best do as your told," she said to Tara.

Tara hated having it said she was doing as she was told. Now didn't seem the right moment to pick a fight, however. She followed Darius into the backyard. He took long strides toward his motorcycle. Tara almost ran to catch up with him. There were more of his men than usual in the yard, all sitting on their bikes, as if they had been waiting.

"I'll meet you out front." He gestured with his thumb, indicating they should go.

None of them said a word, although most took a good look at Tara before slowly driving toward the front of the house.

"What's going on?" Tara watched his mean leave. The conversation in the kitchen with his mama had spurred her curiosity. Now, the presence of more of his men than usual really had her interest piqued. Not to mention, they were armed. She wondered what Darius was leaving to do. She also wondered if he would ever confide in her…that is, if she decided to stay with him.

Darius waited until his men had disappeared toward the front side of the house, then placed his hand on the back of Tara's neck and guided her toward the shed. He didn't let go of her when the small structure blocked their view of his house, and anyone else's view of them.

"You'll tell my mama that you're a Runner."

"What? No. Why?" The moment she asked it became apparent that he was not accustomed to having his commands questioned.

"You'll do as I say," he informed her, and his lips pressed into a narrow line on his well-chiseled face. Darius stroked the back of her neck with his thumb. "I don't have time to explain everything to her. She's asking questions. You'll answer them." He tilted her head back by pressing under her jaw bone. "You'll make sure she understands that you're here because you want to be."

"I'm not so sure this is a good idea."

Darius smiled. It was only a small play at the side of his mouth. Tara had come to learn that for him that might as well be a full grin.

"How do your people handle you?"

Tara didn't hesitate in answering. "They do as I say."

Darius shook his head but then pulled her to him and kissed her forehead. "Behave while I'm gone."

"Where are you going?" Tara sensed some type of military excursion. She wasn't accustomed to being left out of such things. "Your men are dressed for battle."

"There are some rumors." He twisted a strand of her hair between his fingers. "They haven't been confirmed. But possibly, the Sea People are preparing an attack." He tightened his grip on her hair. "Ah, your eyes are glowing. You think this is exciting."

Tara didn't smile though. She didn't need protection from the harsh realities of whatever was going on. "What are the rumors?"

"Just that their armies are moving close to the Gothman borders. I'm riding out now to confirm." A slight breeze lifted his blond curls. It didn't soften the sudden hardened look he gave her. "You will focus on explaining who you are to my mama. She will be upset at first but she likes you. Be gentle with her, give her time, and she will continue liking you as she always has."

"I don't think I could sit by and not fight if you're invaded." Tara knew how much she could help him.

Darius saw more than that. "You're showing your loyalty to Gothman." He leaned down and kissed her. "Be good while I'm gone. Go talk to my mama. I'll be back soon."

He got on his motorcycle and she watched him leave.

An idea came to her as she entered the kitchen, and she approached Hilda with enthusiasm. "My lady, I'd like to invite Reena over this afternoon. I haven't seen her in a while, and I have something I want to tell you. I'd like her to be here for it."

Hilda's face lit up. "Ah, a splendid idea." Hilda grinned broadly and then opened the pantry to inspect the shelves. "While you're doing your morning chores, I'll drive into town and pick up a few things. I hear the blueberries are good and fresh. We'll have some of those, and I'll whip some cream. Cold cuts will work well, don't you think? Set out some potatoes to boil. I'll make a hot potato salad to go with the sandwiches. You might want to pick some fresh flowers for the vases."

Tara smiled. Hilda hurried upstairs to change for her trip into town. For now, she'd made the old woman happy. She grabbed the Gothman communications device, which hung on the wall, and untwisted the thick cord to the mouth and ear piece. Tara placed the call to Reena, who also thought the idea was splendid.

Tara sat in the kitchen by herself and ate another frosted roll for breakfast before starting her housework. She felt bad about not telling Reena she'd only been invited for moral support.

Mulling over in her head the speech she would give to Hilda, it dawned on her that she hadn't asked Darius what questions his mama had been posing. Seeing the guards had completely distracted her. She didn't like that Darius was out in some field going over military tactics while she sat here preparing for a luncheon.

But that was why she had entered Gothman, right? She had wanted to understand a different way of living, this different culture. Yet, she hadn't planned on the *Age Of Searching* changing her life forever. She merely wanted to enter Gothman and observe.

She'd done a lousy job of that. She'd been prepared to remain an outside observer, and instead she'd fallen in love. Tara was sure of it now.

Jumping up, she made quick work of cleaning the kitchen, then moved to the other rooms of the house. She had so much energy, and she didn't question its source. Wiping down woodwork and making sure glass sparkled, Tara smiled while picturing her and Darius racing across the countryside. It would do good for the Lord of Gothman to know the world outside Gothman. She would show him. After all, Darius had shown her Gothman.

Tara had never lived in a structure like this. Although its newness had worn off over the past cycle, the place's magnificence still hung in the air. She would make the place absolutely immaculate for Reena. Hilda would be proud, too. Both women had taken her in and allowed her to explore their people, even though Hilda didn't know that was what she had done. A clean home meant something to both of them. She hummed an old Runner tune as she worked.

The house began to sparkle, but Tara's thoughts became a tangled mess. She cleaned for the old ladies. This big permanent house was impressive, but it wasn't her home. Nor would she ever be able to spend all her days in any house rooted into the ground. She was proud of being a Runner. How could she live here with Darius and maintain the heritage that ran thick through her blood?

Hilda came home and interrupted her thoughts. She'd taken her frustrations out on the house until it was spotless. Hilda was pleased with her work and told her so.

Torgo entered the house, instinctively knowing that food was going to be prepared.

"What's for lunch?" he asked, as he hovered around in the kitchen and sampled the blueberries and cold meat as it was laid out in serving dishes.

"With that appetite, you will be as big as your brother before the new winter." Tara laughed and poked the boy in the stomach. "Why don't we let him eat now, so he isn't bored with the conversation during lunch?" Tara didn't want him there when she explained herself to Hilda.

Hilda nodded her agreement. "I'll fix you a plate, my boy." She smiled, showing a mama's love, as she grabbed one of the porcelain plates from the cabinet and began assembling his meal. "And mind you, let your mama have her visit. I won't have you chattering and underfoot while I enjoy the gossip."

"No problem. Gossip is for women." Torgo grabbed the plate his mama had just made for him and ran out the door.

Reena showed up punctually, carrying one of her wonderful pies. The three women enjoyed scrumptious food. Tara listened as the two chatted away about mutual friends. After eating, Tara cleared dishes from the table while the two women continued to chat. The time for her announcement had come.

"Ah, my dear, this was a grand idea of yours." Hilda sat back and patted her large stomach. "I'm full to the brim. Now then, you said there was something you wanted to tell me. Plans on the claiming, I'm thinking." The old lady smiled and winked at Reena.

Reena frowned at Tara. "You want to discuss your claiming?"

"Well, in a way." Tara hesitated. "If you'll excuse me, I will be right back. I think if I show you something, it will be easier."

Tara ran up the stairs. In her room, she reached under her bed for the bag Reena had given her and pulled out her Runner clothing. For a moment she just sat there, caressing the black leather. She hadn't seen them in over a cycle. The embroidered symbol of her clan made her feel warm inside. This was who she was and that would never change.

Reena's mouth fell open as Tara entered the room with the clothes in her hands. "Child, what are you doing?" she whispered, shocked.

"What do you have there, girl?" Hilda looked up, not seeing Reena's expression go white.

"Lord Darius asked me to do this." She laid the clothing on the table and spread them out.

Reena immediately recognized them. The embroidered symbol of the clan stood out plainly to see. She stared at the red blood drop with the circle around it.

Hilda gasped in horror. "Where did you get those clothes?" She stood up quickly, jumping back, and her hand went to her heart.

"Hilda, they're my clothes. I'm a Runner."

Hilda shook her head as color drained from her face.

Reena and Tara hurried to her side and helped her back to the chair.

The old woman stared at the clothing as if it would bite her if she dared look away. After a minute, she looked at Tara. "What is this you're saying?"

Tara sat next to Hilda. Reena took the chair on the other side of her old friend and held her hand.

"I came to Gothman to learn about your people. I'd heard the stories of a proud, large race of people, so different from my own. All I wanted was to see how you lived. I didn't expect to become so involved with your family," Tara said, letting her last words trail off.

"Ah, so now you have a lord who's gone and claimed you. Let me guess, he can't figure out how to get out of this mess, and so he's sent you to me. What is it you want?" Hilda pulled her hand free from Reena's and fisted it on the table.

"This will be scandal for our family," she hissed under her breath.

"Well, my lady, I didn't know he claimed me when I moved in here." Tara glared at Reena. "He finally admitted to me that he'd announced a claiming. But it was after I found out from Thelga at the grocery store. I was furious and ready to run from this land right then. I told Darius that no one claimed me without asking me first."

Reena covered her mouth to stifle a laugh. Hilda's chair scuffed against the floor when she slid back and turned on Reena. "This is serious, old woman. The Lord of Gothman can't claim a Runner. It will be the biggest scandal our nation has ever known."

For a moment, no one spoke. The two women stared at each other. Tara gave Hilda time to digest what she'd just learned. Regardless of what Hilda now thought of her, Tara would never embarrass her or Darius. But then Hilda looked from Reena to Tara and back again. Her mouth fell open as if she would say something.

Reena's expression changed and she shook her head. She touched Hilda's arm and Hilda closed her mouth. Reena spoke before Hilda did.

"Do you love Lord Darius, child?" Reena asked looking away from Hilda.

Tara saw Reena was trying to help. "I think I might," she admitted voicing her feelings for the first time.

"I've seen the two of them," Hilda said to Reena, although her tone was accusatory instead of sounding pleased. "They act like they belong together. You knew about this, didn't you, old lady? I daresay you planned the whole thing!" Hilda accused.

"She came to me the night she arrived in Gothman." Reena waved her hand in front of her, knocking Hilda's accusations out of the way. "She wanted to know the life of Gothman. I didn't know she was coming."

"Reena, Runners are our enemy. You know she won't stay here. It's not in their nature to stay put. I don't need to tell you--"

"My lady, I'm not your enemy." Tara stressed, interrupting, and putting her hand on Hilda's. "I don't understand why our people consider each other enemies. We aren't a threat to each other."

"And so you think you can change how Gothman feel about Runners, do you?" Hilda shook her head and clucked her tongue. "Is that why you were sent?"

"If she's claimed to the Lord of Gothman, it would be a good start." Reena was quick with her argument.

"You'd like it if that happened, wouldn't you?" Hilda yelled and stood, glaring at Reena. She shook her head at Tara, looking disgusted as her hands went to her wide girth. "My son didn't know you were a Runner when he made the claim. Now he must save face with his people. He has promise to be one of our greatest leaders."

"He did know I was a Runner. He knew all along." Tara wanted to jump up and stamp her foot. Why was she defending him? He should be defending his actions to his mama.

"Did he really?" Reena was smiling again. "Hilda, he knew and he still claimed her. Maybe they were meant to be together."

"What a day that would be for you, wouldn't it, my old friend? I'm not so old that I don't remember what happened over twenty winters ago." Hilda snapped her finger in the air. "My claim knew of your goings on with the Runners. Maybe he should've been rougher with you."

"But he wasn't. I've never said a word. Then was not the time for Runners to be among us. But now! Times are changing. The Runners haven't opposed Gothman for many winters. This generation thinks Runners are enemies, but don't know why. You said it yourself. These two are in love. Tara will challenge him, but is that so bad? Imagine it, Hilda. She will make Darius stronger. I've heard you say a time or two that behind a good man is a good woman. What a match they will be, don't you think?"

Hilda was quiet. She looked at the clothes, then walked around the table, still staring at them. Tara watched her pick up the cloth with the embroidered emblem on it.

Her chubby fingers traced the circle with the red drop of blood centered in the middle. "What is this?"

"It is the symbol of my clan."

"And what is the name of your clan?"

"The Blood Circle Clan."

"Ah, and who are your parents?"

"Patha is my papa, but not by birth. He found me as a toddler and brought me into his clan to be raised."

Hilda started to stomp out of the room. She stopped and turned, looking angrier than Tara had ever seen her as she glared at Reena. "You knew she was coming to you!"

"No, Hilda, I told you already." Reena remained in her chair, but her lips narrowed to a fine line.

An animosity of some kind appeared between the two women, as if some old wound had suddenly been opened. Finally Reena relaxed and stared hard at Hilda as she spoke. "She caused quite a ruckus in the pines that night. The guards were out thick looking for her. She dodged them and made it to my house. I saw her for the first time when she came out of the woods. I didn't know she was coming."

Hilda stood there for a minute, thinking. Then, she picked up the clothes and thrust them at Tara. "Put these on. I want to see you in them."

Tara took the clothes and looked at Hilda confused.

"You've been with us for over a cycle now. You've lived like a Gothman, but you're a Runner. My heritage means a lot to me. Let's see if your heritage means as much to you. Put those on and feel your heritage. Show me who you really are." Hilda's voice shook with emotion as she pointed with a shaky finger to Tara's clothes.

Tara clutched her clothes. She trotted up the stairs, feeling queasy with excitement. In minutes she would be out of the flimsy Gothman dress. She rubbed her finger over her leather pants. Taking the stairs a couple at a time, she hurried to her room. She was also a bit nervous. Changing into her own clothes didn't bother her. Darius had taken most of his personal guards with him. There would be a few of the lord's guards on duty outside, not that she would tolerate any of them upsetting Darius' family if they saw her in Runner clothing.

There was something going on between Hilda and Reena that she didn't understand. The two of them kept exchanging looks. Tara didn't want to fathom a guess what the two of them might be hiding but it had something to do with Runners. Once Hilda was calmer maybe they would enlighten her. Unlike the two of them, though, old gossip didn't interest her as much as second-guessing what would happen in the future.

The leather was cool against her skin. Her feet rejoiced to be in her boots again. She pulled her headscarf over her face and headed back downstairs. She didn't make a sound as she approached the dining room, and the two women didn't hear her return.

"I won't have her having my grandbabies, then steal away during the night. Those clothes will bring her back to reality. She's been pretending, and she'll come to her senses now."

"You want her to leave," Reena spoke quieter and her voice sounded strained.

"You can't make her stay anymore than you could make her papa stay," Hilda snapped.

"You'll not speak of that. I have your promise!"

"You think if she quits pretending that it will change everything?" Hilda sounded downright hateful. "You're a fool, old woman, and you always have been."

"I am not pretending. I've known who I was the entire time I was here," Tara interrupted, not understanding, or liking the way Hilda was speaking to Reena.

The two women looked up as the Runner entered the room.

Hilda shrieked and covered her mouth, staring wide-eyed at Tara.

"I've taught your youngest son to ride a motorcycle. I've raced his lord through the hills on my motorcycle. Lord Darius had it brought here. It's in the shed right now. I've behaved the way you've wanted but have never ignored who I am. If I stay here, I'll stay as a Runner, and Darius knows this."

"I see. Well Darius asked you to tell me and so you have. Now I know. If my son is asking for my blessing, he knows how I feel about Runners. That hasn't changed. You have a good heart, Tara, but you're a Runner." Hilda sat back down and looked exasperated.

Tara moved to the old lady, bent, and kissed her on the cheek.

She then did the same to Reena. "I don't know what yet, but you have a secret and I mean to learn what it is," she whispered in Reena's ear.

"Well, child, you best get back out of those clothes before someone thinks you are attacking us instead of kissing us." Hilda grabbed her cloth napkin and dabbed her cheeks and neck. "Go now."

Tara noticed the woman's hand shook. But she did as Hilda asked, ran upstairs, changed, and returned her clothes to the bag under her bed. She came back down in time to see Reena gathering her things and preparing to leave. Tara followed both women to the front open room.

"I'll be seeing an announcement to a claiming party before long, I expect." Reena walked across the yard to her groundmobile. "We'll have to make her a dress for certain, old woman. Goodness knows she can't sew a stitch."

"I wonder why she's more excited to see me claimed to your son than you are." Tara watched Reena drive away before turning to face the plump older woman.

"I can't go and tell you her thoughts. She'll have to do that herself." Hilda headed upstairs, claiming a headache. "And she won't ever do that," she called down, closed herself in her bedroom and locked the door.

Torgo ran to greet Darius when he and his guards pulled around the back of the house and parked that following afternoon.

"I'll help fight if you need me." Torgo sounded delighted at the thought.

"Will you now?" Darius climbed off his bike and stretched. He looked exhausted and dirty, very much like a warrior who'd been on the road a couple days.

"I can ride my motorcycle pretty well," Torgo continued. "I can run errands, or do anything you want."

Tara smiled as Torgo sought his brother's approval. She'd been walking through the pines and returning to the house when she heard Darius' motorcycle pulling into the backyard. She wanted to run and greet him and let him know how she had missed him. Instead, she stood, sheltered by the branches surrounding her, and watched Darius push his bike around the back of the shed.

Torgo ran to get water and rags to help Darius clean the mud from his bike. He returned just as his older brother was opening the shed. The young boy disappeared inside along with Darius. Tara hurried across the yard to join them, ignoring the guards when they scowled at her.

Torgo saw her first and ran to greet her. Darius turned and their eyes met. He looked exhausted and more serious than she'd seen him look before.

She imagined him creating strategies and hearing reports from his scouts while she sat and dined with old women. She should have been at his side. She had knowledge of the Sea People. She had heard stories around the fires of the strange race.

The Sea People were greedy and paranoid. Many of the stories she had heard over the winters said they were a race addicted to some type of opiate drug. If what she'd heard was true, the Sea People's actions would be hard to predict in battle.

Darius pulled her into his arms the moment she reached him.

"I can't wait to hear your stories," she told him, knowing it was a Runner greeting shared between spousal warriors.

Darius only smiled. "I will be..." he whispered in her ear, but wasn't able to finish.

"Tara, oh my dear, there you are. Come at once. There has been a call to the house." Hilda stood at the door to the house gesturing wildly. "Darius, I'm glad you're home. This is bad."

Tara started toward the house with Darius following. They entered the kitchen and found Hilda rushing about, a distracted look on her face. She didn't offer any further explanation but began moving items around on the pantry shelves. Hilda glanced over her shoulder. "I'm losing my mind. There aren't good times ahead."

"Woman! Hell be doomed. What's wrong with you?" Darius spoke from behind Tara.

"Darius, I answered the caller." She pointed to the receiver, with its stretched cord on the counter. Hilda had forgotten to return it to its cradle on the wall.

"You said that already. What is so incredible about the caller?" Darius' frustration strained his voice. He picked up the receiver and put it on the cradle.

"Reena called and asked for you Tara, but I didn't know where you were." Hilda began, and brought several small jars out of the pantry. Her pallor didn't look good. "She has company. She said some of your, uh--" She paused as Torgo slipped into the kitchen eyeing a plate of food on the counter. "Tara, your family has arrived. She needs you to take these herbs to her. I know they are used for medicinal reasons, so someone must be hurt."

Tara didn't wait to hear more. She rushed from the kitchen and up the stairs to her bedroom.

"Tara!" Darius' bark echoed off the walls.

She ignored him as she ran to her closet and quickly flipped through her dresses until she found one more practical than the frilly thing she had on at the moment. She chose one made from a knitted material and hurried to change.

"What are you doing?" Darius appeared in her doorway, then leaned against it, watching her.

She'd forgotten to shut the door. Already having taken off one dress to put the other on, she worked desperately to get the zipper in back to close. "Would you help me with this?"

He walked toward her, turned her around, and zipped her dress. "You'll take the herbs and come right back."

"I'll be back as soon as I find out why there are Runners at Reena's." She squatted down on all fours and reached under her bed.

"There are Sea People ready to attack Gothman. I'll not have you running around the countryside."

Tara ignored him. She took her Runner clothing out of the bag and set them on the bed, then slipped into her leather boots.

This was the first Darius had seen of her Runner clothing. More curious to him though was the small, silver bang stick she pulled out of an inner sleeve in the bag. Tara checked it like a seasoned professional. Then she opened another flap in the bag and pulled out a larger weapon. This one grabbed his attention. Darius leaned over and picked up the small laser to look at it. "This is what you used to shoot the trash can that day, isn't it?"

"Yes." She continued to get herself ready.

He put down the laser, then picked up the larger weapon, strode over to the balcony. Darius opened the doors, aimed the Runner weapon at a group of trees at the far edge of the meadow, and pulled the trigger. A branch on a tree a good half-mile away fell to the ground. Darius grunted as he scrutinized the weapon closely.

Tara reached into the bag and pulled out a small case. She opened it and removed a small flat disc. It was more minute than any coin and as flat as a piece of paper. She placed the disc on the edge of her finger and moved behind Darius.

"I like this one." He held up the large weapon.

"It has four more shots in it." She reached around him and pointed to the attachment on the side. "It works best at a distance. If it's used at close range, it emits a large explosion. You may keep it. I'll do with my laser."

Darius put his arm around her waist and yanked her up against him. He held her to him in a possessive grip. Darius kept the powerful weapon in one hand at his side. But he held her in a death grip with the other arm.

Tara wrapped both hands around his neck and gently stuck the small disc on to his flesh just under his shirt at his nape. It held its place under Darius' curls, and she prayed he wouldn't detect it. Although she'd never used a tracker before, they were virtually undetectable, waterproof and would give her peace of mind if trouble was about to occur.

"It's important that you listen to me. Gothman is going to be attacked sooner than I anticipated. I want you to be safe." Darius searched her face as he spoke.

There wasn't time to rejoice in the compassion she saw on his face, in spite of her heart skipping a beat. Tara pushed away and slipped a harness over her dress, then she slid her laser in it. "What do you know of the Sea People? Have you had contact with them before?"

This was a side to Tara he hadn't seen before. She was preparing for battle. It would take many guards, and probably locks and chains to keep this woman at home. Tara was a Runner, something he'd always known, and staying put wasn't her nature. Up until now he'd had no problem keeping her at home. The moment she heard word of her people, she prepared to leave. She wasn't asking his permission to go; she was just going. He wondered if he would ever be able to tame that part of her.

Tara appealed to him because she was wild, untamed, outspoken and beyond sexy. Would taming any of those qualities make her less appealing? He worried the answer to that was yes.

"This is the first time the Sea People have come this close to Gothman. I'll not stand for them pushing into my borders, though."

"They've communicated with you?"

"I've received messages saying the Gothman have grown too large and they don't intend to honor the hold I have on my land."

"That isn't true. The Gothman borders run into the Freelands. Darius, have you never been out of Gothman?"

He frowned and his gray eyes darkened. He wasn't pleased that she questioned what he knew, or didn't know. "Are you saying I can't rule this land because I've never been outside its borders?" He scowled. "My papa didn't need the help of outsiders and neither do I."

"Understanding your enemy helps to defeat them."

"So now you are telling me how to rule." He looked fierce when he smiled and stroked her cheek. "You have until sundown to go and return home."

Tara put her black leather jacket over her dress. Grabbing the bag, now empty and ready for Hilda's herbs, she headed for the door.

Darius grabbed her arm. "Did you hear me? Before sundown."

"I'll be fine." She went up on tip toe and rested her hand on his shoulder. She was reeling from the shock of him just saying this was her home. "I know this will take time for you to accept," she whispered and brushed her lips over his. "Not only would I be safe outside after dark, but I would be the danger others should worry about."

Tara reached up and pulled a band off his leather jacket sleeve that bore the Gothman seal and shoved it in to her bag.

"I'll represent two nations today." She smiled and kissed him again.

"You'll be home before dark because no respectable Gothman woman is out after the sun goes down," Darius grumbled, his expression still dark and dangerous. Then his voice went oddly flat. "Tell your leader that Gothman would be honored if the Runners would enter into battle with us against the Sea People."

Tara stared at him, stunned. "Okay, I will," she said, before turning and leaving the room. Now her head was seriously reeling as she ran down the stairs.

Hilda looked at Tara's outfit when she reached the bottom of the stairs, but didn't say anything. Her son stood at the top of the stairs with the large Runner gun in his hand. Hilda opened her mouth, but closed it and handed the keys to her groundmobile and the herbs to Tara.

Nothing she would say would make any difference. There had been many times since her claim, Jovis, had died that she'd been glad he wasn't around to see what was happening. Jovis had encountered Runners many winters ago. Their culture and beliefs were very different from Gothman. Their nomadic nature had been proof enough to her claim that they were unreliable with no true honor or sense of commitment.

"They will infiltrate our society and breed weakness into our strong Gothman code of values. My warriors are superior because they've known since they were boys that they would be part of a powerful nation. Gothman is a mountain that can't be crossed. Runners will never be allowed to impress upon my people their nomadic ways."

Jovis had ordered any Runner entering Gothman to be shot on sight. Before that decision, her claim had left for Reena's many times. Even as a girl, Reena had insisted on remaining in the forest outside of Bryton after her parents died. Hilda had feared her good friend was becoming a mistress to claimed men. Hilda's fears had escalated when her claim had started riding out to the secluded home of her unclaimed friend.

Hilda already had two babies – two sons. She was claim to the Lord of Gothman. Some claims weren't based on love but Hilda had loved her claim. It had been an early morning when she'd followed Jovis to Reena's. That's when she'd seen Reena with the Runner.

The Runner wanted Reena to leave with him. Hilda had rushed out of her groundmobile and wrapped her arms around Reena. She'd been a fool to doubt her claim's love for her. Now all that mattered was saving Reena. Hilda had cried that she couldn't stand living without her best friend. Jovis had held Hilda in his arms, soothing her, and forbade Reena to leave Gothman. The Runner had told Jovis if he gave Reena a claim it would mean war.

"You've tainted this lass, Runner," Jovis had barked. "No honorable Gothman would want her. But hear me now. If a Runner ever enters my lands, mingles with my people, they will be shot on sight." He'd sliced his hand through the air with the finality of his command.

Hilda blinked away the memory and stared at Darius holding the Runner weapon and the Runner leaving with Hilda's groundmobile. If she'd given up her best friend all those winters ago maybe her claim's justified fears wouldn't be coming true today.

Hilda's groundmobile moved a lot faster than Reena's, but it still took too long to get through the town and up the hill to Reena's house. Two Runner motorcycles were parked in front of Reena's house when she pulled up. Tara immediately recognized Patha's. She got out of the groundmobile and ran to the house.

There was no one in the living room, and the house was too quiet. Tara pulled out her laser and aimed it in front of her as she moved toward the hallway.

The door to Reena's bedroom was open, and she pointed the gun at the empty room. Tara walked to the window and looked out at backyard. She didn't see anyone. A group of five framed images on the dresser next to the window caught her eye. The first image she saw was of a small child picking flowers in a meadow. Others depicted the same girl at different ages.

The last image was of a girl in her adolescence sitting on a small motorcycle. Tara cocked her head sideways in puzzlement. The motorcycle looked very familiar. She looked back at the other images again.

They were all of her!

Tara's heart tightened in her chest. She wiped her suddenly damp palms down her hips while staring at the images. For the sake of Nuworld! What was Reena doing with pictures of her at different ages? She hadn't even known the images had been taken.

"Tara?"

She spun around and aimed her laser at the open bedroom doorway. The front door closed. It sounded like several people had just entered the house. Tara grabbed the framed images and walked down the hallway, laser in one hand and images in the other.

Reena called out again. "Tara?"

"I'm here." Tara stopped at the end of the hallway.

Reena stood in the middle of the room while Patha and one of his guards struggled to help a Runner she didn't recognize to the couch.

"Did you bring the herbs?" Reena asked.

Tara nodded and pointed to her bag on the edge of the couch. She then hurried to the large old man, setting her laser and the images on the table beside her. "Patha! It's so good to see you."

Patha turned to greet her and she jumped into his arms. Patha lifted her up off the ground and hugged her tight enough she lost her breath.

"What brings you this far from home?" No matter how many winters she had, she would never tire of Patha's hugs. "What happened?" she asked, nodding to the injured Runner.

"Reena's the best doctor in the area, and we needed her. We aren't with the clan right now." Patha squeezed her wrists with powerfully large hands. "Look at you, Tara-girl, all dressed up like a Gothman." He held her hands out in front of her and took a good look. "I do believe she's put on a little weight." Patha looked at Reena for confirmation. "What do you think?"

"Maybe Gothman suits her." Reena finished mixing together a salve from the herbs Tara had brought and knelt to coat the Runner's wounded leg. She finished by tying a bandage around it then stood and moved to stand by Patha. "Your man should be fine. Mind you, those wild boar lashes can get infected, but I've got him good and cleaned up."

"We're closer to you than the clansite right now," Patha explained. "I knew you could take good care of him."

"I'll be fine," the Runner on the couch promised.

"Unlike that wild boar who threw you off your bike." Duru, who was five winters older than Tara and had returned from his *Age Of Searching* before she'd left, laughed and slapped the man on the shoulder.

The two men joked about what had happened but Tara turned to Patha. "I've really missed you. I can't wait to tell you what has happened."

"I look forward to your stories around the fire." Patha beamed and looked over her. "Gothman won't know what's hit it."

"Tara, what have you here?" Reena interrupted, and picked the images off the side table.

"I found them on your dresser when I was looking for you. They're images of me. What are you doing with them?" Tara watched Reena glance up at Patha. Patha looked at the images. He then looked at Reena and the two of them were silent for too long.   Tara narrowed her eyes at both of them. "What's going on here?"

Reena turned away from Tara. "How does that bandage feel?" She asked her patient.

"I'll be fine." The Runner started to stand and Duru helped him to his feet and allowed himself to be used as a crutch.

"Let's put him in the bedroom on the right," Reena instructed. "I'll watch him for a bit just to make sure no infection sets in."

"Reena, you didn't answer me," Tara persisted, after watching the two men disappear into the bedroom.

Reena didn't turn around but stared at the hallway and the open bedroom door where the two Runners were. "Tara, I'm your mama," she said, her voice barely a whisper.

"What?" Tara gasped, and grabbed Reena's arm to spin her around. "It sounded like you just said—"

Patha reached for Reena. "Tara," he said in that soft warming tone that used to make her jump to do as she was told.

She wasn't a child anymore. She stared at Reena, who was holding Patha's arm as if she might fall over if she let go. "Reena, it sounded as if you just said -"

"I did," Reena interrupted. Her face was white as a sheet. "I am your mama."

Tara reached for the back of the couch to steady herself. The room started spinning. Reena wasn't making any sense. "My...mama?" She barely uttered the words. "I don't have a mama."

"Come outside with us, child." Patha pulled Tara to him and placed his other hand gently on Reena's shoulder. "It's time you knew the truth."

Duru appeared from the hallway, and Reena turned to him. "Slice some pie for you two," she said, gesturing toward her kitchen.

Tara noticed Reena's hand shaking and turned to the kitchen. "I should help him." But she didn't move. Her brain wasn't working.

"I can handle it." Duru smiled at Tara and waved the group toward the door. "Go share your stories. If there is pie in the kitchen, I will find it."

"You better save a slice for me." Patha chuckled and again placed his hands on the two women, guiding them to the door.

Tara walked outside in a dazed stupor. She settled on the steps and frowned when Patha and Reena sat on the open room's swing together. Patha's large fingers wrapped around Reena's small hand and the two held hands.

She stared at their hands, interlocked. "You told me that my mama died and that you never knew her name. You said you found me when I was three winters old." She shook her head. None of this made any sense. "And what is this?" she demanded, staring at their hands.

"Child, I don't know where to begin." Reena's eyes welled with tears. Now there seemed to be too much color on her face. "Patha and I have known each other for a very long time. He would come see me from time to time, but staying for too long was not his way. Patha and I fell in love. He wanted me to move to his clan but Lord Jovis would not permit me to leave."

Patha patted Reena's hand. "Lord Jovis ordered me to stay out of Gothman but I continued to come see you," Patha chuckled, and Reena nodded, both silent for a moment as they relived a memory. "I wasn't too good at following orders."

"I do believe you threatened a war over me." Reena beamed at Patha.

"No." He shook his head and smiled at Reena in a way that Tara had never seen him smile before. "You're remembering wrong. I would never have done that."

"You didn't want any other man claiming me."

Patha leaned over and kissed Reena's forehead. "I still don't."

"Hey, what about me?" Tara demanded. "None of this makes any sense."

Seeing Patha this happy made it hard to be angry, but Tara was definitely confused.

"How are you my mama?" she demanded of Reena.

"When I found out I was pregnant I was so happy. I had a part of Patha that would stay with me, and I was free of the claiming forever. I had hoped, at first, that Patha would settle down with me here. Lord Jovis wouldn't hear of it, and Patha was not the settling down type. I kept you until you were about three. Oh child, you were beautiful even then."

"Why didn't you keep me?" Tara pulled her knees to her chest, forgetting the Gothman dress she wore. She turned on the open room's steps and faced both of them, engrossed in the story of her past. Try as she would, though, she didn't remember Reena, or this home.

"When Lord Jovis learned I was pregnant with a Runner's child he wanted to have you claimed to his son," Reena explained.

"In spite of hating me, he believed my child would give way to great warriors if bred with his blood," Patha intervened, sounding proud. His eyes glowed as he stared down at Tara.

"Now know that was his first-born son," Reena continued, nodding as she spoke. "With you and Juro both being just children." Now she began shaking her head as her mouth flattened into a strong, disapproving line. "Tara, it wasn't the life I wanted for you. I wanted you educated, free to make your own choices. You never would have had that in Gothman. The next time Patha came through we talked about it, and he agreed to take you with him and make you part of his clan." Reena began crying. At first she wiped the tears that streamed down her flushed cheeks. She gave up and smiled at Tara, letting the tears flow. "My dear child, you don't know what it's like giving up your daughter, especially one as perfect as you." Her voice cracked and she looked at her hands.

Patha put his arms around Reena and she relaxed against his large barrel chest. "You never gave her up," he whispered into her hair, then kissed her forehead.

Reena nodded but then continued on as if Patha hadn't just said something. Her voice was muffled, but she turned her head, resting it against Patha's chest as she spoke. "It was the hardest thing I've ever done in my life. I never saw you after that. We couldn't risk you entering Gothman, even for a short visit. It was almost impossible pretending I didn't know you the night you arrived here."

"I had no idea." Tara was already comparing features between the two adults on the open room's swing and herself. She looked more like Reena, she decided, who was her mama. Her throat was thick, and she'd started trembling. "Patha, why didn't you tell me? You really are my papa? I wish you would have told me. I've never had real parents and now I have two."

"Reena didn't want you to feel any obligation to visit her. She was afraid you'd be claimed once Lord Jovis knew you were back. He wanted you for his son almost before you were born.

The man knew you came from good blood." Patha chuckled and reached for Tara. She scooted across the open room and sat at their feet. Patha took her hand and held it on his knees. "As you grew and became more beautiful, we both knew the second you returned to Gothman, the first man who saw you would have you. When you left for the *Age Of Searching*, I knew you would end up here. I also knew no man would be able to claim you if you didn't want it. You're an incredible warrior now, not the helpless child you once were." Patha shook his head at his daughter. "I almost pity the man who would take you on. You've two very stubborn parents, child. And you definitely inherited that trait."

Tara didn't try to stop the tears. She let them fall as she absorbed this incredible news. Then sniffing, she wiped her teary face on her sleeve.

"So, suddenly I'm no longer an orphan. I've never thought to search for my parents because I thought they were dead. I didn't bother trying to ask questions about them because they were from another clan. No one would have known them. This is too much. I should be mad at both of you."

Tara swallowed a deep breath and turned to look at the tall pines surrounding them. Patha had raised her as his own. Her mama wasn't dead. She had sent her away. She searched her emotions and didn't feel angry. Maybe she should feel abandoned. But she was grateful for who she was and not a Gothman female, living in ignorant suppression. Tara was educated, a warrior with knowledge of Nuworld. She was on the *Age Of Searching* and had the freedom to come and go as she pleased. She would make her own decisions about her future. Patha and Reena had suffered in silence to give her all of that.

Tara stood and stared at the watery-eyed woman who looked up at her. She saw concern and worry in Reena's face. The woman feared Tara would hate her for the choice she had made. Maybe she'd lived with that worry for winters. She'd made a heart-breaking, selfless sacrifice and had given Tara a life of opportunity. Tara was the heir to the leader of all Runner clans.

"Hello, mama." Tara couldn't keep her voice from cracking as she held her arms out to Reena.

"Oh Tara!" Reena cried, and fresh tears streamed down her face as she leapt up and wrapped her thin arms around her daughter.

"I guess there are many stories to share," Tara mused. She buried her face in Reena's gray hair and breathed in the smell of spices and soap. This was her mama—her very much alive mama. "I hope we have time to do that very soon," she whispered.

Tara looked over Reena's shoulder at Patha, who smiled at the two women in front of him. Having only known her mama for a few brief seconds possibly made it easier to put stories of her to the side, at least for now. There was more to discuss, and it proved more urgent.

She stepped out of Reena's arms and cleared her throat. She needed to know how much danger Darius might be in. "Patha, I'm afraid there is about to be war."

"You refer to the Sea People." Patha's smile disappeared.

"Darius rode with some of his men to his borders and returned with stories that don't sound good."

The Patha she'd known all her life sat before her. The almost soft, gentle side of him that had appeared while sharing his story with Reena was gone. Tara straightened, staring into his calculating gaze. She needed to know what he knew.

"Patha, Lord Darius will have the Runners stand with him if they're willing. If there are battles coming, he needs us. Darius has no knowledge of the world outside of Gothman. He doesn't even know who he's fighting. I gave him an Eliminator, but he'll need much more than that."

Patha's eyes widened. He didn't bother to hide being surprised. "So, the son of Lord Jovis is not narrow-minded and full of hatred? Did he say he would have Runners ride alongside him into battle?"

"Yes. He's not full of hatred at all, Patha. Darius is cocky. And he's arrogant," she added. "But he's intelligent. He might never admit it, but he knows that there is much he doesn't know of Nuworld. Otherwise, he wouldn't have asked me to give his message to the leader of my people."

Tara's eyes were moist with tears. There was no missing how her face lit up at the mention of the Lord of Gothman. Patha noticed that, and much more. He watched his daughter's expression transform when she began explaining the thinking of the new, young lord.

"You've been in Gothman almost two cycles," Patha prompted. "You have Reena curious that you might be staying."

"Oh. I – uh…" Tara hesitated. She shifted her weight and looked away from both of them. Without ceremony, she plopped down and sat cross legged. Tara tugged on that Gothman dress she wore under her Runner jacket. When she pulled her jacket around her, Patha saw the symbol of the Blood Circle Clan on the sleeve. But she'd slipped a ban over the sleeve of her jacket – the symbol of the Bryton house.

"The truth is he had my bike," she told them, laughing then looking down and tracing her finger along the tip of her boot. "It's okay, though. You should have seen Darius when I let him ride it."

"How did Lord Darius know you're a Runner?" Patha had already guessed but wanted her story.

As he always had, when his clan was close enough to Gothman borders for a transmission to go through, he'd contacted Reena. He'd hurried to Gothman as soon as Reena told him that Lord Darius had claimed Tara. With the Sea People ready to start trouble his clans were primed for action. Patha had left with only a few of his men, knowing they'd travel faster that way. For now, the clan was safe where they were, although he'd left them on alert and was maintaining open transmissions in case the Sea People got stupid while he was away.

He didn't want to attack Gothman. Now both of his women were here. The last thing he would do was start a war and risk either their lives. However, Patha would make it clear to Lord Darius the same way he had with his sire. Patha would kill to protect his family.

"I told him I was a Runner." Tara put her hand on Patha's knee. Her face glowed when she smiled up at him. "He had figured it out, but Darius thinks he has everything figured out. At first I thought he was an idiot, because of his laws about women. But don't worry, Patha. Darius won't make me do anything I don't want to do."

Reena stiffened and fell clumsily back onto the swing next to him. Patha gave her shoulder a gentle squeeze. Tara hadn't said she wanted to stay in Gothman.

"Have you fallen in love with this Gothman lord?" Patha saw his answer when he looked at his daughter. He'd never seen such a glow in her face.

"Yes, maybe. I think so." She blushed and looked from Patha to Reena. "He's a good man. He claimed me, but I told him I wouldn't be claimed until I was ready. He could have had me killed. But he didn't. That speaks so much louder about his character than any of the stories do, don't you think? He told me when they heard a Runner had entered Gothman territory they hunted me, and he found me. Darius wouldn't have me killed on sight. He told me that he didn't see a threat, and like me, wanted to know why the law to shoot a Runner on sight existed before implementing it."

Lord Darius is willing to wait for you to accept his claim?" Patha searched her face for more of an answer than she would give him with words.

"Gothman don't feel a need for their women to accept a claim." Tara rolled her eyes but was still grinning at both of them. "I think I'm going to claim him, though."

"Does he know this?"

"I haven't told him yet."

A small smile appeared on Patha's face. His daughter would never do anything she didn't want to do. That was his Tara, stubborn as she was beautiful. She was also one of the best warriors he'd seen in all his winters. A union between Tara and Lord Darius would end the ban of Runners in Gothman. Runners would be even more powerful with Gothman under their wing. "I'll have several thousand Runners here within a quarter-cycle." Patha turned serious. "Where's his army?"

"I believe the Gothman armies are preparing to head south."

"Why are they heading in that direction?" Patha looked surprised.

"He told me his scouts saw the Sea People heading in from the south."

"There are no Sea People there. We've come up from the south after trading with the River People. When we rode north outside of Gothman we spotted several Sea People camps. My scouts report that they are travelling with tanks and heavy artillery. They've already attacked several clans north of here. According to the transmissions, there have been quite a few casualties."

"Oh Patha, this is horrible." Tara was mortified. She'd been out of communication with the clans for almost two cycles.

"If I hadn't spoken with you just now, I would have allowed Darius to take his army south. Gothman would have been unprotected. "Patha, somehow Darius has some bad information. I need to warn him!"

Tara hurried to her feet and ran into the house to grab her bag. She pulled out the flat landlink. It seemed to take forever to activate. She punched keys the second she had a signal. The tracer she'd put on Darius' neck appeared as a red dot on a grid map. He was already heading south.

"Patha, Darius has already left." Tara yelled, but when she turned Patha and Reena were right behind her. Reena moved to the stove and reached for the kettle. "Reena, I'd like to send Hilda and Torgo to stay with you for the time being. I believe they'd be safer here. If the Sea People target the area, they would go after Darius' home. This place is isolated, and we could post guards to protect you. Will you have them?"

Patha gestured to the Runner who sat on the couch with a landlink on his lap. "I can leave Duru here with you for the time being. He can monitor the area."

"Of course, child. They can stay here." Reena walked around the counter and put her hands on Tara's waist. "That is, if Lord Darius will allow it. You will go to battle with your claim?"

"Oh yes," Tara said. "I'd be of no help staying in hiding with the women."

Reena smiled but looked serious, almost sad. "My daughter finally knows me, and she wants to leave for battle."

"Reena, don't worry. I'll be back."

"Tara, you're with child. You know this is true, right?"

Tara and Patha both stared open-mouthed at Reena.

"How could I be?" Tara was ready to disagree.

"There's only one way." Reena smiled.

Tara looked down at her flat tummy.

"I'd say just over a cycle. I know the glow and I've never been wrong. You take very good care of yourself and my grandbaby, you hear?"

Tara glanced at Patha, but didn't say anything. Instead she grabbed her bag, and ran out of the cabin. That last bit of information was one piece of news too much.

Reena watched as Tara drove down the hill in Hilda's groundmobile. "Tell me we did the right thing." She looked up into Patha's face for reassurance.

"We've discussed this for winters and now suddenly you're worried?" Patha walked into Reena's kitchen and helped himself to a slice of her pie. "Did you see her, Reena? She wore symbols of the Blood Circle Clan and Gothman on her sleeve. She is quite possibly the first person on Nuworld to do that."

"She ran out my door more excited to tell Lord Darius about a war than of being pregnant." Reena still wasn't convinced they were doing the right thing. "You were right, though. I daresay you always are. Lord Darius claimed her as soon as he saw her."

"Of course he did. She's as beautiful and smart as her mama."

Reena walked up behind Patha, wrapped her arms around his middle and rested the side of her face against his back. "I remember when your flattery, and your just being here, took all my worries away."

"You remember?" Patha complained and turned in her arms. "Remember? You think I'm too old? I'll show you too old." He lifted her without asking and plopped her on the counter next to her pie. Instantly, his large competent hands slid underneath her dress and up her thighs. "Duru, you should go check on Sal."

"Duru, you should leave Sal alone and let him sleep." Reena laughed. When she wasn't strong enough to move Patha, she put her arms around his neck and scratched his short gray hair. "You don't approve of her fighting when she's pregnant, do you?"

"You were serious about that?" The mischief in his green eyes disappeared. "I'll let you know after I meet Lord Darius. What do you know about him?"

"He has a lot of power but he's young. People that get in his way have a tendency to fall into bad luck, so to speak. I don't know whether or not he's good enough for our daughter. But I really hope Tara will stay here. I'd like get to know her. Imagine her living in Gothman as a Runner." Reena pursed her lips, trying to digest the possibility.

Patha moved his hands to cup her face. "It will be tough on her at first, but their union will create the most powerful nation in Nuworld."

Reena stared at Patha's rugged, perfectly weathered, handsome face. She'd seen that incredibly focused, determined look before. It hadn't always been clear what he planned, but she'd always trusted Patha. Not once had he led her wrong.

With that one statement though, she understood Patha's thoughts. He was more concerned about how powerful Runners and Gothman would be if the two were claimed. She was more concerned about her daughter's happiness.

Reena worried that the challenges Gothman, and Lord Darius brought Tara would be enough to satisfy her. Darius would command Tara to stay in Gothman. If she didn't, and Reena understood Runner blood better than anyone, it might start a war.

CHAPTER SEVEN

TARA PULLED up in front of the Bryton house, ran up the open room stairs, and called for Hilda and Torgo. The two of them hurried to her, instantly concerned by the worry in her voice. "I'm going to send you two to stay with Reena."

"Darius wouldn't leave us here if he didn't think we were safe." Hilda crossed her fleshy arms over her bosom and scowled at Tara. "We aren't going anywhere."

"Darius doesn't know how many Sea People are surrounding Gothman right now. The Runners are here and more are coming. With our equipment we can help Gothman. These Sea People are ready to attack. You're safer at Reena's outside of Bryton. I've already arranged for guards to protect you," Tara reassured both of them.

"You talked to Runners?" Torgo's eyes grew large.

"Yes, child," she smiled and ruffled his hair. "It'll be a great story when I tell it to you."

"Now quickly, go get some clothes for the next few days." She followed them up the stairs.

"I don't like the idea of being sent away from my own home," Hilda grumbled. "And by a Runner no less."

"Hilda, I'm not your enemy." Once in her own room, Tara changed into her Runner clothing. Completely dressed for battle, she sat down on the bed and pulled her landlink from her black bag she had taken to Reena's. It didn't take as long this time to activate. Soon she was communicating with some of the Runners outside Gothman's borders.

It felt good to be connected again. Gothman didn't have landlinks and therefore no networks. Now with a Runner clan close to Gothman, she activated and communicated with her people.

"This is Tara of the Blood Circle Clan," Tara whispered the words as she typed. "Requesting any known information on Sea People in the area."

Tara sent the message to the two clans she'd managed to locate. She would check back soon for a response.

"Come on, let's go!" she yelled as she left her room and headed down the stairs.

"Whoa!" Torgo hurried down the steps and froze when he saw Tara fully dressed as a Runner sitting on the couch with her landlink on her lap. "Tara, is that you?"

"Torgo, never fear a Runner." She beckoned him. "A Runner will never attack someone unless attacked first."

"I wasn't scared. You look cool!" Torgo sat next to Tara and stared at the flat screen. "And I guessed you were a Runner all along."

Tara grinned under her headscarf and ruffled his already tousled curls, then pointed to her screen. "I'm linked now so I can communicate with any Runner this way." She pointed to the map displayed on the screen. "I can also tell where Lord Darius and his army are."

"You're kidding. How do you do that?"

"It's Oldworld knowledge. It's easy enough though. It won't take long to teach you."

Torgo was leaning over looking at the screen when Hilda came down the stairs.

"So, you're a Runner now, are you?" She looked at Tara disapprovingly. "Torgo, get away from that thing."

"Hilda, I've always been a Runner." In the older woman, Tara saw some of the prejudice that had obviously kept her son ignorant of the world outside of Gothman. "Now go, both of you. Reena is expecting you. Remember, if you see any Runners at her place, they aren't your enemy."

"Can't I stay with you and fight, Tara?" Torgo pleaded, not moving when his mama insisted. "Why are you sending me away with the women? I'm not a child anymore, you know."

"I know." Tara stood with Torgo, snapped her heels together, and clasped her hands behind her back. "Stand at attention, and let me give you your orders."

Torgo imitated her stance and became serious, his large gray eyes glowing with fascination.

"These women need protection. Right now I have no soldiers to send with them. You will escort your mama to Reena's. You will stay there, guarding them with your life. Understood?"

"Yes. Understood." Torgo broke out in a grin, and before Tara had time to react he reached for her and gave her a quick hug. "Be careful, okay?"

Tara smiled when Torgo released her. "I always am."

Torgo hopped out the front door ready for the adventure. Hilda didn't look at Tara as she left. Since the old woman and Reena had been friends for so long, Hilda probably had known about Tara when she was a little girl. Although she'd probably never hear it, knowing Hilda's side of the story about Tara leaving Gothman might have been a good one, or at least interesting, if not educational, to hear.

As soon as the front door shut, Tara jumped up and ran to the shed out back. There was a lock on the door this time. Tara sighed and looked around the yard to see who might be watching. No one was in sight. She pulled out her laser, and a small blast caused the lock to fall to the ground. Within seconds, she rolled her bike out of the shed and snapped her landlink on it.

Tara narrowed in on Darius' signal. He was south of town and from what she could tell, twenty or so others were with him. She scanned for local roads and was surprised to find a map of Gothman. She took off at top speed.

Who would have led Darius to believe he should go south? This was now the question at hand. There was really only one reason she found plausible.

Tara considered the matter. The Sea People approached from the north, but had come from the west, which made sense since they lived along the West Sea. Darius would be protected from any attacks if he was in the southern region, but Gothman would not. Someone wanted Darius out of the way so Gothman would be defenseless against a hard attack. Who would want to place Gothman in such a danger?

When her dot was practically on top of Darius's dot on her landlink's screen, Tara parked her bike and scanned for Gothman communication. It wasn't hard for her landlink to pick up their simplex form of transmitting. Static crackled through her sound transmitters. Her equipment wasn't designed to receive such antiquated forms of communication signals. Tara was lucky anything came through at all.

She adjusted her frequency and managed to tap into the Gothman conversation. Normally, Tara used her comm, which wrapped around her ear and came down to her mouth, to hear anything or communicate with anyone. The Gothman audio transmission wouldn't work with her technology. She was forced to turn up her volume on her landlink and listen that way.

Tara glanced around at her surroundings warily. There were definitely Gothman nearby. They picked up on her landlink although she didn't see, or hear them.   Adjusting her sound transmitters to a very low volume, she then leaned forward on her bike, keeping alert to any movement around her, and listened. The audio was poor but leaning forward she heard conversation through the small boxes attached on either side of her handlebars.

Every inch of her tensed when the first man's voice crackled through her sound transmitters. She became acutely aware of the slightest breeze moving branches, as well as any sound she picked up that didn't come through her landlink.

"He'll be within sight in a few minutes. Be ready now."

"Have you had any further communication?"

"I have. They're coming across Runners."

"Is that a problem?"

"It's a passing clan. It shouldn't be."

Tara remained straddled and pushed her bike forward with her feet into the forest so she was better hidden. She then stopped and froze. Up in a nearby tree, a Gothman was lodged between two branches holding a walkntalk in front of his mouth.

Tara pressed her ear to her sound transmitter, turned the volume down further, waited, and listened.

She didn't have to wait long. Tara heard voices and saw movement through the trees ahead. So did the Gothman in the tree. He pulled a bang stick from his jacket and aimed at the group approaching.

Tara watched the Gothman focus on his target. She shifted her attention when she heard Darius. He barked orders, and the booming sound of his voice carried easily. Then it dawned on her. Darius was the target!

Tara slid off her bike, moved to the tree where the man was perched, hoisted herself up and knocked him off balance. Before he had a chance to yell out, she shot him in the back. The man's body slumped over a thick branch. His bang stick fell to the forest floor with a quiet thud. Blood flowed down the tree from where she'd sliced him open with her laser. It formed a sticky dark pool over the bang stick. She pried the man's walkntalk from his hand. Tara leapt free of the stench and crept behind some nearby bushes. The dead man's companion had to be nearby.

"What is that smell, my lord?"

Tara froze and watched as Darius came into view with a group of his men.

"I smell it too. It smells like something's burned," another guard answered.

Darius passed by without seeing her. "It smells like burnt blood."

He stopped so close to her hiding place she easily smelled the scent of his soap, and the smell of him she'd grown all too fond of.

"How does blood burn?" an older, stocky warrior asked.

"Should we search the area, my lord?"

The group of men stopped around Darius. Their boots shuffled over the undergrowth, crunching crumpled leaves, dried pine and twigs underfoot. They weren't concerned about concealing their whereabouts. Nor did they notice the dead man hanging in the blood soaked tree not far from them. The walkntalk in her hand crackled and a voice came through. If the guards hadn't been so noisy, the sound of it would have given her away.

"Why didn't you get him?" a voice said. "Mikel will be furious."

Tara frowned. Her heart skipped a beat, and a pain tightened in her chest. She fought for a soothing breath as reality hit her. Mikel was Darius' brother.

Something moved in a tree beyond where Darius and his men stood. Scooting past the bushes, Tara moved crab-like until she was sure Darius and his men wouldn't see her. Now all she needed was time to find the other man on the walkntalk, kill him, and get back to her bike unscathed, and undetected. Right now she would keep Darius alive. Later she would learn why Mikel wanted him dead. Someone jumped from the tree and shot at her.

"Who is firing?" one of Darius' men yelled.

"Over there!" Darius barked the command. "I see movement."

"You're a Runner," hissed the man who had jumped from the tree. He aimed his bang stick directly at her chest.

"And you're a dead man," Tara whispered through clenched teeth. The whistling sound from her laser pierced the air. The man fell to the ground.

She took a second look at the Gothman's ugly face. It was the guard who had tried to attack her the first day she'd visited Daruis' home. Now why didn't that surprise her? At the sound of Darius and his men approaching, she damn near rolled into the bushes. Then scurrying for distance, she crouched where she could see him between trees.

"This is the smell." Darius stood over the second man she'd shot.

His men coughed and covered their mouths with gloved hands as they stared at the man who had been sliced wide open by the laser.

"What was Judo doing back here?" one of Lord Darius' soldiers asked, as he stared at the charred body.

Tara watched Darius as he studied the dead man. She guessed he'd never seen a man killed by a laser before. Yet his expression remained blank. If his emotions were that much in check, then he was a better warrior than she. Her emotions swarmed in her head, making it hard to concentrate. Darius needed protection. Gothman might be attacked and at the moment stood unprotected. And for some unknown reason, Darius had an internal problem.

"Judo was supposed to be with the other troops, my lord," a guard standing next to Darius said. "Maybe he was trying to get word to us about who ever shot at him."

"We've been all across this land. There's no indication that any Sea People have been here. If he wanted to tell me something, he would have used the walkntalk. It's right here." Lord Darius squatted to take the walkntalk off the dead man and studied the laser wound. He searched the foliage and was silent for a moment.

No Gothman bang stick would have killed in that fashion. Tara pushed the button on the walkntalk in her hand. "I need to speak with you alone," she whispered into the rectangular-shaped black box.

She took a chance contacting him in that manner, but it made sense that the walkntalk by the corpse and the one she'd taken from the other dead man would be on the same channel. The dead men had been collaborating with Mikel. She needed to warn Darius.

Darius stared at the walkntalk in his hand. Then taking his time he took a good look at their surroundings. Tara had just spoken to him. He seriously doubted she was trying to reach Judo. That told him two things. One, she had one of his other men's walkntalk, and Darius seriously doubted they loaned it to her. And two, she was watching him right now.

An intense desire to wrap his fingers around her Runner neck distracted him for a moment. Tara was risking her life out here, and not knowing where she was at this precise moment pissed him off and terrified him. He was going to enjoy the challenge of taming his Runner claim.

"Let's head back to camp." Darius stood and kept a shrewd eye on their surroundings. "Something's not right here. I want to confirm that the Sea People are south of Gothman. Grab Judo and haul him back."

His men began dragging the body toward the bikes. Tara was somewhere in the woods. What was she up to? He thought about all the stories he'd heard about Runners over the winters. They were rumored to be better warriors than Gothman. While he questioned that, Tara had just proven she did some things as well as a man. There was no doubt that she'd killed Judo. The blood still flowed. She'd just killed him, and he hadn't noticed she was here before she spoke through the walkntalk.

She was perfect in so many ways with that tempting mouth, long soft strands of hair, and elegant slender neck. He could feast on those breasts all day. Those toned thighs she wrapped around him had the strength to make him forget about a nation. But she was so much more than a luscious female who warmed his bed.

Darius listened. Concentrated. He squinted and looked in the direction where he thought he'd just heard something. There! Through the bushes! Something in black. His men were at their bikes, working in solemn uniformity wrapping Judo's body to prepare for the trip home. Judo had died in combat, a warrior's death. His life would be celebrated and his claim a valuable commodity. Many men viewed it as good luck to claim a woman who'd fucked an honourable warrior til death.

Darius would consider it good luck to capture one hot and incredibly disobedient Runner without his men learning what he was doing.

He took care moving though the tress. He spotted Tara as she reached her bike and straddled it. He crept up from behind, wrapped his arms around her and cupped his hand over her mouth.

Instantly, Tara lurched backward off the bike. She shoved herself into her aggressor. Her body had more pack to it than he might have guessed. She pulled her legs up and slammed her heels into his knees. The pain was damned annoying, but determination prevailed.

Tara must know it was him. She was trying to convince him how well she fought. She twisted her body and thrashed against his. He tightened the arm around her chest until he was afraid he would smash her rib cage if she didn't succumb.

Darius was impressed. More than once he struggled to keep his balance. Finally he tightened his grip until she was gasping for breath. She stopped thrashing her legs.

"What are you doing here?" he whispered into her ear.

Tara relaxed. He slowly removed his hand from her mouth and slid it possessively down her neck.

"You've been fed wrong information," she whispered as she coughed in air. "Hopefully, your spies are dead. I don't detect any other Gothman in the area other than those behind us and about twenty or so down the hill." She spoke quickly then stopped and inhaled sharply.

"What are you talking about?" He flipped her around and gripped her arms, fighting the urge to shake her until she made sense.

"The Sea People are north and northwest of Gothman. They're heavily armed and driving metal groundmobiles loaded with artillery. You need to move all of your troops now." She paused for a moment, confirming they were alone. She pulled her shirt down and adjusted her face cloth. "I'm pretty sure Mikel fed you false information to get you out here and kill you."

A look Tara couldn't identify crossed Darius' face. "I didn't know he was warrior enough to try such a stunt."

"I heard your men talking on their walkntalks." She tried reading his reaction to what she was telling him. "There'll be several thousand Runners meeting you at your northern borders in about two days. Your defense needs to be strong to hold the Sea People off until then." Tara turned and began punching keys on a flat pad between her bike's handlebars. It hadn't been there when her bike had been in his shed. "Patha's on line. He's verified reinforcement."

"Patha of the Blood Circle Clan?" He frowned. "How do you know Patha?"

"He's my papa." It would confuse matters to tell him she'd just found this out today.

"I see."

Tara thought Darius already knew who she was. They'd never discussed her clan though. At least she had the satisfaction of knowing he hadn't tried claiming her because she was heir to all clans. If he didn't know her clan, or her relation to Patha, then he wouldn't know where she ranked among Runners. It wasn't much better that he'd initially claimed her based on her looks. Something told her that more than her body appealed to him now.

Darius looked away from her and murmured, "My papa knew him."

"So I've heard."

Darius took his time looking at her again. Although it was only a brief moment, he stared at her and it seemed a silent understanding passed between them. There was history the two of them would discuss. But not now. Now was time to prepare for battle.

"I'll confirm your information." He started to walk away but then turned to look at her. "I'd hate to think of what might have happened if you hadn't interfered."

"I'm not interfering."

A small smile played at his lips.

"What are you going to do about Mikel?"

"He'll be taken care of." His voice was quiet, and his gray eyes melted her insides. "He's not my priority, though. Gothman comes first. Trust me, my lady, Mikel won't interfere with my securing the strength of my nation. I won't allow it."

Tara grabbed her handlebars and started her bike. She believed him. His gray eyes might seduce her with a look, but they also held the gleam of a warrior. Not only would Darius fight to the death to maintain Gothman, the thought of doing so created the excitement in him that she saw now.

She rolled the bike forward, its motor a quiet purr. "I've made my decision." She gave him one last look. "The claim stands."

Tara didn't wait for a response, but hopped on her bike, accelerated and left him standing there.

Arriving back at the house, she set up camp in her bedroom. She propped the landlink on the desk and opened the balcony doors. The fresh air made her feel less boxed in and she'd hear any Gothman bike approaching. Confirming she was still activated, she again searched for Runners in the area.

This is Tara, of the Blood Circle Clan, she typed, after detecting one of the clan leaders on line.

Greetings. This is Jaree, wife to the leader of the Red Star Clan.

Before long, she was deep in conversation explaining to Jaree what to expect when her clan arrived at the north Gothman border.

The Red Star Clan is loyal to Patha and the Blood Circle Clan. Jaree's typed message appeared on Tara's screen. *You can count on our help if you need us.*

Tara worked into the night, briefing clan after clan that had either heard from Patha or from another clan leader. She joined a transmission with several other clan leaders, including Patha who was on his landlink at Reena's house, and argued the pros and cons of a Runner and Gothman union.

I see you claim two titles now, Patha typed in a private message to Tara, while both of them continued to discuss political issues in the group transmission. *You're not only my heir, but now you're the claim to the Lord of Gothman?*

I need to show that I'm dedicated to helping Gothman. Tara felt her fingers cramp as she hurried to express her point to Patha, while continuing to comment in the group transmission. *Runners and Gothman have always believed they were enemies. Sharing news of my claim will help strengthen the alliance.*

As the evening wore on, news travelled of the union between the Runners and the Gothman.

Is it true? One of her friends from her clan sent a transmission that popped up on her screen. *How have you become the claim to the Lord of Gothman?*

The questions from Tara's clan members were justified. She typed and typed until her fingers were numb and her eyes watered and burned from staring at the screen so long. The Runners needed reassurance, though, that Gothman would now be a formidable ally.

Tara fell asleep before Darius returned that night and woke up with the cool morning breeze blowing through the open balcony doors. She was starving and the walkntalk she'd brought back with her beeped next to her. Getting up and stretching, Tara experienced a wave of nausea. It terrified her that Reena might be right.

Hell and doomed! Now wasn't the time for a pregnancy. The truth of it was Tara had never given thought to being pregnant, or raising children. She was a warrior. Protecting her people, insuring their freedom, and doing whatever was needed for Runners in general had always been her top priority. The walkntalk beeped again and Tara pressed the flat button on the side, allowing the person to talk.

"Tara?" It was Hilda's voice. The older woman muttered something to someone else. She then yelled. "Tara, are you there?"

Reena yelled too. "Tara, are you okay?"

"Yes. I'm fine. What time is it?"

"Oh, for Gothman's sake. We woke her up." It was Hilda again. "Reena thinks you're pregnant. Is that true?"

Tara forced herself to ride out the nausea and hurried to dress. Last night she'd been alone in the house. One glance out the open balcony doors and she knew it was well pass sunrise. She didn't know who was in the house now. Tara was definitely not ready for two meddling old women to squawk a word like *pregnant* through a walkntalk loud enough that others around her might hear them.

"I don't know, Hilda. What did you want?"

"She wants to know what we need," Hilda said, her voice breaking up when she kept the button pressed and spoke to the background again. Hilda shouted into the walkntalk. "We want to make sure you're okay. Is my son there?"

Tara was suddenly grouchy and nauseous. She bit back her urge to snap and demand to be allowed to go back to sleep. Tara needed Hilda to believe she was okay or the woman might very likely try contacting Darius with news that Tara wasn't ready to share. She sat on the bed and found her landlink under the blankets.

"Your son is out with his troops defending Gothman. I'm fine, Hilda. I promise. I don't want you to leave Reena's house. Do you have enough food?"

"The Runner, um, Patha, is here. And yes, my dear, I daresay we have plenty of food—even for Torgo."

Tara dropped the walkntalk on the crumpled sheets, then typed a message to Patha. He wouldn't like doing it but Tara begged him to keep Reena and Hilda from telling anyone she might be pregnant.

"After all," she read to herself after she'd finished typing the message. "There's no proof that I am and a false rumor would do more damage that good right now." Satisfied, she sent the message.

Nothing in the kitchen looked good. Tara settled on some grape juice. She then returned to her bedroom, sat cross-legged on her unmade bed with her landlink and planned her strategy for the day. She remembered the walkntalk and found it between folds of the sheets. Could she reach Darius on it?

Tara might not have knowledge of such antiquated devices, but she was sure they were not a secured means of communication. How had a nation become so large on such primitive equipment? Wit and brawn – there was no other logical answer.

What information she'd obtained last night led her to believe the Sea People had obtained more sophisticated equipment. Gothman would have to be armed with better weapons than Oldworld technology if they were to survive. Something needed to be done about it immediately. She prayed Darius wouldn't be too stubborn. She had to take matters into her own hands.

Tara carried her landlink out of the house to her bike. The few guards on duty were alongside the house talking. Darius would have to train his men better. But for now, she was glad they didn't notice her climb onto her bike and disappear around the other side of the house.

The morning air was cool and the sky a magnificent blue. She travelled north on an obviously seldom-used rocky road heading toward the location indicated on her screen. Half an hour later, she noticed several black trailers coming across the meadow to her west. Within minutes, many motorcycles became visible as well. It was a Runner clan and a rather large one at that. The scouts leading the clan approached her first, and she slowed to greet them.

"Identify yourself, Runner." The voice was female although with her headscarf and large jacket it was hard to determine her gender if she hadn't spoke.

"I'm Tara of the Blood Circle Clan." She scanned the open area as more motorcycles came into view.

The Runner spoke into her comm clipped around her ear and extending to her mouth. The comms were used by most clans, proving the easiest way to communicate while on a bike. Tara knew that one of the black trailers contained the clan's base unit, and the female Runner was informing those inside the van of her contact.

"I'm to tell you that Redo of the Red Star clan greets you. He's received your communication and has brought his clan to assist."

"I'm very grateful to all of your clan for your willingness to help with the Sea People. I'm on my way to meet Lord Darius of Gothman. Will you ride with me?"

The woman spoke into her comm again, then grinned. "Lead the way."

Darius' exact location was beyond the oncoming hills. She and the clan began making their way toward him, slowing their pace over the rough ground so the trailers would be able to keep up with them.

Pride in her people grew as Tara rode with a scout on either side of her. The remaining members of the clan rode behind them. She and her fellow Runners were creating history. The noise of their approaching motorcycles—several hundred in all—roared over the hills like thunder, stirring up clouds of dirt like a tornado, and sending tremors through the ground as powerful as an earthquake.

The scout to Tara's right pointed to a large number of parked bikes, and scores of tents being assembled. They'd arrived at the Gothman camp. As the Gothman became aware of the approaching Runner clan, all hands dropped what they were doing. But while a commotion stirred in the camp, the Gothman warriors had obviously been notified of the Runners' pending arrival since no shots were fired. Nevertheless, Gothman guards at the edge of the camp pulled their bang sticks and stood alert.

The clan's warriors accelerated around the scouts, now leading the way, and Tara alerted them to slow down. She stopped the clan within twenty feet of the Gothman. It would appear to any bystander to be quite a standoff, with Runners lined up over a hundred bikes thick and Gothman mostly on foot tense with bang sticks in their hands.

"Hold your clan and wait for my instructions," Tara told the nearest scout.

She accelerated and parked alongside the Gothman guard who wore the armband of highest rank.

"I'm Tara of the Blood Circle Clan. This is the Red Star clan, here to assist the Gothman. Inform Lord Darius we await his instructions."

He yelled to another guard who was standing next to him, and that man turned and ran into the camp toward one of the tents.

Tara didn't move. The Red Star clan remained parked with the Gothman watching them. Over five hundred people were silent in the meadow. Birds didn't dare fly overhead. The silence was deafening. Tara wondered if prejudices could be put aside long enough to fight this battle together.

Something rumbled behind her. Tara turned, as did those behind her. Behind the Red Star clan, at the bottom of the hill, another clan approached.

Tara shouted to the Gothman warrior, "Tell your men to hold their position. I will see what clan this is."

She rode back to the Runner scout, who was already on her comm. "Have the clan identify themselves," Tara instructed. Ask them to hold their ground and wait further instructions.

Tara turned back to the Gothman at the sound of a motorcycle weaving around the Gothman men. She breathed a sigh of relief at the sight of Darius.

"Lower your weapons, Gothman!" He bellowed with enough ferocity that his men turned on a dime to face him. "The Runners are here to assist us. Get back to work and get this camp in order!"

His men returned to assembling the tents and preparing the camp for battle, although many kept their eyes on the arriving Runners. Darius accelerated around the Gothman guards and pulled up alongside Tara.

"How many Runners are here?" Darius' tone was demanding and harsh, although he spoke softly enough only Tara heard.

She glanced at him but he wasn't looking at her. His tone wasn't controlling, but instead demanding information as a leader of people would to another. "I don't have a count, yet. I'll get one."

She looked at the scout parked on the other side of her. "Lord Darius wants a count of Runners. How many are there in the Red Star clan?"

"We are two hundred and fifty," the woman responded and glanced past Tara to give Darius a curious once over. "Two weeks ago, our clan numbered over seven hundred. The Sea People attacked us because they thought we were destroying a field where some opiate plants grow. We were all but destroyed by them. It's an honor to join the other clans and the Gothman in battle. The Sea People are a no good race of drug addicts. Nuworld is better off without them."

Tara saw the anger in the woman's eyes as she spoke.

The woman pressed her hand to her ear, listening to someone through her comm. She then glanced at Tara and smiled. "The Blood Circle Clan is behind us. They number twelve hundred, and Patha sends his greeting to you, Tara."

Tara's face lit up. Her people had come. Not that she'd ever doubted Patha. She started to turn back toward Darius when the woman raised her hand.

"Wait," she said. "Patha is coming forward. His clan will maintain their location until further orders, as will ours. Patha says no further action is to occur until he meets with Lord Darius."

Patha was not only leader of all clans but loved and respected by all. He'd established the large networking system existing among Runners today when he was a very young man. It was due to Patha's ingenuity that the clans were able to communicate with each other no matter how far away they might travel. His focus had always been protection of all the clans. It would be tough following in his footsteps.

Tara was proud of Patha, her papa. She straightened when she spotted him approaching the front line of Runners. She glanced at Darius. He too sat tall and watched Patha ride toward them.

"It's Patha. He'll want to speak privately."

Darius nodded but focused on the large man on a larger version of Tara's bike. Completely covered by Runner attire, and adorned with metals of victory, a muscular man, not quite Darius's size, drew near. In spike of his headscarf concealing his appearance, Darius saw what he needed to see in Patha's eyes. Patha never once looked away from Darius. The man looked intelligent, shrewd and incredibly focused.

"Patha, I'm so glad you've arrived." Tara said when Patha stopped, facing them. "May I present Lord Darius."

Patha looked from Tara to Darius. "I'll speak with you two alone now."

CHAPTER EIGHT

THE GOTHMAN camp was large and well-organized. Very tall, powerfully built warriors stood all around the edges of the encampment. Metal-clad groundmobiles heavy with artillery looked ominous parked along the northern boundary. Tara spotted two towers constructed from wood with ladders rising to a platform where more warriors were posted. At least three large circles of tents were assembled in the level section of a grassy meadow. Each tent stood well over six-foot tall and blocked her view of the rest of the camp as they rode nearer.

Soldiers ceased their target practice or slinging large hammers that drove stakes as tall as she was into the ground, to stare at the two Runners. Did all these men know she was claimed to their lord? Did they know she was the reason the Runners were here to fight alongside them? If they weren't victorious, Runners and Gothman would not only despise each other worse than before, they would hate her. Tara would only focus on victory.

Darius pulled his bike alongside a tent larger than the rest and parked. As tall as the tent was, Darius ducked when he led his way inside. Two large screened windows allowed sunlight to naturally light the interior. A heavy tapestry divided the tent in half. Darius stopped at a large table with maps and outlines scattered across it. He sat at a tall-back wooden chair and gestured for Patha and Tara to sit as well.

"Welcome to Gothman, Patha." Darius's low, cool baritone rang with pride for his nation. That edge of arrogance that Tara already knew was in the backbone of his personality shone through in his relaxed expression, and in how he commanded the room the moment he draped his body over the chair he sat in. "We are honored to have your men join ours in battle."

"You're the son of Lord Jovis." Patha took his chair at the opposite end of the table and laced his fingers against his muscular stomach. He stared at Darius a moment. "I had dealings with your papa many winters ago. He didn't care much for Runners. It appears you don't share your papa's opinion of us."

Tara sat very still in her chair. If Darius hated Runners he would have killed her and this union wouldn't be happening. Patha didn't speak to hear himself talk. She waited to hear his point. If Patha mentioned Reena's belief that Tara was pregnant, it would put a hitch in these proceedings. Patha had more sense than that.

"I'm aware of your associations with my papa." Darius looked very relaxed in his chair. "That was a long time ago. I know you're Tara's papa, and Reena is her mama."

Tara blinked and looked into cool grey eyes. How long had he known Reena was her mama?

Darius wasn't looking at her, though. He focused on Patha. "All warriors in this camp have families. They keep their personal life at home and are here to fight a war. There's no room for thoughts other than the strategies we need to prepare."

"If there are no thoughts other than strategy and combat, you turn your warriors into machines," Patha countered.

"They would become machines if they quit thinking," Darius said easily. "And machines break down."

"Very true." Patha rubbed his chin and looked at the netting over the tent window while he gathered his thoughts. He returned his gaze to Darius. "So, you allow for emotions and personal feelings to be integrated into your strategy?"

"We fight for Gothman. Our nation is powerful, and we are proud of who we are. That is an emotion." Although Darius sounded as if he spoke from his heart, his expression remained masked, his eyes focused and alert. "And as for personal feelings, a good warrior is always affected by war. I wouldn't want to fight next to a man who was immune to the blood and death around him."

A slow smile crossed Patha's face. He stood and walked around the tent, continuing to look outside. Turning, he removed his headscarf and nodded for Tara to do the same.

"Very good, young man. We'll review your strategies. I will have one thing made clear first."

Darius' expression didn't change as he watched Patha.

Tara had no idea what was going on in his head at that moment. She was impressed by his manner, though, and hoped Patha was as well.

"Do you want the Runners' help in this war?" Patha walked to the table and leaned his fists against it.

"Patha, I will accept your assistance in defeating the Sea People." Darius leaned forward as well and looked Patha straight in the eye. "Now, I'll ask you a question." Darius got up and moved behind the chair where Tara sat.

Tara froze, wondering what the question would be. She wasn't sure, but she thought she saw a hint of amusement in Patha's eyes. Tara guessed her papa enjoyed the way Darius reacted to Patha, as if they were equals. Patha didn't have many people who made that assumption around him. But by rank, the two men were equal.

Darius put his hands on the chair. His fingers brushed the back of her neck.

"What's your opinion of the Gothman, Patha?"

Patha looked the young man square in the eye. "I've worked most of my life to incorporate a belief that a person should be judged by his or her actions and not by their race or gender. We are all of Nuworld, Lord Darius. I see before me a man who rules a race of people, but has little knowledge of the world around him. There's a law in this land stating if Runners enter Gothman territory, they are to be shot on sight. You intentionally broke your own law. I believe you had a glimpse of the world outside your own through Tara and it intrigued you."

Patha paused, looking from Tara to Darius. He had their undivided attention.

When Darius didn't respond, Patha returned to his chair and sat. "Tara has shared her feelings with me, now I must hear yours. What are your intentions here?"

Darius placed his hands on Tara's shoulders. "Patha, I love your daughter."

A tremor shot through her and quickened inside her. Darius just said he loved her. Did he mean it, or was he saying what Patha wanted to hear? She had seen affection in his eyes, but she would have been inclined to think of it as possessiveness more than love. Maybe to him that was love. After all, claiming a woman meant owning her without concern to her thoughts or beliefs. That was the only world Darius knew.

"I hope the two of you have the same meaning of love." Patha smiled gently at his daughter. "I'll accept that answer. Now, when you unite, you'll bring together two cultures. It'll be hard on both of you. I want this union between you two to be more official than a marriage, or claim, as the Gothman call it."

Patha reached inside his jacket and pulled out some papers he had clipped together. He dropped the papers on the table and looked at Lord Darius.

"This is a treaty of peace between Gothman and the Runners. It will state officially to Nuworld that our two races have united. There will be no race stronger, or larger in numbers, once our signatures appear on this treaty. It states that you'll continue to rule Gothman, and I'll rule the Runners. When I die, Tara is my next in line. She'll be leader of all Runner clans. The two of you will rule almost half of Nuworld. While I'm alive, at least, that rule will be a fair one. Read through this treaty carefully. The Runners will not help you with this war until this treaty is signed." Patha got up and headed to the entrance of the tent. "I'll be waiting with my clan."

Patha walked out of the tent, leaving Tara and Darius alone. She turned in her chair and looked up at him. He glanced down, moving his hands to her head and stroking her hair. His expression softened for the first time.

"How long have you known Reena was my mama?" She didn't know why that was the first thing out of her mouth with all the issues at hand.

"A good ruler must know what is going on in his kingdom." He smiled at her. "I remember hearing about it when I was a boy. My papa was furious when Patha took you. You were claimed to my brother, did you know that? I didn't know you were the girl I'd heard about as a child until you told me your papa was Patha."

"I just found out myself. It appears I'm only half-Runner." She suddenly felt very serious—the rush of excitement was gone.

Darius grinned. "When did you find out that I loved you?"

"Just now."

He laughed and pulled her out of her chair, sat in it and pulled her down on his lap. His arms were strong and sculpted from steel. He held her tight enough she felt the strong pulse of his heart thumping hard and solid in his chest.

What a man he was! He'd just been put on trial as leader. Patha had tested Lord Darius' knowledge, and Darius hadn't hesitated with any of his answers. Sure he would have researched Patha and known what he wanted to hear. But Tara believed he hadn't hesitated because his answers came from the heart.

"My lady, we're meant for each other. At first I thought I needed to break you, but now I see that would be a mistake. It's the excitement in your eyes when you're challenged that I love. I wouldn't be happy with a passive woman. They all instantly bored me. Oh, I knew you were a Runner. Patha was right. I broke my own laws. But I didn't know a woman like you existed."

"I'm definitely one of a kind." Tara shifted in his arms once he relaxed his grip. Then running her fingers through his blond curls, she stared into his unique gray eyes. They definitely weren't cool anymore. The smoldering lust she saw there had her hoping there was a bed on the other side of the tapestry.

"You'd be wise never to forget what a good match we are," she whispered, and brushed her lips over his.

Darius grinned. "Is that all you have to say?"

She smiled. "I'll challenge you. There's not a passive bone in my body, Darius. We're equals, and I have no problem teaching you how to accept that. Neither of us surpasses the other in any way I can see. I'll say this much, you proved yourself as leader to Patha. He was impressed, and so was I." Tara wrapped her arms around him and kissed him passionately.

Darius stood and scooped her in his arms. "I would love to impress you some more."

"I might let you." Tara ducked her head when he pulled the tapestry to the side and carried her to the other side of the tent.

A large down mattress was on the floor with several quilts thrown over it. He let go of her and Tara straightened, her body sliding against his until she stood before him. That quickening in her gut became swollen need, pulsating deep in her womb. Darius had told her he'd never met a woman like her before. She'd never known a man like him. He was aggressive, dominating and so sure of himself. Tara smiled and pressed her body against his. They really were equal in every way.

"If there were time, I would ravish you right now," Darius growled and began slow kisses up her neck toward her ear.

"If there were time," Tara began and clasped her hands behind his neck. She stood on tiptoe, leaning her head and allowing him room to continue sending her places she ached to be. "I would demand you satisfy the fire you've lit in me."

Darius chuckled. "And if I refused?" he asked.

"I would have to take you by force," she whispered and stretched to press her lips against his when that damned cocky grin appeared on his face.

Darius deepened the kiss until Tara was mad with need. She hated that there wasn't more time. Troops were making camp outside, and both of them had work to do. She sighed and loosened her grip.

Darius kissed the tip of her nose before releasing her. "I do want to know when you planned on telling me that you're pregnant." He walked out of the room.

"What?" Tara yanked the tapestry to the side and hurried after him. "How could you possibly know if I'm pregnant?" She snapped at him so hard that he raised one eyebrow in surprise.

"I told you I know everything that goes on in Gothman." He sat in his large chair and picked up the treaty. "Patha put some time into this," he mused, and chuckled as if that pleased him.

Tara snatched the treaty out of his hands. "I don't know that I am pregnant and nor does anyone else."

He leaned back in the chair and looked at her. "A true warrior eagerly takes on the challenge of battle. The look in your eyes over the thought of defeating the Sea People matches the feeling in my soul. Our battle will begin soon, and the satisfaction of their blood on our hands will be yours as well as mine. You're an outstanding warrior. You've proven your abilities, and I need your skills. As a good warrior, I know you respect the chain of command. The simple truth is, I outrank you. I am lord. Therefore, I assure you, my lady, the second you start to show signs of carrying our child, the future ruler of the greatest nation on this planet, I will see to it that you are taken out of battle."

His voice was so low and calm. It pissed her off further. She hated that he was right. If one of her warriors were pregnant, Tara would remove her from the line as well.

Tara stormed toward the tapestry, but then turned as if to leave the tent. The thought of not being in control of her own body, of something else taking over, was unfathomable. She was not one to be owned. Being pregnant would be a total loss of her freedom. Having a child wasn't a top priority for her, but then, neither was falling in love. She was a warrior!

She stormed outside and plucked her landlink from the bike, then returned inside the tent and flung herself into the chair next to Darius, desperately trying to discipline her thoughts. When that didn't work, she slammed her fists on the table, causing everything on it to bounce.

Darius knew the temper of a warrior should be treated with its due respect. He thought his words out carefully and spoke gently. "My lady, do you not want this child?"

She glared, not softened by the gentle look. "Darius, how could you possibly understand?" She didn't understand herself. "Now's not the time for this. There's so much to do. The crisis before us is great. One wrong play and a dangerous, unpredictable race could take over. This…pregnancy…would only be a distraction. Not to mention, there's no proof. We can't rely on some woman believing she saw a certain look."

"Time will be proof enough. I'm sure there are doctors in your camp that would ease your mind, if you wish." He smiled and covered her hand with his. He was seeing a side of her that he rather liked. Tara had an incredible temper. "I have faith in Gothman doctors, my lady. I know some Runner ways are different from ours. I've heard stories of how Runners try to control when they have a baby. I have heard that some women decide not to be pregnant, even after they are. If you don't want this right now…" he paused and looked at her, doubting she knew how hard this was to say. "This time, I will allow you to choose not to be pregnant. But hear me, I won't allow it a second time."

Tara hated the look on his face. Gothman women wouldn't consent to abort a pregnancy. All the women she'd met so far built their lives around being claimed, having babies and raising a family. Tara leaned back in her chair and studied Darius's radiant gray eyes and the dark blond curls bordering his face. He was so damned good looking that it made her hurt inside. What appealed to her most, though, was what she saw in his eyes. He possessed something that most men didn't. He didn't take things for granted because of tradition. Darius challenged life. Laws and social expectations didn't faze him. The man existed by what he saw as right in his heart. It might not be the way he lived, or what he believed in, but she saw that his offer was sincere. Darius wasn't narrow-minded. He wasn't so self-focused that he couldn't see how others lived differently. And(omit "And") even if he'd never been out of Gothman, he was a good enough ruler to research the people he'd be associating with. Tara knew at least several women who had found themselves pregnant and had aborted their unborn child. Each woman's reasons guided her conscience and allowed her to accept her decision without remorse.

"No. If I'm pregnant, I would stay that way. We didn't plan this but if I am then it's meant to be." Tara knew a pregnancy would bind them together more than a Gothman claim or Runner marriage ever would. She felt her stomach tighten at the thought.

"I knew that would be your answer, but the choice exists for Runners, and I will not deny you your heritage." He squeezed her hand, and stared at her thoughtfully. "We conceived the first time we were together, I'm sure of it! Even more proof that we were meant to be together, my lady." He leaned over and kissed her, his lips soft and tender.

"Promise me our child will know no prejudice, not over race or sex. That is, if there is a child," she added, and wondered if Darius might ever want his people to know life that way, too.

"I'll do my best, my lady."

Darius took the treaty she'd snatched out of his hands and pulled her chair next to his. He draped his arm over her shoulders and set the papers where they could read together.

Patha put a lot of thought into the papers. It was full of the necessity of equality among all men and women. It emphasized that the Runners and Gothman were setting a standard the rest of the world would strive to meet. Nuworld would need to become one united nation. It stated this would be the only way all war and hostility could end. The treaty stated all cultures should always be honored and respected for their diversity. No race should ever be asked to give up its traditions or religious beliefs to adhere to the beliefs of another race. If two cultures chose to unite, it would be their responsibility to peacefully combine their cultures.

The treaty was incredibly idealistic, Tara thought. What a wonderful world it would be if the treaty could be enforced to the letter. Patha didn't take into consideration that both Runners and Gothman viewed their way of life as better than the other. She saw the two races tolerating each other at best.

Darius shared her concern as they mulled over different sentences and argued certain points. The day was well over when they finally emerged from the tent.

"Here." Tara stopped him outside and put the comm around his ear. "You'll need to learn how to use one of these." She adjusted the device so it would reach his mouth then secured it.

"What is it?"

"It's similar to your walkntalks. You can choose who you wish to talk to, however, and the main landlink will secure your line. We call them 'comms'."

He felt the mouthpiece and blew into it.

"There's a switch right here." Tara showed him. "Flip it on and say that you want to speak to Patha. You don't have to speak loudly. The microphone is very sensitive. A whisper can be detected."

Darius pushed the switch and requested to speak to Patha.

Tara watched the look of fascination on his face as he listened.

"We'll ride to the Blood Circle Clan and meet Patha there," Darius told her after talking with Patha. "Do you think we can get more of these?"

"I'd think they should be supplied to all your men. I can confirm with Patha, but I'm fairly sure we have an ample supply. It would be difficult to fight a war without them." Tara climbed onto her bike. "I guess we're already incorporating part of that treaty. In some ways out cultures will unite."

"Our cultures are too different." Darius stared across the meadow as his men prepared for nightfall. Uniting Gothman and Runners was a strong possibility, but combining the two cultures would be impossible. Darius saw how their cultures might learn from each other. He wasn't willing for his and Tara's relationship to become the glue to secure the bond, though. More than once he'd wanted to demand obedience from Tara. She'd accepted his claim, was pregnant with his child, and had said how they were equal. Darius needed to slow things down. With both their lives uprooted and battles to win that wouldn't be easy to do. He needed time to train Tara. He was Lord of Gothman. With his people, and in his world, Tara would have to honor him and submit. When they were alone, he rather liked her feisty nature and way of thinking. But in public, she would have to learn the Gothman way.

"We'll have to be the example to our people as a couple," Tara said, as if she sensed his thoughts and decided to challenge him.

"We can do that when we reach your clan." The two drove through the Gothman camp. Campfires were lit, and talking and laughter filled the early evening. Cheers and whoops, and just a few catcalls rang out as Darius and Tara drove past men huddled in groups around the fires.

The small Runner clan they drove through next was much quieter. Trailers and motorcycles were parked in a large circle with large fires burning inside that circle. The Runners watched with curiosity as Tara and the Gothman lord drove past them. Tara guessed the Runners probably already knew of the treaty. Patha would have made an announcement about it upon his arrival.

Darius saluted the Runners they passed, and the Runners acknowledged the deference with raised arms of greetings.

This was promising, Tara thought, although she knew the Runners would face less change with the treaty than Gothman. Her people already saw each other as equal. As well, they respected each individual's ability to excel in whatever they were good at doing. Their nomadic existence provided opportunities for them to continually experience different cultures and understand that different didn't necessarily mean wrong.

The Blood Circle Clan stood and cheered the second Tara and Darius were spotted, outdoing the noise the Gothman had made. Runner children ran beside the motorcycles encouraging the two along. They were forced to ride slower but finally Tara pulled up alongside a large trailer and got off her bike.

"Leave it to you, Tara, to draw out a crowd." A young woman approached. Her Runner outfit showed every curve of her female body, and her black headscarf didn't conceal her sneer.

"Tasha, I didn't know you'd returned."

"How could you when you were off playing house with some Gothman lord? Although why you chose such a primitive race is beyond me. I never took you to be the submissive type." The young lady eyed Darius and flashed a flirtatious smile. "So tell me, did you have to beat her terribly to get her to obey?"

"Not terribly." Darius let his gaze wander over the young Runner.

"Lord Darius, I would like you to meet my sister, Tasha."

"No, she wouldn't like you to meet me." Tasha sashayed in a circle around Darius before coming back around to face him. "But, I wouldn't miss this for the world. From what I hear, it sounds like the two of you are trying to rule Nuworld."

"Come on." Tara took Darius' hand. "Patha is waiting."

"I'll say this," Tasha continued as they walked away. "He's much better looking than Kuro was."

"Who's Kuro?" Darius growled.

"He's a guy I was with when I was a teenager." She waved her hand, dismissing the comment her sister made. "Tasha's trying to start trouble. It's her nature. You aren't jealous, are you?"

"Do I have reason to be?"

"No." Tara hated her sister for saying whatever she could to make Darius not trust her. Hopefully, Tasha had failed.

They spent several hours with Patha, going over the details of the treaty, discussing military strategy, and explaining the comm along with other military equipment that the Runners were willing to supply to the Gothman. When finally the two left the trailer, it was quite dark, and the Runner camp had settled. All was quiet.

When they returned to the Gothman camp, Darius informed the guards he wanted his men assembled so he could speak to them. Thirty minutes later, the soldiers gathered in the meadow, looking curiously at Tara as she stood next to their lord.

Tara listened and studied Darius's men as he explained the treaty and the new equipment to be provided by the Runners.

"Today is a great day in Gothman history." Darius' voice boomed through the sound transmitter. "The Runners presented a treaty to me, asking Gothman to form a truce with them, and to exist as their allies. Runners are a race different from many since they have no land, and move from place to place in order to survive. They have learned about many races on Nuworld and know Gothman are the strongest and most powerful. So, they come to us seeking allegiance, and I have granted it. This is an excellent move for Gothman. The Runners have obtained knowledge that will now be readily available to Gothman. We go down in history today for discovering this race and seeing the advantages they can offer us."

His speech was moving and the Gothman cheered loudly when he was done.

"Very soon each of you will receive a new communication device." Darius held the one Tara gave him up in the air. "The Runners call it a comm. You will be instructed how to use it. This will become your principal way to contact others."

Darius took it upon himself to demonstrate to those leaders who reported to him later how to wear the comm and how it worked. Not once did he ask Tara for assistance. She stood next to him without saying a word. When he was done with the demonstration, he led the way to his tent.

She followed. "You were rather impressive out there." She secured the tent flap once they were inside.

He sat in his chair and kicked off his boots. "I have to be confident in front of the men always. You know that. Your equipment may be different than ours, but it's not complicated to understand. I agree all our forces should be using the same means of communication." He leaned back in his chair and stared across the dark tent. "You may think we're more primitive than you because we don't use these landlinks or have your advanced technology. But just because we are different doesn't make one of our races better than the other. I have a tight rule over those men out there. I know how to speak to them. This war will be won, and Gothman will remain strong because of its leadership." He paused and studied her face.

"Don't let the words of my sister affect you. Just because she referred to you as primitive, don't take it personally. She was out of line, as she usually is." Tara sat next to him and took off her boots as well. "She doesn't speak for Runners, or they wouldn't be here."

She draped her long legs across his and leaned back in her chair. "You best believe she doesn't speak for me, or I sure wouldn't be here."

Darius ran his hand along her inner thigh. Then without another word he lifted her legs, got up and went into the other room.

She sat there, leaning back in the chair completely exhausted. She was almost asleep when he returned. She opened her eyes and saw him standing in front of her. His shirt was off, and his bare chest distracted her out of her sleep.

Tara studied the different shades of golden curls that covered hardened chest muscles. She didn't bother to wake up enough to talk, nor did she see reason to lift her eyes to his face. The view she had at the moment pleased her.

Darius must have noticed that she enjoyed the view, because he didn't move. After a minute, Tara looked up and met his gaze.

"I have something for you. Come here."

"What?" She followed him but stopped when she noticed a small box sitting on one of the pillows at the opposite end of the down mattress. "What have you done?" she whispered.

"Look for yourself."

Shadows were casted over his face but she studied him for a moment. He was so large, a full-fledged killing machine of a warrior. More than likely he'd trained since childhood, as had she, to defend his people and fight for a world safe for them to live. But as she stared at him, even with his expression masked, she saw more. It wasn't his first nature, but she swore she saw compassion. Possibly he did love her in the same way she loved him.

Tara walked around the mattress and picked up the small box, which was made of tree bark sanded until it was smooth as glass. She opened the small box and pulled out a delicate chain with a small gold circle on it. In the middle of the circle, a tear-shaped ruby was fused to the side. The deep crimson of the ruby glittered in the dim light.

"It's the symbol of my clan," Tara gasped, almost choking on her words. Tears welled in her eyes, and she looked away. She didn't remember the last time she'd cried for any reason. Sitting on the mattress, she made a show of admiring it while composing herself.

Darius sat next to her and lifted her face. He wiped her tears with his calloused thumb. "I had it made for you shortly after I first saw you in town. I tell you, my lady, it was love at first sight. You and I were meant to live this life together."

That did it. Tears streamed down her cheek.

He laid her back on the bed, wrapping his arms around her. Darius slid off her coat and lifted her shirt over her head. When he stood and began removing his clothes, Tara silently cursed the darker half of the tent for robbing her view.

"I suggest you take off those pants, my lady." His voice was as dark as his shadowed face.

Another time Tara might have challenged him telling her what to do. But she wanted this and decided she'd choose her battles later.

Darius lay on top of her naked body, and his flesh touching hers urged her need forward until she was basking in it. She wrapped her arms and legs around him. He rose to his elbows and stared down at her for a moment.

"Do you like your gift?"

"You know I do." She almost told him no one had ever given her anything so thoughtful. "Thank you," she said instead.

His kisses caressed her flesh. Several times she tried to roll over and take charge of the lovemaking, but he pinned her and continued to make love slowly, taking his time enjoying her body.

She fought to control the speed at which desire swelled inside her, but he controlled even that. When he finally entered her, she attempted to thrust upward and bring him to a climax. Darius took her legs and pressed her knees to her shoulders. He had her captured in a frenzy of molten heat and swarming desire. There was no stopping him, unless she begged. No way would she do that. Not that she had words at the moment. Surrender was required to enjoy the moment. Tara might not have control, but she wouldn't deny herself this pleasure. She refrained from screaming as he penetrated deeper than he ever had before.

"You are mine, Tara."

She blinked to focus. Blond curls shifted around his face each time he thrust and sunk further into his heat. Pressure built until it exploded and boiled over, searing her entire body as her release ruptured through her insides. Darius let out a low growl. Every inch of him stiffened. Then he came deep inside her.

"You won't ever own me," she managed to gasp.

CHAPTER NINE

SEVERAL LONG cycles passed at a gruelling slow pace. There was no indication the Sea People planned to attack. But, they were out there. Landlinks detected them in vast quantities just beyond Gothman borders. There was heavy artillery spotted throughout their camp. Yet they just sat there. Hell be doomed! It was irritating.

Darius' men were restless. They were geared up to fight. He'd sent his scouts to physically observe the Sea People along with Runner scouts, who used viewers, which were long cylindrical tubes that magnified items in the distance. Most of them grumbled they should attack instead of waiting for the enemy hovering on their borders to attack first. They didn't belong there. The point was to force their retreat. They could have destroyed this drug-infested people and been home to their women by now.

His men began circulating rumors doubting the accuracy of Runner landlinks. When Gothman and Runner scouts verified thousands of Sea People with large amounts of artillery, those rumors stopped. It didn't stop how irritable his men were, however.

"I wouldn't be surprised if the Sea People discovered Runner clans camped with Gothman so are waiting for reinforcements," Tara suggested to the small group sitting around the table in Patha's trailer.

"And who would they be waiting on?" Geeves, Darius' personal assistant, stared at the Gothman map spread over the table and didn't glance up.

Tara stood at the kitchen counter where she finished slicing a block of cheese. She didn't take it to the table. No way would she would wait on Darius' men. Leaving the sliced cheese on the counter, she plopped a piece in her mouth and moved to stand behind Darius, who sat next to Patha.

"More Sea People to arrive," she grumbled with her mouth full.

"I say we attack." Darius looked at the others around the table, and Geeves grunted his approval. "Gothman won't tolerate our borders lined with Sea People."

"Runners don't attack unless attacked first." Patha didn't raise his voice and focused only on Darius as he spoke.

"Tension builds among the men, my Lord," one of Darius' commanders said from behind Tara. He leaned against the wall by the trailer door. "They are ready to fight, and we have them sitting around like women."

Tara cleared her voice, letting the commander know she didn't like his comment.

"I can't justify leading the Runners into combat." Patha paid no attention to Tara but continued giving Darius all his attention. "The Sea People sit in Freeland territory, not on Gothman soil. Granted the Sea People are suspiciously close to your borders. It's all their artillery that makes their intention clear."

"So Gothman will sit and do nothing?" The same commander behind Tara raised his voice a bit with the question.

"I don't like it any more than you do." Darius scraped his chair against the floor as he pushed away from the table, almost backing into Tara. Darius came around the table to face his man. "In all of Gothman history, no attack has occurred before the enemy crossed Gothman borders."

"We shall wait for the Sea People to make the first move." Patha didn't bother to stand.

Tara experienced the mounted tension everyone else fought to cope with when she left Patha's trailer and rode through her clan. No one was pleased with their current circumstances.

The days stretched on and were growing warmer. Tara lay on the mattress in Darius' tent and worked to pull her pants over her hardened belly. This had become a routine, trying to get her clothes to fit, but this particular morning it wasn't going to happen. She absolutely could not fasten her pants. Time had given her what she hadn't taken time to hear from a doctor. An answer. She was definitely pregnant.

Tara groaned at the thought that she might have to concede to wearing Runner pregnancy clothes. She stared at the ceiling of the tent, her hands still gripping button and button hole of her pants, and her fingers burning from trying to pull the material together over the growing bulge of her baby. She'd be forced to obtain some temporary clothing while her child grew within her, even though such articles would hamper her ability to climb on a bike and perform military maneuvers.

Tara decided to drive over to the Blood Circle Clan site and say hello to Balbo, her brother through Patha's marriage. She'd been too busy with planning and training maneuvers to have visited him yet. Darius and Patha had decided mock battles, and mixing the races in combat, would help ease tension and the growing irritability among their warriors. Gothman and Runners would learn from each other. Darius had gone out early that morning to observe the battles. This left her the opportunity to leave camp without any questions. Besides which, Balbo might be able to help her with the clothing issue.

Patha had two wives over the winters, although Tara had known only one. His first had died in battle. His second wife, Cloya, raised Tara but died giving birth to twins when Tara had fourteen winters. One of the twins died with Cloya, and the other twin was sent to Cloya's family to be raised. Tara had a sister, Tasha, and a brother, Balbo, who had been Cloya's children when she married Patha. Balbo was older than Tara, but since he was not of Patha's blood, was not heir to Patha's clan. Balbo was a good man with little interest in leading the clans. He had always been supportive of Tara. Right now she needed a favor.

Balbo hugged and kissed his sister on the cheek when she entered his trailer. Then, looked confused after hearing her request. "You want what?"

"I need a pair of pants. Mine don't fit anymore." She privately begged that he wouldn't ask why.

"Eating too much of that Gothman food?" He laughed but then scowled. "Tara, your face is gaunt. And why are there dark shadows under your eyes? Have you been to a doctor lately?"

"Why would I see the doctor because I'm tired? I just need a larger pair of pants."

Balbo sighed and shook his head. But he brought her a pair of pants. As he handed them to her, he gave her that brotherly look she'd hoped not to see. "Tara, I've never interfered with your life, and I won't start now. But, what's the harm in stopping in and seeing Dr. Digo while you're here?"

"We'll see." She hugged her brother and thanked him for the pants. "I wanted to say hello to a few people I haven't seen in awhile. Maybe I'll see the doc, too."

Dr Digo had been her doctor all her life, or as long as she remembered. He'd tended her first laser wound and set more bones than she cared to count. He was a good man, and she didn't mind stopping in to hear the latest stories.

"Tara, child, how you've grown. Why, you're not even a child any more, but a beautiful woman. I've heard the stories about you…how you started a revolution. Doesn't surprise me a bit. Here, have a seat, tell me a good story." The old man patted the chair that was reserved for his patients and assumed his doctorly position, leaning on the examination table.

"Okay, here's a story." She squirmed in her seat, trying to get comfortable. "This young girl has reached the *Age of Searching* and is drawn to places she's never seen. She enters a culture so different from her own. Doctor, I tell you, she is exposed to a way of life she had only heard about in many exaggerated stories. An old lady takes her in and teaches her about the culture and provides her with clothes so she will look like one of them. It was harder to give up her way of life than the girl thought it would be. Then, one of the men in this culture takes an interest in her. He knows her for who she is, but she doesn't know this. She thinks she has him fooled. She comes to discover later that he not only knows her for who she is, but he knows more about her than she knows herself. I guess it was inevitable, fate some may call it, but she falls in love with him."

"And, this man, does he love her too?" Dr. Digo looked interested.

"Yes, he tells her he loves her, and proves it by his actions. It's just that their cultures are so different. She's not sure they define love the same way."

"So, what happens next?"

The old doctor had already moved over to the cabinets alongside the wall of his trailer and started opening drawers.

She ached from the tight pants she wore and tightened her grip on the pants in her lap. "I don't know."

Dr. Digo pulled a syringe out of the cabinet and moved over next to Tara. "Shall we find out?"

Tara didn't answer but took off her jacket and pulled up her shirtsleeve.

Dr. Digo smiled as he drew the blood. He'd seen this look of concern and worry on many young women's faces. They always approached him with the obvious staring him in the face and telling him they didn't know. He never argued and always let them be the first to admit it out loud.

Tara remained quiet as Dr. Digo took the blood over to his equipment on the counter. He turned the monitor so Tara saw the results as soon as they were available.

"Tara, you're definitely pregnant. Would you like an examination?"

She consented and it was done.

Tara left the office wearing the pants her brother had given her. They fit much better but she knew they wouldn't work for long. Dr. Digo told her she'd have a baby in five cycles, right before the New Winter. Only five cycles before her entire life would change—she would be a mama!

She rode away slowly, lost in thought, which is probably why she didn't pay much attention to the young Runner standing outside Dr. Digo's trailer.

The young boy leaned along the backside of the trailer watching her as she mounted her bike and disappeared into the camp. As soon as she was gone, he reached up and turned on his comm.

"I found her. She just left Dr. Digo's trailer."

Darius and Patha left at the same time and drove to Dr. Digo's trailer.

"Come in, Patha. You're not hurt, are you?" The doctor's smile lessened as Lord Darius entered the trailer behind Patha. He looked at the tall blond man, who stared back, his expression unreadable.

"Digo, my friend, I'm not hurt." Patha accepted Digo's extended hand and shook it with both of his. "I'd like you to meet the Lord of Gothman. Lord Darius, this is Dr. Digo. He's cared for my family as long as I've had one."

Darius appraised the stocky older man, guessing his age to be close to Patha's. The doctor looked nervous. Darius decided he didn't care as long as the doctor told him what he wanted to know.

"Digo, we won't take up much of your time." Patha crossed the room and sat in the chair behind Dr. Digo's desk.

Darius moved into the middle of the room. He sensed the doctor studying him. It made Darius wonder what Tara might have told the doctor about him.

"We're here to talk to you about Tara." Darius didn't want to waste time on civilities. He wanted to know why Tara had been here, and more importantly what the doctor told her.

"Patha, you're an old friend, but you know I can't talk to you about my patients."

"As Patha said," Darius interrupted, facing the doctor in the middle of his office. He didn't like speaking to the doctor, then having the doctor address his answers to Patha. "We won't take much of your time."

"What can I do for you?" The doctor continued to focus on Patha, and noticeably relaxed.

"What did you find out while Tara visited you?" Darius knew the tone he used had a quiet, unquestionable authority.

"I can't tell you that." The doctor rubbed his hand through his hair and sighed deeply. "This is a very sensitive situation."

"How pregnant is she?" Darius knew in his heart that the child was his, but he had to hear it from the doctor. He had to make sure Tara didn't arrive in Gothman already pregnant.

"Answer the question," Patha ordered when the doctor hesitated.

"About four cycles," the doctor sighed again. "She'll give birth before the New Winter."

"Thank you," Patha said and stood.

Darius had no regrets paying the Runner boy to follow Tara once his men had reported that his claim had left camp. Tara would learn soon enough that the Lord of Gothman's claim would always be watched. She may view a claiming as demeaning, but to Gothman, she was a valued woman.

When the boy reported that Tara was in the trailer with the Runner doctor, Darius had contacted Patha out of respect. Patha had told Darius he would go with him when Darius said he planned on visiting the doctor. Darius had accepted Patha's offer, knowing the Runner leader would play diplomat.

"There's more." Dr. Digo looked directly at Darius. Maybe the doctor had never been nervous, because he certainly didn't look that way now. "She shouldn't be in this environment. It's not good for the baby." He then turned and looked at Patha. "While Tara has always been good about ordering ladies in her command to step down when field maneuvers become dangerous for the unborn child, I detected confusion in her. I fear you might need to remind her it's time to remove herself from the battlefield."

Patha and Darius looked at each other and left the trailer. Neither one looked forward to having that conversation with Tara.

Tara woke the following morning alone on the down mattress. She and Darius had made love most of the night. Apparently now she'd overslept. She had procrastinated the night before in telling Darius about her visit to Dr. Digo. Darius had acted preoccupied until they went to bed. Now, he had left without waking her, and she had no idea where he had gone.

She lay there a moment trying to convince herself to get up. It wasn't like her to be this exhausted first thing in the morning. It was time to remove herself from duty, but she had responsibilities here. Of course, there were several good candidates she trusted to take over. But damn it, she wanted the action.

Tara jumped to her feet when a large explosion shook the tent. Screams, and people running outside followed. Instinct took over. Tara dressed in a flash, hobbling to the entrance of the tent as she shoved her second boot on her raised foot. Another explosion rocked the ground before she got out of the tent.

"Darius," Tara shouted, struggling to wrap her comm around her ear. "Where are you?" She left the tent and jumped on her bike. "Hell be doomed!" she howled as another explosion created an unnatural light around her.

For a moment there was no sound. Her head rocked from the impact of it. The explosion had been closed. Tara slowed her bike and finally reached the middle of camp, joining several soldiers squatting behind large barrels of water. "Report!" she yelled through the noise and understood when none of her Runners looked at her. Their eyes were on the sky.

Tara's comm beeped, and she slapped at the small button to activate it. "Yes," she yelled.

"Five aircraft just flew over us," one of Tara's commanders shouted in her ear. "We got one of them, but the others should be flying over you soon."

Tara squinted at the dark gray sky. "I see two approaching." She didn't see the other two.

"They're coming back around," the Runner next to her yelled, and jumped behind the Gothman who squatted with an Eliminator resting on his shoulder.

The powerful weapon was more than capable of destroying the aircraft flying overhead, if the shooter had good aim. Once Tara had arranged for Darius' men to be equipped with eliminators, it immediately became their weapon of choice. There wasn't time to take the eliminator from the Gothman and give it to a more skilled shot. She prayed the warrior had excellent marksman skills.

"On my mark, fire," Tara ordered. She hurried to give the Gothman space, knowing what kind of kick the thing had.

"Fire!" Tara yelled.

The Gothman pushed the large button on the side of the Eliminator, and then fell backward as a zinging sound pierced the air. Tara didn't focus on the Gothman, but strained her neck to look at the sky and the two dark gray crafts now shadowing the ground.

"Take cover! Take cover!" Someone screamed, but the advice wasn't needed.

A massive explosion overhead sent shrapnel zooming to the ground. Once again her world went silent. The attack in the air was loud enough to pierce her eardrums. A humming sound violated her senses as she crouched to the ground with her arm over her head. She wasn't able to hunch over as much as she normally would. It seemed something prevented her ribs from getting as close to her hipbones. Something was preventing her— the baby growing inside her. It was a harsh reminder that she was not in a suitable environment. Tara never would allow one of her warriors to endure direct fire if they were pregnant.

"It's a direct hit!" The Gothman next to her let out a whoop of excitement then immediately ducked.

"Excellent," Tara whispered as watched the craft ripple with fire. More burning fragments began twirling to the ground. The second plane wasn't hit, and it fired on the camp.

The ground exploded around them. Either large pieces of the aircraft, the hit from the remaining craft, or both, shook the ground hard enough that Tara stumbled to the side. She dug bits of dirt underneath her fingernails when she braced herself, not wanting her body slammed too hard in any way.

She wasn't able to focus on her pregnancy and keeping them all alive. Tara grabbed the eliminator from the Gothman, who had let it go limp in his arm. She swung it with one arm so it rested on her shoulder and aimed at the craft when it hovered over them.

Tara fired and flew backward. She lost her footing and slipped to the ground, landing rather hard on her rear end. All wind was knocked out of her. It seemed the jarring of her body was more extreme than usual. She'd fired eliminators enough times to know how hard their kick was. She told herself it was her imagination that her body seemed to react more to the fire power of the weapon than usual.

A moment after she fired, the aircraft exploded. It was impossible to see anything—the flames and smoke surrounding her made it difficult to see the weapon still in her hands. But the bright flames that burst into the sky was enough to know she'd made her mark.

"Tara! What's going on?" Darius' voice boomed into her too-sensitive ear.

"Four aircrafts were reported. We believe all four are down. Where are you?" Tara coughed as black smoke filled the air.

"Help!" someone screamed.

Tara leapt to her feet but then balanced herself as a wave of dizziness made it impossible to move. *This is no place for a woman in your condition*, the warrior inside her chided. Tara promised herself she'd step down as soon as possible. Runners with spray packs on their backs began hosing down the isolated fires. The water turned the black smoke to gray as it filled the air.

"Where are you?" she asked again.

Tara put her hand over her mouth and nose when she could barely breathe. Her headscarf didn't stop the thickness of the smoke from filling her lungs.

"We're at the edge of the Blood Circle camp. My reports tell me the Gothman camp took the worse hit. Patha says your landlink shows you're right in the middle of it."

"All is under control now. And I'm fine. But what about you? Are you okay?" Tara coughed again and ignored the curses she heard through her comm.

Her comm beeped again, and she reached for the thin wire that ran along her cheek from her ear to her mouth. "Stand by Darius," she said.

"What?" he barked. "Hell be—"

But she cut him off with a sigh, regretting that when she saw him next he would probably keep yelling. "Tara here," she said as she tapped the side of her comm.

"Frig here, Tara," one of the Runner soldiers she had known since childhood responded. "We'll have these fires out in no time. I've got a medic team reporting only three wounded."

"Thanks, Frig."

The attack didn't last long, although it seemed half the day passed. Even though casualties had been few, the soldiers were shaken, and the campsite was partially burned, but functional.

"Darius, were you hit hard?" Tara waited too long before his deep baritone swam through her senses. She wanted to know if he was injured, and if Patha was okay, along with the rest of her family. Darius would view that as a sign of weakness, however. So Tara kept her comments pertaining to the issue at hand.

"A few casualties. Prepare yourselves. More crafts have been spotted!" He sounded stressed.

Any warrior would be anxious under pending attack, but she couldn't help but hope he wanted to be at her side as much as she wished she were with him. "Acknowledged," she said simply and shut off her comm after hearing the termination on Darius' end.

Tara left the minimal protection offered by the water barrels and moved her way through the active camp. She tapped her comm again and addressed Frig. "We have more crafts headed our way."

"Several of my best warriors are armed with Eliminators," he told her. "We'll have the Sea People out of the sky before they're able to attack this time."

"Make sure of it."

A hit of adrenaline surged through her from the enthusiasm in Frig's voice. Well-trained warriors lived for battle. They fought for a just cause, and Runners and Gothman would be triumphant. Tara held her head high as she worked her way toward her bike. Those around her straightened, or moved faster when they saw her. If they only knew how their reaction to her inspired her to hold her own.

Daylight barely managed penetrating the smoke and dust swirling around them. By mid-afternoon, the sky remained a dark gray, and black clouds created from burnt rubble and campfire smoke, hung heavy and low.

Visibility was so poor, Tara barely distinguished the people around her from inanimate objects. The trees outlining the camp were completely obscured. She tracked her warriors' movements from her landlink.

Water used to put out fires had turned the camp into a mud drenched, dark gray world. If it weren't for the energy coursing like electricity through her veins, her surroundings would have been gloomy. As it was, she tapped her keypad and paid acute attention to her screen, which possibly made everything around her more acceptable.

Glancing up, Tara spotted a group of Gothman soldiers through the murk. They continued past her without a glance in her direction. "What are your orders?" she yelled after them.

"Preparing to search the surrounding area, them's the orders." The Gothman only half-turned to acknowledge Tara, an act she'd grown accustomed with many of the Gothman.

"The area surrounding the camp?" Tara wondered if someone had picked up movement, and she hadn't yet been told. "Who gave you your orders?"

"Lord Darius." This time the Gothman didn't even turn when he answered, but instead signaled his men to begin their search.

"Darius?" Tara asked after tapping her comm.

"What do you need? Are you okay?" The concerned sound in his tone made Tara want to tell him she would be better if she were at his side.

"Have you spotted movement surrounding the camp? Why wasn't I notified?" She heard mumbling through her comm and surmised Darius was speaking to someone with him.

"Your landlinks show no activity," Darius said after he finished talking to whomever he was with.

"Then why did you order men to search the area?" Tara waved at the Gothman leader to halt his men.

He only appeared mildly interested in her gesture, and didn't stop his men.

"To make sure the area is secure."

"Tara, we've spotted the crafts!" Frig waved frantically from several tents' distance. He looked like a dark shadow floating toward her.

Tara's comm beeped in her ear. "Darius, order your men to cease their search. It's a waste of manpower." Tara barked the order, suddenly frustrated with the man for not trusting Runner equipment and belittling her authority by issuing commands she didn't know about.

She hit the small button on the silver stem of the comm to acknowledge the next call, cutting Darius off in mid-rebuttal.

"Eliminators are ready," a Gothman grunted in her ear.

At least the Gothman stationed at this camp recognized her authority. Granted, she was in the Gothman camp, and Darius was at the clan site. Not that she didn't doubt for a moment he was in communication with all his men. She was the highest ranking here, though, and that fact couldn't be questioned. She might be the claim to the lord of Gothman, but in this battle, she was the second highest ranking member of all Runner clans.

Tara ran back to her bike, ignoring the stitch cutting from her lower abdomen down her leg. She started the bike with one hand and moved it slowly while attaching her landlink to the handlebars. "When you have them in target, fire," she ordered, deciding to monitor the attack inside one of the nearby Runner trailers.

An explosion shook the ground. People flew into the air not too far from Tara's right. She accelerated, hugging her bike, then swerved to avoid falling debris.

"One of the crafts has a different type of artillery on it," one of her commander's shouted through the comm.

"Get those blasted things out of the air!" Tara yelled over the growing confusion around her.

Another explosion shook the ground.

Tara was forced to stop her bike when several Gothman bolted in front of her. Then she heard the zinging sound of an eliminator.

"Yes!" Several cheered as one of the crafts twirled and burst into flames.

She moved around barricades and soldiers issuing orders until she reached the spot where two Runners stood next to each other, aiming eliminators at the second craft. Tara parked, jumped off her bike and stood as close as she dared to the marksmen, watching the sky the whole time.

Eliminators were fired. A fiery inferno burst into light as bright as the sun in the otherwise, dark greyish black sky.

"Well done!" Tara cheered, grinning at the bleeding red colors spilling to the ground.

"Thank you." The man had a big toothy smile as he looked at the dismembering craft. He then hugged the warrior next to him and the two men kissed.

Tara allowed them their moment of celebration and hurried to her bike.

"I want a report of damages," Tara continued issuing orders through her comm as she mounted her bike and headed with more speed to the nearest trailer. The ground billowed smoke, and the stench of burning metal, rubber and human flesh turned her stomach. "Get this camp in order and prepare for any further attacks."

Over the next few weeks, the Sea People challenged the Gothman borders, but Gothman and Runners managed to keep them at bay. Tara remained in charge of all Runner's in the Gothman camp, in spite of Darius' men continually challenging her command.

Patha and Darius began to bond, with Patha taking the role of mentor. Tara knew Patha looked ahead to a time after his death, when she and Darius would rule both races. To this end, Patha considered it his highest priority to train Darius, to help him understand the Runner way.

It was late one night when Tara ventured to the front line to find Patha and Darius. The rocky ground jostled her bike, and when she stood after riding, mild stitches shot down her legs from her pelvis. Knowing the discomfort came from overworking the muscles holding her baby in place, she stood still until the bits of pain subsided and she could walk without discomfort.

As she glanced about her at the busy clan site, now turned into a military operation on the front line, Tara saw Patha and waved. Idly, she noticed that he appeared to stop speaking into his comm as soon as he saw her.

Flicking off the device, he waved back, and after saying something to the Runner he was with, began walking toward her, smiling. His smile warmed her. She narrowed the distance between them, taking care not to jolt her body as she stepped on uneven ground.

"It appears we've a break in the action. The report I received this morning showed the Sea People have regrouped and returned to their camp." Patha looked tired, but happy as he greeted her.

"And how are you doing?" She slid her arm around his and walked with him into camp.

"I'm fine Tara-girl, just fine." Patha chuckled and patted her arm. "Darius and I plan on preparing our next method of attack today. You're just in time. Come to my trailer."

"We've three more clans arriving from the east," Darius said, without looking up as Patha and Tara entered Patha's trailer, which was the newly converted main headquarters.

Darius sat at the landlink reviewing incoming transmissions from his commanders and a newly arrived clan, the Kill Water clan. He responded with orders, telling the clan where to set up camp. Then he turned and spotted Tara. As she tossed her jacket on the back of a chair, he immediately noticed bones showing at the top of her shoulders. He stood and removed her headscarf without asking.

Her blue eyes searched his features before meeting his gaze. Dark, puffy circles rimmed her eyes and her face was gaunt. Her skin looked gray, partially from lack of sleep and partially from dirt and campfire smoke. She smelled of the smoke and anti-inflammatory powder.

What had he done? Darius kept his expression placid. The slightest inclination that he found her lacking, and she'd be outraged. Tara looked worn out enough, yet spiking on adrenaline at the same time. He knew from experience that often led to quick tempers, even in himself. But Tara didn't look well. He'd been so wrapped up in battles, strategy, and protecting Gothman from an unpredictable enemy that he hadn't given enough thought to his claim and unborn child.

He'd issued his fair amount of lectures over the winters in drills, scrimmages, and even recently during battle that his men keep their claims out of their heads. The moment any man started thinking with his dick instead of his brain was the day he died a dishonourable death. Had he intentionally followed his own advice a bit too closely because, if he hadn't, it would have meant pulling himself from the front line to deal with his pregnant claim?

Not that he hadn't wanted to see her. Hell be doomed! He'd ached from the very fibers of his being to have her fighting at his side. He had definitely wanted her warming his bed at night. The only time he had mentioned his place was in the Gothman camp to Patha, he'd quickly been shot down. Patha wanted Darius by his side to uphold the reality of Gothman and Runners fighting together. He'd also pointed out how it was good for Tara to learn to give orders to warriors who didn't already follow her blindly. Darius saw now that as much as he liked the old man—he'd wished his own father had been half the man Patha was—that he should have stood up to him and insisted on seeing Tara. Because he hadn't, his claim looked ready to collapse. Darius should have known she would never have pulled herself from duty.

Tara was too thin. She no longer wore her skin tight Runner clothing. Was she wearing another man's clothing? He almost growled at the thought but didn't want the conversation he was about to have beginning with a fight. His claim was dirty, exhausted, and smelled.

It struck Darius that he still found her incredibly beautiful. He had made a promise to the doctor to remove her from battle. A promise that now had to be carried out.

"Sit, Tara, have something to eat." Patha took her from Darius and guided her into a chair at the round table, which sat to one side of the spacious living area.

Tara complied and almost collapsed into the chair. A wave of exhaustion hit her. Holding up her head with her hands, she ran fingers through her hair. She was not thinking clearly and guessed fatigue was taking over quickly. A few hours' sleep and a hot shower and she'd be good as new.

"I can help." Tara tried standing.

Patha began pulling food from his cold box.

"Sit." Darius stopped her with a hand to her shoulder.

Patha placed several plates of food on the table.

"This looks so good." Tara eyed the sliced meat, smoked boar with the fat trimmed, and cold duck legs. Several chunks of cheese were still wrapped in thin, almost transparent cloth. She reached for a vine of grapes out of a chilled bowl.

The men joined her and they ate in comfortable silence for a few minutes.

"The Blue Horn clan reports all units are ready for battle," Darius said with his mouth full and a peeled duck egg in his hand.

"Good. I want all clans to report in before the end of the day." Patha stabbed his boar meat with his eating knife, then added a chunk of cheese. "Something to drink, Tara-girl?"

Patha leaned back to the wooden counter behind him, which divided his living/working area from his kitchen and grabbed a ceramic pitcher. He poured iced grape juice into mugs for all of them.

"Thank you," Tara said between bites.

Darius pondered how to bring up the conversation of Tara stepping down. He gave less thought to relieving his seasoned warriors of duty when necessary. Darius knew why, too. None of them would dare argue with him over his decision.

"Don't let those clans dawdle in getting their updates to you." Patha waved his silver eating knife at Darius, a gift Tara had given him when she'd been a child. Its tip, similar to Reena's knitting needle but with a sharper end, had remnants of cheese on it. "If all clans haven't reported in before sundown, send them notice, or they'll receive the last available slots when I position everyone for battle."

Patha slid his chair from the table, then stood and patted his belly.

"Are you leaving? I'll walk with you," Tara said. She wanted to talk to him about her and Darius working together instead of in different camps.

Patha chuckled. "Not this time, Tara-girl. I can tell you aren't done eating. And when you are done, enjoy a shower. I know living out of that tent you've been in all this time has denied you such luxuries."

"A shower would be nice." Tara stood and began carrying the plates to the other side of the counter. She waited for Patha to leave before speaking again. "Your Gothman warriors still have trouble acknowledging my authority."

"It will take them time. A culture doesn't change in a few cycles." Darius slid her hair across her shoulders and kissed the back of her neck. "Go enjoy that shower now, my lady," he whispered against her skin, sending chills down her body.

The water was hot and had never felt so good. Tara let it spray over her body, praying it would revitalize her. She was so worn out it took effort to scrub herself. Water was rationed and not wanting to use all of it for her own comfort, she did her best to hurry.

Tara stepped out of the shower long before she wanted to and wrapped herself in a large towel. She wasn't wearing the clothes again that she'd removed to shower. They were stained, and they smelled. She would have to send for fresh clothes. The large bulky towel wrapped around her accentuated the size of her growing tummy.

"You've got to come out sooner or later." Darius leaned patiently against the wall at the end of the short hallway as Tara opened the bathroom door and turned the other direction. Nothing but that white towel separated her from Darius.

Tara headed into the spare bedroom, hoping Patha might have something stored that might fit her. Darius followed and came up behind her. As she turned to face him, he grabbed the towel and pulled it off her.

"Woman, you're so beautiful." He gazed at the growing bulge between her disappearing hipbones. "Look at you. I should have you home with plenty of servants waiting on you."

"I'd be bored senseless," she complained, making a face at him. He stroked her hair, pulled her to him, and rubbed her stretched tummy. His child grew within her. That child would be healthy and strong if his mama didn't carry him into battle every day. She must return home, to a safe environment, and if he worded it right she would go willingly.

"We're warriors, I don't need to be taken care of," Tara added, but made no attempt to move out of his strong hands. She wanted to stay by his side, with him helping her through this strange transformation she was experiencing.

"I love you, and our child," he whispered in her ear as he picked her up and shut the door with his foot.

He laid her on the bed shoved in the corner and caressed her sore muscles. Darius kissed the bruises on her body with lips that seared her skin. Her weary muscles had the consistency of over-boiled potatoes. All she wanted was to reach up and run her fingertips over his skin. She wanted to feel those tight, coarse curls that sprinkled over perfectly chiselled chest muscle.

As sleepy as eating and a hot shower had made her, Tara was more awake than she'd been over the past cycle when Darius spread her legs and began kissing her inner thighs. Heat sprang to life inside her and grew unbearable. She felt a slight contraction as she lifted her hips to meet his lips. It was oddly pleasant.

That sensation was quickly replaced by another, more carnal, and desperate. Darius took her places she'd only dreamt of night after night, alone in his tent, in his camp. It took no time before her orgasm followed.

When Darius entered her, his velvety round tip glided over her soaked walls. His thick, hard shaft sunk deep inside, straight to her core. He wasn't gentle, but she didn't want gentle. She wanted her warrior in all his magnificence. She wanted him aggressive, dominating and controlling her senses. Because right now she doubted she could do anything other than enjoy him.

Tara took all of him and cried out for him more. With each plunge, he brought her closer to the edge. She clung to him, and to the moment. She didn't ever want their lovemaking to end. The edge was right there but it felt too good to take the plunge yet.

Darius was a relentless lover. His body rippled with power. She felt that power fill her. But then he adjusted his angle. He'd been toying with her, letting her think she controlled when she came. It showed on his face the moment he impaled her and hit that spot. Tara came so hard that her world shattered before her eyes. He followed with a few hard grunts, then exploded deep in the recesses of her flowing, molten heat.

Darius leaned on his arm next to Tara, enjoying the half-smile on her face and the glow in her sapphire eyes. Her body relaxed and her expression turned peaceful. This is how he wanted his claim; satisfied with his love for her, and looking content instead of stressed and overworked as she had when she'd entered the trailer. He wouldn't have her seen in public again showing such extreme signs of battle fatigue. This beautiful woman would carry his child and glow with satisfaction that she belonged to him, needing nothing and not entangled with worries.

"What?" Tara demanded after a moment. That sated smile remained on her face. "Why are you staring?"

"You're glowing. Pregnancy suits you very well. We should have lots of children." Darius traced his index finger along her cheekbone and down to her mouth, allowing her to suck on it while her wide blue eyes stared up at him.

Tara pushed his finger out of her mouth with her tongue. "Oh right, that way you can order me to my room as soon as I start to show."

"Tara, you know you can't stay here. I don't need to tell you that." He lay next to her and tightened his grip when she tried pulling away. "I'm going to reassign you—but your skills won't go to waste. I promise. The Sea People have attacked Bryton as well."

He hurried to speak when she would have interrupted. "I have warriors assigned there, but I don't have to tell you most of them are here. Bryton is full of women and children. I need someone to watch over them. My men there are too young, or too old, to be here. Hilda and Reena can see to your needs as well as any other lass you wish to have help you. I've stationed soldiers around the house, but I need someone for them to report to who can keep me informed."

"How long did it take for you to think up that one?" She smiled at him, pleased she would still have responsibilities, although she'd be out of the heart of battle.

He didn't return the smile, but his eyes twinkled.

"I'll leave in the morning," she decided. She snuggled up next to him, and tried organizing in her mind what she would do in town. She would organize the women to supply the troops with food and clean blankets. She thought of ways to get his men to listen to her, but soon sleep took over.

Darius listened to Tara's gentle breathing. Life couldn't be this good if he'd planned it. He ran his finger up and down her outer thigh. She'd been so submissive during their lovemaking. Agreeable even when he reassigned her to home, where she'd relax and let the warriors tend to the duties of battle.

Just thinking about how she'd obeyed his orders got him hard all over again. Could it possibly be that she'd accepted that he was in charge? If he gained Tara's submission to him completely, he'd rule Gothman *and* all the Runner clans.

Darius ran his hand up her body and fondled one of her exposed breasts. She was so beautiful, the perfect woman for him. Tara wanted to be in charge, too. But there was only one leader. She would advise at his side, and he would control both nations. Darius smiled as he played with her nipple and delighted in her quickened breathing even though she remained sound asleep. He'd captured a beautiful Runner, and now she walked proudly by his side. He would defeat the Sea People and soon control all of Nuworld.

When Tara woke, she was alone. There was an outfit folded on the chair next to the bed, a Runner's maternity dress. Tara got up and pulled it over her head. It slid down her body easily. She was thrilled not to have to struggle so her clothes fit, only to feel cramped in them all day. She ran her hands down the black material and turned to the full-length mirror that still hung next to her door from when she was a child.

Tara wrinkled her nose at her scraped knees and bare feet. She turned and searched the room and noticed black leggings, which had been folded underneath the dress. Of course, she had seen women dressed like this many times. The leggings were easy to slip into, and Tara decided the end result was tolerable. She slipped her laser into her pocket and went on a search for food.

After finding sweet rolls and grapes, Tara sat with her landlink and ate while tapping through the screens, catching up on communications with the other clans. A groundmobile pulled up outside the trailer.

She waited to see who would come through the door, assuming one of Patha or Darius' commanders had arrived with news or questions. Instead she heard the sound of a motorcycle being started. Tara rushed to the door and shoved it open. A runner was sitting on her bike!

"I'd get off of that right now and find your own," she said coolly, stepping out of the trailer with her laser pointed directly at the man's chest.

The foolish man leapt off her bike, his eyes large behind his headscarf. "Look, I'm just following—"

"I can see what you're doing." She shot the laser at the ground in front of his feet and the Runner took off running.

Tara spun around at the sound of someone laughing. Patha and Darius stood alongside the trailer. The longer Patha stood there, the harder he laughed until he was holding on to Darius' shoulder to keep from falling over. Darius' baritone chuckle only annoyed her further.

"The poor lad." Patha shook his head as he wiped his eyes.

"What's so funny about someone trying to steal my bike?" Tara wanted nothing more at the moment than to slap the large grins off both their faces.

"My lady, the man was following orders." Darius must have sensed her anger, because his smile disappeared, although slowly. "We asked him to drive your bike up to the shed behind the house."

"Why?"

"You'll drive this groundmobile." He walked over to the groundmobile parked next to her bike.

"You're taking away my bike?"

"It's doctor's orders, Tara-girl." Patha still smiled although he tried to stifle it when he saw her expression.

"And you asked the man to bring the groundmobile to me?" Tara was quiet for a moment and then smiled at her own mistake. "That poor man will never come near me again."

Tara slipped her laser into her dress pocket and patted her bike. When Darius approached her, she smacked his chest. "Well, what are you waiting for, man? I can't very well drive both of these into town. You need to get someone over here to drive my bike to the house."

Darius moved before she could stop him and wrapped her into his arms. "Is that an order, my lady?"

"You bet it is," Tara informed him. "Now let me go. I've got a town to organize."

Darius watched his claim drive away from the campsite and hoped his town would survive his Runner claim.

CHAPTER TEN

"SHE'S HERE," Reena yelled from the living room. "Oh, goodness, old woman. Hurry up. She is here!"

"I'm coming." Hilda waddled down the stairs as fast as her plump legs would carry her.

Torgo galloped past his mama and flung open the front door. "Wow, do you look pregnant!" He ran down the front open room stairs to greet Tara.

"And you have grown." She smiled at the boy as she got out of the groundmobile.

He greeted her with a big hug and a smile that went from ear to ear.

"Miss me, did you?"

"It was awful boring with two old women bossing me all the time." Torgo peered into the back of the groundmobile at all of the landlink equipment. "Especially with a war going on. What's all that?"

"I'm in charge of the soldiers in town. I need this equipment to help me keep track of what everyone is doing. I'll set up in my bedroom."

"Oh, Reena, look how big she is." Hilda clasped her hands to her mouth.

"Of course she's big. She'll have that baby in a couple cycles." Reena sounded sure of herself.

"I wish I had only a couple cycles to go," Tara said with a laugh as she kissed each woman on the cheek. "But the baby won't be here until around the New Winter."

Tara instructed the guards standing in the driveway to unload the equipment and take it up to her room. There was no time like the present to show them who was in charge.

"I'll be wanting to do a thorough exam, lass." Reena rubbed her chin as she studied Tara's belly. "I'm wondering about that fancy doctor of yours."

Tara doubted it would do her any good to argue. "I'll make sure you get to do your exam."

"And soon," Reena said, and wagged her finger. "Don't be putting me off."

"As soon as I have everything in order with the troops," Tara promised.

The women hovered a bit longer, but bored quickly when Tara began arranging her landlink. They left her to her business with promises of a warm meal as soon as she was settled.

"Can I help you?" Torgo hovered in Tara's doorway. "Or I'll just watch if you'll let me."

"Come on." Tara smiled at the boy and he joyfully leapt to her side.

"I'm a quick learner, you'll see."

"You watch and see what you can figure out. Once I know all is in order, we might have time for a lesson."

Torgo took to the landlink like a natural. Over the next few days, Tara organized shifts for the men in town, established military tactics, confirmed the layout of the town on the landlink was accurate, and discussed procedures with Patha and Darius. Since the schools were closed for the safety of the children, Torgo had plenty of time to learn. He was careful not to get in the way, and Tara enjoyed his company and enthusiasm.

"Tomorrow morning I'm going to drive into town and take a look at the damages." Tara leaned back and scratched her stretched-out belly. Fatigue was setting in after a day of handling what seemed like one crisis after another.

Torgo decided that Tara was one of the most unfeminine women he'd ever met. He liked that about her. She didn't snap at him to sit up straight or tuck in his shirt. In fact, she didn't seem to notice when he plopped down in her room with dirty shoes or clothes.

"I can show you exactly where the bombs hit." He wanted so much to be part of it all. "Some of the buildings downtown are all the way gone."

"Did many families lose their homes?"

"Uh, I'm not sure. My mama won't let me wander too much. I saw the buildings downtown when we came back from Reena's. They're rubble on the ground. That's why Mama says I have to stay near the house." Torgo looked at her, hoping she wouldn't make him stay home, too. "Please, can't I go with you?"

"I guess that would be up to Hilda."

There was an argument at the breakfast table the next morning. Not only did Hilda not want Torgo to go, neither Hilda nor Reena thought Tara should go into town.

"I'm not convinced that Runner doctor is right about your baby coming around the new winter. You're just too big." Reena still wanted to give Tara an examination.

Reena was convinced Tara would have the baby in the next two cycles. To make matters worse, the first snow had fallen the night before. The women had noticed how cautious Tara was walking on the uneven ground. They knew she would have a difficult time maintaining balance in the snow. Both women ganged up against Tara, saying it was not wise for her to go anywhere. Torgo looked forlorn when the two women looked triumphant with their argument.

"Are the two of you quite through?" Tara leaned back in her chair after eating and stared at both women. "I'll be driving into town today. I've spent many days in much colder weather than this, and I'll be fine. I think it might be a good idea to take Torgo with me. Look at it as a compromise. He can be my chaperone. It will help to have him with me."

Hilda threw up her hands in the air. "I don't have the fight to keep up with you, girl. Will it be anytime soon that you'll act like a Gothman claim?"

"How's this," Reena suggested, saving Tara from having to answer. "You take the boy, but when you get back, I do the examination. Will that suit you, Hilda?"

Hilda looked at Tara.

"I reckon it suits me. It's man's work inspecting what's left of those buildings. He'll be a man soon enough. I guess it's time he learned how to be one."

"Great!" Torgo jumped up from the table. "When do we leave?"

"Soon." Tara helped herself to more bacon.

"That's right. Sit, boy." Reena smiled. "She's eating for two now."

"Dr. Digo says that's the type of thinking that makes women fat," Tara said in between bites.

"Ah, and this same man says you're due in four cycles as well, huh?" Reena shook her head and scooped more food onto Tara's plate.

Downtown looked so different than it had before. Tara remembered coming to the stores for the first time with Reena. As she parked the groundmobile and walked with Torgo hardly anyone was around, unlike before when women and children bustled about chattering. The grocery store was open, but most of the other shops were closed.

Tara pointed to the side street where she'd first met Torgo. The two buildings on either side of the service road were gone. They walked past the rubble. Two women hurried across the street with long coats pulled tightly around them to block the cold. Neither one of them looked their way—unlike Gothman women who another time would have eagerly welcomed gossip about how the lord's claim looked good and pregnant.

"We need to organize a team to clean this up. These people need hope. Gothman isn't used to the hardships of battle, and I fear morale is low. The town will have to be rebuilt sooner or later. If we have a crew start on clean up now, it will help everyone's morale."

"None of the men are here to do it," Torgo pointed out.

"What's wrong with the women, and all of you young people too young to fight, doing it? There's no reason why you can't help. You've nothing else to occupy your time with school closed. It'll keep the kids out of trouble. And I'm sure the women want to help, too. That way, when the men do come home, they can focus on rebuilding."

"I'm game, but I don't think many of the women around here would help. We aren't like you, Tara. If the men came home and found their women had been doing their work, they wouldn't be happy."

Tara thought for a moment and then looked up smiling. "I have an idea, come on." She hurried back to the groundmobile.

"What are you thinking?"

Tara drove toward the camps. Torgo held on as she bounced over the rough road. He got excited when he saw where they were heading.

"My brother is going to be mad." He was grinning.

"Don't worry about your brother. I can handle him."

She drove to the Blood Circle clan.

"I've never seen so many Runners," Torgo whispered.

"They're people just like you." She pulled up in front of Balbo's trailer and got out of the groundmobile. She didn't see her brother, but his daughter came out and greeted her. Syra had fourteen winters and was of age to wear the full Runner clothing. The young girl bounced down the trailer steps to greet them, wearing her headscarf, which Tara guessed she had put on when she noticed she had company. Tara remembered reaching the age when she could finally don full Runner garb, and how anxious she had been to wear it at every opportunity.

Tara noticed the looks Torgo and Syra gave each other. They were the same age. Torgo hadn't mentioned any girls to her, but appeared to be appraising Tara's niece with interest.

"Where's your papa, Syra?"

"They should be returning soon. I just got word from him." The young girl tilted her hear and studied Torgo, who sat in the groundmobile. "He went down to the front with the other men last night."

"If he returns before I do, let him know I wish to talk to him, okay?"

Tara got back in the groundmobile and headed to the battle site, which was also the same direction as Patha's trailer. She didn't make it to Patha's trailer when he and Darius came toward them on their bikes. She was delighted that she was able to see Darius while here. A quarter-cycle without him made her heart ache. Torgo, however, slouched down in his seat.

"You are about to meet my papa, who is also the leader of this clan." Tara looked at the boy as they pulled up in front of Patha's trailer with a rumbling motorcycle on either side of them. "Be sure to show all signs of your warrior training, understand?"

"Yes." He straightened.

"What are you doing here?" Patha had parked his bike and approached them with long strides.

She climbed out of the groundmobile and Torgo scurried around the front to stand by her. "Patha, I'd like you to meet Torgo, younger brother of Lord Darius." Tara ignored the question and instead offered the introduction.

She swore a slight smile appeared on Darius' face when the young boy stood alert, did not smile, and showed all the signs of a future great Gothman warrior.

Patha acknowledged Torgo with a solemn nod, as he would a grown warrior.

"I've come to recruit several young people to take care of some work I want done in town." Tara looked from one man to the other.

"What work is that?" Darius pulled her into his arms without asking. "You shouldn't be doing any work, my lady."

"I won't be doing the work. Several of the buildings downtown are nothing more than rubble."

"Which buildings?" Darius frowned at the news.

Torgo looked ready to respond but a sharp look from Tara reminded him of what she'd taught him. A young warrior doesn't speak to a superior unless spoken to directly.

"The building next to the grocery store is gone. It'll need to be rebuilt. A few others are badly damaged. Almost all of the shops are closed." Tara pushed against Darius's chest when her belly started constricting. The rest of her reacted as well to all of that hard packed muscle. She stretched her fingers over the steady beat of his heart in his chest and stared into his seductive gray eyes. "This is necessary, Darius. The pride of the Gothman people has taken a stab, which is normal during war. If we show we're ready to rebuild, it'll boost their spirits. They need to see that life as they know it will return soon."

"It's a good idea. But that doesn't sound like work for children," Patha frowned. "Hauling rubble is dangerous work, Tara-girl."

"The Gothman women won't do the work. I want teenagers too young for fighting to work. The school's been closed, and they need something to do. I want Runner, as well as Gothman teenagers, to start hauling this rubble. It'll allow them to get to know each other. And if the Gothman girls are allowed to work also, it will help them start to learn how to work alongside men, doing the same task."

"Could you do this work?" Darius now addressed Torgo.

"Yes, I could." Torgo stood tall as he spoke.

Darius then looked down at Tara, his tone changing to a soft rumble when he spoke. "And what do you think the young girls' mamas will say when you tell them you want their not yet claimed daughters to do a man's job?"

"I've seen the kind of work these women do around the town. They could rebuild the buildings themselves with instruction. My first thought was to have the women do the work. It was Torgo who said they would fear what their claims would say when they returned. I know they'll be reluctant. I hope if they see Runner girls working it will show them that it won't ruin their daughters to let them help."

"Whether they can do the work or not isn't the point." Darius rested his chin on the top of Tara's head and moved his hand over her growing belly. She looked so pregnant. He was sure she'd almost doubled in size in the quarter-cycle since he'd last seen her.

There was a folding chair by the trailer, and he set it next to Tara. Placing his hand gently on her shoulder, he made it clear she was to sit. "Some things are simply men's work," he tried explaining. "Your culture isn't as different as you'd like to think. A man will carry heavy items while the woman takes care of the children. Your women may be warriors, but they don't mind the chivalry of a man."

Tara smiled, determination clear in her eyes. "I still want the children."

"Stubborn as they come," Darius said to Patha.

"The town people won't go for it, Tara."

"They will if you tell them to."

"Could we ask your niece to help?" Torgo spoke up, forgetting about not speaking unless addressed.

"What?" Darius turned a foul expression on his younger brother.

"Nothing."

Tara ignored Torgo and kept her attention on Darius. "Your people will do what you say." She was not going to give up. "They follow you blindly."

Darius turned from her and walked toward the groundmobile. He wasn't going to argue the obvious.

"I'll issue an order," he said slowly, mulling over how he would word it.

Darius decided to worry about that later. His thoughts shifted to what was more important at the moment. He scrutinized Tara. She still looked tired, but she was clean and there was more color in her face. Her eyes glowed, and she seemed pleased with her victory, but he was looking deeper. He wanted to see excitement about her becoming a mama. He knew she loved the life of a warrior. Would she love being a mama as well? He wanted her to…desperately. The thought of her raising their child kept him going in this dreary and tiresome war, a war he wished would end.

"When's your next doctor's visit?"

"As soon as I get home."

"Good. I expect a raving report." He kissed her, wishing he had time to do more. "The Sea People are showing signs of weakening. This war will be over soon."

Tara was glad he approved her plan. She would have implemented it even if he had said no; she'd already made her mind up about that. It wouldn't have been hard to tell the people he'd given a command. They wouldn't have found out otherwise, not until the deed had been done. But going behind Darius' back wasn't how she wanted to do things. The two of them needed to be a team, not working against each other.

Balbo agreed to send his daughter to town; several other Runners agreed as well. That was the easy part. Back in town, Tara took Torgo's suggestions on which houses to approach. The women who answered the doors were reluctant at first, but when they were told Lord Darius ordered it, they also agreed. Most of the women looked at her as if she were crazy. A few questioned if she told them the truth. It stabbed at her pride when Torgo, a child, assured them that he'd heard his brother agree to let teenage girls do the work. That's when they agreed. The next morning, the young people would meet downtown and begin cleaning up Bryton.

Reena was ready for her the moment they returned home and scooted Torgo out of the house. She wouldn't have a man under the roof while examining a woman.

"Now then, I am going to see if your cervix is softening, I am." Reena waited as Tara got comfortable on her bed and Hilda looked on.

The examination was uncomfortable but, regardless of what any doctor may say, there's no way to examine female organs without some discomfort. Tara put all her attention into keeping her face expressionless. She'd handled laser wounds, broken bones and other injuries with dignity, but the unusual pressure she felt as Reena probed with her fingers made Tara want to yell and slap at her to stop.

Reena poked and prodded and pushed on Tara's tummy. She would stand back and look at Tara and then continue with the prodding.

"That's interesting," she said once. "Well, I'll be," was another response.

Tara watched her and strained her neck to see what Reena was doing, although it was difficult with her big tummy in the way. Finally, Reena seemed done and washed her hands.

Hilda handed Reena a dry towel and studied her friend's face, then turned and patted Tara's shoulder.

"Do you want anything, Tara-girl?" Reena asked, using Patha's term of endearment.

"No." Tara put her legs together and started trying to sit.

Reena pushed her back until Tara was flat on her back. "Stay there then. I'll be right back."

Hilda followed Reena out of the room. Tara strained to hear their words as they walked down the hall.

"Why?" Hilda asked.

Tara thought Reena sounded irritated. But then all she heard were the two women descending the stairs.

She must have drifted to sleep, because Tara awakened to the sound of voices in her room. But they sounded so far away...she was content to ignore them. Slowly, she opened her eyes and was rather surprised to see Dr. Digo standing there looking at her with Reena and Hilda at his side.

"You needed that sleep." Reena smiled at her daughter.

"How long was I out?" Tara tried to sit up, but a cramp slowed her down.

"Not long, dear." Reena's hand fluttered toward Tara but her attention was on Dr Digo. "Just long enough for me to call in a second opinion about a small matter."

"I'd hardly say Lord Darius' heir--" Hilda began.

Reena made a fierce clucking sound. "Enough out of you, old woman."

Dr. Digo stepped in front of both women as if they weren't there. He pressed his large palm on the middle of Tara's belly. Instantly, both women peered around him, their eyes wide and their mouths pressed in thin lines. If Tara hadn't picked up on the tension and wanted to know what was going on, she would have found the scene comical.

"Do you cramp often?" he asked.

"I guess so. I don't give it much thought."

He lifted a suitcase she hadn't noticed until then and opened it to display a portable landlink.

"How can I help?" Reena looked at the foreign equipment.

"A bowl of very hot water might help. This ointment is always cold for some reason. It would be better for Tara if we warmed it up."

Hilda rushed out of the room before Reena could. It was obvious she was bothered about something and that alerted Tara.

"What's going on, Doc?"

"I'm going to do a sonogram. Ever had one of those?"

Tara allowed Reena to adjust the sheets so just Tara's protruding belly showed.

"No, but I've heard of them. Can you tell me if my baby is a boy or a girl?" Tara wasn't sure why Reena sent for Dr. Digo, but she looked worried. "Is everything okay?"

"I'm sure everything is fine, but we'll take a look to make sure. If you want, while we're checking, I can tell if you are going to have a son or daughter." He smiled at her and accepted the hot water when Hilda returned, then placed a tube of ointment in it.

After setting up to the sonogram machine, Dr. Digo spread the ointment over Tara's tummy. The women watched as he turned on the machine and placed a flat disc on Tara's stomach.

"That won't hurt the baby, will it?" Hilda looked more nervous than a cat.

"Goodness, no, ma'am." Dr. Digo tried not to smile at the ignorance of the question. "Look at the monitor, and you'll be able to see what's inside Tara's uterus."

"For Gothman's sake," Hilda breathed.

Tara couldn't tell if Hilda's response was a result of the extraordinary equipment or at the doctor mentioning a female reproductive organ so casually.

"I can't tell what I'm looking at." Tara watched the movement of the black and white picture on the screen.

"You were right," Dr. Digo told Reena.

"I was?" Reena clapped her hands to her mouth. "But what does it mean?"

"Knew what?" Tara looked at each adult hovering over her, confusion and fear settling hard in her gut. "What does what mean? What's wrong?"

It hadn't crossed her mind until that moment that something might go wrong with the pregnancy. She'd seen her fair share of pregnant women in the clan. Other than getting bigger, they never acted any different and continued with their lives just as before.

"I'm not sure anything is wrong," Dr. Digo said slowly. "What I can say now is that Reena discovered you are carrying two babies."

"Twins?" Tara let her head drop to the pillow in disbelief. "Are you sure?"

There's only one heartbeat," Reena blurted out. "Two babies and one heart."

Tara forgot to breathe. She began stroking her belly and felt the life inside her respond to her touch. "One of them is dead?" she whispered, choking out the words.

"No. No!" Dr. Digo repeated, pointing a finger at Reena, then the monitor next to Tara's bed. "There are two very active babies inside her."

Reena and Hilda looked at the monitor. Tara did, too. After a minute it was easier to pick out arms and legs. Twins? How would she handle two babies?

"Maybe they have the same heartbeat," she mused.

"Each baby has their own heart. We should hear two heartbeats. I've heard twins in the womb before," Reena said. She crossed her thin arms over her small chest and shot Dr. Digo a side glance.

He looked at her at the same time. "Each baby has their own heart." He nodded and was silent.

"Then I have happy, healthy twins." Tara was still trying to get it all to sink in. "You scared me for a minute."

"And for some reason their hearts are beating as one," Dr. Digo said, his voice sounding oddly strained.

"I've never heard of such a thing," Reena murmured.

"Dr. Digo sighed. "Me either." He patted Tara's knee. "You've got a unique situation here."

Tara looked into his clear focused eyes. "What is different about my babies? Maybe we are hearing two heartbeats and they are just the same."

Dr. Digo smiled but looked concerned.

"It's just mighty strange," Reena muttered, speaking before Dr. Digo said anything. "Their heartbeats should be overlapping each other. Two babies don't have heartbeats that beat in unison that strongly together."

"Apparently mine do." Tara said defensively, holding her belly and the very active lives inside her. "And none of you will speak of my babies as if there is a problem. You just said they are fine. My babies are happy and healthy and that is all you will say."

"Carrying two babies is a lot harder than carrying one." Dr. Digo turned his attention to Reena and Hilda. "She is going to need to keep her activities to a bare minimum from here on out."

"Oh no! I can't do that." Tara tried to sit up and cursed when her large belly stopped her, not only with its size, but with shooting pains that stole her breath momentarily.

Reena noticed the look of defiance she'd grown accustomed to seeing. "Now we know that your babies are fine and you'll not go anywhere until they are born." Reena let her daughter see where she got some of that wilfulness.

Tara opened her mouth to rebut.

Reena lifted her hand to make it final. "Her cervix is a lot thinner than I expected it to be. She shows all signs of a woman preparing for birth in a cycle. But I'm thinking we don't want those babies coming before they are done." Reena spoke to the doctor, but caressed her daughter's head, letting Tara hear the reality of what could happen if she disobeyed this order to rest.

Reena might be conferring with the doctor, but she still watched him warily. She wasn't comfortable with him being here. The twins' situation had been unique enough, and Reena cared that much to have brought him here.

"Well, these babies are not ready to be born yet. We need to do everything we can to keep them in her for at least another cycle and a half. The longer, the better. "Dr. Digo leaned back against the dresser, aware of the fact that he would not be able to do an internal exam with the two old ladies present. "Tara, you're not going to like this, but I want you to stay in bed as much as you can. If you move out of that bed, it should be to a chair. Do as little walking as possible. The more you move, the more those babies will move around in you, and the thinner that cervix will get. Now they haven't turned yet, and that's a good sign."

Tara groaned. Her babies were okay, but staying put for the next cycle and a half? She'd never heard of other women having to do that. But then apparently her twins were unique. Already she knew this was knowledge that would never be public. Darius would agree with her. Her babies would rule nations and Nuworld would know them as perfect.

One of her babies was a boy, but Dr. Digo said the other was being bashful and he couldn't tell its sex. As Dr. Digo packed up, the women stood anxiously watching him and helping to organize his things. Tara knew they were anxious to share the most exciting piece of gossip they'd come by in quite awhile. She was sure every soul in town would know Lord Darius's claim carried twins before the day was out.

"Not a word to anyone about their heartbeats," Tara instructed the three of them. "I mean it. Gossip all you want about them being twins. But you will say they are healthy and happy. Am I clear?"

"And can't wait to greet Nuworld and claim their birthright, "Hilda added clutching her pudgy hands together and nodding in agreement.

"There are always private family matters that no honorable Gothman woman gossips about," Reena explained.

"The Lord of Gothman will have twins. One of them is said to be a boy." Hilda was inching toward the door.

"And you'll stay in bed so those babies remain healthy," Dr. Digo insisted. "You may move to a chair, but that's it."

After assuring all three parties she would stay put and call if she needed anything, Tara found herself alone. She slowly got up and moved over to her desk and her landlink. The homing device was surprisingly still on the back of Darius' neck, and she was able to locate him without difficulty. He was at Patha's trailer. She reached for her comm to see if he'd respond.

"Darius?"

No answer.

She resorted to the landlink and sent him a message to see if he was on one of the transmissions.

Patha answered the message and told her Darius was in the shower.

She told her papa to send him at once indicating it was very important. Patha said he would send him.

Tara logged off. She stared out the window, not seeing the beautiful view. She'd grown accustomed to the thought of having a baby by the new winter, which was still two cycles away. She was familiar with the amount of work involved. She'd helped with the younger children in her clan. But two babies…double the work…she'd not once entertained that thought. It was so overwhelming. The cruel bite of fear started the contractions all over again.

She needed to hear Darius tell her he'd help her with the babies. She'd known in her mind all along that when the baby came she'd do most of the raising. The thought hadn't bothered her too much. He would rule the nation with her guidance, and she would raise the child with his guidance. By the time she became ruler of the Runner clans, this child—her children—would be much older.

Darius would help feed them, change them, and get up when they cried at night. But she didn't want anyone else to assume responsibility of her armies. Tara had worked hard to gain Patha's respect—her *papa's* respect—so that he would give her all the responsibility she now had. Her days already were full with overseeing all the commanders, not to mention the tasks that she would need to undertake once this war ended. How could she possibly handle working all day with her clan and being the mama to two babies? Tara let her thoughts absorb her and after a bit laid her head down on the desk and started to cry.

"Tara?"

Tara lifted her head at the sound of his voice and smiled at Darius, then wiped her eyes to clear her blurred vision.

"I'm so glad you're here," she whispered and pushed herself to her feet before falling into his arms when he moved across the room. "I've just found out that we're going to have twins, Darius. How are we going to handle two babies?"

"We're going to have twins?" Darius' dace instantly lit with pleasure.

Tara looked up at him and frowned. "That isn't good news," Tara said and pushed away. "That means twice as much work. I've got responsibilities, and so do you. How will we handle twins?"

"Together, my lady." Darius pulled her to him again. "We will handle them together. I'm not that ignorant to the raising of a child. You forget that Torgo came along when I was old enough to help. Papa didn't have much of a hand in raising him, but I did."

"You helped with Torgo when he was a baby?" Tara's voice cracked through her tears, and she walked over to her dresser and pulled out one of her handkerchiefs, then blew her nose.

"Yes, my lady. My papa wasn't around too much, and the lad often put my mama at her wit's end." Darius sat on her bed, and patted the spot next to him. "I know my share about changing diapers and feeding time. You and I will do just fine."

Tara smiled and hugged him. The man said exactly what she needed to hear, and now she felt like crying again, because she was so lucky to have him.

"It doesn't seem right that it takes two people to make the baby," he stroked her blotchy cheeks, smiling gently, "but just one is expected to raise the baby."

"I can't believe you just said that," she whispered as he pulled her close. "Do you really mean it?"

"Having you in my life has brought out what I already knew was in my soul." He pulled away far enough to look at her with penetrating gray eyes of his. "We can't have you all upset like this, now can we? You'll rest now. That's an order, my beautiful warrior."

Had he truly meant all those things he'd just said? She knew only time would tell—and she hated that she would have to wait and see Darius in action to find out if he spoke the truth.

"There's more," Tara began.

"More?" He raised an eyebrow. "I doubt you can make me happier than I already am."

Tara told him about the heartbeat, and how the twins' hearts seemed to beat as one. "It's as if their hearts are in perfect unison with each other."

Darius stared at her large belly. "And this is odd?"

"Apparently not for out babies." She held his gaze when he gave her a quick look. "Our babies will rule nations, my lord," she whispered. "All of Nuworld must know that these twins are perfect."

His gray eyes sharpened and narrowed. "Who knows of this identical heartbeat?"

Tara told him.

"None of them will say a word," he said with a fierce finality.

Darius closed her bedroom door after Tara fell asleep. It was time to hire servants. He thought about what Tara had just told him. Pulling out his comm he fixed it around his ear and tapped the bottom to turn it on.

"Dr. Digo," he said. If his children were unique, he'd know everything about them before they were born.

The next cycle moved along uneventfully. Tara moved from room to room, changing her environment, so she wouldn't go stir crazy. She went outside a few times—although the oncoming winter made it easier to stay inside. She wasn't exactly bored. There was plenty to think about. Especially since Reena had returned from town a few days before with news. Rumors in town claimed the war was all but over.

"We finished clearing the last of the rubble today." Torgo joined Tara at the table, carrying a hot bowl of soup he'd brought from the kitchen. "The women are going to have a gathering for everyone who helped."

"That sounds great." Tara sipped at her own soup and smiled when Torgo offered her a slice of bread from the platter in the center of the table. He'd smeared butter on it, and she took a bite.

"I think some of the Runner kids are going to be there." He wasn't sure why, but he decided not to mention his friendship with Syra. He'd never hung out with a girl before, but she was cool.

"You're experiencing history in the making." Tara smiled in between bites. "Already our cultures are accepting each other."

Torgo slurped his soup just as Hilda entered the room.

She slapped the back of his head. "Reena should be here soon." Hilda sat at the opposite end of the table from Tara and placed a large cloth bag in front of her so Tara couldn't see her face. "I wanted to show you some of the material we will use on the baby quilts."

Tara had seen so many different materials for the quilts; she couldn't keep straight what they'd look like when they were done. She humored the woman though and watched attentively.

The front door opened and Reena entered, bringing a gust of cold air with her. "I daresay that one is my favorite." Reena ran her hand over a flowery print Hilda had just pulled from the bag.

"I'm going to meet some of the kids in town." Torgo stood, grabbing his empty bowl. "All this quilting talk is for ladies."

"You behave now, boy," Hilda scolded, but smiled before returning her attention to see Tara's reaction to the material.

"I have to agree with Reena." Tara dunked the crust of her bread into her soup. "I like that material, too."

Hilda seemed pleased and folded the material before placing it back in the bag. "Now are you sure you'll be okay left alone for a time?"

The pair appeared anxious to go, and Tara hurried to reassure them. "I'll be fine. Get going you two. We'll need those quilts soon, I expect." Tara stood and walked around the table, then made a feeble attempt to hug the two women. She watched as they left the house.

Soon after that, Tara headed out the back door to enjoy a walk through the snow. The weather was crisp, and she felt her lungs freeze with her first gulp of air. A path was shovelled through the snow, and Tara stuck to it. It led through the yard to the driveway, which had also been shovelled. Small mountains of snow towered on either side of her. Snow from the path rested on the pristine, sparkling white yard.

Tara desperately wanted to wade into the snow to reach the shed and the backfield. There, she could truly enjoy the winter's beauty. She had to admit trudging through the snow sounded exhausting and so behaved, and stayed in the cleared area. She reached the end of the path and began walking toward the front of the house along the driveway.

Suddenly, she stopped in her tracks. A red spot soiled the ground in front of her. Something had been dragged from the spot through the deep snow to the other side. Tara moved closer and recognized the mark as blood. One touch told her the liquid was still warm.

Tara pulled her comm out of her pocket and hooked it around her ear. "Darius," she whispered as she looked around her, remaining alert.

"Yes?"

"There's something wrong at the house."

"What is it?"

"I don't know. There's blood in the driveway. I think one of the guards has been dragged off. Darius, I'm outside and I'm not armed," she continued and started toward the back door.

"We'll be there in a minute. Who's there with you?"

"I'm here alone." Tara heard the comm go dead as soon as she'd spoken those words. She wondered where Darius was and how long it would take him to get there. Her laser was in her room. The women had thrown such a fit about her carrying it in her condition. Plus, Darius's men were stationed everywhere. At the moment, though, it seemed eerily quiet.

She looked toward the back of the house and then to the front. Four guards were supposed to be stationed out here. She saw no sign of them.

Tara moved as fast as she dared along the shovelled area and hurried inside. There was no way to tell if anyone was in the house, due to its size. She crept up the stairs to her bedroom and her laser. Grabbing it, she headed back down the stairs.

No sign of life was evident through the windows, and from the front open room she noted the snow was undisturbed except for the footprints along the driveway. Then she saw it—

more blood along the snow in the front yard and indications that someone had been dragged.

Whoever did this was still nearby.

An icy breeze made Tara to shiver, and icicles shattered to the ground from a nearby tree. Tara stepped carefully to the bloodstained snow and looked off into the direction where crushed snow appeared to form a path. The snow was deep, and she moved slowly so she wouldn't lose her balance. With every step her huge belly constricted. Her babies were being exceptionally still at the moment, however, as if they sensed something was wrong, too. A hard fall to the ground would send her into labor. She hugged her belly as she searched the yard.

"Isn't it inappropriate for someone in your condition to be out in this weather?"

Tara turned quickly to face a Runner standing on the path by the house. She didn't recognize the man through his headscarf, and something was strange about his voice.

"Who are you?" She wrapped her fingers around the laser in her pocket.

"This is rather a shame," he stated, ignoring her question. "It's not really you I'm after, although I guess you should die as well."

Tara listened to the voice carefully. It was Gothman.

Just then, she heard the sounds of motorcycles approaching. The Gothman in Runner clothing pulled out a laser from his pocket and aimed it at her head.

"Drop it, now!" Darius pulled his bike to a stop and aimed his gun straight at the Runner.

"Oh, what perfect timing. And how heroic. Don't tell me you came alone." The intruder turned his laser on Darius.

Tara pointed her weapon at the stranger and approached slowly. "Hold it right there."

The intruder pulled a second laser from his pocket and aimed this one at Tara. "I won't let this continue."

"You won't let what continue?" Tara took another step toward the stranger, feeling the snow crunch under her boots.

The stranger didn't acknowledge her question, although the laser remained pointed at her. He looked at Darius. "You've destroyed the Bryton blood line. You have no respect for anything but your power. To think how many bastards you have running around out there. That was bad enough."

"What bastards? Darius, who is this?" Tara didn't take her eyes from the man, and his laser didn't waver as she pointed it at him.

"Who knows when someone might show up claiming his right to be Lord of Gothman?" the man continued as if she hadn't spoken. "But then, you go and do something like this." The man waved his laser at Tara. "You'll allow a half-breed to be our heir? Darius, that is unacceptable!"

"Mikel, put down the gun." Darius spoke with a cold authority that the other man didn't possess.

Tara's mouth fell open in disbelief. This masked stranger—the one holding a laser to her head, dressed in the garb of people he claimed to despise—was Darius' brother.

"I may die, brother, but so shall you." Mikel raised both of his hands and wrapped his fingers around each trigger. "You murdered Juro. I can prove that, you know. That alone gives me the right to kill you. What do you think our papa would say about this?" He gestured his gun at Tara. "You disgust me, Darius."

Darius' shot rang through the air with a high-pitched whistle.

Mikel was thrown backwards from the close impact of the laser. As he slammed into the side of the house, both of his lasers went off, one into the air and one straight toward Tara.

Instinctively, she threw herself to the ground, feeling the loss of air in her lungs. She turned to land on her side, holding her belly with both hands, as her laser fell into the powdery snow next to her. The ground came fast and hard, and the pain was so intense she wasn't sure if she'd been shot or not.

Darius was by her side instantly.

The discomfort and pain racking her body made it hard to speak. She fought to focus as her world blurred. "Something is wrong, my lord."

"Shh. Be still." Darius lifted her into his arms and was up the open room stairs and into the house within seconds. He didn't care about his dead brother lying out front, but focused only on Tara's condition. He took the wide stairs three at a time and had her on the bed before she realized it.

"What about your brother? You can't leave him there." Tara watched Darius as his hands went over her body, as if searching to see if anything had broken.

"Don't worry about him right now, my lady. It's you I am concerned about."

A sharp pain riveted through Tara's body, starting somewhere in her middle and ending halfway down her leg. Tara caught her breath and exhaled when the pain subsided.

"How do you feel?" He stroked her hair and looked way too calm.

"Am I shot?"

Darius was talking into his mouthpiece. "Patha, I need Dr. Digo sent to the house immediately." He was silent for a second before turning off the comm. "Where's Reena?" he asked her gently.

"She's working on the quilts with the other ladies." Suddenly, Tara was confused. "Darius, I think I'm okay. I guess I knocked the wind out of me." She attempted to sit, and a sudden pain flashed through her gut and down her legs.

Darius eased her back down.

She grabbed his hand with both of hers and squeezed harder than she'd ever squeezed before. The pain subsided as she lay back down, and she eased her grip.

Darius' face was expressionless. He tapped his comm again. "Send someone to find Reena. I believe she is at one of those quilting meetings."

Tara felt another wave of pain, and Darius offered his hand again, which she squeezed without mercy. She cried out from the intensity of the pain, and watched Darius' mouth move, but couldn't quite make out his words.

"And I don't want a trace of blood visible," she thought she heard him say, but another wave of pain hit her before the last one completely ended.

It seemed like hours passed before Dr. Digo appeared. Not long after, Reena arrived. Tara heard Hilda's excited voice although she didn't see her. Whenever she opened her eyes, it was Darius' face she saw.

He watched her, his expression assuring her everything would be all right. Her claim stroked her head with a damp cloth, which felt better at that moment than she could have imagined.

Then she felt his cheek brush hers, as he placed gentle kisses on her forehead. She focused on his touch, as wave after wave of biting pain violated her body.

Tara tried turning her head to see the activity in the room. Everyone around her seemed surreal. Reena appeared to be bouncing from one side of the bed to the other. Dr. Digo placed a needle in her arm, and everyone suddenly seemed very far away.

Tara heard everyone talking but had a hard time focusing on words. Her thoughts kept going inward. She vaguely paid attention as her legs were lifted, her boots removed and her feet placed on cold metal. She blindly obeyed when Reena stood between her legs and instructed her to push.

"Tara," someone was speaking to her and there was cold water dripping slowly down the side of her forehead. She lifted her hand and brushed the water away. "Tara-girl, open your eyes."

She obeyed and this time the room was in better focus than before.

"Say hello to your son, my lady." Darius stood by the bed holding a bundle of blankets.

Tara focused until she saw the baby in his arms. She had done it. Tara sat so easily it made her dizzy. She looked around the room at her exhausted audience. She should feel as tired as they looked, but instead she was exhilarated and overwhelmed with happiness.

"Where are my babies?" Her throat was too dry, and her voice cracked.

Darius sat next to her and placed the bundle of blankets in her arms. Hilda approached with another bundle. Tara wrapped her arms around the two babies and looked down into their squishy pink faces.

"We have a boy and a girl." Darius ran his fingers through her hair and lifted her face to his. "I must say, you were quite impressive." He leaned forward and kissed her on her chapped lips.

She smiled when Darius gave her breathing room, then glorified in her babies. "Hello there Andru and Ana," she whispered.

"Andru and Ana is it?" Darius smiled and nodded. "So be it. Andru and Ana are perfect in health and stamina. Both doctors agree. Our children shall rule the greatest nations on Nuworld. I have no doubt they will do great things."

Tara didn't need anyone to tell her it was true. She saw it in her son and daughters beautiful faces. She wrapped Andru's tiny fingers around her index finger and watched with curiosity as Ana's fingers curled in the air, as if she wanted a finger to hold, too.

Later that night, Darius crept into the dark room where Tara lay, cradling her sleeping babies. She smiled as he leaned down to kiss her.

"I wanted to wish you good night," he whispered. "But I fear I woke you instead."

"I've been sleeping when they do, I guess. But I'm glad you're here."

"You were wonderful birthing our children, my lady." And when he kissed her again, she smiled against his mouth and returned the kiss until he backed away a few inches to study her.

"I'm sorry about your brother," she whispered.

His expression darkened. "I only have one brother, and he knows nothing of my papa's philosophies."

"Darius?" She looked up anxiously as he turned to leave. "Do you have any other children?"

"No."

The door closed, and the room became completely dark again.

CHAPTER ELEVEN

"COME ON, you can do ten more." Tara was dripping with sweat.

"Can't we take a break?" Torgo dropped to the ground. "If I do one more push up, my arms will break."

"Okay, a little break." Tara laughed and fell to the ground as well. Her muscles burned with exhaustion and it felt so good. "You don't know how happy I am to be back in shape."

"You look incredibly good, my lady." Lord Darius walked toward them and looked at his claim and brother lying on the ground. "Duty calls, however, the twins are up from their naps."

Tara jumped to her feet and straightened her shirt. "I guess we'll continue your training later."

Torgo tried hard not to sigh with relief. He had a hard time keeping up with Tara. Fortunately, no guards were around to see him continue to lie in the cool grass.

Tara hurried upstairs to greet her beautiful children. Each had their own cradle and smiled at the sight of their mama. She'd grown accustomed to picking them both up and laying them at opposite ends of the table where their diapers were. The two children would kick each other giggle when she blew on their tummies, changed diapers, and dressed them.

"I can't believe how much you two are growing." She kissed fingers and toes. "You're six cycles old today, did you know that?"

"Oh, good, they're awake now." Hilda entered the nursery with a bag in her hands. "I bought these while I was in town this morning. They were such cute outfits I couldn't resist. Don't you agree?"

The two outfits were made from a smooth, soft material. One was a pair of overalls and the other a dress with straps like the overalls. Hilda also produced a white blouse to go with the dress and a white shirt for the overalls. The two women struggled to get the lively children into their new outfits then placed them on the floor.

Tara laughed as Andru tried to inspect the shiny buttons on his sister's outfit. Ana slapped at his hands for his efforts, but at the same time tried fingering his buttons.

"I heard news in town this morning, you know—catching up on the gossip so to speak."

"Oh?"

Tara never appeared interested in any of the goings on of the community, but Hilda was determined to teach her new daughter the fine art of gossiping.

"Ah, yes, I did. I heard Patha is planning to head south for a few cycles. It was Gertrude's daughter who told me, you know the baker's claim? It was while I was showing off these new outfits that she told me."

Tara was less interested in the source of the gossip than the news itself. "Patha is leaving? I just saw him the other day, and he didn't mention it. Do you know when?"

"Now that I don't know, but here is the best part." Hilda lowered her voice as if someone might be listening. "I heard that he asked Reena to go with him."

"What did she say?"

"Well, I would think she would say no." Hilda thought the question absurd.

Tara picked up the babies and walked into the large adjoining bedroom she now shared with Darius.

"Where are you going?"

"I'm going to say goodbye to my papa." Tara pulled a clean headscarf from her top dresser drawer.

"You're taking the babies?"

"Can you tend them?"

Hilda shook her head. "I'm having tea with some of the ladies over at Roga's. You really should hire one of the girls in town to be a nanny." The old lady scurried off to prepare for her outing.

Tara was left alone with her babies. She thought about asking Torgo or Darius to go with her, but neither was to be found when she loaded the babies into the back of the groundmobile. It took some effort to remove the two plastic sections that made up the roof of the groundmobile, but Tara managed. Fresh air blew her hair off her neck when she finally sat behind the large steering wheel.

"It will get you accustomed to riding on a bike when you're older." She watched them look up at the endless blue sky.

Andru and Ana's blond curls fell around their creamy white, pudgy faces. Their deep gray eyes, which were the same color as their papa's, took in everything and didn't miss a thing. Watching her children at times made Tara feel as if she had double vision. Andru watched a bird fly overhead, and so did Ana. One twin didn't parrot the other. Both twins moved as if controlled by one thought.

Tara saw how intelligent her children were. They were beautiful and perfect in every way. Once they got older, and came into their own personalities, she didn't doubt they'd quit being so identical. Until then, she allowed herself to marvel in their unique behavior.

"Shall we go see the people you will one day rule?" Tara tapped Ana's nose.

If it were her call she would allow the twins to grow older before deciding which would lead which nation. Darius had laughed and tried getting her to admit that their son would be the better ruler. He insisted his son had been born first and was the rightful heir of Gothman. Reena had told her Ana was born first, but then later insisted she didn't remember. Tara was sure regardless of which of her children were the elder, Darius wouldn't budge on his decision that Andru would lead Gothman and Ana be heir to all Runner clans.

Her children quit looking at the sky. They gave her their attention and kicked their pudgy legs. Tara laughed at their baby babble.

"Then let's get going." She double checked the straps secured around them in the special infant sized seats Darius had installed in the back seat of the groundmobile. Then turning and facing the wheel, she accelerated and the rumble of the motor drowned out the chatter.

"And we're off," She laughed and glanced over her shoulder to see her babies laughing, too.

Her clan was definitely preparing to leave. Doors stood open as trailer interiors were dismantled. Breakable items were being boxed before being placed in compartments under the trailer. It was summer and the best time to travel to cooler land north of them that wouldn't be passable when it got close to the new winter.

Tara felt a pang of regret that she wasn't going. It surprised her. She'd been so busy with the babies and so wrapped up with her love for Darius that it hadn't dawned on her until now how long she'd been in one place.

The clan would move around for the next four to five cycles before settling in right before the new winter when the weather turned bad. The alliance built with Gothman enabled the Runners to leave some of their possessions on the land, with Darius promising protection. Patha and Darius agreed that the land just to the northwest of Bryton would be Blood Circle clan property.

The townsfolk had grown accustomed to Runners entering their stores. It was a first for the clan to own land. Times were changing in so many ways. Thinking about it always gave her tingles of excitement. She forced herself to feel cheerful as she waved to clan members and weaved around trailers in the groundmobile.

"Hi, Syra." Tara pulled up to Patha's trailer and smiled at her niece. "What are you doing?"

"Nothing." Syra sounded sulky.

Tara was about to ask her what was wrong when Patha and Balbo came around the other side of the trailer.

"I heard you were leaving." Tara greeted her papa as she reached for her children.

"In the morning." The old man smiled and headed for his grandbabies. "These babies will be walking by the time I get back."

Tara handed Andru to his grandpapa and held Ana in her arms. "What's wrong with Syra?"

"Believe it or not, she doesn't want to go." Balbo shrugged his shoulders at his daughter's behavior. "I don't understand her lately."

"Why not let her stay with me? I need a nanny for the children. I could pay her, and she could have her own room. It would help her save money for her first bike. She's about ready for one, you know."

Patha looked at Balbo, nodding his approval of the suggestion.

"She's growing up so fast." Balbo shook his head. "Nothing I do is right for her anymore. Are you sure she would be a help with the babies?"

"I was caring for babies at her age if not younger. Besides, Balbo, it might make it easier to find another wife. Syra is quite the young lady, and another woman might think she has competition with her around."

"Another wife?" Balbo started coughing and his face turned red. "I don't need to leave my daughter behind to find a wife. What stories are you hearing around the fires?"

"Nothing." Tara didn't remember when she had last sat around a roaring fire and listened to the stories. "I really need help with Andru and Ana."

"Don't try to argue with her, Balbo." Patha laughed. "Sounds like she has her mind made up."

"Okay. I'll speak to her. That is, if she'll talk to me." He walked over to the sulking girl.

Tara watched her papa play with her son. "I'll miss you. You better stay in touch with me."

"Don't you long to travel, Tara-girl?"

"I hadn't thought about it to be honest with you until I entered the clan and saw everyone tearing down. The twins and Darius keep me so busy." Tara squinted from the sun and looked around the clansite. Runners loaded bags onto their bikes and locked down trailers. "Coming out here does put the yearning into a person, though."

Patha looked at her, but instead of saying anything he moved closer when Andru reached for Ana. He stood next to his daughter while his grandbabies wrapped their pudgy fingers together and held hands. He didn't know a lot about twins but it seemed these two were exceptionally connected to each other. Patha glanced at Tara. As always, his daughter was playing strong and trying not to show how torn she was over decisions she'd made in her life.

She noticed the look of concern in Patha's eyes. "Don't worry about me. I am happy. Really I am. I've found a good man."

"Good. You have an obligation here. The Runners have never had land like this before, and a lot of that is due to you, Tara-girl."

"I know." Tara knew the Runners were talking about her being responsible for a pivotal turn in their history. Maybe she didn't join in on stories around the fires the way she used to. She did make time to read communications between clans on her landlink. She received more respect from them due to the Lord of Gothman claiming her than she did from the Gothman.

Balbo and Syra returned from the side of the trailer. Tara noticed the young girl was all smiles.

"Can I really stay with you?" Syra looked from one twin to the other, her smile growing.

"You can work for me." Tara caught the girl's eye. "You'll be in charge of the babies, and you'll go to school. It won't be fun and games."

Tara knew the teenager had had exposure to young children. Tara realized Syra would be one of the few girls in her class. Syra wouldn't let anyone bully her. Still, she was breaking the mold by attending school while Gothman girls were discouraged from going. The Gothman believed their girls learned what they needed to know by staying home and helping their mamas. Tara had done her best to encourage girls to attend, but it was a slow process.

Darius had approved Runners enrolling their children in the Gothman school. That was a slow process too, encouraging Runners to take advantage of the Gothman schools instead of home-schooling their children, as had always been the custom.

"I won't let you down." Syra bolted away and ran toward her and Balbo's trailer. She yelled over her shoulder. "Just let me get my things."

Syra couldn't believe her luck. She would see Torgo every day. This sure beat spending the next several cycles cooped up with her papa. Torgo would be a lot more fun. He was so cute and so tall. Ever since they'd finished the project of clearing rubble for the Gothman, all she did was think about him. This change of events was too good to be true.

"I'm ready." Syra ran back to Tara who was still talking to Patha and Balbo. She took Ana just to make sure Tara knew she could do the work.

Tara handed the baby to Syra but didn't pause in her conversation. "Why are you going south instead of north?"

"The River people at the southern edge of Southland are trying to form a new government, and I thought we would start by going there," Patha said. "I want to make sure they know the Gothman and Runners have united. We'll show our respects to their new government and see if they'll welcome our union by letting Runners enjoy their community."

"Honestly I thought you'd go north for milder weather," Tara admitted, watching as Syra struggled to strap Andru and Ana back into their seats. "I guess the travels aren't about survival anymore."

"They are, Tara-girl, but in a different way. Runners and Gothman are building a new nation," Patha explained. "And to survive, we must make sure all of Nuworld knows. Defeating the Sea People gave us strength. There are other nations who need to acknowledge us."

Tara knew there was oil in the ground down there. It was thick in the ground just north of the border, then continuing into Southland. Patha and Darius had probably discussed this. Gothman had very little oil. Runners had bartered with nations all over Nuworld for winters to secure enough oil for their travels. Darius was aware of his lands limits. Securing relations with the River people would greatly help Runners and Gothman.

Syra had loaded the babies and her bags into the back of the groundmobile. She sat in the passenger seat waiting for Tara. Hugs were exchanged one last time, then Tara and Syra headed back to town.

"I can't believe it. The house is so big. Isn't it weird how all their houses are fixed into the ground?" Syra watched in awe as Tara drove along the gravel driveway toward the Bryton home.

"You get accustomed to it. Let's get you settled first." Tara parked behind the house. Tara gave Syra a quick tour of the home and showed her where her bedroom would be. She gave her old room to the girl, knowing Hilda wouldn't mind. After Syra seemed somewhat familiar with her surroundings, Tara decided to put her to the test and announced she was going to take a short ride and would be back in a few hours.

"Reach me on the comm for any reason." She made Syra promise then left her playing on the nursery floor with the twins.

Her bike felt so good underneath her. She revved up the motor then took off toward town. Darius wasn't answering his comm so she decided she would go look for him. It had entered her mind, while she was showing Syra around, that she would now be able to spend more time with him. She wasn't sure where he was at the moment and hadn't taken time before leaving the house to track him on her landlink. After driving through Bryton, she wondered if he was out joyriding, too.

Tara rode around town, taking her time and enjoying the aroma of blooming flowers. It was fun riding through the trees, weaving in and out of the brush. Once she hit the open meadow, she pushed her bike and flew at speeds she'd only dreamed about over the past winter.

Instinctively she headed for the back hills, to the cliff where Darius had taken her on their first motorcycle ride, where the twins had been conceived. Now it was her favorite spot, as well. She imagined Darius standing at the edge of the cliff overlooking his reign, lost in thought. She would sneak up on him, giving her Runner skills a much-needed workout.

Tara smiled, deciding she would take him right there and make love to him. Their lovemaking was often interrupted or hurried since their children had been born. They were way past due for some incredible foreplay and heated sex. She drove faster, skillfully dodging the ruts in the earth, enjoying her thoughts.

She bypassed the rugged rocky road leading up the hill, knowing the motorcycle would make too much noise going over the rocks. It was a slow climb riding around the jagged rocks and through tall grass but she enjoyed it. Her heart leapt when she spotted Darius' bike close to where she'd imagined it would be. Tara parked a fair distance before the trees ended and climbed off her bike. The excited pounding of her heart soon changed when she heard voices.

"Why did you bring me here, my lord?" a female voice said. "It would be nice if you would have me in a bed."

Tara almost tripped over a loose branch before she dropped to the ground and crawled through the grass. She couldn't believe what she just heard. Images of Darius' face, so full of love and concern throughout her labor, appeared in her mind. He had repeatedly told her she was beautiful even though she was pregnant with twins.

After the twins were born, he'd not once complained that he had to wait to make love while her body mended. She had hated rushing through their love making when the babies started to fuss. Not a day went by, though, when he hadn't told her that he loved her.

The pain that burned up her insides as she watched her claim through the trees was unlike any pain she had ever experienced in her life.

"Shouldn't a lord's mistress enjoy better comforts than this?""

Tara saw the woman now. She was facing Darius. He wasn't looking at the woman, or in Tara's direction, but staring toward the cliff.

Her heart seemed to stop beating. She couldn't breathe. The air had turned to poison.

He was with another woman.

How could this be? He'd given no indication he was having an affair. Her blood boiled inside her as she listened to the conversation. The pain she'd initially felt hardened inside her and turned to raging fury.

"Don't presume you're anything that merits a title," Darius said.

Tara saw the woman's face, or better yet, the girl's face, no – the *whore's* face! She was young - too young - more than likely not even twenty winters. Her long reddish-blonde hair fell in a mass of curls down her back. Tara was sure she would vomit. The little tramp was beautiful and looked nothing like Tara.

She watched in violated shock as the girl began undressing in front of Darius. She was experienced; Tara guessed she'd undressed in front of men before, seducing them with a toss of her long hair. And the way she played with each button before releasing it! It was disgusting, revolting. She let her dress fall to the ground. Then she reached for Darius' shirt.

Tara was horrified. Every inch of her began to tremble. She couldn't make herself stop shaking as her fury became too much.

The whore placed her hand on Darius, and he didn't stop her. The man showed no apparent emotion, but he let the whore touch him and didn't make a move to prevent her. His gaze appeared to rest somewhere other than the whore's face.

Tara squeezed her eyes closed, momentarily refusing to accept the fact that Darius, her man, her claim, allowed the whore to playfully pull at his shirt until it released from his pants.

He placed his hands on her breasts.

Tara grew livid.

"You'll have me, my Lord, won't you?" The whore ran her hands up Darius' chest underneath his loosened shirt.

Tara flew off the ground and ran into the open. "No, he will not!"

Every muscle in her body spasmed; she feared she might collapse in front of Darius while the disgusting whore still had her hand on his chest. Tara's legs felt mechanical, but they didn't fail her. She pulled her laser free from where it had rested at her hip and aimed it at the woman. The woman screamed and tried to cover her naked body with her arms.

Completely taken off guard, Darius dropped his hands from the woman's breasts and stepped back.

"Get dressed and get out of here," Tara ordered, her laser still aimed at the girl.

Darius put his hands out in front of him, his palms facing Tara. "Tara, don't do anything you'll regret."

"Why not? You have."

The blood boiling in her veins showed right through her eyes. Tara saw red dots popping in her vision. She was on anger overload. The fury was too powerful to control. She shot a venomous look at the whore who was frantically trying to get her dress back on. Tara felt a warped satisfaction that the bitch's body shook so violently she could hardly dress.

"Don't bother with the dress, bitch." The snarl coming out of Tara was absolutely evil. "Just run. Run naked! Let the whole world see you for the fucking whore you are."

The woman froze and stared at Tara in absolute horror. Darius started moving slowly to Tara.

"Run!" Tara screamed and raised her gun to the woman's head.

Now the woman screamed and with dress in hand took off toward the trees.

Tara's body didn't move when she fired the laser, sending the whore's naked body flying into the trees.

Darius lunged at Tara.

She dodged his attack and turned her laser on him, forcing him to a dead stop.

"Tara! Put it down."

"Don't speak to me. I don't need words to add to the scene I just witnessed." She pointed the gun at his head.

"Put down your weapon. It's done."

"You won't get out of this that easily." Tara breathed in gulps of air, as if she'd just run up the side of the hill.

He looked at her, not saying a word.

She stood there thinking for a minute. Her hand was too steady. The laser didn't budge from its target.

"Please then, my lady, put down the laser."

Tara noticed something she hadn't seen in Darius before: fear. The recognition of the emotion seemed to also allow her to witness every other fault the man possessed. She cocked her head and studied Darius, as if truly seeing him for the first time. She lowered her arm.

Darius exhaled noticeably.

Tara watched him. She saw Darius with unyielding clarity at that moment—as if every trait, character defect, every emotion that made the man who he was, had been labeled clearly on him for her appraisal. Tara didn't see good looks, she didn't see sex appeal, and there was no hint of the magnificent warrior. What she saw was a man, impure and tainted, and she wasn't impressed.

Intentionally and with premeditation, Tara raised her laser again and felt a calming satisfaction as his eyes widened, and his lips parted. Then without hesitating, she shot him in the foot.

He went down on one knee and grabbed the bleeding foot with both hands.

"I am no longer your lady." She turned and walked away. Bile churned within her, and sudden spasms made her muscles quiver, but she managed composure. Darius wouldn't see her break from his deed. She wouldn't give him the satisfaction of seeing how he had affected her.

"Tara, where are you going? Come back here."

She heard the pain in his voice, but wasn't sure if it was from being shot, having been caught, or having heard her last words. So much anger and pain racked her entire body that she could no longer speak. She passed his bike and headed to the forest. On impulse, she turned and shot the motor out of his bike.

"Tara, you can't leave."

That was the last she heard him say. She ran. Reaching her bike, she climbed on and destroyed the ground and most of the foliage surrounding it as she spun around and put distance between her and the life-destroying scene.

Her fury surpassed any pain she might otherwise have felt. The horrific scene kept repeating itself in her head. How he had betrayed her! Shit, the woman was no more than a girl. How could he have done something like this to her, to them, to the twins, their new family? He'd brought that tramp to their magical spot. Did the man have no heart, no soul?

As she rode toward the house, she began to wonder how long he'd been unfaithful. She remembered the words Mikel had spoken before Darius had killed him. They haunted her.

Anger so intense she shook from it coursed through her. She couldn't go back to the house in this condition.

Tara rode to the Blood Circle Clan, intent upon talking to Patha. She would leave with him. There was no reason to stay here. Darius had been unfaithful, and he had destroyed their love.

Tears burned her eyes as she drove. No, he was no longer a lord, not in her eyes. He didn't deserve any title of respect. He was Darius, a Gothman, and she'd been fooled into believing he actually thought more of her than he did anyone else.

Her bike slid to a stop in front of Patha's trailer. She jumped off and pulled open the trailer door with a force fueled by the fury wreaking havoc inside her body. Patha was sitting at the table talking to Reena and stood with a start, reaching for his laser, as the door to his trailer flew open.

Tara noticed his surprised expression and knew no one entered his trailer without knocking. She stopped in front of the two of them and yanked the door shut behind her. She was shaking and knew her face was stained from splattering dirt and tears.

"Child, what's wrong?" Reena spoke first as she too hurried to her feet and rushed around the table.

Tara's body now shook uncontrollably, and tears fell so rapidly she barely saw her parents standing in front of her. She tried to speak, but instead savage sobs came out. She gave up and fell into the nearest chair, holding her head in her hands as she cried.

"Tara, control yourself." Reena wrapped her arms around Tara. "What has happened? How can we help if you don't talk to us?"

Patha sat in the chair next to them.

"Something has happened. It's awful. Awful. I just…just can't believe it."

"What? Has someone been hurt? The children? Lord Darius?" Patha asked each question with increasing alarm deepening his voice.

"I found," Tara tried to say the words that would only cause her more pain. "I mean I saw—" She stopped talking and took a deep breath.

Now that she was here, with both her parents looking on with incredible worry, she wasn't sure she could voice the words. She'd have to describe what she'd witnessed and renew her shame, and the betrayal. Saying the words out loud would make it all final, as if otherwise, if she remained silent it might all go away.

"Say it quickly, child." Reena saw the pain in her daughter's face and no matter how much she wiped the tears, more followed.

Tara gave up on trying to focus. If her world remained blurred so might the truth. If she told Patha and Reena that she and Darius had a terrible fight they would believe her. Darius would never enlighten either of them with the truth. He would also see it as a license to do it again. If Tara took care of covering up his unforgivable act, Darius might think it a crime with no true consequences.

Suddenly she saw how women stayed with men who were unfaithful. Some might think that no other man would have them. Tara wasn't a beaten, or defeated soul. But her thoughts did stray toward trying to fix the matter. If she didn't tell anyone but instead dealt with Darius on her own, the matter would go away.

That would simply be lying to herself. It wasn't a healthy, or honorable way to live. If not for herself, she definitely wouldn't exist that way for her children.

"I found Darius with another woman." She quit crying as an incredible numbing sensation crept over her. "I heard them talking…and she was…she was naked. Darius has taken a mistress."

"Oh child, no." Reena wrapped her arms around Tara. "I'm so sorry."

Patha leaned back in the chair and crossed his arms, but didn't speak.

Tara wanted more of a reaction, and decided to keep talking since she'd been able to get out the ugliest of the words.

"I went out looking for him." Her eyes moved from one to the other. "I found him all right. The dishonourable man was with the whore." Anger replaced her tears, and her temper raged once again.

Patha frowned. "Tara, what did you do?"

"I killed his precious mistress, if that's what you're wondering." She stood and walked to the door, then turned and looked at the two of them. "I will get the children, and we'll be back. We're going with you." She reached for the door.

Patha grabbed her arm. "Tara, where is Darius?"

"He's where I found him."

Patha looked her in the eyes, studying her as if seeking an answer he hadn't heard yet. "You didn't kill him, did you?"

Tara yanked her arms from his grasp and turned her rage on him. "How dare you!"

"How dare I what?"

Reena gasped as her eyes shifted from papa to daughter.

Patha, on the other hand, didn't look away from Tara. He crossed his arms, waiting for her answer. He appeared to Tara as he had over so many winters—the patient, but stern gaze that awaited her confession of the truth. Never had she been able to lie to the man, and in truth she had never tried. She saw no reason to change that pattern now.

"How dare you be more concerned for that man than me? I have been wronged! And you're asking if the man is alive or dead?" Tara's voice shook with anger. Her fury locked her jaw. She spoke through clenched teeth as she glared at Patha. "He was going to have sex with another woman. Who knows how many women he's been with? He's a liar and a dishonorable man! In my eyes he no longer has any title, or rank. He's not anyone you should care about at all! You should care about me, papa."

Patha sounded too calm. "You're a strong woman, Tara. You can straighten him out."

"I'm not going to do anything with him." She wanted emotion out of her papa. A reaction—anything. "He's broken my trust and that can't be restored. There will be no second chance."

"Tara, this is bigger than simply your emotions." Patha was straightforward. "The two of you have an obligation to two different races. You must stay and work it out with him. You're under contract. It's as simple as that. These people need your strength."

"I'm not the one who broke the contract." Tara opened the door and ran from the trailer.

CHAPTER TWELVE

TARA SLIPPED her comm around her ear and adjusted its frequency, then contacted the house.

Syra answered the caller, which was the first thing that had gone right since she'd left. It would be easier to get the babies out of the house if Hilda weren't involved.

"Syra, I need you to do something for me." Tara concentrated on sounding as calm and pleasant as possible. Inside her head, her thoughts spun around like a mean wind storm, making it really hard to focus on what she was saying.

"Hi, the babies are fine." Syra assumed Tara was checking up on her.

"Great, I knew you could handle it. Now, I need you to load the babies into the groundmobile for me. Pack a bag with several of their outfits and a blanket or two. I'll also need a basket with some food in it. Can you do that for me?"

"Sure. Where are we going?"

"I thought I'd give you the rest of the afternoon off. The babies and I are going to say goodbye to several people in the clan before they leave," Tara lied. "I'll be there in a minute."

Syra was loading the groundmobile when Tara pulled up. She pushed her bike onto a flat trailer parked nearby. Syra watched with curiosity, but left to get the babies, who were still in the house.

Tara backed the groundmobile up and attached the trailer to the back of it. She then ran inside to her bedroom and hurriedly pulled out several outfits and threw them into her bag. Suddenly the frenzy in her brain came to a stand still. It was as if all thoughts clamouring against each other in her brain stilled. Tara saw, and thought, with pure and perfect clarity.

She paused in front of Darius' dresser. There was a small box buried under his clothes in the bottom drawer. Her hands were colder than ice when she lifted it, rested it on his folded clothes that filled her senses with the painful smell of him. Tara knew there were several small bags filled with gold coins and a few priceless jewels in the box.

One of the bags of coins had been payment for protection. Darius had told her about it. Right after he'd become Lord of Gothman, a feud between several prominent families in Bryton had been brought to his attention. The eldest son of one of the families had been murdered by several members of another family. They'd accused the young man of raping one of their unclaimed daughters, then refusing to claim her. The family with the murdered son had sought retribution and a blood bath had followed. Darius had resolved the feud. At the moment, Tara didn't remember how he'd done it. But the two families had sent Darius a gift of gold coins and rare jewels. Darius had put the coins and jewels in a bag and in this box. It had been his first command decision and the bag was his reward. He planned to never spend it but keep it as if the coins and jewels were a trophy.

She hesitated before dumping the contents into her bag. He'd robbed her, and now she was robbing him. She would need money and Gothman money was no good outside of Gothman. The gold coins and jewels would satisfy any merchant. She dropped the empty bag into the small box and didn't bother burying it back under his clothes. There was a strange empty sensation inside her when she turned and left their bedroom.

Syra was talking to Hilda, who'd just returned when Tara went back downstairs. Tara decided what she would say to the obvious questions as she approached the old lady.

"Did you have a nice time?" Tara asked as she walked past Hilda to go out the back door.

"Ah, it was nice to see everyone." Hilda followed Tara. "I see you took my advice on the nanny."

"Yes, it was a good idea." Tara turned and smiled calmly at Hilda.

"Where are you going?"

"We're going to go say goodbye to several of the Runners before they leave. I'll be gone most of the day. I'm leaving Syra here, if you don't mind. I told her she could have the afternoon off, but I don't see why you can't put her to work if you like." Tara checked to see that she had everything she needed.

"Have fun, my lady. I'll spend the time getting to know the girl." Hilda waved as Tara slowly drove down the driveway.

She followed the road to town until she was sure anyone watching from the house no longer saw her. Tara then pulled off and started heading for a back lane that would turn south. There was no doubt she'd be followed, and all measures would be made to stop her. Her load was heavy, and she would not be able to travel quickly. She turned to look at Andru and Ana who were turning their heads to watch the surroundings move past them. Her stomach tied in knots. She knew it would stay that way until she was out of Gothman.

The first hour passed peacefully. She drove through the meadows on the backside of the hills. If Darius had been up on the cliff he would have seen her. Tara looked in that direction. Even if he stood at the cliff, she wouldn't be able to tell at this distance. More than likely he wasn't in the mood to adore all of the land he controlled. At the moment, he probably didn't feel in control of much of anything.

That thought cheered her up. Even as she decided her happiness came from relishing in his misery, and that someone else's pain had never given her peace before, her mind seemed to relax. She actually started to enjoy the beautiful day and forced all thoughts of what had happened out of her head. If she were going to get through this it was imperative she not think about Darius.

The landlink next to her started blinking. There was little doubt as to what the message might say, and without looking to see who was, she tapped delete. Her comm blinked. Someone was trying to reach her. Tara ignored it. There wasn't anyone she wanted to talk to—and it had to stay that way.

It wasn't much longer before she heard the sound of motorcycles behind her. She'd expected this. Darius wouldn't let her go without a fight. There was no way she could outrun the bikes with her load. Tara drove with one hand and opened the suitcase on the floor of the groundmobile with the other. Inside were several hand bombs and two eliminators.

She pulled an eliminator out and set it on the seat next to her. She had already covered her babies with Runner blankets made out of the same black material as her clothing. The material would repel laser fire, or even shots from Gothman bang sticks. It didn't guarantee Andru and Ana wouldn't be hurt. Nor would Tara rely on the possibility that Darius would order his men not to fire on her or his children. All she had was her own skills and training to protect herself and her son and daughter.

Glancing over her shoulder, several of the bikes were close enough now that she saw the men's faces. She detonated one of the hand bombs and threw it. Three motorcycles skidded sideways across the field as the bomb exploded. Turning to focus her attention on her babies, she spoke soothing words to them and made sure the blanket remained in place around them.

"We'll be through this part soon, my dears," Tara promised, and rubbed Andru and Ana's arms and legs through the blanket. She placed her flat palm on one child's head, and then the other. They were securely belted in, but the rough ride wasn't pleasant and neither infant liked it. "I know you're too young to trust your mama's skills. But I promise we'll live through this. I love you, my sweet babies."

The other motorcycles in pursuit slowed at the explosion. She pushed the groundmobile to go as fast as it was capable.

Gothman territory ended not too far ahead. Then she'd be in Freeland territory. It didn't take long before it was clear the Gothman warriors would follow her outside of Gothman. Darius probably assumed no one would stop him if he chased her to the borders of Southland. He knew so little of Nuworld. Tara counted four Gothman as they increased speed in an attempt to pass and force her to stop the groundmobile.

"Hell be doomed," she hissed, as one of the bikes swerved dangerously close to a front tire.

She couldn't make any sharp turns with the trailer hitched behind her. And she couldn't fire at all four of them at once. "But I can take you out one at a time," she yelled through the wind. Tara leaned around the windshield and shot the rider who had attempted to drive into her.

Tara noticed none of them had drawn their weapons. Maybe they did have instructions not to shoot her. Another guard pulled along the other side of her, while the third came close to the trailer behind her. Tara swivelled her head back and forth in an effort to keep tabs on what all men were doing. The groundmobile bounced over a small gully in the ground, and Tara cursed. Andru howled in protest, and Ana's tiny fists shot forward, knocking the blanket down to the babies' waists.

"We are going to make it through this," Tara insisted, but her babies were crying and didn't hear.

She gripped the steering wheel with one fist, fought to secure the blanket with her free hand, and dared to turn the groundmobile just enough to delay either guard from boarding her.

Tara wouldn't risk shooting behind her, but had no problem eliminating the guard next to her. She was down to two Gothman chasing her.

"You really don't know me that well, Darius, do you?" Tara yelled as she kept her eye on the remaining Gothman. "Not only did you think me easily deceived, but did you think you would capture me with less than an army?"

The guard behind her boarded the trailer and began climbing toward the groundmobile. She wasn't sure where he thought he was going, but if he crawled any closer, he'd be on top of the children. The second guard also mounted the trailer, letting his bike slide on its side to a stop. He successfully detached the trailer from the groundmobile and held on as the trailer slowed to a stop behind her.

She was able to move a lot easier without the trailer attached and yanked the groundmobile in a sharp turn. Andru and Ana were wailing in severe protest. It would take a while to calm them down. Both were hysterical.

"I'll end this soon," she promised them, although she knew neither heard her. They were screaming too loud to hear anything. "How dare you send men after me and upset your babies," she yelled into the air, and her anger toward Darius returned with a vengeance.

The guard hanging on to the back of the groundmobile slid as she spun the vehicle around. She waited until he'd crawled along the outside and was at the door to her side, giving her an easy shot.

Tara fired her laser and the man propelled into the air, then rolled over the ground for quite a distance. Instead of watching his body spin like a pile of clothing caught in the wind, she turned her attention to Andru and Ana. Their faces were red and puffy from crying and her heart lodged in her throat.

"I think we might have pulled this off." Tara smiled at her children, who both acknowledged her with frowns. Ana let out a shriek, which Andru quickly imitated. "Just a little bit longer, sweethearts," she reassured them.

Now for her bike. She drove head on toward the remaining guard, who was struggling to start her bike. The bike was still strapped to the trailer, and he used it as a shield when he watched her approach. If he guessed she would not shoot her bike, he was right. Tara stopped within shouting distance and got out, her laser by her side.

"What are your orders, Gothman?" she asked as she walked toward him.

"You need to come back with me, my lady." His voice shook as he spoke.

Tara noticed he was young. "You won't be successful today in capturing me. Do you realize that?"

The guard peeked at her from behind her bike.

"Are more coming?" Tara pointed her gun straight at his head. He ducked down again behind her bike. She was close enough to hear his breathing. "I'll give you only one more chance to save your life, Gothman. Are more coming?"

"My lady, if we aren't back soon, Lord Darius will send out the next group of warriors."

"I see. Well, if you start running now, you should be seen by them before it gets dark." Tara altered her aim by a fraction, and laser fire sliced through the field, causing several large rocks to fly.

The Gothman shouted his surprise and hunched farther behind her bike.

She walked up to the bike and stood over it.

The guard backed away from her and slowly stood up. He quickly raised his bang stick.

She shot it out of his hand, then cocked her head and gave him a small smile.

The guard turned and ran back toward Gothman territory.

Tara let out a laugh as she let the man go. "Well, my loves, I think we might have won round one."

Andru and Ana must have realized there was a break in the action, because both of them simultaneously let out screams of protest over the experience they had just been forced to endure. Tara hurried back to the groundmobile and the twins.

"It's okay. My sweet babies," Tara cooed as she climbed over the seat and grinned at their outraged expressions.

Both children wanted out of their groundmobile seats and reached for her as she spoke to them. Their screams turned louder now that they had their mama's undivided attention.

"Are both of you okay?" Tara pulled the blanket from their squirming bodies, which resulted in tiny legs kicking even harder. "It appears so," Tara said with a laugh, feeling shaky as adrenaline still pumped through her.

Tara reached behind the seats securing her children and pulled a cloth bag free. "We don't have time to get out and play right now, my dears. But how about a snack while I get us ready for another ride?"

The children fussed, showing their disapproval, but calmed a bit when she produced flat bread and an apple. She peeled and diced before giving them small bites.

It took a long time to hook the trailer back to the groundmobile. The twins were happy while they ate but when they finished wanted to be held. She longed to oblige her children but they had wasted enough time preparing to drive again.

Tara made sure her babies were dry, then calmed them with bottles. It was almost dark when she finally started driving again. While the groundmobile and the trailer left an easy trail in the tall grass for someone to follow, at least night fall made it harder to see. It grew quiet once her children slept. Tara had her thoughts and the pain in her heart to keep her awake.

Patha's comm beeped a second time when he headed off behind Darius' home.

"The less gossip about this matter, the better." Darius said as Patha listened through his comm. "We've accomplished a lot in bringing our two nations together. If word spreads, it will reverse everything we've achieved so far."

"Agreed." Patha decided the lecture Darius had coming to him would wait. "I'm coming to get you."

"Hilda, are you here?" Reena let herself in the back door and moved through the quiet house.

Her friend would be angry, and likely blame Reena for all of it. Hilda had known from the beginning that Tara was Reena's daughter. She'd only seen Tara once, or twice, as an infant. Lord Jovis had been blindly in love with Hilda. It wouldn't surprise Reena to learn that she'd plotted right along with her claim to have Tara claimed to their oldest son. None of that happened. But Hilda had a long memory, and didn't forget. She would definitely find reason for all of this to somehow be Reena's fault. She straightened her spine, ready to go head to head with her dear friend, and walked further into the quiet house.

"Hilda?" she called out a bit louder this time.

"Hello?" Syra walked into the kitchen with a white rag in her hands.

"Ah, it's a good thing you're here. Call your papa, child. He's worried about you."

"He knows I'm here," the teenager said, a bit testily.

Torgo walked through the back door at that moment and froze in mid-step.

Reena ignored the boy's reaction and persisted with Syra. "Tara has left, child. Your papa was scared you went with her. Call him now."

"I still don't understand why I have to check in with him every few hours." She stomped over to the landlink that she'd brought with her from the clan. Her comm was with it and she wrapped it around her ear.

"What do you mean, Tara has left?" Torgo walked over to the counter and grabbed a cookie from a plate that had several more on it. He watched Syra as he stuffed the entire cookie in his mouth.

"I think Lord Darius should explain the situation. All I can say is that Tara and the babies are gone."

"They went out to say goodbye to some of the Runners." Syra said, her tone indicating she thought the old lady was confused.

"Is Hilda upstairs?" Reena wasn't going to explain anything to the children. She didn't feel it was her place, and she knew Lord Darius would be more furious than he already was if he came home to a household apprised of the situation. Reena had been more than willing to not be part of rescuing the injured lord. It would be bad enough facing Hilda. Leaving the two of them, she headed upstairs.

"Hilda, may I come in?" Reena tapped on her friend's bedroom door.

"Reena?" Hilda was working on a sampler for her grandchildren's bedroom wall. "Is something wrong?"

Reena entered the bedroom and shut the door. "Tara has left Darius." Reena pursed her lips. "She and the babies are gone."

Hilda let her sewing fall to her lap. "What?" Hilda asked in disbelief. "You say it like she is really gone. They went to say bye to some of her Runner friends."

"She caught him, Hilda. He should have known Tara wouldn't stand for that behavior."

Hilda gathered her sewing and stood to face her lifetime friend. "How do you know she is gone? Where are the babies?"

"Tara went to the clan site. She came to Patha's trailer," Reena began, watching her friend closely.

Reena then told Hilda about Tara's visit. She stopped talking every time she heard a noise from somewhere in the house.

"She took our grandbabies with her." Reena concluded. "Patha went to get Lord Darius. Your son won't get her back, not unless she wants to come back."

Hilda just looked at her friend. "My son has more power than he can handle. His actions have surprised me more than once." Her words were strained, and Reena knew she referred to her two dead sons. "But don't think your daughter's bullheadedness matches my son's power. If he wants it to happen, he will force Tara to return. And he will get my grandbabies back!"

Torgo and Syra didn't give any thought to the conversation taking place upstairs. They leaned on opposite sides of the island counter in his kitchen and stared at each other.

"So after my clan leaves, I'm staying here and helping Tara with the babies." Syra leaned against the counter and studied the golden hair on Torgo's arm. "Of course, I'm sure I will have plenty of time for other things, too."

Torgo had just put another cookie in his mouth and almost choked on it. "Like what?" he asked with his mouth full and slapped at the crumbs that he spit on the counter.

Syra shrugged. "What do you do around here for fun?"

Torgo had a hard time looking at her face and not her rather large breasts. She looked soft and curvy. He wasn't too sure what he'd do, exactly, if he had a chance to be alone with her. And he meant really alone. The opportunity to find out sounded like it couldn't happen soon enough.

"I dunno." He shrugged. Torgo tried thinking of one thing he did at his house, just to answer her. But he saw breasts, his groin hardened, and he knew he couldn't move from where he leaned over the counter. "I could do something with you…uhh…I mean, maybe show you around…"

Torgo jumped when Patha and Lord Darius bounded through the back door. He panicked that he'd permanently injured himself when his hardened dick banged against the cupboard door beneath the counter.

"Tell Reena to come here," Patha yelled, in spite of the teenagers being in the same room.

Syra ran from the kitchen.

Torgo looked at the blood on his older brother's foot. He wasn't wearing his boot. "What happened to you?"

"Not now." Darius gestured to Torgo, looking seriously irritated. "Help me get upstairs."

A second look at his brother and all thoughts of large breasts and personal injuries vanished. Darius was really hurt. Torgo became a human crutch for his older brother as he helped him to the stairs.

Once Darius was in his room, Reena had Syra on the run gathering necessary items to mend his wound. Torgo loitered in the hallway, catching bits and pieces of the very alarming news.

"Send out four of your fastest riders," Patha said into his comm, as he shut Darius' bedroom door behind him. "She's not to be hurt, you understand? Those babies are with her, and I want them all back here before nightfall."

"I can't believe she didn't take me with her," Syra whined later as she joined Torgo. The house had settled a bit, and they stood in the stairwell, leaning over the banister that opened below into the front entryway. Torgo wanted to suggest they go to his room, but didn't have the nerve and couldn't imagine what he would say to her once they got there. At least she was talking to him, so all he had to do was nod and watch her. "My clan is leaving. Now Tara's left, and I'm stuck here."

"I don't mind you being stuck here." Torgo blushed so deeply he looked down at the ground. He was grateful for the deep shadows in the hallway. "I mean, I get really bored most of the time. It'll be nice to have someone my age to talk to, uh, sometimes."

Great, now he was talking like a bumbling idiot. He glanced sideways at her, hoping she hadn't noticed. Just being near her raised his body temperature.

Syra guessed from Torgo's actions that he hadn't been around many girls. She'd love to teach him a thing or two. It brought a smile to her face that she made him blush and feel awkward. He was so cute, already pretty developed. And, he was a lot taller than she was—that in itself was a bonus—especially since she was taller than most boys her own age.

"My papa and I travel around a lot, and there aren't many people my age to hang out with either."

There were boys her age in the clan, but she didn't want Torgo to think she'd been with a whole bunch of them. And she hadn't, really, just a few.

"He's really lucky she just shot him in the foot," Syra continued, dropping her tone so as not to be overheard. She wanted to keep their conversation going.

"I know. If she shot his foot then that is where she wanted to shoot him."

They were quiet for another moment or two, trying to figure out what else to say to each other.

"Maybe you could show me…" Syra began, but stopped talking when footsteps sounded on the stairs.

Patha approached them and passed, not seeming to notice they were there as he entered Darius' room. It was easy to overhear the conversation beyond the partially open door. "They found her, but she easily got away from them," Patha said.

"I'm not surprised. She isn't going to get caught unless she wants to. Still, I can't let her get away from me like this."

"You've made a mess for yourself, son."

"No lectures, please. Things are bad enough as they are."

"I suggest you let me look for her when we leave tomorrow. We know she headed south, and she'll probably pass through one of the towns to restock. I'll be able to find her."

"Ah, but will you be able to bring her back?"

"Son, you're going to have to do that. You've made a terrible mistake, and she'll not forgive you easily. I'll find her for you, but you'll have to do the convincing."

Patha came out of the room, and Syra and Torgo tried to look as if they hadn't been eavesdropping. Patha still seemed uninterested in them, but he paused and turned to address them before he reached the stairs. "Syra, I guess you should come with me, and I'll take you back to your papa. There's no reason for you to stay here." He disappeared down the stairs.

"Great, more time alone with my papa," Syra groaned. "I wish I went with her. This isn't fair." She stamped her foot on the ground before following Patha.

They didn't leave right away, however. Hilda insisted Patha and Reena stay for supper, as it was about ready. Darius hobbled downstairs with his wrapped foot and endured the looks his mama gave him as she set the table.

She finally started to cry over the loss of her grandbabies and the woman who had taken them. Torgo didn't want to hear his brother yell at his mama, so he slipped out into the backyard. His brother had made his mama cry one too many times, and it was more than he wanted to hear right now.

When Syra saw the opportunity, she followed him.

"You know, you're complaining that you have to leave, and I wish I didn't have to stay." Torgo leaned against the shed staring at the star-filled sky. He switched his gaze to her as she approached him.

"Is this yours?" Syra ran her hand over his bike.

"Yeah, and it was Tara who taught me to ride."

"That's why I was here, to earn money to buy my first bike."

The two were silent then Syra had an idea. It was really awful, and she didn't want Torgo to get the wrong impression if she brought it up. He'd started shining his handlebars with his shirt. His blond hair was a mass of tousled curls and his gray eyes were lighter, not as deadly as his older brother's. He'd be nice to have as a boyfriend, she decided.

"Don't take this the wrong way or anything," she began and looked back toward the house to make sure no one else had come out. "Why don't we go find her ourselves?"

"What?" Torgo whispered the word. "There's no way we would get out of Gothman. Both of us together don't have half the skills Tara has."

"It's not like they are going to hurt us if they catch us. It would be an adventure, and I'm going to be bored to death if I have to spend a couple cycles alone with my papa." Syra looked at Torgo slyly. "Are you scared?"

"Of course not!" he declared. "I'm just not going to take off running without a plan. Let me think about it. We also shouldn't leave before supper."

"Can you get out of the house tonight?" Her mind was already scheming.

"I guess so."

"I'll have to leave after we eat with Patha and Reena. You'll leave half an hour after we do and meet me at the edge of the clan site, on the west side. We'll be out of Gothman before anyone missed us. I'm sure of it with the speed this bike probably has. I bet it takes the rough terrain a lot better than a Runner bike." She smiled at him to see what he thought.

Torgo didn't have a better plan. The thought of listening to his brother scream and yell at everyone because he'd made a mess out of his life sounded worse than running away. He nodded and headed toward the house. There was no way he would back out or give her any indication, but he was scared to death to take off on his own. He'd never been outside Gothman territory, and the stories he'd heard didn't make him want to leave.

Syra left with Patha and Reena and headed back to the Runner's camp. She didn't speak to either of them, but then she never did. They were so old and never understood anything she talked about. Instead of sulking however, she made a mental list of things she would need. She walked through her trailer with her bag that already had her clothes and landlink in it. Quite convenient, she thought.

"Ah, there you are, my girl," Balbo said, as Syra entered their trailer. "Hard to believe your papa missed you when you were gone far less than a quarter-cycle."

"No one to show you how you are always wrong?" Syra rolled her eyes at her papa, but found herself smiling. She guessed as far as papas went she had a pretty good one, for the most part.

"I felt lost without anyone to argue with." Her papa returned her smile and reached to pull at her headscarf.

She ducked past him and headed for her room. Once in there she began

pacing as four walls closed in around her. Somehow she needed to get food, and enough for both of them for at least several days.

"Syra, I'll be back shortly."

"Okay, Papa." This was perfect.

In the kitchen, she took things she thought wouldn't be missed immediately if her papa were to look. She did most of the cooking, so she hoped he didn't know what was there. She filled a bag with food, grabbed her bag of clothes, and left the trailer.

Torgo was on the west side of the clan when she got there, looking nervous as he sat on his bike. He had side bags into which she stuffed her belongings. Then she climbed on behind him. Her heart leaped as she inched her legs along his and slowly moved her hands around his waist.

"I thought you'd never get here." His bike rumbled noisily as he left the clan site.

CHAPTER THIRTEEN

"THIS ISN'T on the map." Tara tapped from screen to screen on her landlink as she spoke aloud to herself. She'd driven all night and halfway through the next day. The babies were grouchy and so was she.

Runners seldom travelled into land close to Southland. They knew of scattered towns, but that was it. All morning she'd been traveling through uncharted land, having already left the Freelands. The River People lived near the border but they weren't an organized government and had no officially claimed land. Now a wide river blocked her path.

The river flowed from the west and curved in front of her, heading south beyond her ability to see. Her only choice was to travel alongside it. There was nowhere to cross. She added the river to her landlink map, taking it upon herself to chart the area.

After travelling along the river's edge until the sun was on her back, Tara spotted a large hauling watermobile moored at a small port. Several buildings, their walls warped wood that was well baked by the sun, lined the edge of the river. She parked alongside the nearest building.

Tara put Andru into the back carrier then shrugged into the shoulder straps. She lifted Ana in her arms, and the three walked toward the hauling watermobile. A large man ambled off the dock and tossed several bags onto the ground. He didn't look at her until she cleared her throat.

"Where does this watermobile go?"

"South all the way to the border. If you have good paper." The man spoke with the distinguishable River People accent. He took a good look at Tara and her babies. "Been travelin' a while, have you?"

"Long enough. How much paper?"

"Six dorsels a person, no matter their age." He eyed the babies.

"I have gold."

"Change it over at the building. That way." The large man rubbed his hand over his unshaven face and studied Tara. He couldn't quite figure out her accent but knew he'd heard it before. She'd been traveling awhile...and so pretty...odd she didn't have a man with her. Those two babies would turn most men away, but with her looks...he scratched his whiskers some more. How did he know that accent?

Tara spotted the building, it being the one closest to the dock, where the large man had directed her. She pushed her way inside. It was warmer in the building than it had been outside.

"I need dorsels," Tara said, dropping several pieces of gold on the counter in front of a small wiry man, who straightened where he'd been leaning when she entered.

He handed her a stack of paper and she studied it, not familiar with the currency. The sheets were thin, dyed red, and there was a numeral two in each corner of the rectangular shape. She counted the papers by two and came up with twenty.

"Are you sure this is right?" She only knew what she'd heard around the fires. River People were always out to make the better end of a deal.

The man grunted and handed her three more pieces of paper.

"How much to haul a groundmobile and bike?"

"Ten apiece."

"How far will you take me?"

"To the border. The hauling watermobile don't go past the border." The wiry man tapped the counter with a bony finger. "You pay to come back, too."

"And meals? They're included with this outrageous price, I assume?"

"Yeah, but I don't know that the cook will be fixing food they can eat." He pointed his long finger at the babies.

Tara took the dorsels. She returned to the large unshaven man now loading bags onto the hauling watermobile.

"Where you heading?" He took her money and rubbed his whiskers as he stared at the groundmobile and bike Tara had just paid to have loaded.

"South."

"There's a lot to see down that way."

"Have you been south of the border?" Tara wouldn't mind some good stories, and as unappealing as this man was, he was the first adult she'd spoken to since leaving Gothman.

Taffley studied the young woman and her babies. She was quite brown from the sun and in dire need of a shower. Her hair was stringy from sweat, and her dress clung to her thin body. She was beautiful, though. In fact, she was quite sexy. He liked dirty women.

He didn't entertain too much hope of catching her eye. Women like her seldom had much of an interest in men like him. But there was something off with her. Taffley met all kinds of people on his hauling watermobile. Be them good or bad by nature, he never turned away paper. It was all the same no matter how stained the hand it came from. He scrubbed his jaw and gave his brain a good workout trying to learn where this woman was from without asking. Taffley never had to ask—and he was seldom wrong.

His thoughts returned to her accent. It bothered him when he wasn't immediately able to tell what race a person was. You knew a lot about a person when you knew where they were from and what their people were. Then he noticed a necklace around her neck. It was a circle with a very nice looking ruby in the middle of it.

"Yeah, I've been to a town or two in Southland." He looked at the necklace one more time and it hit him harder than if his watermobile had banked itself. Panic ransacked his entire body. "Go on aboard. Take the cabin on the left side in the hall." Taffley hurried away, afraid his fear would register in his words.

Runners could smell fear.

The man who owned the hauling watermobile seemed nervous about something, but Tara was too worn out to care. She walked onto the watermobile and down a hall with several doors on each side. The farthest door on the left was slightly open. She peeked in and saw a bed sprawled in one corner. A table with two chairs pushed under it filled the other corner. An old dresser stood next to the door. One half-open window provided dim light that barely blanketed the wooden floor and walls. She left her bags in the room and carried her children out to watch the large man bring her groundmobile and bike on board.

Taffley drove the groundmobile with attached trailer up a large plank and parked them on the back of his watermobile. His hands shook as he worked. That pretty little lady he'd been drooling over was a Runner. He recognized the symbol of the Blood Circle clan. The motorcycle matched the clan as well. The most dangerous race in the world. That clan called themselves that because they didn't hesitate to draw blood. He'd heard all the stories.

Why was she dressed like that? Runners didn't travel alone. For some reason, she didn't want anyone to know who she was. This bothered him even more. No doubt about it, she was going to be trouble for him.

He looked at Tara and walked onto the dock, muttering to himself. He didn't need trouble on his hauling watermobile. This was his only means of getting paper—dorsels always preferred but if a deal was to be made, well he owned the hauling watermobile. That always put him at the better end of any bargaining. But with a Runner on board. Hell be doomed! This would be trouble for sure.

A few moments later, he entered the wooden purchasing and exchange building. "Saffle, d'you see that lady that come this way with those babies?" Taffley spoke to the wiry man.

"Yeah, she had gold."

"She's a Runner."

"Taffley, you're water-logged for sure. She wasn't dressed like no Runner."

"I tell you she's a Runner. I know that accent, and she had the sign of the Blood Circle clan around her neck." He scratched his jaw and turned to look at his ferry.

Saffle laughed. "I never heard you to complain a pretty lady's on your hauling watermobile. Did you hear me? I said she had gold. Runners don't have money. They want to barter their services, more exact their protection. Only thing I needs protected from is them," he finished, and laughed some more.

"I knew that accent." Taffley ignored Saffle's laughter and continued staring out the open door toward his watermobile. "But when I saw that necklace. Now you tell me right now who would wear the symbol for the Blood Circle clan around their neck if they weren't no Runner? Tell me that now."

"If what you say's true, you've a problem on your hands." Saffle pulled a piece of paper from under his desk. "This came through with all the mail today. They've been passing 'em out, from what I hear."

Taffley turned from the door and took a wrinkled piece of paper from Saffle's bony hand. His face fell as he looked at the contents on the paper. The top of the page said *REWARD* and a description followed. Oddly enough, it was Gothman writing, and the reward was Gothman currency. It was large: ten thousand Gothman gold coins offered for the whereabouts or return of a lady and two babies. The woman was described as a Runner, but it was said she might not appear in Runner clothing. The babies were twins, a boy and a girl, six cycles old.

"That's a lot of money." Taffley scratched his beard.

"What are you going to do?"

"I'm going to take her to the border. She's a Runner. I'm not going to cross her." Taffley smiled. "You put a wire through and let them know our destination and where they can pick her up. You say I expect payment in full before I turn her over."

Inside her room, Tara pushed the table in front of the door and began exploring. She found a small, connecting bathing room—with only one door. She was thrilled that she wouldn't have to share bath water with another passenger.

Fatigue was taking over, so she decided to wash herself and the babies. Perhaps a cool bath and clean clothes would revive her. She left her laser on the bathroom counter and began filling the tub.

The children splashed the water as Tara scrubbed the dirt and grime from all of them. She then soaked while the twins' delighted squeals as they played helped relax her.

Suddenly, the water in the tub splashed to one side and her babies slid into her. She grabbed them and held on as the hauling watermobile pushed off from the dock. They rocked as it slipped into the river currents. Tara held her infants close to her body until the movement slowed.

After dressing the rambunctious babies in matching one-piece outfits, she put on a clean dress. A bell sounded, and she recognized the large man's voice when he yelled that food was ready.

A long table was set up in the open area at the front of the watermobile. Tara was his only passenger. There was a chair set at each end of the table and to her delight, two smaller chairs with straps were set on either side of one end of the table. Andru and Ana seemed to know they were getting fed when they didn't complain about being strapped in. And if the large man noticed how they used the same hand when they reached for something on the table at the same time, he didn't comment.

The menu consisted of fried fish, new potatoes, and a leafy green vegetable on each plate. Tara hadn't noticed how hungry she saw the food. The twins were equally enthusiastic about getting fed.

"I don't really have food for the babies." Taffley sat at his end of the table. "I found some bread and squash. You can feed them that, if you want."

"Thank you." She smashed the squash on two plates and tore bits of bread. Andru and Ana began snatching the bits of food the instant it was on their plates.

The babies made a mess, and the man ate loudly. Tara didn't mind either. The hot food gave her energy. She enjoyed every bite and willingly accepted a second helping of fish. The babies also ate well and contentedly sucked on bottles of juice after the meal was over. Tara sat back as the man lit several torches and cleared the table. The large wheel rotating under the ferry made a soft swooshing sound in the water. It was peaceful, and Tara began to relax for the first time since she'd left Gothman.

Later, she sat on the edge of the bed rocking her two children until their bodies grew limp in her arms. She'd taken two of the drawers out of the dresser and filled them with blankets. Her babies looked beautiful as they lay asleep in their makeshift cradles. She admired them in the moonlight, and thought of how they looked like Darius.

A noise on deck forced her to push him out of her thoughts. She reached for her laser and held it low as she walked down the hallway.

Creaking boards told her someone was there. She stood very still using the shadows in the dark hallway to hide her position. Taffley was leaning over the front of the watermobile, holding a pole extended out over the water. She heard another creak coming from above the doorway. Whoever was there chose that moment to jump down onto the main floor with his back to her.

The noise startled Taffley, who turned around as the intruder raised their weapon.

Tara didn't hesitate. She shot the intruder in the back. The sound of a yelp followed by a splash told Tara another, much less brave, attacker had been on board. Tara stepped out of the shadows.

The large man approached the dead body. He heaved the limp figure into his arms and dumped it overboard. "Much obliged." He looked wide-eyed at her as he walked to the other end of the watermobile, evidently making certain no one else was in the water. "Damn thieves."

Tara walked to the edge alongside him and listened. She was satisfied they were now alone and turned to look at the man. He didn't say anything, but walked past the table where they'd ate, leaned over and began stirring a fire to life in an iron stove.

Tara turned to go back to her cabin.

"Stay." It was more of a suggestion than a command.

She turned and looked at him.

"I won't hurt you. Heavens knows I'm no match. I'll admit you scare me to death." He smiled and showed off dirty teeth and several dark holes where teeth had once been. "Name's Taffley. Sit and tell one of your stories."

"One of my stories?"

"Come now, all Runners have stories. I've heard some good ones in my time."

"What makes you think I'm a Runner?"

"Several things, lass. You wear the Blood Circle clan symbol around your neck. Your motorcycle is a Runner's bike, and you've just shown me the skills of a Runner." He pointed to the chair she'd used during dinner. "Sit. If you will."

Tara did so and looked up at the stars. Her fingers instinctively played with the telltale necklace. It was unbelievable that she'd forgotten she wore it. Tara loved the necklace and that Darius would give such a precious gift. Although it crossed her mind to rip it from her neck and toss it in the river, instead she let her hand drop and the necklace remain around her neck. Just because Darius had done her wrong didn't mean she had to take it out on the necklace. She watched as Taffley got up and went over to a cabinet built in the wall.

He opened it and pulled out a large bottle and two clay cups. Taffley poured some of the contents into each cup, then set one in front of Tara. "The Sea People make an excellent wine. It's become quite rare lately. Their economy's crashed, you know." He offered the information as if it were common knowledge and leaned back down in his chair.

"You said you'd been south of the border." She took a sip of the wine.

"Yeah, Southland." He took a large drink and made a face, then took another drink and set the cup on the table. "Why d'you want to go there?"

"I haven't been there."

"A true Runner response." He laughed and drank the rest of his wine. He offered Tara more after pouring some in his own cup, but she shook her head. "What's your name?"

"Tara. Tell me what the people are like down there. Are they warriors?"

"Well now, some of them are. None to match you Runners, that's for sure. They were doing pretty well for themselves, had lots of currency to spend 'til the Sea People started that war up north. From what I've heard, they lost pretty badly. They didn't know them Gothman would go and hitch up with you all Runners. Strange people the Sea People are." Taffley stopped to wet his mouth. "Ever met one?"

"No, not personally." Tara wanted to hear about the south, not the north, but decided to be patient.

"They come across nice enough. Gave me a fair bit of business there for awhile. Not very trusting people, though." He sipped more wine and stared at the black water lapping against the side of his watermobile. "Southland is real good for growin' this opiate plant, you see. All I did for the longest time was haul the harvests across the border. That's all done now. The towns down there are hurting pretty bad. No reason to grow their crops because there's no one buying their harvest."

"The Sea People don't want it anymore?"

"I'm sure they want it. They just can't pay for it. They're broke, you see. Plenty of money they owe me." Taffley poured more wine into their glasses.

"What should I expect when I get to the border?" She swooshed the purple liquid around in the cup but didn't take a drink. "How far to the closest town?"

Taffley thought about how to answer. He imagined what she would see when they got to the border. Saffle had sent that wire. Tara would be picked up the second she got off his hauling watermobile. A twinge of guilt ran through him. She'd saved his life, and now he was turning her in for the money. He focused on the reward. It would clear all the debts he'd created when he still thought the Sea People would pay him for his services. It was a good bargain he'd made. After all, he was risking his life hauling this Runner and her babies.

"The first town is Semore. On that groundmobile of yours it will be about half a day ride from the border. There's Pixley, which is further south, but you also have to drive a little west to get to it. The roads starting at the border go to Semore, though. After Semore are Highton and New Hanger. All those towns are under the same government and use the same coins. They've got some good ideas down there. It makes sense to have the same rules and money. I guess you'd have to see how they live to understand." Taffley wondered if she would ever be able to go there.

"Are they all the same people?" Tara tried to picture what he'd described. Her excitement grew at the thought of being the first Runner to explore a new land. "Who's their ruler?"

"Well now, that's where they are real different. They don't have a ruler."

"What? That would be complete chaos!" She took a drink of her wine and pulled her legs up, getting comfortable in her chair.

"You'd think. But it's not. They have a bunch of people in charge. I can't remember what they call it, but all the people get together every five winters and vote on who the people in charge are going to be." Taffley got up and pulled a blanket out, shook it, then walked over and wrapped it around Tara. "Can't let it be said one of my passengers got sick on my watermobile."

"People say who their leader is going to be?" Tara adjusted the blanket around her, pondering the concept. "Who is in charge right now?"

"The main guy is Gowsky, I think. Never met him. Don't have cause to, you see. He's got a mess on his hands. They were all accustomed to plenty of paper, and coins. They had both. Except now, there is none."

Tara never thought how their war might affect so much of Nuworld. People who didn't know her were struggling to keep their towns going because of decisions she and Darius had made.

Tara suddenly came to the conclusion that a ruler would indeed be great if he or she were aware of all of the people around him or her, and not just familiar with a little corner of Nuworld. Darius had never been out of Gothman. Would he ever know what life was like outside his kingdom?

"What you thinking, Tara?" Taffley cocked his whiskery face at her.

"About everything you've just said. I look forward to meeting these people. It sounds like they need help getting back on their feet."

"Well now, how would you help them?" Taffley sounded curious.

"I don't know. You said they grew something the Sea People needed. Maybe there is something else they grow that another race might use." Tara was anxious now to continue her journey and meet these people. "Like I said, I don't know. I'll have to wait and see what their land is like and what they're like. What do they think of strangers?"

"Anyone can come and go through their towns. That's something everyone knows. Though I don't know what they'd think of a Runner. They kind of blame you all for their turn of fate, you see. People say the Sea People could've beat Gothman if it weren't for the Runners. I've heard that the Lord of Gothman got tricked…"

Taffley stopped talking, and his mouth fell open. Now, he'd never been accused of being a real bright man. He liked what he did and tried to keep peace with everyone with whom he did business. Still, he'd learned many things sitting at this table with his passengers. He'd almost said that he'd heard about a beautiful woman, who turned out to be a Runner, and had tricked the Lord of Gothman. That's what he was about to say, but then he figured something out.

"You're the one, aren't you? No wonder there's so much money on your head!" Taffley slapped his hand over his mouth. Hell be doomed! Southland wine always made him talk too much.

"What did you say?"

"Oh, I'm as bad as an old woman." Taffley hung his head and pulled a piece of paper from his shirt pocket. He tossed the paper across the table.

Tara picked it up and held it by the lantern. Slowly she wrinkled it up as she made a fist. Then she started looking really angry.

CHAPTER FOURTEEN

"I CAN'T believe this. The notice makes it sound like I'm his property." Tara began to fume all over again.

"Gothman women are property." Taffley said with a shrug.

"I'm not Gothman!" Tara slammed her fist on the table.

Taffley jumped and knew he'd hit a nerve. Was it a bad decision showing the paper to her? If this made her angry, what would she do when she learned she was floating into a trap?

A loud boom exploded in the night air. Taffley screamed! He staggered out of his chair and reached for the bottle of wine. He didn't have his wits about him before another boom made his heart race too fast to breathe.

Bang sticks!

Tara squatted next to her chair and adjusted her laser to scan for life-signs. Whoever fired was too close. The explosions had been so loud she wasn't able to hear if her babies were crying. Although it was a good guess that they were.

She pointed the laser toward the woods along the river, judging where the shots had come from. People were yelling, and although the red beam on the laser found their attackers, she didn't need it. They were making enough noise to be easy targets. She set her laser to kill just as Taffley grabbed something else out of that closet where he'd pulled his wine. He took off running and the next thing she knew he was climbing the ladder to the top of his watermobile.

Hell be doomed! Someone had, more than likely, scared her children to death, and for that alone deserved to die. Now Taffley was on top of the ferry, and he had started shooting. The darn fool was going to get killed.

Tara shot at three individuals on the bank. A splash in the water and a howl let her know one of them had fallen in. She saw another fall from a tree. The third jumped in the water of his own accord and started swimming toward them.

Taffley aimed his long bang stick at the person in the water, and another loud explosion ran through the air. The man in the water let out a bloodcurdling scream. His arm floated away from his body.

Taffley's bangstick had such a kick she saw him stumble back after firing. For a second, she envisioned Taffley falling down his ladder, but he steadied himself and looked around at the now calm waters.

"Sure are a lot of thieves lately," he muttered as he came back down the stairs. "We live in a land of no laws. Take care of your own, that's the River People's law. I've learned to protect my property. Keeps one on his toes. They say a government will stop all this, but I don't see it happening."

Tara ignored his rambling and ran down the short hall to Andru and Ana. Both of her children were crying loudly. She almost slid into the room and reached for the twins. Tiny hands simultaneously grabbed her fingers and held on as if their lives depended on it.

"You're safe, sweet babies. I swear it," she promised and scooped both children into her arms. It was all she could do to calm her outrage in order to soothe her babies.

Taffley walked to the edge of the hallway, but respecting her privacy, talked to her without coming to her door. "I'll keep a watch tonight. You don't worry none about them babies. I'll keep them safe. Ain't no thief ever boarded my hauling watermobile."

Tara doubted Taffley's ability to keep them safe, but thanked him and pulled the children up on the bed. Within moments, the three of them were sound asleep.

It seemed just minutes later when Tara opened her eyes to the sun streaming through the open window of her room. Ana lay cuddled next to her, sleeping soundly, while Andru played with his feet. He smiled broadly at her when she looked at him. The smile looked just like his papa's. Tara lay there, holding both of them tightly, feeling pain from the loss of the only man she'd ever loved. Tears came to her eyes and she let them flow.

It wasn't long before both babies were fully awake and ready to play. Tara had to put her own thoughts aside and focus on her children. As she sat on the floor of the small room, tickling and playing with them, she heard Taffley whistling through the wooden walls as he prepared breakfast. Every now and then he groaned. She imagined he was either hung over from the wine, or not used to firing that large bang stick of his.

The bell announcing that food was ready came shortly, and Tara picked up the babies and headed out to the table. She was surprised to feel how warm it was outside.

"We've had someone following us through those trees over there," Taffley said as Tara secured the babies into their chairs. "If you want to eat in your room, I can set the table in there."

Tara looked at the trees and heard the low rumble of a motorcycle. She squinted and saw two people riding the bike. They were matching the pace of the hauling watermobile and staying just out of view through the trees.

"If you'd help me push the babies chairs to my room, I'd appreciate it."

She walked back to the room, pushing Ana in her chair. Taffley followed with Andru. Her son talked gibberish in a very demanding tone. It made her think of Darius. Not the gibberish. Andru spoke in such an insistent manner. He sounded as if he had the answers and wasn't too patient about explaining them, just like his papa.

Once again she shoved the man out of her head. Andru would never be like Darius. Tara would raise him to be better than that.

She watched the bike through her window as she fed the babies their breakfast. Why wasn't its rider attacking like the others? They paced the hauling watermobile—watching, learning, yet not attacking. It was a Runner strategy, but that wasn't a Runner bike.

"Tara?" A voice shouted her name.

She jumped, startled, and rushed to the window. "I don't believe it!" She ran out of the room and onto the deck.

"Stop the watermobile," a voice yelled.

"Not on your life." Taffley raised his bang stick to fire.

"Taffley, no!" Tara cried out, but it was too late.

Taffley fell to the ground as laser fire shot across the water and knocked him off the deck. He yelled loudly and looked at his smoking leg. Dark blood started soaking through the torn material of his pants.

"Put that laser down now!" Tara yelled to the shore.

She ran over to Taffley and propped him up against the deck.

"Tara, you've got to make him stop," Torgo yelled. He and Syra were now visible on the shore of the river.

"Who are they?" Taffley was grimacing from the pain.

"A couple of kids. What they're doing here is the question!" Tara looked back at the two sitting on Torgo's bike.

"Tara, can you hear me?" Torgo yelled.

"Yes, I can hear you."

"You're floating into a trap. There's a mob down there just waiting for you. They'll turn you in for the price on your head."

Tara looked at Taffley, who kept his eyes pinned to the deck. "How do we stop this thing?"

He got up slowly. Holding onto his bleeding leg, he limped to the back of the watermobile. She didn't follow. Her babies wailed. Tara hurried to them, deciding the many mothers in her clan who had always appeared calm as the clan travelled had to have been very good actors.

Taffley yelled at her. "Hold onto those little ones. I'm dropping the catch hold. When it digs into the river bottom, it will cause quite a lurch."

Tara gripped the sides of the babies' chairs and braced her feet as the watermobile jerked to a stop. It was suddenly very quiet all around them.

"Word is traveling all over the place that you are on a ferry headed to the border," Torgo yelled, breaking the silence.

Tara left her children with their breakfast, hoping the calm surrounding them would be enough for them not to cry.

"I wonder how they found out." Tara marched on to the open deck and glared at Taffley.

"All I knew was that you were a Runner. People 'round here's scared of Runners. I'd already let you on my hauling watermobile when I saw the reward being offered." Taffley looked sincerely forlorn as he stared at her. "I don't know why you're wanted, but I can't imagine whatever you did was all that bad."

"I didn't do anything wrong."

Taffley looked at the two kids sitting on the bike on the shore. He nodded in their direction. "If things are as bad as those two say, the thieves attacked us to get to you." He shook his head.

"There'll be more. Probably soon. You'd stand a better chance if you get off on the other side of the river."

Tara studied the water. The river was wide. She spotted a few sandbars ahead of them and nodded in that direction. "How far to the border?"

"Half a day, if you drive. We'll get there tonight if you stay on board. If you drive straight south, you'll cross the desert. Another half a day of heading west and you'll hit the road."

"We need to get the groundmobile and my bike off this thing." She started yelling instructions to Torgo and Syra. "Cross the river up there by the sandbars. Torgo, give it some speed when you hit the water."

Taffley was obviously feeling the pain from his wound as he hobbled around. He didn't complain. To his credit, he made quick work of removing the straps from the groundmobile and bike. More than likely he'd decided it there wasn't a reward in it for him, his hauling watermobile would be safer with her and the twins off of it.

Tara loaded the babies into their seats in the back of the groundmobile, much to their dismay. A bit more of their breakfast, a few select toys, and Andru and Ana seemed content.

"What can we do to help?" Torgo lifted himself out of the water onto the deck. He'd parked his bike on the shore after driving to the other side, then he and Syra had swum out to join them.

"Hell be doomed! What are you two doing here?" Tara showed her rage. "This isn't a game."

"You promised me a job." Syra shrugged, not caring if Tara yelled, and wrung water from her hair.

"You can't stay with me. You'll both get killed." Tara wasn't in the mood for a mouthy teenager.

"You're not so great you couldn't get killed yourself." Syra's eyes flared. "Especially with two babies. You need help."

Torgo spoke up. "My brother isn't going to stop looking for you, or his children, no matter where you go."

"'Scuse me. I hate to break up this family feud, but are you all getting off, or not?" Taffley shifted his gaze from the dripping teenagers to the irate Runner.

"Yes, we are." Tara continued to glare at Torgo and Syra. "Okay, you want to work? You got it. Syra, take my bike off the trailer. It will lighten the load when we drive the groundmobile through the water. Torgo, you help Taffley lower the ramp."

Everyone began moving, and in no time Tara was in the groundmobile, going through the water. The splashing on either side of the vehicle impressed the twins. They watched the spectacle with awe.

"Be careful, Taffley," Tara yelled from shore after they'd secured the trailer to the back of the groundmobile.

"It won't be a welcome committee when I get to the border, that's for sure." Taffley let out a laugh. "Do me a favor, though. When you tell it around the fire, say you shot me while escaping. I don't think I could live it down if they knew I got shot by some kid girl."

"Deal!" Tara smiled. "I'll ask a favor in return. From now on, you be friendly to Runners. We're good people, and no Runner will attack you unless you attack first."

Taffley waved, then started pulling up the catch hold.

"Let's get a move on. You can ride with me as far as the border." Tara was anxious.

Syra ignored her and walked over to Torgo on his bike.

"You'll ride with me," Tara stressed as she climbed in the groundmobile.

"Why? I want to ride with Torgo."

"I can see that." Tara gave Torgo a hard look, and he diverted his attention to the ground. It dawned on her that the two of them had been together all night. "You want to work for me, then get in the groundmobile."

Syra knew Tara would lecture her. After all, she had left without telling anyone. She was with Torgo. And, she'd followed Tara, who had every gold hungry warrior in Nuworld after her. Deciding to pick her battles, she joined Tara.

Syra glanced back at Torgo, who followed behind the groundmobile. He smiled and she faced front. So far, this was the best adventure she'd ever had. It was actually disappointing that they'd found Tara so fast. Riding with Torgo all morning, rubbing against his body, her arms wrapped around him…her mind drifted to the night before.

They'd rode south, following the only map she had found on her landlink. Once they'd found tracks that resembled those a groundmobile and trailer would leave, they'd followed them to the river. That's when they'd decided to take a break.

She remembered Torgo kissing her. The bright moon had made it easy to see. When she'd unbuttoned his shirt and slipped it off his shoulders, every one of his chest muscles were outlined with moonlight. His hands had been all over her. He never even hesitated with his exploring. Maybe he wasn't as inexperienced as she'd thought. Everywhere he'd touched her had set her on fire. She didn't remember how they'd moved from standing to lying on the ground. They'd greeted each other's bodies with excitement and anticipation. While she hadn't been aware of hurting herself at the time, the bruises on her body this morning indicated they'd gotten a bit carried away.

There had also been the…thing she'd done to Torgo. Syra never would have thought to do it, except she'd caught her Aunt Tasha doing it to another clansman one night. Her aunt and the man never knew she'd seen them. But, she'd never forgotten what she saw. It had looked like they'd been enjoying themselves, so she'd tried it last night on Torgo. He'd seemed so surprised when, after making him hard as a rock with her hand, she'd put him inside her mouth.

It was bigger than she'd expected, and she wasn't able to make much of it fit; not like her aunt had. She'd done something right though. Torgo had almost flipped her when he'd arched his back and howled. She'd held on tight and was surprised when he'd soaked her face with his white fluid. It had been salty, but she liked the taste.

Torgo had then laid her down and spread her legs so far apart she'd thought he'd split her in two. When his tongue entered her soft sensitive folds, she'd gone over the edge, lust tearing through her like a wildfire. He'd sucked, licked and kissed. It was more than she'd ever dreamed it would be, and he'd brought her to such an incredible orgasm she had been dizzy afterward. No way would she ask if Torgo had seen Darius doing that to Tara.

Thinking about it made her very anxious to do it again. After another quick glance at Torgo, she shoved the thoughts out of her head. It hadn't been hard to do when she focused on the fact that she sat next to a very angry Tara.

"It would be a lot easier if we ditched the trailer, and you let me ride your bike," Syra suggested after driving for a while in silence.

"Syra, I can't let you go with me. Believe me, I wish I could. You're right, I need the help. But, I just don't have the right to take either one of you from your parents."

Syra reached down, opened Tara's landlink and started to log on.

"What do you think you're doing?" Tara grabbed the landlink from Syra's lap.

"My papa said I could work for you over the summer," Syra started to explain.

Tara tried to stay calm and took a deep breath before she spoke, "If you log on with my landlink, it will instantly tell anyone who is watching exactly where I am. Trust me, they're watching. I've got the heirs of the Gothman and Runner nations on board."

"Okay. I'm sorry."

Tara was startled by the sincerity of Syra's apology.

Syra met her gaze and her youthful energy pulsated in her green eyes. "Did you love him, Tara?"

Tara didn't answer, but she fought the stinging in her eyes from tears that threatened to come. Had she loved him? She *still* loved him. She needed to stay focused and thinking about her feelings for Darius would get her nowhere. They continued in silence with still nothing but rough ground and trees around them.

"We should have hit desert by now, according to what Taffley told us." Tara looked up at the sun. "We're definitely driving due south. Something is wrong."

"Could we use my landlink to see if we can activate a nearby transmission that isn't a Runner transmission?"

"I guess we should try. For all I know, we have already passed the border." Tara stopped the groundmobile, and Torgo pulled up alongside her.

"Why don't you get the babies out and let them crawl around in the backseat?" Tara used Syra's landlink and easily found a transmission, although it was definitely foreign. Images began appearing on the screen.

"Well, there's life out there somewhere," Tara commented as she started to tap the screen. "I found a map. Here it is. There are several cities that appear to be not too far from the border. And I see two roads. One of them comes all the way to the border. We must be farther east than we thought. According to this, if we head west, we should pull out of this rough terrain faster than if we continue south." She studied the foreign screen providing this information and wondered what culture shared the technology.

"Sounds good to me." Torgo squinted toward the west.

"Let's keep moving. Syra, why don't you explore what these cities have to offer while you're back there, and I'll drive. Whatever you do, don't switch transmissions. Hopefully, no one will be searching for us on this link."

The drive continued to be difficult as the trees grew closer together and cliffs and rocks appeared. The terrain almost appeared mountainous, and Tara noticed some of the rock formations appeared to lead into caves. She continually looked around them and listened. No one would stop them, she would see to it. Determination pumped through her, keeping her on edge.

Torgo watched Tara and although he would look in the same direction as she did, he never saw anything out of the ordinary. The more time passed, the more often Tara checked their surroundings. Her actions started spooking Torgo. Although nothing around him seemed out of the ordinary, he started feeling as if they were being watched or followed, just by Tara's actions.

After driving for a time, Tara stopped. While the two teenagers watched, she got out of the groundmobile and stood, listening. She walked a short distance away from them but then hurried back.

"Syra, I want you to turn this groundmobile around and take it back to one of those caves." She reached down to the floor of the groundmobile and grabbed her suitcase along with her landlink. "Take these and put them on." She handed comms to both teenagers. "We need to put them all on the same channel and keep them open."

"What's going on?" Syra looked confused as she watched Tara guide her bike off the trailer.

"Get this thing turned around and go hide in one of those caves we just passed until I tell you it's okay to come out."

"Why?" Syra persisted.

"We've driven into an ambush. Head back toward those caves, and you and the babies will be safe." Tara's tone was enough for Syra to scurry behind the wheel. "Now move."

Syra obeyed and drove off with the babies.

"Torgo, a good warrior always knows when he's outnumbered." Tara flipped open her landlink and turned it on. "I'd say at the moment we are grossly outnumbered."

"Tara, I don't see anyone anywhere."

"Trust me."

"I do." He looked around nervously.

Tara fastened the landlink to her handlebars, pulled out her eliminator, and hooked it to her bike. "Do you have a laser?"

"Of course." He pulled out one of the nicer Gothman bang sticks he'd used for target practice.

She tossed one of her lasers at him. "Use this. It's a little more accurate. Aim it the same way you do yours. Let's go."

Their motorcycles engines roared to life when they took off, picking up speed as they darted around trees and rocks. The terrain was similar to Gothman. Torgo kept up with her nicely, but his loud bike was going to draw more attention to them. Glancing repeatedly down at her screen while navigating her bike, Tara quickly activated the main Runner screen.

Help was nearby—Patha and the Blood Circle Clan were just on the other side of the border. He really pushed his clan for them to be this close. Not that is surprised her, and at the moment she was grateful.

The first shot rang through the air from somewhere behind them. Tara continued to drive at high speed but turned and shot at a vehicle closing in from behind. Torgo did the same, pulling off a decent shot.

An old groundmobile crashed into a tree, making a horrific sound. They'd hit their target. She tapped her landlink screen as fast as she could.

What are you doing?" Torgo yelled through his comm.

"We're too outnumbered. I'm detecting fifteen to twenty people to the north of us, about ten people behind us, and there are three coming straight at us from the west. We'll see them here in a minute. We need help, or we won't make it."

Three men in a groundmobile not too different from hers appeared in front of them. As one of them drove, the other two leaned out, hanging onto the bars. They aimed large bang sticks at Tara and Torgo.

Tara pulled the eliminator faster than Torgo could even react.

The first shot coming her way caused a tree to fall in front of her. She heard men whooping and yelling in excitement of almost hitting her.

Did that reward announcement say *dead or alive*? She wished now that she'd read it a bit closer. From the sheer numbers around her, enough people had gotten wind of her location to turn the situation into a crazed hunt. There was no way she and Torgo could take on this many opponents. Who was to say how many more were on their way?

And they were River People—a crude people with no laws. They had no trained warriors. There would be no pattern, no order, no way of predicting their next move.

Tara aimed the eliminator and shot the groundmobile. The explosion caused several surrounding trees to catch fire. If there was anyone out there who wasn't exactly sure where she was, they certainly knew now.

"Help," was all she was able to transmit without crashing into a burning tree limb directly ahead of her.

"I've got you on my scanner." Tara saw the response to her plea and sighed with relief. She would deal with the wrath of Patha after all of this was over. Right now, she knew her clan wouldn't let her down. She hadn't done anything wrong, and they knew it.

Tara and Torgo continued to drive as fast as they dared into dense woods. A shot from the north exploded through the air, and Tara turned in time to see Torgo's bike slide.

She slammed to a stop and sent rocks and dirt flying as she turned around. If Torgo was hurt, she'd never forgive herself. Relief surged through her as she approached Torgo and saw that only his tire had been blown out. He had slid through the brush and was getting up slowly from underneath the bike. Her heart raced and a cold sweat broke out over her body. Torgo stood and began slapping his clothes. She wanted to leap off her bike and make sure he was truly okay. They weren't out of danger yet, though.

"Climb on." She pulled up next to him. "Tell me you're okay."

"My bike." He looked forlornly at his prize lying on the ground.

"Casualty of war, son. It's what you get for following me." She grinned at Torgo as he climbed on behind her. They both noticed blood on his leg at the same time.

"I'm okay."

Tara took off again, but didn't make it far. At least ten men on motorcycles were driving straight at them. They were well-armed, Tara noted as they spread out and surrounded her, forcing her to stop.

One of the riders in the middle glared at her with cold eyes as he yelled. "Okay, lady. I know you're a Runner, and I'm sure you're well-armed. Slowly, and I do mean slowly, you and the boy get off that bike."

He raised his large bang stick with practiced skill and pointed it at her head. He wasn't nervous, Tara observed. His moves were pre-meditated and calculated. It wasn't the same with the other men. They were shifty and not as certain of their next move.

The man yelling at her thought his mock army would be more intimidating, which made him a fool. A simple diversion would send all of them into a panic. They had a plan by the glances they kept giving their leader, as if waiting for a signal, but she guessed there was no backup plan.

Tara climbed got off the bike. She could easily pull the eliminator and take out at least half of them. But, it would take just one of them to fire back, and she or Torgo would be hurt. Or worse. There would be no brave attempt to escape this time. Her babies needed a mama, and she wouldn't risk Torgo's life.

"I can take the guys on the right, and you take those on the left," Torgo whispered at her shoulder.

"No. A good warrior knows when he's outnumbered. I told you that already. There's always time to escape. Right now isn't the time."

"Silence!" The leader yelled. "Be careful, boys. Runners are sadistic warriors. They keep a calm look on their faces, but their minds are scheming your death."

He gestured at Tara with his bang stick as if using her as an example while teaching young warriors. "Get away from the bike!" He curled his lip as if her looks repulsed him.

Tara complied, walking several steps toward him. She seriously hoped Patha would arrive very soon. She took a few more steps, and every laser instantly bristled in her direction. She was less than a man's length away from the leader.

"Let the boy go." She looked straight at him. "There's no price on his head." She paused. "Let him go and fight me like a true warrior. I'll show you how a Runner does it. Then you won't have to make up stories."

She glared at the leader and tried her best to let the fury in her eyes shine through. He was scared. She saw it now. All she needed was one small distraction.

He didn't need to yell with her so close but did anyway. "The boy is Gothman. I'm sure their leader will pay for him just as he will pay for you. The way they treat their women, I'm sure he wouldn't care if we had a little fun with you first." The leader laughed, and the men around him joined in.

This was all the distraction Tara needed. As she raised her eliminator to fire, the singing of lasers resounded through the woods in all directions. Apparently she hadn't been the only one waiting for that perfect distraction.

She shot the leader. Laser fire took out the other men before they knew what hit them.

CHAPTER FIFTEEN

"I MUST say, this will be the best story for quite a long time. I can't think of many Runners that could have made it this far being hunted, Tara-girl." Patha sat with his family around the fire later that evening. "And you did it with two babies as well."

Tara accepted another piece of apple pie from Reena, who was smiling at her.

"I'm just glad you're all alive and okay. I was worried sick." Reena sat next to Patha and took Ana from him. "This is no life for my grandbabies."

"My grandbabies, too." Patha bounced Andru on his lap. "Traveling is in their blood. But being hunted isn't. What are your plans?"

"I know. You're both right." Tara looked at her babies as they giggled in their grandparents' arms. "Patha, there are towns south of the border. I've heard some things about them, and they sound fascinating. Did you know that people decide who leads them down here?"

"Who'd have thought of such a thing?" Reena looked up from the pie she was feeding to Ana, shaking her head as she tsked. "How do these people know who would be a good leader?"

"Yes, the Neurian government. I've heard of them," Patha nodded. "Gowsky is the head of their council. He's a young man with lots of ambition."

Tara was surprised. Patha seemed to know everything.

"Did you know their main export was a crop to the Sea People? When we won the war over the Sea People, this Neurian government lost its main form of income."

"So you want to help these people?" Patha asked.

"Yes. That's exactly what I'm going to do."

"How do you propose to do this, child?" Patha narrowed his gaze on her. "You don't know these people. They are nothing like Runners, or even Gothman. They live a very different life. You won't be able to waltz into their country, change your clothes, and fit into their culture."

Tara smiled at Reena, remembering her first days at Gothman. "Maybe not. But I'm going to try. It's time I find a new life for myself."

Both Patha and Reena looked up at her quickly as she said this.

"Tara, I..." Patha started.

Tara lifted her hand to cut him off. "No, Patha, please. I can't go back to Gothman. Darius isn't going to change. His definition of love is obviously very different from mine. There's no way we are going to become compatible. I won't put my children through a life where their parents don't love each other."

"It's a little late to be coming to these conclusions." Patha studied his daughter's face. "You don't run away from your problems. That's not how I raised you. You need to place a time limit on this adventure of yours."

"I don't know how long I'll be gone. Now that I've heard about these people, I've got to check them out. They live so differently from anything I've ever seen—and apparently they're doing it well; or they were until our war ended their main source of income."

"She's living her culture, Patha," Reena pointed out. "She's doing what Runners do best. Love isn't going to keep her in one place."

Patha looked grave. "Is there a message you'd like to send to Darius?"

"I would think he would have a message to send to me."

Patha shook his head. "I believe he's sent you messages, but it appears they are deleted before they're read. I'm sure he's sorry."

"Sorry means you won't do it again. Tell him to call off this hunt. I won't have my children continually shot at by gold hungry fools." Tara picked up Andru, who had fallen asleep in Patha's arms.

Reena got up with Ana, who was also asleep. She followed Tara into Patha's trailer and helped put the babies to bed.

"I'm not accustomed to offering motherly advice, Tara. And I know your mind is set. But I want to say something to you." Reena paused outside the bedroom where they had put the twins. "Lord Darius has done you wrong. I don't blame you for your reaction. In fact, I admire you. There are many women who would forgive and do their best to forget. They convince themselves they can handle it."

"I know. And they would look the other way when it happened again and again. I can't do that, Reena. I would kill him."

"I believe you." Reena smiled, but it didn't cover the sadness in her eyes. "I think what Patha wants you to see, and what I want you to see as well, is that you started something in Gothman. It was you who brought Runners and Gothman together. You're the one who insisted women should have rights. You've started something and have walked away without finishing it."

"That's not fair." None of this was her fault. "I loved Darius and would have led our nations together. He said things to me, made promises. He lied to me. He's the one who quit without finishing, not me."

Reena looked away without saying anything.

Tara watched her. For some reason it dawned on her how much she wanted Reena's support. They moved into Patha's kitchen and she sat at the table across from Reena, waiting for the older woman to say something, anything.

Finally, Reena spoke. "Tara, I'm Gothman. I always will be. I have no choice but to be loyal to Lord Darius." She lowered her voice and continued. "I can't help but say that I feel you're more of a man than he is, so to speak. You might just have to make the first move."

"I don't know that I could ever trust him again." Tara felt defeated.

"How long will you be gone?"

"I don't know." Tara got up and moved to the door. "Patha said he'd let Torgo sleep in the spare room tonight. I'll send him in so he can go to bed." She paused in the doorway. "You know, Torgo has been loyal to me. He would make a great lord. But I doubt he'll ever have the opportunity to prove that." She sighed. "I'm leaving tomorrow, Reena. Tonight, I look forward to lying under the stars. It's beautiful out there, and I think sleeping in the night air might help clear my head. Good night, Reena."

"Goodnight, Tara-girl." Reena hugged her daughter. "Don't worry about those babies. If they wake in the night, I'll take care of them."

A short time later, Tara threw her bedroll on the ground next to the fire by Patha's trailer. The stars glowed larger than usual and filled the sky. She didn't have a chance to enjoy them, though. Sleep overcame her the second her head hit the pillow.

It was barely light when Tara opened her eyes. A good night's sleep was just what she'd needed. Now she was anxious to get herself organized and hit the road. The trailer was still quiet when she entered. Tara was gazing at her sleeping beauties when Patha came out of his room.

The old man looked over her shoulder at the two babies. "You'll do a good job with those two."

"They'll be great warriors, Patha. I promise."

"How could they not be? Look at their bloodline." Patha gently took Tara's arm. "Come with me. I've something to show you."

Tara followed Patha out the trailer and across the meadow to another trailer. He unlocked the door and the two of them went inside.

"This is for you."

"What do you mean?" Tara looked at the kitchenette. A table and small couch furnished the living room. An extensive landlink system caught Tara's eye, and she walked over to it.

"This trailer. It's for you." The old man grinned.

"It's mine?"

"Can't have my grandbabies running around without a roof over their heads." Patha walked to the door. "I'll see that your belongings are brought to you."

Tara was left alone in the living room. She walked down the hallway and opened the first bedroom door. A nice sized bed and a tall dresser furnished the room. There were shelves in the closet as well as a bar on which to hang clothes. The second bedroom contained a small bed and another dresser. She gasped when she opened the third bedroom. Inside were the babies' cradles from the house. She walked up to them in disbelief. Who had brought them here? All their clothes hung in the closet.

Tara stood in the little room, stunned by what she was seeing. What did all this mean? If Darius was giving her all of the baby things, did that mean he didn't want them to come back? A wave of panic ran through Tara's body. It had never occurred to her that he might decide he didn't want them to come home. She ran her fingers over a cradle, and her eyes welled with tears.

He wasn't willing to change for her. He'd made the decision and sent her these things. Tara imagined that the empty nursery had been more than he could bear. The man had no use for baby things without babies in the house. Or maybe he thought sending her Andru and Ana's things would make her react just the way she had. It would be just like him to send her everything to scare her into thinking he didn't want her—a bluff to lure her home. Tara wouldn't put an act like that past the man. Originally she'd left in anger but now she wanted to teach him a lesson. She wanted Darius to know she had zero tolerance for what he'd done. Tara wouldn't live continuously wondering where he was, and with whom.

As her finger traced the crib's carvings, it dawned on her that was exactly what she was doing right now. She missed him. Maybe she should have stayed and battled it out.

She shook herself, trying to get her thoughts back to reality. She wouldn't live with a man who didn't respect her. Tara hurried out of the room.

The landlink in the living room was logged on. The screen indicated there was a message waiting for her response. Someone had taken the time to program this landlink to use her pass code. She tapped the screen and saw the message.

Hello, Tara. This is my third attempt to contact you. I hope you'll not delete this message. It's not possible for me to right a wrong when you won't return to allow me to do so. I hope this trailer will show you that my intentions toward you are genuine. I've made every attempt to bring you back. I am now made to understand that you still do not plan to return, and instead are entering Southland. Tara, your place is here. We've united two nations, and you are meant to rule them with me. You, too, are failing your duty, just as you say I have. Return within a quarter-cycle, or I'll sever relations with the Runners, disowning all of you. I don't want to do this. My love for you is strong. Return to me now. Darius.

Tara read the message twice. Her blood boiled. Did Patha know of this threat? She slammed her fist on the table and turned to leave the trailer. As she opened the door, she almost ran into Syra.

"Have you heard the news?" Syra was grinning. She had a bag in each hand as she entered the trailer. "I get to go with you. My papa said it would keep me away from Torgo. What an adventure. Which one is my room?"

Tara stood there speechless. She hurried to regroup her thoughts. No one must know about the message from Darius. She walked back to the landlink and deleted it. She wasn't going to bother acknowledging such an insult. He didn't control everyone's life.

"You want me to go with you, don't you?" Syra apparently misread Tara's silence and looked worried. "I'll help with the babies."

"Of course you can go with me." Tara smiled, trying to force her thoughts to the future. And not the past.

She looked past Syra at the sound of a groundmobile pulling up to the trailer. Patha and Balbo entered without knocking and began bringing Syra's things into the trailer.

Apparently they hadn't considered that Tara might say no to Syra going with her. She glared at the boxes, feeling a wave of grouchiness swell inside her. It didn't make sense. It wasn't as if Syra moving in with her made her trip into Southland more of a definite move. She'd already insisted to Patha that she was going. Patha was simply taking her at her word. Darius's transmission had been an attempt to bully her. She'd already deleted it. Heading south was the right thing to do. And, she'd just told Syra she had no problem with her coming along.

Tara forced a smile on her face. She made her grouchiness go away. The pain in her heart, however, refused to budge.

They put away clothes and hauled furniture. Tara watched Patha closely. If her papa knew of Darius' threat, he gave no indication. He spoke only of his concern that Tara stay in touch and report regularly on what the people of Southland were like.

"Log everything that happens to you daily." Patha wiped sweat from his brow. They had just finished putting her new trailer in order.

"I will," Tara said as she stood outside the door to the twins' room. She watched Syra and Reena sitting on the floor with Andru and Ana as they played.

"You're breaking ground for Runners."

"I know."

"Keep track of every detail, even if it doesn't seem important at the time."

"I will."

"Let me know when you are safely in Semore." Patha hugged his daughter soundly. His eyes looked moist when he pulled away.

"And take care of my daughter," Balbo added, coming down the hallway.

"I will."

"Syra, bring the babies outside. I think we're ready to go."

Tara continued listening to Patha's instructions as he followed her through the trailer and together made sure everything was secure for travel. Countless times in the past they had performed this task together. Except now it was her trailer, and she wasn't traveling with her clan.

"Take care of yourself, Patha," she said before they stepped outside. "And…"

"Yes?"

"Nothing." Tara gave him a fierce hug, not sure what exactly she would have said. What was the point in asking Patha about Darius's threat? This was her private war with Darius and she didn't need reinforcements. Everyone said their goodbyes once she was outside. She hugged Reena, Torgo and Balbo then climbed into the driver's seat.

The town of Semore was unlike anything Tara had ever seen. It was built around ruins from Oldworld. There weren't ruins like these in Northland, at least none she'd ever seen.

Tall rectangular beams jutted into the air like the skeleton of an ancient, gigantic metal beast. Other beams crossed horizontally above the ground. Tara slowed and she and Syra stared in awe at a gigantic sign, as long as her trailer, with strange red shapes on it. It was made of material that looked like hard, thick paper. It wasn't though, but instead a material she'd never seen before.

"What is that?" Syra asked, twisting in her seat as they drove by.

"Ruins from Oldworld."

"We should stop."

"I doubt we'd get a better view. A ruin like that is probably protected."

"Why would anyone care if it keeps standing? It was pretty ugly."

Tara laughed. "Yea, it was. But it's good to keep in perspective that other nations existed before us."

"They must not have been very good warriors."

"Or maybe they were too good of warriors." She didn't want to think about what might happen if she and Darius became enemies. It was one thing to think she might kill him. Tara didn't want to go down in history as being party to destroying two nations.

Her heart once again constricted painfully in her chest. She tried putting Darius out her head, once again, by making mental notes as Semore began spreading out in front of them.

Small flat buildings made out of white bricks lined each side of the road. People walked on smooth, flat stone paths on each side of the road. Tara saw more groundmobiles than she'd ever seen at any one time. Semore definitely had a lot more people in it than Bryton did.

Roads crossed over each other in Semore. As the roads intersected each other, there were round, tall poles like smooth tree trunks with no branches next to the paths where people walked. These tall poles weren't wood, though, but designed from metal, which she guessed made them more durable. What struck her as odd were the lights at the top of each pole. These lights changed color without notice and the groundmobiles around her stopped, as if the lights controlled them. It was similar to a child's game except every driver was very serious about it. When Tara chose not to stop, other drivers around her began yelling.

"If I could understand a word they were saying I might be forced to pull my laser on them," Syra muttered.

"We aren't here to fight but to try and fit in."

Syra laughed when they were yelled at a third time, by a driver who almost ran into them. "Might be hard to do when we're the only ones who don't sound like we're singing when we're talking. And we have white skin and brown hair."

Tara had never seen such dark skin. They had equally dark hair. Everyone she spotted had black hair, really shiny, inky black hair; some short and curly others had long straight thick hair. They were beautiful people but with quick tempers.

Her attention was drawn to oil pumps slowly moving in and out of the ground at the edge of town. Oil was something Runners and Gothman needed.

Ahead on the right, Tara spied a sign that she read easily. It said, "*Rooms Available.*" Apparently they were yelling the same language as hers, just with a thick accent. She pulled the trailer into a parking area covered with small red gravel.

A dark-skinned, fuzzy-haired old man with black eyes and bushy eyebrows gave her an odd look. "Go to the edge of town." He pointed. "Go that way to the last house and ask to park there."

Tara drove to the place he'd specified—a large house set back off the road. It had a flat-roofed open room covering the front of the white clay building. The structure was longer than it was wide. Beyond it, the land turned to sand and seemed to stretch on forever. There were no buildings or roads past the while clay, large house.

"Hello," she said to a young woman leaning against a counter just inside the house. "I need a place to park my trailer for a short time."

The young lady looked past Tara out the window at the trailer. She studied it for a minute before studying Tara. The woman's hair was black as coal. She had it twisted in the back in several braids. Her skin was also as dark as night and her inky black eyes looked curiously at Tara. "Where are you from?"

"North of here."

"North? There isn't much north of here. You live in that trailer?"

The girl's dialect was unlike anything Tara had heard before. She liked it. The girl's words ran together, sounding almost melodic. It took listening carefully to understand what she said.

"I do for now." Tara smiled, knowing her voice must sound equally strange. "I have a couple of babies. We're looking for a new life."

"And you come to Semore?" This seemed to surprise the girl. "Things aren't good here right now. I mean, if you're looking for work, I don't know if you'll find any."

"I'd like to try. May I park the trailer for just a few days?"

"I guess we can't turn away a mama with babies. Pull it around back and I'll bring out the paperwork."

Tara thanked her and parked the trailer in the indicated spot. The young girl came out the back door within minutes. She handed forms to Tara and peeked past the open door of the trailer at Syra and the babies inside.

"I've never seen such blond curly hair before," the girl commented. "Where did you say you were from?"

Tara was saved from answering by two men who appeared in the building's doorway. Both were tall, with dark skin and hair. One of the men, however, caught her off guard. He had long black hair falling to his waist. He was thin with broad shoulders and his black eyes were like radiant jewels when he looked at her. The other man gestured for the girl to come to him, and the three disappeared into the building, leaving Tara alone to fill out the forms.

The girl appeared again before long and smiled shyly when she stopped at the trailer door. "My husband wants to know if someone is going to come after you?"

"I don't think so."

"Do you have money?"

"I have gold. I'll exchange it if you tell me where I can do that."

She shook her head. "That won't be necessary."

The girl took three gold pieces and told her it would cost the same amount for each day she was there. "You're welcome to join us for a midday meal shortly. You'll hear the bell ring when it's ready." The girl took the forms and disappeared into the building.

Tara watched her walk away and wondered which of the two men was her husband. She thought of Darius, then the dark man with long hair and glowing eyes. Darius was much better looking. She pushed both images out of her head and went to her children.

The food was not identifiable, but it was good. The couple served the meals, but didn't eat with them. In fact, over the next few days, Tara and Syra were not sought out by any of the town folk. Nor did anyone pay much attention to them, although their fair skin and sandy brown hair made them conspicuous among the dark-skinned Neurians. Even Tara's attempts at conversation in different shops in Semore were unsuccessful. She'd never been more politely ignored as she was by these people. Taffley had said Semonians were friendly people. His knowledge came from stories. Tara doubted he'd ever been here. Every culture was different. As she paid for clothes that she hoped would help her and Syra fit in better, the woman in the shop accepted her gold without making eye contact or saying a word.

"Everyone is different," she mumbled as she carried her packages to the hectic street and forced herself not to take it personally.

The landlink system in Semore was quite elaborate. It was connected to nearby towns, and Tara studied everything there was to learn about these people. She discovered that every citizen had a group of numbers assigned to them. She was able to obtain a guest number and visit many of the local merchants through their networking system. Her frustration grew, however, when a message continually appeared on the screen saying her "guest status" did not allow her to view her selection. She was prevented from viewing anything about their government.

Every morning, Tara walked down the street to buy papers sold at a corner stand. Newspapers were printed each day. She read about the town's current events, and occasionally political news items, as well.

A quarter-cycle had passed since they'd parked the trailer by the while clay house. Tara was lonely and thinking of Darius as she walked back to her trailer. The time frame he'd given her to return had expired. She'd spoken to Patha every day, but he had never indicated he knew of Darius' threat. Darius hadn't sent her any more messages, and she wondered if he really would disown her, as he'd put it.

She walked slowly along the street, reading the paper, and looking for possible work. If she were home, there would be plenty to do. But here, there wasn't much call for overseeing military training, or resolving conflicts among clan members.

Briefly, she considered who would have assumed her tasks among the Runners. Darius had learned a lot about her people—had he taken on her responsibilities? If so, how would her people react to Darius mediating a clan dispute?

Tara stubbed her toe and let out a curse. Thinking of Darius would not help her right now. Maybe Patha had been right. He'd said she wouldn't be able to fit into this community easily.

As she half-heartedly scanned the paper, a new ad caught her eye. An assistant was needed in one of the government offices to do some landlink work. This was exactly what she'd been looking for. Excited, Tara read the ad again. She jumped back when she walked right into a man coming toward her.

"I'm so sorry." The man looked up from a landlink printout, obviously thinking it was he who had not been paying attention. He seemed to contemplate saying something else.

"No, it's my fault," she began.

"You just arrived in Semore, haven't you?" he asked after some hesitation. He glanced around the street as if to see if there was anyone watching. "Follow me."

Tara followed out of curiosity. The man led the way through a nearby door and down a poorly lit hall. She guessed him five to ten winters older than she, very thin, with black straight hair that fell to his shoulders. He turned toward a closed door at the end of the hall, tapped on it, then opened the door slowly.

Tara patted her pocket, reassured by the hard metal of her laser.

The dark man glanced over his shoulder at her and indicated with a slant of his head that she follow.

Tara entered and faced three men, the one she'd followed, along with two others who sat by a desk in the dimly lit room. One of the seated men was quite heavy; the other had long silver hair pulled back into a ponytail. The silver-haired man looked older than Patha.

They all stared.

She returned their stare, picking up on how nervous they were.

"We, uh…" The man standing by her began speaking, stopped, and looked at the two men sitting. "That is, um, we know who you are."

"That's nice. But I don't know who you are." She forced herself to appear unconcerned.

"Fleeders," the tall man pointed to himself then to his friends. "Snith and Tilk. We, uh, work here."

The room was poorly lit with a useless overhead light and a lamp next to the landlink. There was another desk in the room with a landlink on it as well. The shelves lining the walls were filled with landlink parts and discs. After she'd studied the contents of the room, she turned to stare to Fleeders. "Why did you bring me here?"

"To talk to you," Tilk, the old man spoke up, and the other two looked at him with worried glances. "We've been monitoring your communications."

"You've been what?"

"It's our job," Fleeders said hurriedly, his accent making him harder to understand when his words spilled out. "We understand that you're not happy about this. But, we monitor all landlink activity."

"Gowsky has us do it." Snith wiped sweat from his upper lip. "It's not really common knowledge, but we've been through bad times."

"We know you're Tara, daughter of Patha, who is leader of the Blood Circle Clan. You joined with the leader of the Gothman, and you defeated the Sea People," Fleeders said awkwardly. He added quickly, "We know you're not here to hurt anyone."

There was a chair next to the empty desk, and Tara sat stretching her legs out in front of her and crossing her feet. A small smile crossed her face. These men were terrified of her!

As they should be. It would take nothing to kill all three of them in this small office and return to the street without anyone knowing it. For some reason, they wanted to speak to her. For now, she tried looking as non-threatening as possible.

"So why am I here?"

Tilk and Snith looked at Fleeders. So did Tara. He cleared his throat again, something he'd done several times now in the short time Tara had been in his presence.

"Gowsky learned you were here less than a quarter-cycle ago. Maybe he's known longer, I'm not sure. He's convinced you're here to start some kind of revolution—take over the Neurian Government. We were asked to monitor your communications and give him a report at the end of the half-cycle."

Tara listened closely as Fleeders spoke. She still wasn't accustomed to their singsong inflections. "So you've monitored my communication. And...?"

"We don't think you're here to start anything," Snith said.

"We think you're here out of curiosity," Tilk said. "And to get even with your husband." He mumbled this last sentence.

"You did make one comment about our oil." Fleeders looked at his friends, instead of her.

"So you know all about me." Tara twisted in her chair and looked at the landlink next to her. It was a lot bulkier than a Runner landlink. The three men didn't say anything as she brought up the screen. It displayed a directory the main landlink offered to every Neurian. Tara had already accessed this on her landlink and was somewhat familiar with its contents.

"So what will your report say to Gowsky?"

"That's just it," Fleeders lowered his voice just a little. "That is why we brought you here, or I should say, decided to try to get you to come here."

Tara glanced at each of them when they hesitated.

Fleeders looked at the other two, then continued. "Gowsky stopped by yesterday and told us to infect your landlink so you are no longer able to communicate with your people."

Tilk interrupted. "He told us he was going to pick you up and charge you with—"

"Charge me with what?" Tara interrupted as she leaned forward in her chair and slapped her hands on her knees so hard the three men jumped.

"It's just what we've been told," Tilk said, sounding apologetic. "Charge you with conspiring to start a war."

"I see." Tara stood and began pacing while her thoughts raced. "Any defense I come up with will likely be shot down in your government. I could leave right now, but I would have accomplished nothing." She stopped and stared at the men.

They looked at her glumly.

"Why have you told me all this?"

"Neurians have been devastated by the loss of trade with the Sea People. We could rebuild if we sold our oil. We've researched you and your Runners since we had access to your landlink system any time you communicated with Patha. You're an advanced race. More advanced than Neurians think you are. We'll try to explain all this to Gowsky, but I don't think it will make any difference. He wants you brought to him." Fleeders shrugged and sincerely looked sorry. "We're telling you this so you know the Neurian government is watching you."

"We don't know what you want to do with this information," Tilk added. "Now you know what's going to happen."

"I know exactly what I'm going to do." Tara walked out the door and hurried back toward the street.

CHAPTER SIXTEEN

TARA FROZE as she heard loud voices at the end of the hallway. It sounded like several men headed in her direction.

"It's the government police." Fleeders hissed from the doorway to the office.

Tara hurried back to the three men. "Is there another way out of here?"

A small window was the only other option. Not waiting for an answer, she ran into their office, jumped onto the desk and lifted the window. She was outside, alongside the building, within seconds. The window shut behind her, but she didn't look back as she ran to the street. She slowed to a walk and headed down the sidewalk toward her trailer. It was impossible not to be conspicuous when her skin color was different from everyone else. No one stopped her on the street, and she wasn't followed.

"You forgot the paper." Syra looked up when Tara walked into the trailer and plopped down on the floor next to her children.

They immediately dropped their toys and climbed onto her lap. She hugged and tickled them, but her mind raced. "Sorry. I guess I did."

"Well, can I go get one?" Syra stood up and stretched. "I could stand to get out of here for awhile."

Tara was so caught up by her thoughts; she barely heard Syra. Glancing up, she stared at Syra. "Go ahead. Make sure you take a comm. Call me right away if you have any problems." She looked at the long sundress Syra had on. "Girls here wear pants, though."

"When it's cold, they want me in dresses. And when it's hot, they want me in pants," Syra mumbled as she walked back to her room to change.

The children napped while Syra explored the town, leaving Tara time to ponder what Fleeders had told her about Gowsky. Here was a man, with his government stripped of commerce upon which they relied. These people hadn't anticipated that their main income would disappear. Their opium was ample. It didn't run out. It was their buyers who had deserted them. Now they were frustrated, desperate, and not thinking clearly. On the other hand, the Neurians' precious oil was important to Runners and Gothman. They should want to discuss this with her.

Tara decided she must speak with Gowsky, which shouldn't be difficult since he wanted her brought in. The question was, should she let them capture her? It probably wouldn't be long before his men showed up at the trailer. Or should she seek him out on her own, maybe tonight after the babies were asleep?

She decided to take a walk with the babies. The children squealed in delight as she pushed them in the wagon across the sand and tiny stones behind the trailer. The heat from the sun made the horizon appear wavy in the distance. It was a good sun though—warm and refreshing on her skin.

Tara trudged across the desert that lay south of the town. She passed several large tree-like plants with leaves the texture of rubber. They were quite beautiful and offered good shade from the hot sun.

Something moved out of the corner of her eye. Tara squatted down next to her children, talking to them quietly, as she surveyed the area.

"What do you think it was?" Tara smiled at Andru as he squinted his eyes to look with her. Andru giggled, and Ana kicked at him and squinted as well.

"Look, there it is," Tara whispered to her children and pointed to an animal crossing the field. It looked like a large dog with dark brown hair and a long tail. It moved closer.

Tara knew from experience that most wild animals were not aggressive unless provoked. If she were threatened, her laser would easily kill the animal. She remained squatting next to her children as they noticed the animal and pointed.

As the dog moved closer, the heat rising from the ground distorted its features. The waves drifted up, making the creature appear to be walking on only two legs. As the distance between then lessened, Tara saw it *was* walking on only two legs. What she thought had been a dog was now a person. Had the creature transformed from beast to human?

An old woman now walked toward them. She was hunched over. She had a deeply creased, leathery face with large dark brown eyes. Her darkened skin, a shade more orange than the Neurians, was covered with a loose fitting animal skin dress. Her boots were made of the same material and laced up to her knees.

"A blessing to you, child." The old woman's voice cracked as if from lack of use.

"Hello." Tara squinted from the sun at the old woman, who now standing right in front of her.

"Why are you here?"

"I'm taking my children for a walk."

The old woman moved closer and reached out to touch Ana. Tara tensed and the old woman shifted her attention, noticing Tara's uneasiness. She pulled her hand away from Ana's head and instead placed her deformed fingers on Andru's head. She glanced at Tara again.

"The children will see and learn a lot. But why are you here?"

Was this old woman crazy? Tara looked at her, and the old woman stared back with dark, glassy eyes.

"Do you mean why am I here with these people?"

The old woman gave her a glazed stare and didn't respond.

"We need a new life. We've moved here from the north." Tara tried to change the subject. "Do you live around here?"

"You aren't through with your old life. You still have much to do."

Now it was Tara's turn to stare. The old woman was out of her head, she decided. Old age and the heat of the desert had done her in.

"Crator knows your fears, but also your pride. You must put that aside. There's no time for it. You have so much to do. None of it will happen without you. Do you realize that?" The old woman's eyes were glassier than before and they seemed to penetrate through Tara. It was almost as if they were focusing on the ground behind her.

"I don't understand what you're saying."

"That is your fear. Crator knows you're strong. Overcome it."

Tara didn't know how to pursue the conversation. It was wrong for people to not care for their elderly. The woman was delusional and possibly lost out here. But what she said *did* apply to Tara's life. Was that delusional? She turned and reached into the wagon for a bag of bread pieces and fruit she'd brought for the children.

"Would you like to have a snack with us?" Tara pulled food from the bag and looked back to offer it to the old woman. The woman was gone. A large dog ran away from her across the sand. She watched until it was out of sight.

"There you are." Syra smiled at Tara and immediately got up from the table to help with the children as Tara entered the trailer. "I wondered where you went."

"We took a walk," Tara said, deciding not to mention the lady in the desert.

"Well, that's what I did, too." Syra slid Ana into a chair they'd found at one of the shops that attached to the table with clamps. She then struggled to strap her in while the child pulled her hair. "Folks here aren't too friendly, are they?"

"We look a lot different than they do." Tara managed to get Andru into his seat, then walked to the cold box for two bottles. "Maybe in time they will warm to us."

"Maybe." Syra shrugged and began dicing cheese and apples for the children. "I got a paper and read a few stories in it while you were gone. Sounds like they have an organized group of leaders here." Syra commented on a few of the stories in the paper.

Tara didn't hear much of the conversation. The old woman occupied her thoughts. Who was she? What she'd said made no sense—and yet it had. It didn't make sense that she'd disappeared so fast.

After supper, Syra bathed the babies and prepared them for bed. Tara sat at the landlink and decided to see if the Neurian network said anything about a Crator. She wasn't connected for long when a message flashed across her screen.

Why are you looking for Crator?

She panicked for a second, but a few clicks told her the message was from Fleeders.

Can I talk to you? she typed.

This method of communication isn't secure. Log off.

Tara wondered why anybody cared if she researched the name. Who *was* Crator? She logged off and grabbed her jacket.

"I'm going for a walk," she whispered to Syra who was rocking Ana to sleep.

Andru lay stretched out in his crib. Tara gently kissed his forehead then kissed her fingertip and placed it on Ana's head. She waved bye to Syra and stepped softly through the trailer, so as not to wake her children.

The night air was brisk. A chill ran through Tara's body and she zipped her Runner jacket that she wore over her Neurian clothes. Moving her laser to her front jacket pocket, she began walking behind the trailer. The vast, endless sand lying in front of her seemed dark and forbidding. Who was out there? What was out there?

Another chill caught her body. She'd faced many enemies who had posed a more obvious danger than an old woman who babbled. What was there to fear?

The woman's words bothered her. She didn't deny it. Although she'd written them off as the delusions of an old mind, Tara kept hearing them in her head.

You aren't through with your old life. You still have so much to do.

Tara shuddered as she saw the truth in those words. She was heir to the leader of all the Runner clans. The old woman couldn't have been more truthful when she told Tara that her old life wasn't done. Tara kicked the ground with the tip of her boot and scowled. That old woman had no clue who Tara was or where she came from.

"What do you want to know about Crator?" The voice that came from behind her made Tara jump. She jerked around, pulled her laser and pointed it straight into Fleeders' chest.

He too jumped and his arms flew into the air. "It was just a question. You don't have to tell me if you don't want."

"You startled me." Tara returned her laser to her pocket.

Fleeders' eyes followed it to its hiding place as he slowly lowered his arms.

"Who is Crator?"

"He is why we exist. Crator made all of this. Everything you see."

"Where is he? I want to meet him."

"You can't *meet* him." Fleeders laughed, then sobered immediately. "At least not until your life here is over. Crator created all life on Nuworld. He's a spirit. I'm sure Runners must have a name for Him. Who made you? Gave you life?"

"My parents gave me life. There's no spirit responsible for my life."

"We believe there is. Crator is responsible for all living things and for Nuworld itself. Are you saying Runners have no faith?"

"Faith?"

"What do you think happens when you die?"

"When you die, you're done. You exist no more."

"I don't think I could go through life if I believed that."

"I want more information on Crator."

"There's plenty of information on Crator. But, the council is watching you closely. I wouldn't be surprised if they know I'm here." Fleeders looked around him nervously. "Why this sudden interest in Crator?"

"I met someone today." Tara pointed to the dark, foreboding wilderness.

Fleeders' stared at her finger.

"Out there. She said something about Crator."

"Who did you meet out there?"

"I don't know her name." Tara shrugged. "Some old lady. Her words were mostly babble."

"You met an old woman out there?" Fleeders suddenly sounded very worried. "What did she say to you?"

"I don't remember exactly." She wrinkled her brow and studied Fleeders' face.

He looked back at her anxiously, frowning.

"She didn't really make any sense. She said Crator knew things about me. Things I was supposed to do."

Fleeders stared out into the wilderness blanketed with darkness. It was as if he expected to see this old lady Tara had mentioned. There was a strange look on his face, one of fear and awe.

"Does an old woman, dressed mainly in animal fur, live around here? I thought I would take her some food. She was an odd sort. I don't think she talks to anyone much."

"There's a legend about the Guardians, voices for Crator." Fleeders shuddered and turned away from the field. "There are animals that turn into people and tell us the wishes of Crator. It's just an old legend. No one's ever seen one. She didn't turn into an animal on you, did she?" Fleeders chuckled as he said this, but still sounded nervous.

Tara sensed how awkward the conversation made him. He really believed these legends of his, yet had no proof. She had the proof and didn't believe in them. A people with such faith might be very powerful, and dangerous, yet these people were scared and felt deserted.

"Why don't we go for a ride and see if we can find one of these Guardians?" Tara walked over to her bike.

"You're not going to go out there tonight, are you?" Fleeders stood firm, focusing his attention away from the dark sandy stretch of land behind them. "No one goes into the desert at night."

"There are good lights on my bike. We'll be able to see fine."

Something exploded in the direction of town. Both of them jumped and turned to look that way. Large flames lit up the dark sky.

"Something's on fire!" Tara straddled her bike.

"Oh no! It couldn't be!" Fleeders gave no explanation as to what he thought it might be but squeezed onto the seat behind Tara. She took off slower than she would have liked since obviously Fleeders wasn't familiar with a motorcycle; he kept fidgeting from right to left.

A large two-story building at the other end of the main street was engulfed in flames. As Tara slowed windows blew out from the second floor. People ran from all directions. Most were curious on-lookers. If she were home, guards would have been on site already. But no one monitored the growing crowd.

Huge groundmobiles with long, thick hoses pulled up. Orders were shouted and the hoses were dragged toward the fire.

Smoke began bellowing toward them, blurring Tara's vision and making it difficult to breathe. She wished she had her headscarf. Instead, she covered her mouth with her hand and blinked out tears as the smoke rushed over them.

"Let me off." Fleeders squirmed behind her.

"What's that building?"

"It's a warehouse that's not being used right now. Our whole project was in there. Nothing in that building would have caused an explosion like that. Everything is ruined. Who would have known? Who did this?" he wailed, yelling over the growing chaos.

Tara pulled the bike to the side of the road, and the two jumped off. "What project was in there? Who knew about what?"

"Nothing. It's nothing." Fleeders shook his head and looked very miserable. Instead of elaborating he took off running toward the building.

"Wait! Fleeders!"

But he was gone in the thick, almost unbearable dark smoke.

A big, round-bellied man shouted orders and the large hose flooded the building with water. The fire withered from the attack. Tara noticed another hose still coiled on the side of the truck. Why weren't they using it? The smoke thickened under their efforts. People crowded into the street. Tara moved around them for a better view and no one stopped her.

What project had been going on in this building? Fleeders had looked as if he'd regretted saying what he had just before he ran off. Now she didn't see him anywhere.

The men putting out the fire seemed to move at a snail's pace. They seemed content to let the building burn to the ground instead of exert the effort to put it out. Tara stared through the smoke at group of men who stood across from the burning building. They were talking to one of the Neurian security men who had come onto the scene. Finally, others in similar uniform showed up. They started ordering everyone away from the building.

Tara remained down the street from the fire and avoided the security. She noticed several people trying to get into the side of the building that hadn't burned yet. The security guards were on them instantly, pulling them back.

Tara noticed Fleeders, his tall skinny silhouette easily identified as he hurried through the thickening haze to the group of men standing across the street. He gestured wildly at a broad-shouldered man with long black hair. It was the man she'd seen the first day she arrived. She watched the broad-shouldered man gesture to several others, who took off running. It appeared the long haired man was in charge.

Was he Gowsky? Fleeders said Gowsky had known she was there shortly after she'd arrived. Had Gowsky recognized her when he saw her pull in to town? The broad-shouldered man turned and looked directly at her.

Another window exploded, again on the second floor. A young woman waved her arms frantically and screamed loud enough to be heard over the shouting in the street.

In spite of the thick accent and strange vocal-inflections, it was easy to tell what she was saying. "Help me!" she yelled to the men putting out the fire. "Please, you've got to help me!"

The potbellied man ordering his team with the water hoses looked across the street at the broad-shouldered man Tara guessed was Gowsky.

Fleeders raced toward the building. Several men leaped and grabbed him.

They weren't going to rescue the woman! These people would let her burn. What was so awful about the project that they would let a woman burn for it? She didn't know the answer, but she wouldn't watch someone die like this. Tara took off running toward the building.

"Hey! Get back!" The potbellied man gestured for Tara to move away. "What do you think you're doing?"

Jumping, she grabbed hold of the ledge above the window. She made eye contact with the broad-shouldered man. As their eyes met, he froze, and his mouth fell open. Tara looked away first and kicked the glass in with her boot. If that was Gowsky, she wasn't impressed.

She glanced inside at bleak darkness, then dropped inside the burning building. The intensity of the smoke increased drastically when Tara landed on the glass covered floor. It seeped past her and outside through the broken window. She began coughing before her eyes slowly adjusted.

There was no time to hesitate or get her bearings. She ran into a hallway. Smoke was rolling toward her from one end. Tara ran the other way. It opened into the large warehouse part of the building. Fire crawled along the floor at the far end of this cavernous room. Some of the rafters on the same side also burned. It wouldn't be long before the building started to collapse. To make matters worse, fire swept the stairs, and the woman was trapped on the floor above!

Tara looked around the warehouse. The large space was empty except for boxes tossed in a corner. She ran to them, glad when there was nothing in them. Tara collapsed several and ran back to the stairs.

"Hello? Can you hear me?" She yelled through the smoke. She beat the fire with the flattened boxes until it subsided somewhat. "I'm at the stairs. Are you hurt?"

When no one answered she threw the flat boxes on the stairs and bolted up to the second floor. Fire leapt at her from the walls and ceilings as she entered a large, open room. The young lady was still leaning out the open window. Tara ran to her and grabbed her shoulders. "Come on. The building is going to collapse."

The woman spun around but then looked horrified. "Who are you?"

Tara had grown accustomed to this dark-skinned race reacting to her that way. She doubted most of them had ever seen someone with her pale skin color. The woman was young, of small build. Her black hair had once been pulled up, but long strands fell wildly across her face and down her back.

"I don't know who you are. What are you doing in here?"

"My name is Tara, and I'm going to get you out of here."

The lady, obviously in shock, looked around the room disoriented. She glanced at Tara, then down at the loose papers and a small plastic container she held in her arms.

"This won't stop anything, you know." The lady was obviously delirious. "Why would they want to stop us? They're not going to hurt us. They're stranded where they are."

"Come on." Tara guided her to the stairs.

"We've already communicated with them. I didn't think anyone knew that. We weren't ready to announce it," the lady rambled.

When they reached the stairs, the fire had engulfed the collapsed boxes. The lady tensed, and looked at Tara desperately. "We can't die. We've come too far. They can help us, you know. And we can help them. We call them Lunians, which was my idea. But I don't know if that's what they call themselves."

"We need something to stamp down the fire before it takes out the stairs." Tara looked frantically around them.

The crackling of the rafters and the heat from the floor let Tara know the structure was ready to collapse. The fire was closing in. Tara's skin already was too hot and wherever her clothes touched her body, increasing pain distracted her. They had to move, or neither one of them would make it.

She turned and looked out a broken window by the staircase. The men below still aimed the lone hose at the building. Tara spotted the broad-shouldered man who'd been talking to Fleeders. It looked like he pointed at her, but the thick smoke made it hard to tell.

It was too far down to jump.

"We've got to make a run for it," she said, turning back to the burning staircase.

"What?" The lady looked terrified and began to shake her head. "We'll be killed."

"There's no time to discuss it."

Tara grabbed the lady and threw her over her shoulder. The lady squirmed in protest, but Tara's grip was firm. She dashed down the stairs straight through the flames. Heat singed her hair and her clothes seemed hotter than the fire. The stairs cracked and groaned under their weight. Large popping sounds zapped the air above and beneath them. It was deafening. Her foot broke through the last stair, and she pulled with a vengeance to release it from the torn board. Pain shot up her ankle, her knee, then her thigh when she finally freed herself from the burning wood. She grimaced as she put weight on it and limped through the large open room toward the window where she'd entered. The woman made the job harder by squirming and kicking Tara's thighs.

The ceiling exploded and crashed toward the back of the building, making a deafening sound. Smoke from the collapsing wood weighed in around them, completely blinding Tara. The woman she carried screamed loudly, piercing through Tara's head. The woman's body went rigid with fear, and she made an attempt to jump out of Tara's arms. Tara held onto her with one arm and used her other hand to feel her way down the hallway. She reentered the small room and ran to the window, her boots crunching over the broken glass.

"We can get out through this window." Tara released the woman. "Hurry! Climb out. The ground is just a few feet below."

"You've saved my life." The lady climbed into the open window and turned to smile at Tara. "I know who you are now. You are the Northerner I've heard about. Do you know about the Lunians?"

"No, who are they?"

"They are a colony living on the moon."

Tara froze in disbelief at these words as the lady stuck her legs out of the window and jumped. Another crash sounded behind her and she, too, jumped out the window.

Pain shot up Tara's leg. She fell sideways in response, and the rest of her body hit the hard ground. She still wasn't safe. Using her good foot and both hands, she moved crablike away from the building to a safe distance. When she stood, putting the weight of her body on her good leg, she looked up in time to see the building collapse to the ground.

The girl she'd rescued was gone. The crowd had dwindled, and the thick darkness, from the night and the smoke, made it difficult to see anything. It was impossible to identify anyone still hovering around the building.

Tara turned and limped in the direction of her bike, thinking about what she had just heard. That lady had said something about a colony on the moon. She had called them

Lunians. She said the Neurians had communicated with them. There was no moon tonight. The sky was low enough to touch from all the smoke.

She wanted to know what communication had transpired with these Lunian people. She'd never given much thought to the moon, although she relied on its light at night and had enjoyed its beauty. Maybe with a good viewer she might notice something to indicate a city. Tara wondered what technology the Neurians possessed that had allowed them to discover the people living there.

Without warning, a hand came from behind her, covering her mouth. Then, someone stuck the end of a laser into the back of her rib cage.

Tara turned instinctively and tried grabbing it. Her aggressor was stronger than she was, but didn't know how to fight. Tara pulled the weapon from his grasp. Unfortunately, she then placed her weight on her bad foot. She grimaced in pain and let out a low shriek as she lunged helplessly to one side, unable to steady herself before falling to the ground.

The glow from the fire silhouetted the figure standing over her. The broad-shouldered man with long flowing hair stood over her.

Still holding the gun in her hand, she aimed it up at him as she slowly forced herself into a standing position.

"I'm not foolish." He sounded calm, almost soothing. "It's not capable of firing."

She focused on his Neurian features. His brown skin was unblemished, and his dark eyes matched the color of his pupils. His white teeth almost glowed in the darkness. "I'm aware of your reputation as a warrior, and I had no doubts you'd be able to unarm me." His singsong accent was as distracting as his features. "You have not disappointed me."

Tara looked at his weapon in her hand and tossed it away. Relying on the distraction, she reached for her laser. The distraction didn't work.

The man's grin increased as he pulled another weapon. It looked like a large laser. "This one, however, will kill."

"Fine, you win." Tara held up her hands. "Now what?"

"Can you walk?" The man continued to look straight into her eyes.

Knowing this to be the perfect way to intimidate an enemy, Tara returned the gaze. "It depends on how far. If I'm lucky, I can make it back to my bike."

"We'll get you to your babies. First though, you and I are going to talk."

With no warning, the man aimed and shot his weapon. Tara's world went dark.

CHAPTER SEVENTEEN

HER ENTIRE body reverberated with pain when Tara tried focusing on her surroundings. The throbbing in her foot matched the pounding in her head. She lifted her upper body onto her elbows. Everything around her was spinning. For a second, Tara had no idea why she lay there. She searched her brain, trying to remember what happened before she had laid down. It hurt to concentrate. Tara didn't like the sensation of not remembering. She never blacked out.

Then it came to her. The fire. She had jumped from the window and hurt her foot. Tara turned her head with effort, the blurred surroundings making her dizzier, and looked at her foot. It also appeared a blur. She blinked and allowed her eyes to focus on nothing while she worked her thoughts into order. It made no sense why pain in her foot would make her brain so foggy. And where was she? She needed to find her bike and get to her children. Tara made an effort to sit.

"You'll feel better in a few minutes," a male voice said.

She jerked her head toward the voice. Her vision started returning.

The man who'd shot her sat several feet away in a metal chair. His features were perfect. Eyes like a starless sky stared at her. His long lashes almost reached thick black eyebrows. He had pronounced cheekbones and a long, straight nose. Tara noticed strands of his long hair were braided, but otherwise his hair fell free past his shoulders and behind his back.

His long legs disappeared into boots made of animal skin that were tied with leather straps just below his knees. He smiled, and his dark skin showed off his white teeth.

She noticed her laser sitting on his lap. "Where am I?" Tara continued her effort to reach a sitting position. Her head still pounded.

"You're in my barn."

Tara moved slowly to the edge of the makeshift bed, which felt like nothing more than a bench with several quilts thrown over it. As she shifted her legs over the side, one foot hit the floor, and she felt incredible pain shoot upward. When she leaned over to massage it, she noticed it was bandaged. She grimaced, swiping her hair over her shoulder. For some reason, her hair seemed longer than it should be.

"It was a pretty nasty scrape. Our doctor cleaned it up. He said it would hurt for awhile."

Tara glanced up at the man.

"Would you like something to eat?"

She shook her head, still dwelling on the pain in her foot.

He handed her a plate of sliced light-colored meat and a small vine of grapes.

Although she'd declined his offer, her stomach groaned loudly in protest, and she hated to admit she was famished. Reluctantly, Tara accepted the food.

"I figured you'd be pretty hungry. You've been asleep for several days."

Tara was stuffing one of the slices of meat into her mouth and had begun to chew eagerly when she heard his last words. She almost choked when she heard how long she'd slept. Instantly, she thought of Syra and the babies. What would Syra have done when she didn't come home? Tara immediately feared the worse. There was no satisfactory outcome. Andru and Ana would have cried for her. Syra hadn't known the children that long. She wouldn't have been able to calm them.

"I've been asleep for several days?" Tara spat remnants of meat from her mouth and glared at the man. "How dare you keep me from my children for that long!"

"You were injured." The man shrugged.

"What about my children?" Tara raised her voice and felt the pain increase in her head. She rubbed her hands over her face trying to understand what was happening. "Why are you holding me here?"

"Your brother's daughter has been notified. Your children are fine."

The man's calm demeanor made Tara want to smack him. "You haven't answered why you are holding me here," she said through clenched teeth. "And why did you keep me asleep for several days?"

"I don't run Semore by myself. The fate of all Neurians must be considered. It's obviously no secret how your war has affected us. Northerners are very different...your beliefs, your priorities—"

"And what do my beliefs and where I come from have to do with you holding me and keeping me from my family?"

"We have a duty to the Neurian people to ensure their safety." The man shrugged again.

Tara slowly stood, testing her foot. She started to put weight on it, then stopped. While she probably could walk, she decided it might be best not to let him know that fact. She was also very aware of her laser in this man's lap. "You seem to know more about me than I know about you. Who are you?"

Dorn Gowsky watched her slim figure as she hobbled a few feet away from the bed. He knew very little about Runners, other than they were supposed to be incredible warriors, and they had helped Gothman defeat the Sea People. Tara was beautiful, even in her current state. Those blue eyes...like the color of the sky...and that pale skin...she was quite the distraction. He'd never seen a woman like her before, other than in pictures.

She limped slowly, but there was very little sign of discomfort on her face. He guessed even in her drugged state, she had enough training to prevent her expression from betraying emotion. His best approach would be to not second-guess anything about her, but continue to watch her and learn.

He'd heard that she'd united two nations and could claim leadership over both. What power, what beauty! He wanted to know the type of person capable of mastering such a feat. She would be intelligent, with negotiating skills and the ability to influence others. Otherwise, people wouldn't respond to her. From the research he had done while she had been there, not enough good things could be said about Tara.

He was definitely attracted to her. But if his plan was to work, he had to remain true to the role he'd agreed to play. Crator help him. He hoped he could pull it off.

The council hadn't accepted his ideas on how to handle Tara, at first. Finally, he'd decided to keep most of his decisions about her from the council. They knew she'd been taken hostage. He'd brought her to them after he'd shot her. But they didn't know she was here, at his home. And they didn't know how long he'd kept her here. The council wouldn't have approved, but he knew he acted with the Neurians' best interests at heart. His conscience was clear.

He'd watched her as she lay under the covers, unconscious from the drugs. She became his sleeping beauty. There were nights when her presence haunted his dreams. He could have had sex with her, and she'd have never known. But that wasn't his style. He liked his women able to enjoy his ability to please them. It would have been rape, so he hadn't touched her—except in his dreams.

It had all started when the Runner, Kuro, approached him.

"You know there is a way to turn around the Neurian economy," Kuro had told him one night after they had enjoyed a fair bit of the Sea People's opiate wine. "And it would make you a hero."

"How's that?" Gowsky had asked, although he thought his friend a bit too intoxicated to be taken seriously.

"I grew up in a Runner clan known as the Blood Circle Clan," Kuro had told him. "Their leader, Patha, has a daughter, Tara. She's a manipulative, hardhearted bitch. She is Patha's bastard child, but she managed to lie and cheat her way into becoming Patha's heir. She'll lead all the clans after Patha dies."

"And what does she have to do with the Neurian economy?" Gowsky had no idea why his friend was talking to him about this.

"She charmed her way into the pants of the Lord of Gothman and gave him an heir." Kuro had poured more wine and leaned back in his chair. "This is where it gets good, my friend. Tara and her children have entered Semore. They are right here in your town."

"You are talking about the pale woman I saw yesterday?" Gowsky had been running errands when the young woman had driven her trailer into town. He had listened while she asked where she might keep her trailer, and had offered gold as payment. The woman hadn't impressed him as cold hearted or manipulative, and Gowsky thought of himself as a good judge of character.

"She must be killed, Gowsky."

"Huh?" Gowsky choked on his wine. "Why does she have to be killed?"

"Gothman and Runners need oil. Your land is floating with the stuff. But Tara won't negotiate for it. Right now, she is probably devising a plan to take it without the Neurians knowing. That is how she is, my friend. But with her out of the way, the Neurians would be able to sell the oil to a just Runner leader. Your economy would be better than you've ever known."

"And who would be the new leader?" Gowsky hadn't liked the idea of murder, but reestablishing the Neurian economy was imperative.

Kuro grinned. "Simple my friend. Me."

Gowsky pulled himself out of his reminiscing and focused on Tara. "I'm Dorn Gowsky," he said to her. "How's that foot?"

Tara glanced sideways at Gowsky. He watched her as if determining the answer for himself. That was something Darius often did. Guilt tugged at her. Noticing this man was handsome was no crime, so why did she feel odd? She concentrated on his question and not how he looked physically. "Your doctor's done a fine job. Please thank him for me. I would like to check on my children. Am I free to go?" She knew the answer before she asked it, but decided to play his game and met his gaze with an innocent smile.

Gowsky smiled back. "Your children are fine. I would like to ask you some questions, if I may?"

"I'd like to see my children first. It's important they know I'm fine. I'll be more than willing to answer your questions after I see them. After all, I have nothing to hide from you or your people." She took chance and started hobbling to the door. There was no doubt in her mind he wouldn't let her go, but she needed to make sure. If he had questions for her, he'd better start asking.

"Your children aren't in Semore anymore. Your trailer pulled out of here yesterday."

"You're a fool!" Tara spun around on Gowsky. The rage burned in her eyes and her body tensed. She saw the amused look in his eyes and her anger intensified. "You better let me contact my family so I can tell them I'm all right."

"I might be able to arrange that." Gowsky stood and walked over to Tara, took her arm, and calmly but firmly escorted her back to the bench. "You handle pain well, but I wouldn't give that foot too much of a workout too soon."

She yanked away from him and sat. Once again, her hair streamed over her shoulder. Lifting several strands in her hand, she noticed her hair was definitely longer.

Gowsky dropped into the chair across from her, a serious expression on his face. He stared at her once again.

She glared back. "Go ahead with your questions."

"Why did you come to Semore?"

"I've never been south of the border. I simply wanted to visit your town."

"You were looking for a job with our government."

"I liked it here. Your people have…" She hesitated.

"We have what?"

Tara reminded herself she had nothing to hide. "You have oil. We need oil. Getting a job with your government seemed like a good way to convince you to trust me so I could begin negotiations."

Gowsky was surprised by her answer. Was it possible she was telling the truth? He suddenly worried he'd made a grave mistake. But he didn't make a mistake. He knew he hadn't. There had been so many hours of meditative walks while praying to Crator. Every morning he'd awakened with the same thought clear in his head. Keep the Runner here. He was doing Crator's will. It wasn't his place to question that based on what Tara said to him now. He told himself her beauty preoccupied him. If she were manipulative, as Kuro suggested, she might be a very good liar.

"Neurians have had their way of life stripped from them. Many of our people are without jobs. Regrettably, the dire situation has made us suspicious." Gowsky got up and stuck her laser into the top of his pants. He opened the door to leave. "I'll see if we can contact your trailer so you can talk to your family."

Tara stared at the door after Gowsky left, hearing the lock click into place. Cold air rushed her face and Tara frowned. It felt like it was almost the New Winter outside, but if Tara understood the climate pattern this far south, winter shouldn't be here for another five cycles.

She cuddled into the thick comforters spread over the bench and observed the dimly lit room. The floor was nothing more than smooth, packed dirt, and the ceiling was wooden. There were no windows, although sunshine peered through the walls, which were just slabs of wood. Her prison appeared to be a type of shed, yet Gowsky had said she was in his barn. The Freelanders had barns. They were very large and animals lived in them. Apparently Neurians only used theirs to keep people prisoner.

She noticed several different sets of footprints leading from the door to the bench and back again. It looked as if she'd had many visitors she slept. She could only imagine who they might have been.

Tara rubbed her leg above the cloth wrapped around her foot. Whatever medicine they'd given her was leaving her body. She lifted her sore foot slowly onto her other leg, unpinned and unwrapped the bandage. There was a three-inch line of stitches along the side of her foot by her ankle

She studied the injury. There was no bruising and just a little swelling. As she ran her hand slowly over it, she noticed something odd. Next to the stitches was a faint scar, a scar she didn't remember, and it wasn't old. How strange, she thought as she rewrapped the injury and secured it with the pins.

Standing up was easy enough, but she worried about how soon she would be able to walk. She tried putting all her weight on her injured foot but wasn't successful. Once she mastered putting weight on her bad foot, she could kick through the wall with her good one. Her prison was not that sturdy, but her injuries made escape impossible at the moment.

She hobbled over to one of the walls and looked through the slits in the wood. All she saw were dirt yard and two trees. No other buildings and no roads were visible. She heard no sounds of animals, and no talking. Would Gowsky live outside town by himself? If that were the case, all she had to do was get out of this dilapidated structure and overpower one man. Child's play, if she weren't injured.

Had she really only been there several days? She thought about the faint scar on her foot. Had she done that climbing out of the burning building? So, why the new scar? Was somebody trying to make it seem like she'd been out of it for days when, in reality, it had been cycles?

Tara's heart began pounding, and icy fingers crept over her flesh. Something was wrong. It was definitely cold outside. How long had she been asleep? She thought of her children, of Syra, and of Darius. What did they think? Had they tried to rescue her? She wondered why Gowsky wanted her to think she'd only been asleep a few days.

Tara didn't see Gowsky for almost a quarter cycle. She spent every waking minute exercising, trying desperately to rouse her atrophied muscles. Her physical condition proved beyond doubt that she'd been asleep a long time. She was weak and out of shape. Her body had always been in prime physical condition, and her lack of strength annoyed her.

Someone brought her a generous plate of food several times a day, usually dried meat and fruit. The same person never visited her twice, and no one talked to her. Quite a few people worked for Gowsky. She also sensed the fear in each person who brought her food when they slid the plate through the gap between the door and the dirt floor. They fled from her wooden prison as soon as their task was done.

Her foot mended quickly, but she decided it was best to give no indication of this. The barn she was in was old and unstable. A quarter or half-cycle of recuperation and intense calisthenics, and escape would be easy.

In the meantime, icy breezes tormented her, mingling with dreams of her babies and loved ones. The blankets she kept wrapped around her provided little comfort. Tara's imagination made things even worse. She worried her family was sick with worry, doing everything in their power to search for her, and growing frustrated when they couldn't find her. Yet while their images plagued her, they also added incentive to endure the cold and bring back her body to health.

Gowsky visited her a half-cycle after she awakened. It was a bitter cold morning, and he pushed open the door with one hand and carried a pitcher with a steamy, hot fluid in the other. The morning glare was behind him.

Tara fought to keep her eyelids from shuttering against the light. He'd awakened her, and she forced her mind to clear before she moved.

Gowsky stood above her for a minute before sitting. Her body was stretched out under the comforters. She was on her side and the comforter curved over the outline of her hip. One of her arms draped across her body and her long fingers fell gracefully off the edge of the bench. Her sandy brown hair fell in strings.

"I do believe it's time to bathe you," Gowsky decided, doing his best not to imagine sudsy water sliding over her naked body, and failing.

Tara focused one eye on him but didn't move. Every muscle in her body ached from the intense workout she'd put herself through the day before.

"I've been bathing myself successfully for many winters now," she answered.

Gowsky chuckled and placed the pitcher on the ground next to him. "Does a hot bath sound good to you?" he asked and produced two mugs from his coat pocket. The steam floated up to the ceiling as he poured some of the dark liquid from the pitcher into each cup. It looked incredibly tantalizing, whatever it was. She licked her lips.

"It's good." He held out one of the mugs. "It also helps wake you up."

She opened the other eye and stared at him.

"Come on. You'll like it." He waved the cup under her nose. "Come on."

She felt its warmth brush her face. Sitting up slowly, she tried appearing to be in more pain than she actually was. The warmth of the mug in her hand felt so good that she wrapped both hands around it and sipped. The liquid was thick and had a sweet honey and chocolate taste. She took another, longer drink, then looked at Gowsky again. He had filled his mug and took a large gulp before setting the pitcher on the floor.

"How's your foot?"

She didn't respond, but instead situated herself on the bench carefully. She had taken the clothes she'd worn since she'd been there and laid them at the end of the bench while she slept. At the moment, she only wore her white pullover undershirt.

Adjusting the comforter over her legs, she noticed he watched the action. His gaze locked on her bare legs, not looking away until she'd covered herself. Whether he noticed her muscles weren't as atrophied or simply enjoyed seeing a partially naked woman, she wasn't sure. But something told her he enjoyed watching her. She knew interest in a man's eyes when she saw it. How much had he watched her? For whatever amount of time he'd kept her here, he'd kept her unconscious. He might have enjoyed any part of her, and she wouldn't have been able to stop him.

When she met his gaze, he didn't look away but instead smiled.

She didn't smile back. "Why'd you tell me I'd only been asleep for several days?"

Gowsky's face looked completely innocent as he raised his eyebrows. "And what makes you think you weren't?"

"It's almost new winter. You've intentionally cut my foot and stitched it up so it would look like the injury from the building. How long have I been here?"

"You've had plenty of time to think in here, haven't you?" Gowsky leaned back in his chair, crossed his arms, and stretched his long legs out in front of him. "Well, it's true. We made certain you'd remain unconscious longer than a few days. It was necessary."

He said this so nonchalantly, the words stung. Anger brewed through her veins, building to a boiling climax. The Neurians had held her prisoner for cycles.

"I assume the Gothman and Runners believe me dead."

Gowsky looked at her with dark eyes and sipped from his mug. "Like I said, it was necessary."

"So why did you bother to wake me now?" She matched his look of apathy. Her mind now, however, focused on a method of escape.

Gowsky shifted position, drawing his long legs underneath the chair, but then stretching them out again. He thought of the best way to answer her question. It was one he had anticipated being asked and had thought of several convincing responses. Telling her it was the suggestion of another Runner wasn't an option. He wouldn't say, *Sorry lady, it was politics, and Neurians need an income.*

He'd almost talked himself into doing away with her when Fleeders came forward and told him that he believed Tara had talked to a guardian in the desert. Gowsky was a man of faith. He'd seen the dog-woman in his dreams a lot lately, and that made him uneasy. He took it as a sign to take Tara out of her unconscious state. If anyone discovered her here, Gowsky knew he'd never be elected to another term.

He wanted to confide in Tara and tell her everything that had happened. The woman possessed a calmness, a sense of authoritative ease, that led him to believe she could talk through a dilemma and find a solution better than any of his council members. He wanted to share his dreams that he'd had during her time in captivity. He knew it meant Crator guided him when he dreamed of a Guardian, and he wanted to share this with her. Tara wouldn't understand. She was a Runner, a member of a race without Crator. If she had seen a Guardian in the desert, it only validated his dreams. It didn't mean she understood Crator.

From the way he hesitated, Tara knew Gowsky wouldn't give her a straight answer. Her mind raced. Darius thought she was dead. Had he claimed another? Was someone else raising her children? What about Patha and Reena? Did her parents believe her dead, as well?

If so, Patha would name someone else to be his successor over the Runners. She would have to fight for her rightful title if someone else was named heir in her absence.

Her children were the heirs to two nations. When they grew up, Andru would lead Gothman. Ana would lead the Runners. She would not have that right taken from them. If Tara lost her title, she knew Darius would see that Andru became Lord of Gothman when he grew up, but Ana would be without a title.

Tara looked into Gowsky's dark eyes. He had a very handsome face. She liked his high-set cheek bones and his long, straight nose. His dark, smooth looking skin added to his definite sex appeal. Unlike Darius, who had a way of burrowing into a person with a hard stare, Gowsky looked more curious. Darius demanded loyalty, and readily fought for ownership and submission. Gowsky stared at her with those black-as-night eyes and tried to analyse her. It was as if he wanted to know everything about her. Tara wasn't sure what he'd do with the information if he did know her. Darius would never have to worry about her being unfaithful with this man, though. He was quite possibly as gorgeous as Darius, but Gowsky had ruined her life.

"The Gothman were prepared to attack us when they thought you were a prisoner. We're not in a position for such an attack." Gowsky swallowed. "You died a warrior's death, saving one of our scientists from a horrible death. We escorted your family safely to a rendezvous point where they joined one of the Runner clans."

"How long ago was all this?"

He sucked in a breath before answering. "Six cycles ago."

Tara's muscles lurched. She fought hard not to leap from the bench and attack from midair. She wanted to pounce on him, pound his face and destroy those good looks. She wanted to kill him.

It took every bit of power she possessed to remain calm. Years of training were called into play. She stayed wrapped in the blanket, masking her feelings. "So now what?"

"We're not murderers. You were put to sleep to protect our nation. Time has passed and our nation is no longer threatened." His voice was so calm. He believed he'd pulled off his deceit-filled plan against the runners.

"And so now you send me home." She didn't make it a question. Tara seethed with outrage. "Just like that?"

Gowsky reached for the pitcher and stood. "We'll discuss this further once you've calmed down." He walked to the door and opened it, letting cold air rush into the small barn. "Get dressed if you want a hot bath."

Tara sat in the same position for a long time after Gowsky left. Sunlight reached her between the cracks of wood. She watched dust rise and swarm in rays of light that were paper-thin angles reaching the hard floor. She wanted to scream. She wanted to kick and punch the wooden walls around her until there was nothing left of this barn she'd been housed in for six cycles like she was nothing more than a caged animal. Neurians thought nothing of the Runners. Maybe her people weren't scientists. More than anything she wanted to show Dorn Gowsky what a Runner was capable of doing. If she destroyed him and everything he owned it wouldn't be enough. She held on to the bench with both hands on either side of her, digging into the wood with her nails. That scream threatened to rise past her throat. She leaned forward letting her hair fall in strings and shroud her face. Tara squeezed her eyes shut and worked past her fury until she felt the pain.

The Runners and the Gothman believed her dead. Darius had mourned her six cycles and quite possibly be ready to move on with his life. Andru and Ana would be over a winter old now. They would be walking and climbing and exploring their home.

Where was their home?

Were they with Patha? Or with Darius?

Darius would keep his children. They would grow up in his large house, exploring from attic to basement. The fields and hills surrounding it would be their world. All of Gothman would be their playground. Tara groaned. The pain came in waves. She missed them. All of them. They needed to know she was alive.

Tara dressed and threw the comforters to the side. The cotton pants she'd been wearing the night of the fire offered little to keep her warm. Her shirt sleeves were short. Her flat leather boots, with their flimsy soles, would not do if she had to walk any long distance. Not only would her clothing not protect her from the elements, they would not protect her during battle, either. Somehow she needed to obtain different clothing.

She stood in the middle of the shed and jogged in place. Her foot had mended. It was sore, but she could live with that. She dropped to the ground and began doing push ups. She needed her stamina back up to where it was six cycles ago.

Tara surveyed the walls of the shed. She glanced through the cracks in the wall and saw no one. Her time was limited. She took one of the blankets and carefully wrapped it around her leg. Using the laces of her shoes, she tied the blanket around her foot and leg. She stood and made sure the blanket wouldn't fall jumping up and down. The blanket didn't move. It would protect her from the tearing through her flimsy clothing and into her skin. She'd already tested the sturdiness of the four walls and knew which wall was the weakest.

Tara jumped into the air and kicked the wall. Several boards cracked and a hole appeared. The blanket got caught though, and Tara fell to the ground with her foot stuck up in the air. She struggled with the laces and finally yanked her foot loose. Pushing to her feet, she stood to the side, waiting. It was silent. She peaked out through the hole.

There was still no one in sight outside the shed.

"Next step," she whispered, planning as she began to hurry.

Tara rolled up the blanket tightly. She re-laced her boot. Then draping the other blanket over the hole so it covered the splintered and broken wood, Tara jumped out of her prison.

The bitter morning air slipped easily through her thin clothes, and she shivered. Tara pulled the blanket out of the hole and wrapped it around her. Carrying the other under her arm, she glanced at the clear sky and got a sense of her direction.

Semore was north. All indications showed Gowsky's house to be on the southern edge of the town. She'd work her way west before heading north again.

There was still no sight of anyone. However, she had no warm clothing, no food, no weapons, and no way to communicate with anyone. The odds for survival were not in her favor.

Within minutes, she stood surrounded by a clump of trees at the edge of the large yard. Tara turned back and looked at the house.

"That was too easy." Tara didn't see anyone. "There are no guards, no servants – no one."

Did he want her to escape? Gowsky had said they weren't murderers. Maybe he didn't know what to do with her. Was he just going to let her go?

"No," Tara decided, and she pulled the blanket tighter to fight the chill. "It would be stupid to let me go back to my people and tell them I was kept unconscious for six cycles by the Neurians."

She looked around at the trees and focused on the land south of her. Aware of how technologically advanced this society was, she searched the topography yard. Maybe there were traps she couldn't see. An icy breeze rustled around the trees. Was it her imagination or did the trees half a dozen yards away not appear affected by the breeze? She picked up several rocks and threw one toward the trees in question. The rock came back to her with so much force she almost didn't duck in time.

So that was it. He had a force field of some kind. She walked in what she believed to be a parallel path to the invisible field, determining its location by tossing rocks. They all bounced back at her. No wonder no one was pursuing her. She was fenced in.

Again, she studied the house. Were they watching her? Studying her? Figuring out what abilities she possessed?

Tara was perplexed. Without a landlink, she had few skills to handle her current situation. She didn't have a way to determine what the force field was made of, determine where it began and ended, or identify weak spots. If she threw rocks all day she might not learn a thing.

She climbed one of the taller trees to see into the distance. Her blankets slipped and attempted to trip her several times, but she managed to settle on a branch, relatively hidden by dead leaves, and wrap the loose blanket around her again. The force field had her stumped, but she would figure something out.

Sooner or later, someone would be sent looking for her. Then at least she'd have the chance to disarm them and have a weapon.

Runners taught their young warriors that patience was a virtue. Tara had never done well with that lesson. She was impatient. How long had she sat on this branch?

She listened for sounds other than leaves rustling. It seemed forever. Eventually two Neurians approached her from either side. She immediately thought of the five Gothman she'd taken out in the forest the day she'd entered that nation. That seemed like a hundred winters ago. She'd thought of those Gothman warriors as nothing more than an obstacle course. Even taking on Darius, when he might have killed her, had been a glorious adventure. Now, with these Neurians, everything seemed more serious, more focused. Maybe it was because she had more to fight for now. Andru and Ana needed their mama. The memory brought a smile to her face.

Two men, each carrying those large Neurian lasers, wandered through the trees toward her. They were looking in her direction, but didn't see her. As they approached each other, they turned around, then walked in circles, focusing on the area beneath her. Their landlinks had led them to her.

She waited until they were within a hand's reach of each other. Slowly, the two men looked up into the branches of the tree above them.

Wait. Wait. She mouthed the words, bracing herself.

Tara's muscles tightened, her adrenaline spiked. A breeze brushed against her neck. Icy fingers crawled down her spine. The excitement of the hunt sent chills rushing through her. Her body and mind had been deprived of this for too long. She inhaled the cool air deeply.

Wait. Wait. She watched two heads tilt back, and two sets of dark eyes look up until they spotted her.

Now!

She leapt off the branch. The comforter acted like a net that she used to try and drape over both men. One of the men aimed his large laser at her. She grabbed the front of it as she fell. With the force of gravity to assist her, she shoved the butt of the gun into his face as she landed on the ground.

"Do you plan to kill me?" she hissed.

The butt hit square on his nose, and he howled as Tara spoke. His own blood blinded him. Grabbing the gun from his hand, she turned and shot the other in the face.

"You broke my nose," the man howled, as he covered his face with his hands.

"I'm sorry, but I don't like it when people point lasers at me." Tara tugged her blanket free from under the dead man and seized his laser as well.

Turning, she hardly had time to aim as a third Neurian, this time a large woman, lunged at her. The target was close, and Tara took her down easily. Two more Neurian women were right behind her. They, too, proved easy targets.

An incredible blow from behind sent Tara flying forward.

She hit the ground with excruciating force. Tara endured the pain from the rough ground tearing into her flesh. She scurried to her knees and crawled to the Neuriam laser that had flown out of her grasp when she fell.

"Hold it right there." Tara aimed straight into the mouth of a young Neurian man. His eyes doubled in size as her finger tightened on the trigger.

"That's enough!" A voice boomed through the air, jerking every muscle in Tara's body as she jumped in surprise.

She turned to look at the man who'd shouted the command. "You steal six cycles from my life, and then tell me this is enough?" Tara pulled the trigger and shot the Neurian in the mouth. She then fired on the man who had issued the command.

The sound of him falling to the ground, with half of his face missing, echoed through the surrounding trees. Then, all was silent.

Tara turned, arms outstretched, aiming the Neurian lasers and at anybody fool enough to make their presence known. Seven dead bodies lay on the ground around her. The smell of blood and burnt flesh drifted as the breeze increased. Breathing hard, her body tensed. She listened to the silence and continued glancing in all directions.

There were more. She heard the occasional leaf crumple, or a small twig snap. Gowsky walked slowly out from behind a nearby tree. His hands were outstretched, his movements slow and deliberate. She aimed one of the large lasers at him.

"Do all Runners fight like you?" He raised his hands higher, letting her know he was not armed.

"If they're good, they do." Tara aimed at his face.

"We definitely have a problem on our hands." He smiled at her. "Do you shoot someone who isn't armed?"

Gowsky must have believed she wouldn't shoot him, since he appeared before her with outstretched arms. But she knew he didn't trust her when four Neurians appeared from behind the trees. They aimed their lasers at her.

CHAPTER EIGHTEEN

"I ONLY shoot if necessary." Tara dropped her lasers to the ground. The breeze whipped through the trees. This time, her sweat-soaked body felt the chill.

Gowsky noticed how seductive she looked in spite of her dirty clothes hanging on her thin body. Tara had many sides to her personality, he noted. Those who didn't know her well would think she was simply a happy mama with two small children, looking for a new life. He'd seen what he wanted to see, however. She was the most incredible warrior he'd ever witnessed seeing. Gowsky was more than a bit put out that Kuro hadn't given him better warning of her unbelievable fighting skills.

Tara watched Gowsky aware that he was summing up her abilities. Had he set her up simply to see what she could do? If so the man had sent seven of his warriors on a suicide mission to test her. Tara had no problem showing the Neurians her skills, or letting them know she would fight for her freedom. Now, she was curious what Gowsky planned to do with this knowledge.

There was no movement beyond the surrounding group of trees. Tara shifted her attention and looked through the trees. Something moved again. It was the old woman from the desert! She stood partially visible behind one of the farthest trees, returning Tara's stare. Had she walked all the way here by herself?

The woman was definitely very old. Her wrinkled skin was leathery and her watery eyes almost glassy. It Tara didn't know better she'd say the age had stolen the old woman's sight. Her dress and boots were made of animal skin. Thick, white, straw-like hair was wrapped loosely around her head in a twisted bun. For an old woman who had obviously walked so far she was relatively clean, probably a lot cleaner looking than Tara looked at the moment.

There was another thing Tara noticed about the old lady. She was out here on the edge of Gowsky's property. Possibly she'd just witnessed Tara kill Neurians. The old woman didn't look stressed, though. If anything, she seemed relaxed, content with her surroundings and at peace.

Gowsky glanced in the direction Tara was looking. He didn't see anything, yet she was alerted by something. He stared harder. Still nothing. What was she doing?

Tara narrowed her eyes and scrutinized the old woman, who had finally stepped out from behind the tree and had begun walking toward her. There was obviously a break in the force field for the old woman to get on Gowsky's land. Tara had to figure out where it was.

Tara returned her attention to Gowsky. The four Neurians still held their weapons on her, and Gowsky was giving her a hard look. None gave any indication they noticed the old woman approaching. Tara looked down at the ground and slowly lifted her eyes in the direction of the old woman once again.

She walked into the open, allowing herself to be seen by the small group. Yet they didn't appear to notice her.

Were they testing her again? Tara tried to give no indication that she noticed the old woman approaching. The woman stopped next to Tara. She looked up and met Tara's eyes. It was definitely the same woman she'd seen in the desert.

"Why are you here?" the old woman asked. Her deeply creased dark brown face appeared healthy.

Tara didn't respond. Instead, she looked at Gowsky, who was giving her an odd look.

The old woman continued. "You have a lot of work to do. Tonight, you need to go home." She turned and walked back through the trees.

Tara made mental note where the old woman left, then looked at the four men, still aiming their guns at her, before focusing on Gowsky.

"Take her inside," Gowsky instructed the four armed men.

Tara was escorted past the damaged barn to the house. She wondered what Gowsky normally used the small wooden structure for since she didn't notice any animals on his property.

Her thoughts returned to the old woman. Who was she? Tara remembered Fleeders' explanation about guardians roaming in the desert, but this woman had been flesh and blood, not a hallucination devised from the imagination.

Gowsky led Tara inside his home, dismissing the guards before they entered. She found herself surrounded by warmth for the first time in days. As she entered a large room, Gowsky didn't seem to mind her self-guided tour, so she studied the room's contents.

Tara glanced behind her at Gowsky, who stood just inside the door pushing buttons on a wall-mounted pad. Tara wished she had her landlink with her; she could then determine if force fields surrounded the house.

Tara stood in a long, narrow room. She noted a closed door at the other end of the room and a hallway to her left, which was shrouded in darkness. The room was possibly used for brainstorming political tactics, judging by the number of chairs and sofas arranged in it. The floors were covered with thick, braided carpet, and the walls made of clay.

A door opposite her opened, and a woman appeared. She stared at Tara but made no move to enter the living area.

"You can show our guest to her room, Saysil," Gowsky said.

The woman walked across the room, heading for the dark hallway. Tara guessed she should follow and did so.

"These clothes should fit you." The woman, who was about the same age as Tara, opened the door at the end of the hallway.

Tara entered the room, noticing Saysil backed to the doorway. She gestured silently to clothes draped over a chair, before closing the door and locking it.

The dark khaki pants and wool sweater she'd been given to wear were actually comfortable. The small room where she'd changed had a large bureau and a small bed. Possibly it was a spare room for guests—or for prisoners.

The room she'd been given in Gothman, when she'd first come to live with Darius, had been much nicer. Darius had also considered her a prisoner of sorts, although at the time Tara hadn't known it. Gothman were obviously a lot more skilled in their tactics than Neurians.

Clay-plastered walls slowly closed in around her. Pacing the length of the room agitated her further. The walls had no pictures hanging on them, and only one thin blanket spread over the bed—certainly not enough cover for the new winter.

Left alone, Tara explored the room's contents. The bureau only had a few items in it, possibly forgotten by a previous guest. She found a pouch-like bag with straps that she tied around her stomach and hid under her sweater. She also discovered long underwear in the bureau and pulled off the khaki pants to put them on before donning the pants again. It would be wise to dress warmly if she took the old lady's advice and headed home that night. Even though she had no idea how this plan was to be executed, she decided to prepare just in case. It would be colder the further north she traveled.

The only window in the room looked out over the backyard. A large pane of glass was enclosed in a wooden frame that slid up and down on ropes. It easily unlocked, and she slid it up. The screen on the other side of the window would pop out easily, she determined after studying the manner in which it attached to the window frame.

She looked out the window at the side yard. Not too far away was another, much larger barn. The barn door was open but it was impossible to tell if anyone was inside. Four guards had accompanied them to the house, but she didn't see any of them at the moment. She didn't see the small barn that had been her prison, but knew it was on the other side.

Carefully, she removed the screen and held on to it until the bottom touched the ground, then let go. Gowsky obviously didn't use his house to hold prisoners. Possibly he relied on a landlink system to protect his home and decided there was only one way to find out. For the second time that day, Tara planned her escape. She slid out the window, landing easily onto the ground.

Tara walked several feet away from the house and froze. At the corner of the building, Gowsky stood talking to another man. They hadn't been noticeable from the window. The other man faced her, but Gowsky had his back to her. If she made a move toward the trees she would be noticed.

The man talking to Gowsky pointed a finger in her direction, and Gowsky turned.

Tara saw him throw up his hands as if exasperated and steer the man in the other direction. That's when Tara realized the other man was Fleeders!

Fleeders looked hard at her, saying something to Gowsky.

Tara seized the opportunity and bolted toward the barn. She heard Gowsky yell her name. He was running after her.

Tara got to the barn in plenty of time to shut the door and lower the wooden lock. She moved away from the door as Gowsky lunged against it.

"Open the door, Tara."

Tara ignored him and moved farther from the door, looking around her. Farming equipment surrounded her. Irrigation supplies lined the wall. She saw several horse stalls and started examining each in turn. They appeared empty. She passed a pitchfork and picked it up as she continued investigating the stalls.

"Tara!" Gowsky yelled loudly this time, his frustration apparent.

"Where are all your animals?" Tara decided to feed his anger.

"Dead. Now open the door!"

"Dead? That's odd. How'd they die?"

"All the animals died, Tara." It was Fleeders' voice.

Tara reached the fourth and last stall. "Perfect."

She stared at her motorcycle parked in the space. It was covered with dust and straw. She brushed off the seat as she pulled it out. The landlink was missing from the dash. Would it run? Not far without fresh gas and oil.

Several laser shots hit the door, Gowsky yelled from the other side. "Aim at the lock."

A final shot broke the metal piece holding the wooden lock, and it slid across the hard dirt floor. The door swung open.

"Where do you expect to go on that?" Gowsky stood at the door, focusing on Tara who'd mounted the bike. "The force field surrounds the yard."

Tara smiled. She pushed the necessary buttons, and the bike started easily. "I guess I will have to have faith in your Crator."

She wouldn't know how hard her words hit Gowsky. He looked at her with complete bafflement. Gowsky snapped his attention at Fleeders, then back to Tara. "You don't believe in Crator."

"Well, it seems your Crator believes in me." Tara raced her engine, allowing the gas to flow through it.

"You have no right to speak about Crator. You know nothing about Him," Gowsky sneered. "Crator would have anything to do with a Runner."

"If you say so." Tara shrugged indifferently. Her expression didn't change as she looked up and saw that he pointed laser gun at her. "You know I saw her again today, don't you, Gowsky?"

"You saw her?" Gowsky inched closer, maintaining his aim on her.

"I saw an old woman." Tara had no doubts that Gowsky would shoot her. But if he got just a bit closer, she'd disarm him. "She told me to go home."

"How convenient," Gowsky snapped.

Tara lunged the bike forward with no warning. Straight at Gowsky. He jumped to the side and fired the laser. Tara reached out and smacked Gowsky's wrist, causing the it to fire into the rafters. A blizzard of hay descended on them.

Tara maintained her grip as Gowsky yanked back.

Her hand moved with him as he yanked, offering no resistance.

He was prepared for her to pull back, assuming she'd try to take the laser from him. He used too much force and lost his balance. Which is exactly what she wanted.

As he hesitated, trying to regain balance, she stole the laser, pulled the handlebar of her bike hard in the other direction and sped out of the barn.

Tara was amazed. She was properly clothed, armed, and had her bike. She knew her skills exceeded those of the Neurians, but the accomplishments she'd just achieved almost appeared to be handed to her. Maybe that old woman wasn't as delusional as she looked.

Gowsky was right, she knew nothing about Crator. She'd never been asked to have faith in something she knew nothing about or had never met. She'd had faith in other Runners before, during battle. She knew they would do their part and if she did her part, they would be victorious. She'd had faith in Patha all her life. He provided for her and taught her everything he knew. That was the faith she would use now.

Still if Gowsky and his people believed in something they'd never seen, what would it hurt if she tried to do the same? Someone or something had just helped her escape.

She skidded the bike around the barn and headed to the point in the force field where the old woman had left. Tara didn't slow down or hesitate in any way. This Crator-being, or the old woman...someone...had faith in her. She would reciprocate. She rode at high speed straight into the force field.

Gowsky dove at Tara's bike but missed. He tore at the ground with his shoes as he broke into a full run toward his house.

"Turn off the force field!" he screamed, running through the house, knocking over an end table, heading for the small room off his living room. He screamed again, "Turn the force field off now!"

Fleeders was right behind him as the two stormed into the small room, startling the young woman sitting at a landlink.

"What?" She turned in her chair, looking surprised and bewildered at the unusual request.

"She'll electrocute herself." Gowsky almost knocked over the confused woman as he reached for the console in front of her. A beeping sound began, and a red light flashed next to one of several monitors. "She thinks she has some gift from Crator and can just drive straight through that thing."

The trio watched the monitor and saw Tara riding at full speed through the backyard toward the trees. Another light began flashing, indicating the force field had been dismantled. Tara drove around the trees and disappeared from the screen's view. Gowsky raced out of the small room.

"You let her go!" Fleeders followed him.

"You heard her. She said she saw Crator. She was going to run right into that force field. Her bike is completely electronic—she'd have been fried to a crisp."

"She told me an old lady talked to her in the desert one night, and she just said she saw an old lady again. Maybe Crator is talking to her," Fleeders whispered, afraid of being overheard. He looked around the empty living room. "She told me the woman disappeared into the darkness and then she saw a large dog. Gowsky, she knows nothing about the Guardians. She wanted to research Crator through our network but I told her..." Fleeders' cut himself off. He made eye contact with Gowsky and shuffled from one foot to the other, suddenly very uncomfortable.

"You never told me that you discussed Crator with her. What did you tell her? And when did this conversation take place?"

"Well, uh, I told her it would raise suspicion if she started researching Crator."

"When did you talk to her?"

"Uh, the night that…" Fleeders hesitated, searching for words. He wanted to say the night that Gowsky burned down his life's work, the night their communication with the Lunians ended. "It was the night you brought her here."

Gowsky stared at Fleeders for a moment. So Fleeders had been communicating with Tara when he was supposed to be spying on her. The man possessed outstanding landlink skills, but his religious faith bordered on the superstitious. It amazed Gowsky that even the most intelligent of people allowed something as simple as faith in Crator to consume their life and affect rational decision-making.

Gowsky didn't have time for this. He gave Fleeders a look that said the conversation was not over. He straightened the small table he'd knocked over, opened the small drawer in it, and pulled out another laser. Shoving it into the side of his pants, he once again ran out of his house.

Tara didn't shut her eyes. She didn't blink. She didn't slow down. She looked straight ahead as the trees cleared and the desert lay ahead.

She had done it. She had driven through the force field.

Was this the act of Crator? Who was this Crator? She looked around to the vast openness, glanced behind her to see the trees fading. Suddenly the frigid wind hit her skin, causing her to shiver uncontrollably.

Gowsky would follow her. Escape would not be this easy. She needed direction. West. She needed to go west.

Ignoring the waves of cold air streaming across her body, she veered the motorcycle. She wasn't used to navigating without her landlink. But one of the tests she'd passed as a young warrior was finding her way back to the clan without the aid of her navigation program. She'd been one of the first Runners to make it back, and she remembered how proud Patha had been. He hadn't shown it in front of the rest of the clan, but that night, as she'd cleaned her bike, he'd told her. She'd never forget the look in his eyes—unconditional love.

Tara's eyes burned. She hated crying. The tears felt like fire, burning her face as they fell down her cheeks. She tasted the salt in her mouth even though it was firmly shut to keep her teeth from chattering. She struggled with the tears as they persisted, fogging her vision.

Patha thought she was dead. Had he cried? She'd never seen him cry before. He was a true warrior and strong emotions would cloud judgment. Patha wouldn't cry. It was more likely he'd been angry—furious that he'd let her go to Southland. He berate himself for not forcing her to stay and tame Darius. Somehow she needed to let him know she was alive and coming home.

Tara looked up at the sky, noticing the sun was moving to the west. The desert would freeze once nightfall hit. However, the farther north she drove, the colder it would get. In spite of better clothes, she still wasn't properly dressed and would freeze to death without some form of shelter, and the means to build a fire.

Looking ahead once again, she veered hard to avoid a large animal directly in front of her. Her bike slid in the sand, and for a moment she thought she would lose her balance. Tara cursed the clothes she was wearing. If she injured herself, she would only freeze faster. She slowed the bike and regained control.

As she turned, Tara's mouth fell open. The same old woman sat next to a fire, stirring something in a pot that hung over the flames.

Tara steered her bike up next to the woman and got off. "We meet again."

The woman didn't look up. "It's almost ready. Hurry and change clothes." The old woman pointed the wooden spoon to something behind Tara.

A large tan tent was set up next to her bike. She was shocked, afraid to move. Something akin to panic hit her. She felt fear, and her shivering became uncontrollable. The tent had not been there a second ago. There was no question. Tara was sure of it. Was she somehow experiencing delirium from the drug she'd been given over the past six cycles? Maybe none of this was real.

She slowly turned to the woman who was still hunched over the fire.

"You'll freeze if you don't change. Your clothes are inside. I'll make you a plate."

Tara left the old woman and walked to the tent, touching it gently, not completely convinced it was actually there. The roughness of the animal skin stretched over wooden poles scratched her fingertips. Tara pulled the flap covering the entrance to one side and stepped inside. Immediately, warmth engulfed her. Her eyes adjusted to the dim interior and she saw a small folding canvas chair in the middle of the tent. Her Runner clothing was folded neatly on top.

She stared at the folded pile of black woven silk and smelled the crisp black leather before carefully touching them and picking up the top piece of clothing. It was her silk black undershirt! As she held the piece of material in front of her, she inhaled the familiar scent of her clothes—the sweet, fresh smell, as if they had just been washed.

None of this made sense. Her bike was outside. She'd parked it there. This tent hadn't been there when she'd stopped her bike. She hadn't been lost in thought and not noticed it. This tent that she was standing in now, that she'd touched with her fingers, had not been here a moment before. Something more powerful than anything she'd ever known, or anyone she'd ever gone up against in battle, was at play here. The old woman was obviously not how she appeared. Patha would advise learning everything possible about this new being and bringing the information back to the clan. Tara would do just that.

As she finished dressing and put on her black leather jacket, Tara noticed her laser in her right pocket where she always kept it. She left the tent, trying to decide what to say to the old woman.

"Ah, that's better. Here, sit." The old lady gestured at her with a plate of steaming food in her crooked, wrinkled hand.

Tara took the plate and sat on the ground next to the old woman's feet. "How did you get my clothes?"

"Crator got them."

"Who is Crator?"

Their eyes met and the old woman smiled. "You'll know when your heart is ready, I guess." She nodded at the food. "Eat up. It's potato stew."

"Potato stew?" Tara looked down at the steaming plate of food. "This was my favorite meal when I was a child." Did the old woman already know that?

Tara hoped she hadn't dishonored the old woman. Not once while eating had she offered any stories as they sat by the fire. She had devoured the stew without saying a word. Tara stood and took her plate over to the fire. Her insides were warm, and her body rejoiced at the comfort of her own clothing. She picked up her headscarf and wrapped it snugly around her head, securing it in the back. "You've been very kind to me. I wish I could repay you, but I have nothing."

The old woman ignored her and started to clean the dishes in a bucket of water on the ground.

"Let me clean up." Tara squatted in front of the bucket and picked up her dirty dish.

"Don't worry, child." The woman took the plate from Tara. "You don't need to repay me. I'm simply a Guardian. You need to get that bike in order. You have a long trip ahead of you."

"What is a guardian?"

"I serve Crator and do as He says."

"Where is he?" Tara hoped the old woman would give her a different answer then she had when she'd first met her with the children.

The old woman chuckled. "Crator is everywhere, my dear." She looked up at Tara and again pointed with the wooden spoon in her hand. "You'll find some tools behind the tent, I think." She sounded distracted, like an old person who wasn't sure where she'd left something.

"Do you live around here?"

"I go wherever I'm needed. Crator sends me."

Tara sighed. She wanted to know more, but wasn't sure which questions to ask. "So Crator takes care of you?"

"Child, he takes care of you, too." The old woman placed the leftover stew in a bowl and put it into a travel bag. "Your faith shall grow, child, don't worry. You are young."

"My mission here wasn't too successful." She paused, studying the woman's leathery face and searching for the right words. "I'm glad I've learned of your Crator, though. I wish we had something like him in Northland."

The old lady slowly took her time standing. "You've learned exactly what you were supposed to learn while you were here." She took Tara by the arm and, at a snail's pace, escorted her around the tent. "Child, Crator is everywhere. He will provide for you as you know Him." She let go of Tara's arm. "Now take care of your bike, child."

Tara wasn't completely surprised to see exactly what she needed to tune up her motorcycle—all necessary tools and a large metal can, which, after smelling its contents, Tara realized was full of fuel.

As it grew dark, the bike was finally in prime condition, ready for the long journey north. Tara cleaned the tools and returned them to the place where she'd found them.

As she walked around the tent, she noticed two things at once.

First, a large dog lay protectively next to the fire. Second, a vehicle approached the small campsite.

Tara pulled out her laser, ready to fight for her life.

CHAPTER NINETEEN

THE LARGE beast showed off deadly looking teeth and growled as the vehicle slowed just feet from the tent. Its hackles rose and it lowered its head. Just as the animal prepared to leap on the intruder, a piercing hum sliced through the air.

A horrific scream violated the campsite, curdling Tara's blood. The ground shook under her feet when the large dog collapsed to the ground.

"No!" Tara wailed and leapt out from behind the tent, firing her laser.

Gowsky stood next to his groundmobile, but his return shot missed her completely as her laser shot sliced through his right shoulder. This time the scream renting the night air belonged to Gowsky as he hit the side of his groundmobile and crumbled to the ground.

"Try again and you die!" Tara ran straight over to Gowsky and ripped the laser from his hand. She hurled it into the night.

"Your clothes," Gowsky struggled to speak while gripping his blood-stained shoulder. "They were returned to your family."

Tara ignored him. She hurried to the lifeless animal and collapsed to her knees. She stroked its bloody coat and sobbed as she pressed her cheek so the side of its head. I didn't hear him coming. I'm so sorry." She wept freely, and her tears mixed with the blood on the animal's coat.

Tara ignored Gowsky's groans as she murmured apologies to the dead animal. "I never even knew your name. I'll give you a proper death ceremony," she whispered into the ear of the dead canine and looked up to survey the contents of the campsite. "You died an honorable death and shall have an honorable ceremony."

Gowsky crawled into his groundmobile, pulled out a small first aid kit and began to treat his wound. Tara didn't give him any attention as she began building up the fire.

There was an exceptional amount of logs stacked by the fire that Tara hadn't paid attention to until now. She squinted through her tears into the darkness. There weren't any trees around them.

"Did you know you were going to die?" she whispered. Then with shock had a hard time stomaching her next thought. "Is my life worth so much that you would die for me?"

"Why do you care so much for that thing?"

"She took care of me, more than once."

"It was going to attack me. I know you would have done the same thing."

Tara turned and gave Gowsky a long hard look. She studied the handsome face and the onyx eyes. "Do you have any idea who you've killed?"

Gowsky looked at the dead animal, then at Tara. His expression was blank, but she thought she noticed trepidation lurking in his eyes. He pressed a cloth, already blood-stained, against his shoulder as he climbed out of the groundmobile. Gowsky walked up to look at the dog lying still on the ground. Standing over the dead animal, he said, "Obviously an animal you cared about."

"She was one of your Guardians. And you are a fool. She's been helping me ever since I've arrived in your nation. She provided this camp, food, and the tools to ready up my bike. This entire setup was here when I arrived, with an old lady attending it. When you pulled up, she turned into a dog."

She watched him look around at the campsite in wonder. Tara turned and yanked the cloth away from the wound. "You'll live," she snarled and slapped the cloth back over his shoulder, glad when he winced. "I came to Semore to see if you'd be willing to start trading with us." She felt frustrated she hadn't accomplished that task, but now all she wanted to do was go home. "We need your oil. But shunned me and kidnapped me. Your people shall suffer for that."

Tara watched him stiffened when she continued. "And there's nothing I can do about it. I could ask that you're given another chance to prove yourselves as allies, but I fear your crimes are too serious. Crator will decide what to do with you."

Gowsky didn't say anything when he walked to his groundmobile. He secured a bandage to his shoulder. Then returning, he lifted the dead animal and placed it on the logs she'd piled. He watched as Tara started the fire. Gowsky watched her graceful movements and thought how incredibly beautiful she was, and how deadly. With the power she now possessed, she could eliminate the Neurian race. Yet somehow, he felt she had no desire to do so.

He was worried. When Tara reappeared after six cycles, plenty of questions would be asked. And what would the council do?

Dimly, he heard her say, "I'm leaving, Gowsky. Go home to your people."

He paused next to his groundmobile as she continued watching flames leap around the dead animal. After a minute, he climbed into the vehicle, started it, and drove toward Semore. Suddenly, he turned the vehicle around and headed back to the gun lying on the ground. Skidding to a stop, he jumped out, grabbed it and squatted next to the groundmobile aiming at Tara.

She didn't budge from her ritual.

He watched as she remained squatted by the fire. After a short time, Tara stood and moved to the tent. She began to disassemble it. The Runner had to be aware of his presence, yet she completely ignored him. Not once did Tara look up at him. How could he shoot a woman who simply ignored him?

Gowsky decided she must think he posed no threat. She must view Neurians as a soft race she might simply dismiss. Tara was challenging his warrior abilities, and he was furious.

After all, his pride was at stake. He couldn't turn and humbly leave as she suggested. Gowsky would show her that Neurians knew how to fight! He jumped back into the groundmobile.

Tara folded the tent and pulled the twine attached to its outer side until it was a compact bundle. She secured it to the back of her bike. As she reached for the tent poles, she saw Gowsky approaching at high speed—straight for her.

Jumping on her bike, Tara skidded out of the way just as he ran through the small camp, sending pots rolling across the desert as he ran into them. Twenty yards or so past the camp he slammed on the brakes and turned around, preparing for a return drive-by.

She aimed her laser and shot his back tire. Tara accelerated toward the groundmobile and slammed on her brakes, skidding to a stop within arm's distance of Gowsky.

Aiming her laser at his head, she said, "I told you to leave."

This time, Gowsky was prepared. He grabbed her wrist and yanked her hand holding the laser. His strength overcame hers, and he pulled her forward off the front of her bike.

Tara came at him full force. The two flipped out of the other side of the groundmobile.

Gowsky twisted his body and landed on top of her. He slammed her hand against the ground and the laser fell free from her fingers. She completely relaxed her body underneath his, which caused him to relax his grip on her, although he watched her warily.

Instantly, Tara brought up her leg and kneed him hard in the crotch. He lunged forward, fell to the side, and she squirmed out from underneath him.

"You insult my fighting abilities and mock Crator," he snarled, doubled over on the ground from pain. "Do you really think our Crator would protect a Runner from a Neurian laser? Crator protects Neurians—not Runners!"

"I'm not insulting Crator, Gowsky. But I am protected from your gun. A Runner's outfit is laser proof." Her blue eyes were radiant with emotion.

Gowsky raised his laser at her.

Tara jumped, kicking him straight in the chest. He fell backward, and she pushed him to the ground.

This time, she was on top of him. Tara grabbed the laser and tossed it, while pressing her other hand against his chest. Raising the laser to his face, she snarled, "I could kill you right now, and it would be completely justified."

"I can't just let you walk away."

She shoved the laser into his nose. "Then you die."

He looked into her eyes and knew that she meant it. "We're not prepared to go to war again."

Tara jumped off him. "You won't try to stop me from leaving again?"

Gowsky scrambled to his feet, staring at the laser in his face. It was way too close for comfort. "I don't have much of a choice. You've disabled my groundmobile, and you have a laser in my face." He tried a reassuring smile but her expression remained hard. "Tara, I wish we could have known each other under different circumstances."

Tara backed off, but kept the laser pointed at him. She walked through the campsite, looking at what was left, but continuously glanced at Gowsky to make sure he didn't try anything. The tent poles were bent and broken. The smell of burning fur and flesh was as strong as the flames were high. It made no sense to burn the dead animal. Maybe it was a Runner ceremonial way to celebrate the death of special people. Tara really believed that dead dog was a Guardian. Guardians didn't die. Not to mention, he knew Crator. Crator wouldn't care about Runners, or Gothman, or anyone as Oldworld as they were. The Runners and Gothman war against the Sea People had taken away the Neurians largest buyer of opium. Crator would never send a Guardian to help someone who had hurt his people.

Crator might have sent Tara to him. He hadn't figured out why though. Gowsky watched Tara's profile waver from the heat of the flames. She squinted in his direction before returning to her bike.

She rode the bike slowly until she was next to Gowsky. "Good luck with your Southland."

Tara left him in a cloud of dust.

Gowsky brushed dirt off his face and scrambled for his laser. He fired but to no avail. Her motorcycle disappeared from sight as he stood at the ruined campsite, next to a burning dog, with a disabled groundmobile and an injured shoulder.

Tara rode due North at high speed well into the night. She mentally tried calculating how long, at this speed, it would take to reach Gothman. Yes, she would go directly to Gothman. Her children were there. She was sure of that. Patha would not oppose Darius in raising his own children, especially if Patha thought their mama was dead.

It had taken her a day and a half to reach the border with much slower transportation. However, without her landlink she didn't know the best way to drive north. As she tried to determine her route, Tara's mind flickered to her children, Patha, Reena, Hilda, Torgo and Syra. And Darius.

She wondered if he'd claimed another woman. It was a recurring thought she'd had ever since Gowsky had told her how long she'd been unconscious. Or maybe he was having sex with every woman in Gothman. He better get it out of his system.

Tara imagined Andru and Ana walking. Her pudgy infants would now have legs strong enough to stand on. Which one had taken their first step? Tara guessed Ana would have taken the first step—she was the one who appeared more daring, more curious to check out new things. But Andru would run first, because he had to be fast to take everything from Ana and inspect it. Her heart constricted with pain at how much she had missed in her children's lives. It was hard to breathe from the pain. With a ragged sigh, she told herself she would see them in less than a quarter-cycle. Then she would work to make them know her again.

And what of Darius? If he had another woman in his life, perhaps she had attempted to make the children her own. Tara hated the thought. No one else would raise her children. Not even Darius would be able to prevent her from being with her children, no matter what happened when she returned.

She set up a makeshift camp when she grew too tired to drive safely, tore it down the next day, and continued north without coming across anyone. Late that afternoon, she was riding along a high prairie trying to remember if she had been this way before. The hills and trees grew thicker the farther north she drove, but after traveling for hours, all hills and trees appeared the same. She worried she had somehow altered course, although she still drove north.

Then she saw it. Ahead in the distance, several trails of smoke filtered slowly up to the sky.

Tara slowed her bike, her senses alert to an oncoming situation. Her muscles tensed as she readied herself for a possible altercation. The smells around her became more apparent. Any movement to the right or left caught her eye immediately. She heard every bird sing, every rock pop under the wheels of her bike.

Tara wasn't familiar with people living this far south of Gothman in Freelander territory. This land had always been uninhabited. There was no reason she would be considered an enemy unless whoever she was approaching feared Runners. Still, caution was in order. Tara veered out of the prairie and decided to approach the camp through the trees bordering nearby hills.

She was ecstatic when she spotted trailers and parked motorcycles. The black outfits of the men and women walking through camp were a welcome sight.

Several Runners noticed her approach and pulled their lasers. Their equipment wouldn't acknowledge her as a Runner without her landlink.

"Hold it right there," the closest Runner approached her motorcycle as she slowed within yards of them.

Tara stopped her bike and held her hands out to show she came in peace but did not speak until questioned. She knew the routine.

"Runner, where is your landlink?"

"I've been to Southland. It was stolen. I'm lucky to be alive." She dismounted to show her non-warrior intentions as was customary. "I'm glad to see a Runner clan."

"You're welcome to hear the stories at the fire." This was the usual greeting offered to a visiting Runner, and Tara smiled her appreciation.

"I've got much to catch up on. I've been traveling for awhile."

"Come back for the test, have you?" They were walking now, and the two Runners led.

Tara pushed her bike. "The test?"

"Well, you have been out of circulation for awhile. No landlink, too. You navigate well."

"I wasn't sure I was, to be honest. What test?"

"The Test of Wills."

Tara stopped walking and stared at the Runner who had just spoken. The Test of Wills was given when the leader of a clan died or stepped down and had no heir.

"We will be continuing north in the morning. Most clans are headed that way. You're more than welcome to travel with us. We'll take you to Rolko, but I'm sure he'll give consent."

As Tara walked, her mind raced with questions. Why was the Test of Wills being offered? What happened to Patha? She remained silent. If she made her presence known after a Test of Wills had been issued, it would stir up commotion among the clans. Tara hoped she would learn more when she listened to the stories around the fire, without having to ask questions.

Rolko permitted her into the Four-Circle clan as a traveling warrior. This meant she could sleep by the main fire, use their water supplies, be fed during the main daily meal, and if she still had her landlink, use their main board to transmit. To refuse their acceptance as a traveling warrior would dishonor the clan, especially since they were going in the same direction. So even though she would have arrived in Gothman much sooner if she traveled alone, Tara graciously thanked Rolko for allowing her to share her stories.

Tara was left alone to move through the campsite after leaving Rolko's trailer. She immediately walked to the main fire, hoping for food and, if she was lucky, details of Patha's death. She bit down on the bitter taste of fury. Patha wouldn't be dead if she had been with him. If he hadn't denied her leaving with her clan, Tara never would have gone south. As well, if she hadn't been kidnapped by Gowsky, and had been able to stay in touch with Patha, she would have known if there was trouble. One thing she knew for certain, Patha didn't die of natural causes. He had been in his prime.

"Hey, wait up!" The voice came from behind Tara. "I'm Male, Rolko's daughter." A girl several winters younger than Tara hurried to join her. "Papa asked me to come get you and offer my hospitality. My trailer's over here if you'd like to clean up or anything."

Male's trailer was simple. The floors were bare; a wooden tile covered the eating and living area. The countertops were spotless, and two overstuffed matching chairs with a rectangular wooden table between them, provided all the furniture for the small living area. A folding table extended from the wall of the kitchen and a shelf mounted on the free wall of the living area housed her landlink.

Male pulled a ceramic pitcher out of the small cold box in the wall. Handing a chilled grape drink to Tara, she sat in the one chair at the eating table. She gestured with her cup to the matching chairs. "Sit. Share your stories." She smiled and pulled off her head cloth, revealing dark curls. "I hear you have no landlink. And that you've come all the way from Southland. Where are you going?"

"North, for the test," Tara lied.

"What were you doing in Southland? My papa will probably report you, you know."

"Report me, why?"

"Why? Because it's forbidden, that's why."

Tara wasn't sure what to say. What was forbidden? Male saw the confused look in her eyes and squinted at her. "How long have you been without a landlink? You do know Runners are forbidden to enter Southland, don't you? Patha of the Blood Circle Clan passed the law himself. That's why we're having the Test of Wills. His daughter died down there."

Patha was alive! At least, it sounded like he was. If he had officially announced her death, she guessed her login number would be deleted. Tara would need a new number in order to access a landlink, any landlink. How would she explain no login number without revealing who she was?

"Would you like to contact your family?" Male asked.

"Would it be all right if I took a shower first?"

Male jumped up and walked down the six-foot hallway, opening the first door and turning on the light. She entered her room and returned immediately with a thick towel.

The shower felt incredible. Male had left her alone in the trailer. The landlink was turned off. Somehow Tara needed on that network. Tara decided to walk around the camp. As she approached the main fire, she saw ten to fifteen Runners surrounding it, sipping ale and chatting among themselves. A large woman dipped wooden mugs into a barrel and handed them out. Tara slipped in inconspicuously and accepted the mug of ale offered to her.

She tried to remember the last time she'd enjoyed this Runner tradition. Gatherings around the evening fire at the end of a day, listening to the old Runners tell their tales of victories and places traveled—these were good memories. She recalled hearing the news from travelers of other clans, enjoying the screams and chatters of the younger children as they ran and played on the outer edge of the circle. These were the parts of her childhood of which she was most fond. This clan made her feel right at home.

The stories she heard that night shocked her. It was Rolko, himself, who explained the latest conflicts between the Gothman and Runners. Lord Darius wanted to be part of the judging for the Test of Wills. Rumors also circulated that several

Gothman wanted to partake in the test. Many Runners had complained loudly to Patha. The test was for Runners only. Rolko assured everyone around the fire that Patha would not allow Gothman participation.

Tara wanted to say this was true. She knew her papa, and he would want a Runner to succeed him. They had an alliance with Gothman, but she knew he wasn't ready to integrate the two nations that quickly. Chaos would result if they did.

Tara was called upon to tell her stories of Southland. She found herself telling the Runners about Crator. She explained that the Southlanders believed that Crator made the planet and all races on it. She told about the Guardians, saying that they brought messages to the people from Crator and could take the form of animals. The Runners loved her stories and applauded as they refilled her mug.

She sat at the fire well into the evening, sipping the ale and catching up on the tales of the Runners. She felt relaxed, at peace and very much at home as she walked slowly back to the trailer later that evening. In a few days, she would have her children in her arms again. Then there was Darius. Would she make peace with him? She wondered once again if he'd found another woman. What would she do if he had? Probably kill her. Tara giggled to herself and realized the ale had hit her.

No other woman would be able to prevent her from returning to her life. She hadn't asked to be gone for six cycles, and she never intended to be separated from Andru and Ana. It tore into her like a jagged warrior's knife that her children might not recognize her. Every time she thought of how the twins might react to her, the pain from missing them grew even stronger.

Male was sitting at her landlink when Tara pulled open the door to the trailer. "Did you catch up on all the latest gossip?" Male didn't turn around as Tara entered.

"It was great to sit at a fire once again and hear all the stories." Tara sat in one of the stuffed chairs and glanced at the monitor.

She leaned forward when she noticed Male had logged onto the Blood Circle Clan site. Tara scanned the screen, trying to see what the clan was broadcasting. She tried to sound nonchalant as she looked over Male's shoulder. "What are you looking for?"

"I'm going to submit the written part of the Test of Wills." Male glanced up at Tara and smiled meekly. "I don't expect to win or anything. Papa thinks it would be good experience. You'd have to understand what it's like to be the daughter of the clan leader, I guess."

Tara understood more than she could say. "Why don't you print one off for me too?" she suggested. "There's no harm in trying, right?"

"Sure, as long as we don't get killed in the confrontation part." Male groaned. "I can handle the first part of the test, I think. But, I don't know about the second portion. Papa has never been too satisfied with my warrior skills."

"Maybe I can help you."

"If you want to take the time. It couldn't hurt."

Male printed two tests and handed one to Tara. She clicked through the information on the Blood Circle Clan and stopped on an article with a large color picture of Darius.

Tara's heart skipped a beat.

"Isn't he handsome?" Male leaned back and breathed deeply. "I hear he's an incredible warrior. He was able to defeat Patha's daughter, Tara."

"When did he do that?" Tara asked the question without thinking.

Male turned to stare. "I guess not everyone follows this news as closely as I do. That's how he claimed her as his wife. She wasn't able to tame him, though. So she left."

Tara smiled and felt a longing as she stared at Darius's picture. "Has he found another woman?"

"No. I hope to see him in person when we arrive at the Blood Circle Clan," Male said. "I wonder if he's as good-looking in person."

Tara wanted to say that he was much more handsome. She gazed at the picture of Darius on the monitor. Her body warmed as she studied the blond curls and deep gray eyes. She hadn't realized how much she missed him until that moment.

She wondered if she could trust him again. But then, only Darius could answer that. He would have to earn her trust through his actions. And that would take time. The longing inside her turned to sexual need and she knew she would offer him that time.

Darius definitely had his work cut out for him. That is, if he still wanted her as his claim. She decided she might not give him the option.

At least now she knew she wouldn't have to kill anyone.

CHAPTER TWENTY

THE SUNSHINE seemed a little too bright the next morning as Tara wiped down her bike and prepared for the day's journey. She declined breakfast, but eagerly worked on her second cup of coffee. One of the advantages of being befriended by the clan leader's daughter, not everyone had access to the rare drink. It worked miracles on the day-afters brought on by too much ale the night before.

"It's just occurred to me that I don't know your name."

Tara looked up to see Rolko speaking to her as he and two other Runners approached. "Good morning." She tried to sound polite as her mind raced for a response. "I'm Leetha," she decided.

"Leetha, we've brought a landlink for your bike." He gestured to one of the men with him, who produced a small flat black panel. "Which clan are you from?"

"The Blood Circle clan."

"Well, we really are taking you home, aren't we?" He smiled, but the look in his eye let her know he had more to say.

She stood silently, showing her respect.

"You violated our law by entering Southland, Leetha. Male has told me you plan to enter the Test of Wills. I can't permit you to do that. I'll turn my report into Patha and make him aware of your violation. You'll have to approach him personally to argue your case once we arrive at our destination, before your entry can be accepted. I'm sure you're aware of the laws."

"Yes, I am. Thank you for the landlink." Tara remained still until the men were finished with her bike and had left her. Her heart sank. The only way to enter the Test of Wills now was by using her own login number. Furthermore, she knew the second Patha received a transmission saying a Runner named Leetha—from his clan—had just come over the border, her cover would be blown.

There was no Leetha in the Blood Circle clan that she knew of. She hoped Patha wouldn't review the reports from the clans right away. After all, there was a lot going on to distract him.

Somehow she needed to remain undetected until the Test began. She knew she could prove herself in battle. In fact, unlike Male, she looked forward to that part of the test.

Tara tested her landlink, and the travel plan for the day appeared on the small screen. They were scheduled to arrive at the Blood Circle clan that evening. This was perfect. Arriving after dark would be to her advantage.

She shut down the landlink and entered Male's trailer. Tara already knew the young girl was not there. She'd taken off earlier to help some of the mamas organize their children for the day. It was a job that had often been assigned to Tara when she was that age. Male would be gone for a while.

She sat down at the landlink and took a deep breath. This would either work or it wouldn't. She held up her fingers, hesitated for a second, and then typed in her login number. The landlink buzzed, and the proper lights lit up accordingly. Her heart thumped when it seemed to take forever for the network to appear. Male wouldn't be gone forever. Tara wanted to submit the answers to the written test through the network before she was discovered. Her landlink had never moved so slowly.

At last, the picture on the monitor flashed and the selection screen appeared. It worked. Her logon number hadn't been deleted. That meant she hadn't officially been announced dead. Why then, were they conducting the Test of Wills? She had no time to ponder this mystery but instead selected a blank page and began answering the questions that Male had printed.

She was familiar with the test but still read over each question carefully. Because the leader of the clans would have to know all the laws of the Runners very well, each test question asked about a particular one. Also required was the origination of laws, which one best suited a particular situation, and how she would interpret several selected laws. Tara typed quickly yet answered each question thoroughly.

After Patha reviewed the tests, he would name those who qualified to compete in the confrontation. This part of the test was no longer a fight to the death. That law had been changed over one hundred winters ago because too many good warriors had been killed. The fight would last until the surrender of one of the competitors. Nevertheless, this still resulted in a fight to the death all too often, at least according to the stories. There'd never been a Test of Wills called as long as Tara had been alive.

Her fingers ached, and her back was sore. Over an hour passed. Tara clicked on submit and leaned back in the chair.

It was done.

Whether this would cut her throat or lead her to victory was undetermined. Tara knew if the test with her logon number was identified before she got to Gothman, Runners she didn't know would arrest her, and she would be delayed. But if she made it to Gothman before her test submission was discovered, she would be able to convince Patha of her need for the test to continue, even though, strictly speaking, it was unnecessary. She imagined Patha would be outraged that she'd enter the Test of Wills instead of simply acknowledging she'd returned.

She stared at the blank monitor for a minute, wondering who would first notice a written test had been submitted with her logon number. Would they think it a fraud, or would they suspect it was her?

Tara leaned back and smiled. Could she actually win the Test of Wills and be heir to Patha twice over? If so, she would rule the clans completely. Her authority would be unquestioned. And then there was Darius. She wanted him to see her earn her way to victory, conquering each hurdle every step of the way.

The winner of the Test of Wills wore the title of Head Warrior. It was the highest honor a Runner could receive and always fell upon the ruler of a clan. Not as many women won as men did, but Tara knew she hadn't lost a competition in winters. She didn't know of a warrior she couldn't defeat. If Darius witnessed her taking the title of Head Warrior, he, as well as all of Gothman, would see that a person's sex had nothing to do with what skills they possessed. Taking the title would be one more step toward earning the respect Tara needed from Darius, and from his people.

Her heart ached and her blood warmed as she thought of battle. Her pregnancy might have stopped her from participating in the last war, but nothing would stop her from using her warrior skills for the test. She was free to soar to her highest potential.

Who would the other contenders be? Would they be allowed to use weapons on a field, or would it be in an arena with hand-to-hand combat? How many finalists would there be? Tara had studied a few Tests of Wills before her *Age of Searching*, and knew the leader of Runners had complete control over how the test would be conducted. Tara hoped for an arena. More people would witness the victories that way.

Questions continued to swarm in her head as Tara stared across the trailer. The sounds of starting motors brought her back to the moment, and she jumped up. Turning off the landlink, she hurried outside to her bike.

By the middle of the afternoon, Tara began to recognize the countryside.

They were coming up on the southern tip of the Gothman nation. The ground was hard, and the dark gray clouds hung very low. Her eyelids burned from the cold wind that had slapped her face for the past few hours, and she guessed snow would fall before they arrived on the western side of Gothman where the clan site was located.

She suspected her logon number had been discovered by now. It wouldn't be difficult for the authorities to determine its source. It was quite possible Rolko would be notified that one of his landlinks had transmitted using her logon number. Then, they would search for the one who had used the number.

Tara wondered how much information Patha would give the clan leader. Would Patha tell Rolko that an illegal number had been used? Or would he specifically say that Tara's number had been used? She continued hoping they arrived at their destination before Rolko was contacted.

Over the next hour, snow began to fall, drastically limiting visibility. Tara was forced to slow down, as was the rest of the clan. She strained to see the passing countryside, trying to determine how far into Gothman territory they'd come.

The wind picked up. For a brief minute, she thought she saw something in the distance, but then it was gone. She focused on the ground immediately in front of her. Several riders ahead yelled, and she looked up. One of the Runners was pointing to something, and Rolko pulled up alongside him.

Tara looked in the direction they indicated and made out several brown figures ahead. She squinted and refocused, watching through the snow as the figures drew nearer.

Four Gothman approached. Rolko, with the surrounding Runners, slowed to a stop. Her heart pounded against her leather coat as she watched the men talk to Rolko. It was impossible to tell who the Gothman were.

The one speaking to Rolko was long-legged and broad-shouldered. Through the blowing snow, she wasn't able to determine his hair color. He turned his head to scan the Runners scattered across the meadow. Rolko gestured for the Gothman to follow him. They rode on their loud Gothman bikes through the hundreds of parked Runners.

Tara watched the four Gothman approached. One of them was Darius!

He passed within a few feet of her motorcycle, head held high in the blowing wind. Blond curls stuck out from underneath a black hat.

His hair was longer. Everything inside her reached to him like a magnet, yet he never glanced her way as he drove by.

The Gothman and Rolko drove back to where the trailers were parked with the Runners congregating in their wake. Tara was near three Runners, and several others joined them to discuss the possible reasons for the Gothman's arrival.

"They said something about a wrong logon number being used."

"That doesn't seem like a reason to stop us in this bitter cold."

"The Gothman are looking for an excuse to search our clan."

"Why would Lord Darius come himself?"

The chatter continued. Tara quit listening. Rolko would figure out what landlink transmitted the illegal number, and when the transmission had occurred. Once he had that information, he would know either his daughter, or she, had sent the transmission using the illegal number.

She couldn't conveniently disappear—she was surrounded by clan members. Even if she slipped away, the snow was blowing hard enough to get lost. Not to mention the fact that they could easily track her with the landlink they'd assembled on her bike.

Tara was trapped.

She waited for the inevitable to happen. Within a short amount of time, it did. A motorcycle approached their group, and one of the Runners who'd been with Rolko gestured to her.

"Come with me." He said nothing else.

She followed through the snow. Some of the Runners watched her pass, but for the most part they huddled together in small groups, preoccupied in conversation. No one was concerned that she'd been singled out.

Torgo sat in the corner of the living area sorting through incoming tests. They'd been arriving by the thousands. Earlier that quarter cycle the program that received and graded the tests had quit working. Patha was impressed by Torgo's ability to save the submitted tests and fix the program. Now it worked twice as fast and sorted the tests, eliminating those with more than one mistake. This made the job of reviewing the tests much easier, and Patha praised Torgo's landlink abilities.

"He's a natural," he told Darius with Torgo sitting right there. "What he can't do on the battlefield, he makes up for on the landlink."

That comment stung at Torgo's pride, but he'd kept a straight face.

"I want an hourly report from you on all written tests," Patha ordered. "Request any assistants you may need to help you."

Torgo had immediately sought out Syra. The perfect tests, and those with one mistake, automatically printed out with the logon number at the top. For the first few days, only one or two tests were printed. But as the day of the Test of Wills approached, several more tests printed out. Torgo had Syra manually check the answers before they were turned over to Patha.

"Here's Kuro's test," Syra said as she leaned back in her chair. Torgo came up from behind her and rubbed his hands down the front of her shirt as he leaned over.

"Not now, silly," she giggled and pushed him away.

"Perfectly answered, I assume." Torgo didn't like Kuro. It annoyed him the way Kuro was a bit too friendly around Darius.

"Of course," Syra shrugged. "Looks like he'll win the Test of Wills. I don't know about the rest of these people, but Kuro's quite the warrior."

"Well, I guess I'll take these reports to Patha for review. One of the clans reported a Runner who admitted coming up from Southland. She's from the Blood Circle Clan. Her name's Leetha." Torgo grabbed the reports and stacked them. "I can take those tests to him while I'm at it."

"Uh-huh." Syra wasn't listening to Torgo. She was busy looking at a test that had just printed. "Torgo, look at this."

He studied it, then looked at her, confused.

She grabbed back the test. "Look! It's Tara's logon number. We forgot to delete it. Didn't Darius ask you to do that a while back?"

"Hell be doomed! Yeah, he did. The transmission crashed and I forgot all about it. I don't understand. How come it's on this test?" Torgo reached around Syra and began tapping buttons on her keypad.

The images on Syra's screen flashed. She tried to follow what he was doing, but his landlink skills were beyond hers.

"It was submitted from a landlink in the Four Circle clan." He continued to type. "They're just south of us."

"What are you going to do?"

"Report it to Patha and Darius, I guess. Those are my orders." Torgo took the tests from Syra and walked to the door.

Syra jumped up and followed him. This was the most excitement they'd had since they'd started gathering the tests.

Patha and Darius weren't in the house. After discussing it, they decided to ride to the clan site and look for the two leaders. They rode together on Torgo's bike, believing their information vital enough for it to be overlooked that they were together on the bike.

Balbo disapproved of the time Torgo and Syra spent together, considering his daughter too young for the physical relationship he was sure the Gothman boy would instigate. If her papa only knew how much she'd educated Torgo.

Torgo drove straight to Patha's trailer, which was parked next to Balbo's. Snow started to fall, and no one noticed the two of them climb off the bike. Darius and Patha's bikes were parked outside the trailer. Torgo knocked on the door.

"Come," Patha barked.

The two hurried inside, shutting the door behind them to prevent snow from blowing into the trailer.

Patha looked up at the young people questioningly. Torgo handed him the two separate stacks of tests. Darius sat at the landlink with his back to the two of them, not acknowledging their presence.

"You rode through the snow to give these to me?" Patha glanced at the papers. "I planned on getting them from you later today."

"There's something I wanted you to see," Torgo spoke calmly. He was working on mastering the coolness of voice his brother possessed.

Patha leaned back in his chair. "Go ahead."

"One of the written tests used Tara's logon number."

Lord Darius spun in his chair. "I told you to delete that number," he bellowed.

Torgo hated how his brother always yelled. "When the transmission quit sending the tests, I spent so much time fixing it that I forgot to delete the number."

"Let me see the test," Patha said.

"The answers are almost identical to the answers you gave us to grade the tests," Syra pointed out.

"There's something else." Torgo wished Syra would let him do the talking. "It's probably just coincidence but I thought I'd—"

"What is it?" Darius snapped impatiently.

Darius was too mean since Tara had left. "The Four Circle clan reports a Runner has joined them from Southland." Torgo held out the report to Patha. "Her name is Leetha, and she's a member of the Blood Circle clan."

"There's no Leetha in my clan." Patha rubbed his head, then looked up at Syra. "Is there?"

"No, there isn't." Syra came out from behind Torgo. "I checked before we came."

Patha handed the papers to Darius to study.

Darius glanced at them but then looked at Torgo. "So what are you saying?" He handed the papers back to Patha.

"We're saying it's a mighty strange coincidence," Syra spoke before Torgo did. Lord Darius made her mad with his continual grouchiness. Once, she'd thought he was cute, but not anymore. He had done something unforgivable, and she wished he'd just get over trying to make everyone miserable because he was an idiot.

She kept talking while she had everyone's attention. "A Runner joins the Four Circle clan from Southland. The report shows she didn't have a landlink on her bike so they weren't able to verify her identity, but she says she's Leetha with the Blood Circle clan. The leader of the clan reports she's staying with his daughter. The next day, a written test is submitted from that clan on the daughter's landlink, using Tara's logon number. And the test answers match your answers almost perfectly. It just seems odd, and we thought you should know."

Syra glared at Lord Darius and then gave the same look to Patha. "Come on, Torgo, let's get back to work." She turned to leave.

"Wait a minute." Lord Darius growled.

Syra turned and crossed her arms, waiting for him to speak.

"Are you saying this is Tara?"

"If it's her, then why is she trying to sneak back up here?" Patha thought out loud and all three people turned their heads to look at him. Patha looked at the test answers more thoroughly and all three stood quietly, watching him.

The answers were almost verbatim to his. He could almost hear her vocal inflection in the writing style. It was a mighty odd coincidence. He glanced over at Darius, nearly forgetting the others in the room. "It's always bothered me that the Neurians were never able to produce a body." He stood. "I want you to check this out."

Darius quickly grabbed his coat.

"Find out who used that number. If it's Tara—" but Darius was already out the door.

"Did you submit a written test for the Test of Wills after I told you not to?" Rolko barked as Tara got off her bike.

"Identify yourself, Runner," Darius spoke a fierce cruelty that made her heart pound.

All she could do was stare at Darius. Even though snow fell steadily, it was no longer cold. Her gloved palms grew damp from sweat. For a moment, she forgot the name she had created to conceal her identity.

Darius stood in front of her, and in spite of his obvious intention to intimidate her, all Tara saw was how incredibly sexy he looked. Six cycles had passed since she'd had sex, and her body screamed for him now. Physically, she no longer cared what he had done. It was the emotional side of her that was torn in two at the sight of him.

She wanted to hear how he had missed her. She wanted to hear how sorry he was that he made her leave. Tara wanted, more than anything, for everyone around them to disappear and leave her alone with the man she loved.

His presence almost overpowered her. Why did he make her feel like this? He had committed the ultimate of crimes and needed to beg for her forgiveness. She fought for words. "My name's Leetha."

Her voice hit him. Darius wasn't able to conceal his reaction to the sound of her. He stood staring, completely shocked.

His guards gave him a questioning look.

"I'll speak to her inside the trailer." His scratchy whisper sounded cruel, even to him. Darius made certain his expression appeared as harsh as he sounded. In no way would anyone see how desperately he needed Tara.

Darius wanted to grab Tara and run. He wanted to leap and do anything to prevent her from moving an inch. He wanted to hold her and make sure she never left his side again. Darius didn't do any of those things. The Lord of Gothman wouldn't be seen at the mercy of a woman. He stared into those blue eyes behind her headscarf.

She never once looked away.

Rolko grunted and gestured to the trailer. "Be quick about it, we have a clan to get settled."

Darius held out his hand for her to lead the way, and she obliged. He entered the trailer behind her and shut the door.

"There is no Leetha of the Blood Circle Clan. Who are you?" His growl was low as he watched the Runner walk ahead of him slowly into the trailer.

She walked farther into the room before turning and glancing up at him again once she'd reached the landlink. He watched her every move, waiting for her to speak again.

Was this Tara? Damn! He wanted this to be her body, her voice. She was in full Runner uniform wearing the Blood Circle clan emblem. What was she doing with this clan after all this time? And why was she entering the Test of Wills? "I asked you a question, Runner."

She put her gloved hands into her leather jacket pocket. "Do you have Andru and Ana?" She asked.

Darius' didn't answer. There were no words for a response. Of course, he had their children. Tara would already know that. There were so many other things to say. He'd had so many thoughts about things he'd never thought about before. There wasn't any way to put into words these thoughts that he wasn't used to having. He was a warrior. The best in Gothman. He conquered, claimed what he wanted, and controlled all that was around him. Apologizing wasn't part of his thought process. Nor were there words in his vocabulary to do so.

Not that he had apologizing on the mind. He had known nothing but pain for six cycles. It had corrupted the blood in his veins, turning it toxic, until every inch of him eternally burned with a longing for her. At first, he had lived with regret and anger due to a trivial act he may or may not have committed. He regretted putting himself in the position to decide. He had been angry that Tara had wrongfully taken that choice from him.

Darius understood the mixture was self-destructive. Before he had rid himself of regret, and overcome the anger, Tara's niece and the twins had been returned to him. The cycles that followed would always remain a dark, torrential blur of unwanted emotions for him. Every morning he had awakened with knowledge that Tara was not with him. That knowledge had festered his ability to think or make command decisions.

Throughout those cycles he had been unable to accept Tara's death. Now he knew why. He ripped the headscarf off the Runner. Tara's light brown hair fell past her shoulders and over her face.

She reached up and shoved the hair from her eyes.

That festering disease of regret and pain vanished the second he saw her. "Yes, I have them." His voice cracked with emotion, and he touched her cold cheek with his fingertips.

"I need to see them," she whispered.

He pulled his mouthpiece out of his pocket and wrapped it around his ear. Sliding his hand down it, he reached for the switch to activate it.

"No, don't." She grabbed his hand. "You can't."

"What do you mean, I can't?" He took her hand in his before she could pull away, put her fingers up to his mouth, and kissed them. "I am telling Patha."

Tara pulled away her hand. "You can't. It will ruin everything. If I announce I'm back, the Test of Wills will be cancelled. That would cause an up rise among the clans that can't be allowed to happen right now."

"There is no longer a need for it. You're Patha's heir. It's your right to lead, my lady. You're not giving that up."

"I have no intention of giving up my right to rule the clans." Defiance put color in her cheeks. "I've entered the contest and shall win."

Darius never thought he'd be so happy to see her insubordinate nature. His Tara had returned to him.

In spite of her intention to remain aloof, Darius' presence in front of Tara was too overwhelming, and arousing. She didn't have the strength to stop him when he lifted her off her feet and into his arms. Darius held her with one powerful arm and lifted her face to his with his other hand. Without hesitation, he covered her mouth with his and kissed her. His overwhelming power and aggressive masculinity softened her defenses and she melted.

Passion that had been dormant for too many cycles soared to life. Tara was instantly intoxicated from need that surpassed her rational thought. She wanted to rip this man's clothes from his body and make love to him, forgetting the rest of the world existed. She wanted him to hold her, and talk to her for hours and hours, until they both knew each other's hearts again. But Tara also wanted to hear Darius swear unconditional loyalty and love—to her and their family. He needed to prove his love through his actions, and not his words. Although her heart wanted the words, too.

It was harder than she thought it would be to put her desire for him to the side. Her arms didn't possess the strength to push him away. Already his hands were underneath her shirt, searing her flesh. His mouth had left hers and his lips pressed sexual promises down her neck.

"No," she gasped before she was able to raise her head. Already, it had fallen back to give him free reign again.

She wanted him inside her now. But it would have to wait. A political agenda existed, and it must be handled first.

"My lady, you think you can defeat all the other warriors?"

She fought against his grasp now. Darius held her with one strong arm, and struggle as she would, she couldn't release herself until he let her go. She backed up and faced him as if he'd just challenged her.

"My lady, do you know how strong some of the entries are?" Darius' gaze dropped as he looked her over.

"I will be triumphant. There's no doubt about that. Now, what you need to do is tell Rolko that I am Leetha, and you've agreed to let me take my argument to Patha when we reach the Blood Circle clan."

"Why would I tell this lie?" Darius grabbed the side of her head, wrapping her hair around his fingers, and pulled her to him.

Tara pushed against Darius' chest but felt his breath when she looked up at him. "You can't create more of a scene than you already have. These people are primed for the Test of Wills. I've heard the stories around the fires of their predictions of victory. If I announce my presence, there will be so much adrenaline, and nothing to do with it. It will cause a stir and create unrest among the Runners. A true warrior prepares for battle and then wants to fight. The Test of Wills can't be reversed once the process has started."

Something cold and brutal melted in those gray eyes. Darius' expression softened considerably. "So you'll put your life on the line to keep peace, will you?"

"I will live through this, Darius," she whispered, as she searched his face, and her hands went from his chest up to his shoulders.

"You'll be an outstanding leader, Tara. Your point is taken, and I'll inform Rolko."

"You should do that now," Tara said, but any strength to leave his arms was gone.

"I'll not lose you again," he whispered. There was a snarl in his voice, almost animalistic, definitely possessive.

"That means you've learned how to behave." Her whisper was just as harsh, and she hoped the fire in her eyes brought his blood to a boil.

"We will discuss that later."

Tara found her strength and tore away. "There are cold Runners out there." She ripped her headscarf out of his hand and put it on her head. Then she opened the door and walked out into the cold.

CHAPTER TWENTY-ONE

THE BLOOD Circle clan was alive with festivities. The snow had stopped, and along with low hanging gray clouds created an insulation that made the night air crisp but tolerable.

Tara heard music and singing as she rode into the camp. Nostalgia crept through her. Several huge bonfires sent streaks of fire shooting up into the thick gray sky. She heard loud drunken yelling and laughter coming from the fires as mugs were passed and ale poured. There were so many familiar faces, unaware of her presence. There were also many newcomers who had arrived at the clan. But no one bothered to look up as she drove by.

She knew there was no way she'd be able to slip into one of the circles around the fires this evening. She'd be recognized the second she spoke. Tonight wasn't a night to hear stories around the fires.

There were two people she had to see immediately, her children. Darius said he had them, so she knew they would be in their bedroom, probably asleep. She wouldn't wake them but she had to see them, to touch their soft skin. Her heart ached as she slipped away from the clan and slowly drove through the thick trees around Bryton and toward the large house on the hill.

It would take a skilful eye to track Tara as she moved through the woods. She knew how to stay invisible. However, it was just that skilful eye that watched her now.

Darius sat motionless on the side of the road and observed her every move, following her as she passed among the trees and the large rocks jacked up out of the earth. He had known it was Tara the moment she rode away from the clan. His landlink picked up the code from the monitoring device that had been installed on her bike. Not that he needed confirmation.

Now she was moving at almost a dangerous speed, considering the limited visibility from the night and the snow. It suddenly occurred to him where she was going. He left the roadside and tore through town to his house. More than one head turned and more than one body jumped out of the way. Darius slid to a stop in front of the house and ordered the guard to take care of his bike as he ran inside.

Reena and Hilda looked up astonished as he bolted in the front door.

"Do not come upstairs." He barked the order and leapt up the staircase, taking three at a time.

The excitement in the community had proven to be an excellent distraction. Tara found herself behind the old familiar house without drawing any attention. She parked the bike in the seclusion of the trees and bushes and slowly moved into the shadows of the large home.

The best place to enter, she decided, was through her old upstairs bedroom. She easily climbed the trellis, free of ivy right before the new winter. Tara hoisted herself onto the walls of the balcony and hopped nimbly onto the floor outside the closed door.

The room was vacant and dark, and the warmth from the house created moisture on the windows. As she opened the door an inch to peek into the room, she heard voices coming from downstairs. The upstairs appeared to be quiet, and she entered her old room, then started down the hallway to the nursery at the other end.

She was surprised to hear a low, quiet voice coming from behind the partially closed nursery door. It was Darius, and she was very much surprised to hear him softly singing a Gothman folk song. He wasn't visible through the half-closed door, but from where she stood, she spotted Andru sitting in his crib watching his papa.

Tara froze at the sight of her son. He was so big! So grown up! Had she only been gone six cycles? He didn't look like a baby. His blond curls fell loosely around his head, and his eyes were large and a deep gray. She watched him move his small hands and wiggle the toes that were sticking out from under his blanket. He was pudgy but not fat, very cuddly looking.

Tears welled in her eyes. Her vision blurred. She swatted the tears away, now wanting anything to stop her from seeing Andru. There was nothing to stop the pain building inside her. Part of her son's life was lost to her. She's never get that back. It was a physical effort not to run into the room and scoop the small child up into her arms. She wanted to bury her face next to his and whisper how sorry she was. She wondered what kind of adjustment he and his sister must have gone through. How traumatized had losing her been for them?

After several minutes of staring at her son in the dark hallway, laughter from downstairs brought her back to the reality of her situation. She stepped away and entered the bedroom she'd shared with Darius. The door adjoining the room to the nursery was closed, and all Tara could do was stand and listen to the song Darius was singing. He ended the song. Long moments of dark silence followed. She pressed her ear to the closed door and listened, trying to determine what Darius was doing. She heard nothing.

Suddenly, the door to the nursery flung open, causing her to jump backwards. She struggled to regain her balance in the dark room and not trip over furniture. Before she had her bearings, a large hand wrapped around her neck. Instantly she was lifted off the ground.

"What is it that you plan to do, my lady?" Darius' whisper was more like a snarl.

She wrapped her fingers around his hand and struggled to no avail.

He threw her back.

She slid across the floor, skidding to a stop before she hit the wall. Tara flipped her legs around and looked like a cat ready to pounce as he came at her again.

"You are not taking these children anywhere!" This time his snarl was more apparent than the whisper. He lunged toward her.

She rolled out of his way and sprang to her feet. "Darius, all I wanted to do was see them." She stood there ready for him this time. "If I wanted my children to leave this house, I wouldn't have crept down the hallway while you sat in the nursery obviously waiting for me."

"Why should I believe you?" He reached out to grab her.

Tara dodged his hand and punched him squarely in the stomach.

He didn't flinch but instead, leapt at her.

She tried to turn away, but he locked her in his arms with her back smashed against his body.

"I guess you'll just have to trust me," she said, relaxing her body in his arms. With that comment, he released her. She looked toward the nursery door and then back at Darius. His expression remained wary, and the anger was still there. His gray eyes appeared almost black.

"Please, Darius, my children…our children…I need to see them." Her voice cracked but her desperation for her children didn't sway her. Tara took off her headscarf and draped it over a chair. "Please, I need to hold them. I need to see if they remember me."

Darius walked over to her and wiped a tear from her eye. "Don't let them see you crying. Andru and Ana have heard many great stories of their warrior mama." He took her by the hand and led her into the nursery.

The two children lay in their matching beds. Tara couldn't stop the tears as she stroked their hair and squeezed their tiny hands. Ana pulled Tara's hand up to her face, and Tara felt the small child breathing gently against her skin. She knelt down and stared, stroking her beautiful baby girl's hair with her free hand.

Darius was behind her when she stood, and he wrapped his arms around her waist. "They're absolutely beautiful children, my lady," he whispered into her ear. Then he gently kissed her neck. "You'll be amazed at how smart they are and how they chatter all day long."

His grip around her waist tightened, and she placed her hand on his and squeezed back. "When I found out how long I'd been gone, all I could think about was getting back to my children." She turned around in Darius' arms and looked up. "I thought about you, too. I wondered if you believed I was dead." She wanted to add, and I wondered how you felt after I left you, but didn't voice the thought."

With his hand on her back, he led her out of the nursery and back to the bedroom. "The Neurians escorted Syra and the children back here and offered their regret that you were killed in a fire. They said you died a warrior's death, that you saved one of their best scientists from burning alive." He put his hands on her shoulders and squeezed, then squeezed her arms and finally her waist. "You are so thin." His large hand held her face up to his. "And, my lady, you are out of shape. What did they do to you?"

Darius didn't share his feelings with her. She would allow him this much. If he wanted to discuss the facts first, that would be fine. But she would hear his formal apology and his desire to keep her in his life, without any other women.

Tara stood in Darius' arms and told him everything.

His arms tightened in anger as she spoke, and he pulled her very close to him when she'd finished. "I wouldn't accept the fact that you were dead. My mama kept saying I was denying your death and that I would be happier when I accepted it." He pulled her so close to him she could hardly breathe. "I had the strangest dreams, though. They kept repeating themselves. I was assured you were alive, and you would come home."

Tara whispered, "Was it an old lady who turned into a dog?"

He stood there, shocked. His whole body went numb. "How did you know?"

"I met her. She helped me escape. She told me my work here wasn't done. I know my muscles have atrophied, but I will be triumphant in the Test of Wills. Crator is behind me. I don't understand Him yet, but he wants me here."

"Crator is an old woman who can turn into a large dog?" Darius asked, frowning his confusion.

"No. The old woman isn't Crator. I don't know who Crator is. The old woman seems to know Him though. She has told me more than once what Crator wants me to do, or not to do. When I listened, things worked out the way they were supposed to."

"You will ask her to take us to see Crator." Darius decided. "Yes. That will work well. We will negotiate with him to help us further when we need it."

Tara laughed and touched Darius' cheek. "My lord, I don't think it works that way. All you have to do is believe in Him."

"Believe in his what?" Darius frowned.

"Believe he exists," Tara said.

"Easy enough."

Apparently Darius decided their conversation about Crator was finished. He picked Tara up and carried her to the bed, and was on top of her immediately. "I'm afraid your work here will never be done," he whispered, and kissed her.

She returned his kiss, but was the first to break it off. As desperately as she wanted him, she wanted his apology. If he was going to take his time, she would continue their conversation.

"What were your dreams about?"

Darius propped up onto one elbow and looked so damn hungry. Lust made his gray eyes more intense. Her insides burned for him but her mind knew how it had to be. She did her best to look calm as she waited for him to answer. "Ever since you left, I've had this one dream that comes again and again. It's not like that usually. My dreams are of war, victory, making love to you." He kissed her again.

She felt him harden. His arousal ignited the fire smoldering deep inside her, an ache growing painfully. More than anything at this moment, she wanted to make love to him and hear him cry out his unending devotion.

"In this dream I was a child," he continued, but began nibbling on her on the neck as he spoke. "I'm walking with a large dog—it's protecting me. Then I'm walking with an old woman, and she's teaching me. It's very important that I learn everything she says, I know." He slid down on the bed and unzipped her coat. "I wrote down some of the things she's said." His hands now worked on her black leather pants. "Remind me to show them to you some time."

"Why can't you show me now?" Tara ran her fingers through Darius' curls and held his head as he kissed from her belly button to her hip bone. He slid open her pants and tugged.

"I have something else to show you now." Darius' breath tickled her when he spoke. He continued to pull her pants.

She arched her hips, making it easier to remove them. "Do you?" Tara pushed herself to her elbows, kicking her pants to the floor when Darius had them to her ankles. She grabbed his shirt when he turned to crawl toward her and pulled it. "What do you have to show me?"

Darius crawled until his face was inches from her, and on hands and knees, he covered her body with his own. "It will take a lifetime, my lady."

Tara moved her mouth to say the word, "oh". But nothing came out other than a mere whisper of the word. The man had rendered her speechless, and although her thoughts leapt at what might take a lifetime to be shown, she wanted – no - needed to hear it.

Darius kissed her curved lips, sucking on her lower lip, then nibbled enough that she gasped at the tingles of electricity he sent through her with the action. She straightened her arms and collapsed onto her back, then reached for his shirt with her hands and tugged it up his torso. Darius pushed himself to his knees and pulled his shirt off.

Her fingers immediately tangled through his dark golden chest hair. "Tell me Darius," she whispered. His muscles jumped underneath her fingertips as she traced patterns down his chest to his pants. "Tell me what will take a lifetime."

"My lady, it will take a lifetime to show you all the love I have for you." Darius flattened the lower half of his body against hers, preventing her from sliding her fingers into his pants. He lowered his mouth over one of her nipples.

Tara gasped. The heat from his breath through the material of her shirt, and his words, brought her to her first quick orgasm. Darius smiled against her breast as she came.

Tara grabbed her shirt and pulled it over her head, and smiled up at him when his eyes feasted on her breasts.

"Do you love me, Tara?" Darius didn't make eye contact with his question, but instead lowered his body until he rested on his elbows and began sucking on her nipple.

"Oh." Tara arched into Darius and held his head in place as he adored her breasts. "I... You... Don't stop doing that."

Darius lashed her nipple with his tongue, rolled it gently with his teeth, then sucked the hardened nub until Tara contorted her body, heat saturating her.

"Darius," she whispered. "Please."

Darius moved away from her breasts. Her nipples were still damp from his attention, and Tara suddenly felt chilled and exposed.

He began a trail of kisses down to her belly button. "I asked you a question," he whispered into her belly button, sending shivers throughout her body.

"You did?" Tara lifted her rear end off the bed and pushed down on Darius' shoulders.

He chuckled as he scooted lower on the bed, then placed a hand under each of her legs, lifting and spreading them apart.

Tara kept her knees bent and reached between her legs with both hands to stroke herself while he watched. She touched herself, running her fingers over her soaked flesh until need swelled inside her again. She slid a finger inside herself, and then pulled it out, spreading the fresh wetness over her swollen nub, gasping as she did. Her muscles tightened and released. She watched Darius' gaze fastened on the action of her fingers. She inserted a finger inside herself again, then pulled it out and extended it to his mouth.

Darius sucked her finger readily, and she smiled.

"Do you love me, Tara?" Darius asked when she pulled her finger free.

When he stroked her soaked, tinder flesh, Tara almost leapt off the bed. Then he lowered his face between her legs and kissed her.

Tara felt another explosion surge through her body, gathering inside her, increasing the swollen sensation. "Oh please," was all she managed to gasp, as Darius teased her with his tongue. She heard his question, but her need to explode fogged her senses. She knew there was an answer but at the moment couldn't find the words.

Darius made love to her with his tongue until she thrust her hips into his face and grabbed his hair. Her orgasm tore through her.

Darius freed himself and pulled away. Her vision blurred as she watched him strip. Finally, he stood at the end of the bed naked, his hardened erection dancing in anticipation.

She didn't say a word but simply watched as he positioned himself over her.

"I need to know Tara, please." Darius made no attempt to touch her, but simply knelt between her spread legs.

She blinked several times and cleared her thoughts. "I never stopped loving you," she whispered.

Darius' grin melted her heart.

"My lady, I will show you that I deserve that love. If it takes a lifetime, I will show you that you never have reason to leave my side again."

"There will be no other women." She knew his people didn't view his horrendous act as a crime. But she did, and he answered to her now.

"Tara, you are it for me. I promise." His expression bordered on dangerous, his expression so intent.

She prayed he meant what he said, but knew only time and his continual show of loyalty would convince her.

"Then prove that to me now." Tara reached for him, gripping his hardness in her hands, and stroked the velvety skin that moved over his harder than stone erection.

Lifting her legs and spreading them at the same time, he knelt before her, pressing his hardness against her oversensitive entrance.

Tara watched those smoldering gray eyes. His expression didn't change when he shoved his steel hardness deep inside her.

Fire ignited inside her, spreading with a fury she didn't try controlling. Darius glided his massive shaft over her inner muscles, and she reached for him. "Darius. Please." The words were hard to form. More than anything, she needed him to soothe an itch that was driving her mad.

He spread her legs further while he pulled slowly out. When he plunged back inside, she screamed.

"My beautiful Runner," Darius growled.

Tara managed to keep her eyes open. She watched when he threw his head back and pounded into her. Tara climaxed again and again. When she thought he would explode, Darius stopped and pulled out.

"Roll over." His voice sounded rough.

Tara pulled her legs from around him and struggled to flip over. Darius helped her but then gave her rear end a sharp swat.

"Ouch," she cried, but she loved the sound of the spanking, and the brief warmth it brought to her rear end. Once she was on all fours, Tara arched her back.

Darius slid into her easily, and the new position had him pushing against the most sensitive part of her insides. She kept her arms locked, pushing back against him. Sex with him had never been so good.

Tara had no idea how much time passed as he moved her around and took her in every position they could master on the bed. She was numb and sated when he finally allowed her to collapse into complete exhaustion. The smell of their sex and body sweat filled the air of the room. Even though it was very cold outside, neither of them felt a need to find a blanket. She fell asleep with his arms and legs wrapped around her.

"Darius?" a voice called.

Tara jumped with a start as she recognized Torgo's voice. She sat up quickly and reached for a blanket.

"Are you awake yet?"

"I'm awake, Torgo. I'll be down in a second." Darius rolled over and pulled Tara down on him.

"Hurry. The candidates are starting to assemble." Torgo's voice cracked as he spoke.

Tara imagined how much he'd grown. She pulled away from Darius and rose from the bed to walk across the room to the shower.

"How do you plan to get from here to the arena?" He admired her naked body as she picked up her clothes

"What did you say?" Torgo's voice came from the hallway.

"Go downstairs!" Darius' voice boomed, and feet were heard scurrying down the hallway.

"I'll make it." She smiled and shut herself into the bathroom.

It was Syra's voice Tara heard as she came back into the bedroom. She was on the other side of the closed door leading to the nursery.

Her heart leapt as she also heard two small babbling voices. Her twins were content and happy. She heard an occasional squeal as one of them decided they deserved the toy the other possessed. Tara listened for a few minutes, anxious for the time when she would be sitting on the nursery floor, exploring the toys with her children.

Finally, she crept to the hallway and back to her old bedroom. Darius was nowhere in sight, and she knew he believed she'd be able to sneak back out of the house. The house was completely silent, other than the noises from the nursery, and Tara assumed everyone had left to watch the test, leaving Syra to stay with the children.

Tara used the staircase by the kitchen and closed the back door silently behind her. She stood motionless in the yard for a moment, listening. Two guards stood on the far side of the house, laughing over something. Tara edged alongside the house in the opposite direction, and wondered if her new friend, Crator, had anything to do with her bike being parked where she had left it.

"I don't know who you are," Tara whispered as she grabbed her handlebars and pushed her bike away from the house. "But if you are taking care of me, Crator, I really appreciate it."

Tara started her bike once she was away from the house, then drove over the rough countryside, around the town, and toward the clan site.

Hundreds of bikes were parked in a lower field. After she left her motorcycle with the rest, Tara began to hike the incline to the arena. The clan site buzzed with activity, considering the early morning hour, and she pushed her way through Runner and Gothman until she reached a roped-off area. Four large poles had been shoved into the ground to form a square, and several ropes were wrapped around the area providing a fence for the arena. Stakes stuck into the ground created an opening for contestants. Outside this area, competitors were checking in at several tables. Tara headed straight toward them.

"And to think, we'll be working together by tomorrow. You haven't noticed any competitor that you think could beat me, have you?" The voice caught Tara off-guard.

"I don't know all the Runners that are fighting. I've only seen the written tests. Can't really judge a person by what they write."

The second voice belonged to Darius, and Tara turned to see where he was. But that first voice, she knew that first voice. Who was it? She spotted Darius. His guards blocked her view of the other man. She continued moving through the crowd toward the tables.

"That's true. Drink with me to victory, my lord."

"It will definitely be a day to remember."

To whom did that first voice belong? Tara turned again, and this time she saw him. The man talking to Darius was Kuro.

She'd almost forgotten him. Kuro...her first love. How unimportant he seemed to her now.

They had met as teenagers, and at eighteen winters he'd pressured her to marry him. They were madly in love, completely inseparable. But she thought she was too young to marry. She wanted the *Age of Searching*. He wanted to rule the Blood Circle clan by her side. She'd refused his proposal, and in anger and humiliation, he'd left the clan.

That was five winters ago.

Now, here he stood, talking to the papa of her children, the man who had claimed her, and the man whom she loved as a woman.

It made sense that he'd return now. Here was his chance to do what he'd always wanted to do: rule the clan.

How had he met Darius? Had they become friends? And what was Kuro saying? He obviously assumed he would win the Test of Wills.

If he still possessed the warrior skills she remembered, it would be a challenge fighting him. Darius must have known she would fight him. Why hadn't he said something to her?

Suddenly she wondered what Kuro might have told Darius about her. Had he mentioned knowing her growing up? And if so, what else had he told Darius?

Kuro turned at that moment and caught sight of her. He gave her a distant look. Then, his eyes widened and he looked at her again.

Darius turned to see what he was looking at and both of them caught her eye.

Tara turned and disappeared into the crowd. She scanned the row of tables, and approached a Runner she didn't recognize.

"You here to check in for the Test of Wills?" he asked, as he grabbed an armband.

"Yes. I'm Leetha with the Blood Circle clan." Her heart pounded against her coat as she was given a white cloth to tie around her arm.

"Bordo, with the Kill Water clan." A booming voice next to her announced his arrival.

Tara glanced at the man and shuddered. His arms were thicker than her waist.

"And he's going to win!" A shrill female voice announced this information loudly, and several other Runners surrounding the large burly man began to cheer.

Tara was forgotten and shoved to the side, as Bordo's supporters pushed their way to the tables.

"Oh Crator, I'm doing the right thing, aren't I?" Tara mumbled. She wrapped her coat around herself tightly and hurried back through the crowd.

CHAPTER TWENTY-TWO

IT WAS only a matter of time before someone recognized her. The best thing was to remain in earshot of the arena, but find an isolated spot to wait—and hopefully remain unnoticed. Tara moved to the edge of the clan site, doing her best to avoid any Runners she recognized. Once in the trees, she climbed to a large branch and got comfortable on her perch. She would wait here for the competition to start.

Tara realized she'd been dozing when she heard Patha's voice boom through the sound transmitter. She'd dreamed of the old lady. Tara had sat next to her at the campfire in the desert. The old lady had kissed the white cloth tied around Tara's arm.

"Crator will guide you to victory. Have faith in Him."

Then she'd disappeared. Tara balanced on the large branch and blinked herself awake.

"Number eight and number three will present themselves at the side of the arena," Patha announced. "The Test of Wills is about to begin."

The crowd exploded with cheers, and everyone began moving at once. All those who had been standing and visiting now hurried to get the best seat to watch the fights. Rows of wooden benches surrounded the arena and the dull thumping of people climbing to an available spot vibrated through Tara's tree branch.

Tara slid to the ground and headed to the arena. She was number three. She would be in the first fight. Was it good to be the first fighter? How had they determined who would fight first? "Quit worrying and have faith," she muttered quietly. *Crator will guide you to victory. You have faith that He'll do that, don't you?* She knew that she did. He'd proven his abilities. Whatever He was, He wanted this for her, and she would not let Him down. If it hadn't been for the dog woman, Tara wouldn't be here now. There was no better way to honor her memory.

Tara had to fight her way to the arena. The crowd was thick, and no one seemed interested in letting her pass. Her toes were stepped on, and more than one elbow jammed into her by the time she removed her coat and entered the arena.

A neutral Runner she didn't recognize confirmed her armband number, and grabbed her hand and the hand of the other contestant. "Round one of the Test of Wills shall begin." The woman yanked Tara's arm and the other Runner's arm into the air.

Multitudes of bodies tested the strength of the ropes surrounding the arena. They screamed their encouragement at the neutral Runner's words.

"Let the fighting begin."

Tara looked at her opponent for the first time.

"I guess you'll do for warm-up," the tall, thin young man said. His pale green eyes mocked her through his headscarf. The man lunged at Tara.

She responded with a hard blow to the side of his head, and he flew backwards, crashing to the ground.

His head fell back and hit a rock. He lay motionless.

Tara stood tall over the fallen Runner and secured her gloved hands together behind her back. The crowd cheered, and she waited for the next contestant to enter the ring.

The next two fights were similar to the first. The fighters would aim one blow at Tara before she flattened them. A hard punch to the abdomen, a kick in the face, each caused the other fighter to fall, defeated. The third fight lasted for several punches.

A young, stocky woman came after her with full vengeance. She knocked Tara backward and punched her twice before Tara regained her balance.

Tara came back at her with several kidney punches, and the crowd groaned as they felt the woman's pain. As her opponent struggled to regain control, she once again stood still with her hands behind her back. The crowd screamed for her to attack again. Tara looked at the crowd surrounding the arena. It was not a fight to the death, and she refused to hurt the woman any more than necessary.

The woman finally pulled the white cloth off her arm and threw it to the ground, indicating her surrender. Part of the crowd moaned. Apparently, she'd been a favorite of one of the clans.

In between the following fights, Tara scanned the crowd. The Gothman were sitting on one side of the arena, and she spotted Darius easily enough. One of his guards was talking, and Darius was listening intently.

She caught his eye when he looked at her, and he smiled. She glanced away first and looked at the crowd of Runners. For the first time, she laid her eyes on Patha. He was staring directly at her. It was harder to pull her gaze away from him.

Did he recognize her? Of course he would, she decided. Then Tara noticed Reena sitting next to him and also staring.

Suddenly Reena's hands went to her mouth. Patha steadied her, putting his hand on her arm.

She watched as Reena looked at Patha and said something. He nodded and they both turned and looked at her again. Reena started to get up, but Patha pulled her back. He then leaned back and crossed his arms across his chest. His face wore no expression.

Tara was forced to pull her attention away from Patha as she took on the next contestant. After several more fights, Tara's adrenaline soared. She ignored the crowd now and focused on each contestant. By the tenth fight, she began to feel more evenly matched. She and one fighter, a large burly man, fought for almost an hour.

Nothing she did would make him fall. He was thick as a tree trunk. His punches served only to increase her drive to fight. At one point, he grabbed her from behind and slowly began to squeeze the life out of her. With sheer determination Tara managed to reach behind and grab him by the neck. A hush fell over the crowd as she slowly turned until his neck cracked and he slumped, lifeless, to the ground.

A sense of battle took over all of Tara's thoughts. She no longer cared that Patha or Darius watched. She was a merciless machine, and each contestant who entered the arena felt her fury. Tara lost count of how many contestants she'd eliminated. The noise of the crowd came back to her when Patha's voice exploded over the sound transmitter.

"There will be a ten minute recess. Several of the contestants have withdrawn their application for the Test of Wills. We'll begin again shortly with the last ten contestants."

There were only ten more contestants? Two large Runner warriors strolled into the arena and escorted Tara through the crowd. She knew both of them as Patha's personal guards.

Fortunately, they paid more attention to everyone surrounding them and didn't look too closely at her.

"Make way for the next leader of the Runners," a young boy screamed not too far in front of Tara.

"You'll defeat the others, don't you worry," came another voice from beside her.

"Never seen anyone fight like you, lady," a man yelled.

Patha ordered her to be secluded in a white tent near the arena. She was given water as the two warriors stood outside the tent preventing Runners and Gothman from entering to offer their allegiance.

Tara's hands shook as she sipped the water. The crowd outside pushed against the canvas, and more guards yelled at them to step to the side. Tara exhaled and watched her breath appear as a puffy cloud in front of her in the chilly air. A Test of Wills hadn't been called for in over a hundred winters, and Tara couldn't recall from her history lessons if another warrior had successfully won every round. She felt exhilarated and nervous at the same time.

"I'm meant to lead the Runners."

The crowd outside the tent and throughout all the benches buzzed with the excitement of the day. The same questions were repeated everywhere.

"Who is she?"

"Can anyone defeat her?"

"Which clan is she from?"

The Blood Circle clan members knew exactly who she was. Whispers circulated through the crowd. "Tara is dead. How is it that we watch her fight?"

Kuro pushed his way toward Patha. He demanded permission to speak with the leader of the clans. Patha ordered his guard, who stood next to Kuro, to inform the young man it would be inappropriate to speak to a contestant during the test.

"You know who that is out there." Kuro looked past the guard and spoke to Patha anyway. "What are you going to do about it?"

Patha didn't answer and the guard stood between Patha and Kuro. "Patha will not speak with a contestant."

Disgusted, Kuro left Patha for the other side of the arena. It had been well over six cycles since Kuro had spoken with Dorm

Gowsky. Granted, the Neurian leader was no warrior. He had been, however, a means to an end. There had been no reason for Gowsky not to believe what Kuro had told him about Tara. And Kuro had believed Gowsky when he'd said Tara was dead. He'd been so excited with the news that he hadn't investigated to learn if it were true. Kuro would have unlimited power leading the clans. He'd been so close when he was younger, but Tara wouldn't have him.

The bitch! It wouldn't have surprised him a bit if she'd spread her legs for Gowsky in order to stay alive. Then she'd plotted her escape. That's what Tara did best – fucked men, then ran from them. She would not make a good leader of the Runners, he thought with bitter disgust.

He searched through the Gothman, looking for Darius. The Gothman were whooping and hollering and faking punches as they downed Runner ale. Darius was still sitting on the bench with several men around him, including his little brother.

Kuro pushed aggressively through the men and confronted Darius. "That's Tara, isn't it?"

Kuro had bellowed the question, and Darius looked annoyed at the rudeness. The other Gothman pushed Kuro back and grumbled something about showing respect to the Lord of Gothman. He had no intentions of respecting this race of people who possessed an Oldworld mentality much longer.

"She's supposed to be dead. What's going on here?" Kuro ignored the other Gothman and demanded an answer.

"You know as well as I do that Gothman aren't allowed to have anything to do with the Test of Wills." Lord Darius showed no expression as he downed his cup of ale. "We're just here to observe."

"No one can fight like that," Kuro snarled. "Except maybe Tara."

Darius stared blankly, and Kuro was furious. "I haven't seen her in five winters, and I can tell you without any doubt that is Tara. If you aren't so sure, then maybe your claim isn't as strong as you think. After all, you weren't able to keep her here the first time."

Darius leapt from where he was sitting and struck Kuro with his body while in midair. The two tumbled down the stadium benches to the ground. Gothman hurried out of the way in all directions, clearing a path for their lord so he could fight.

Kuro landed on his feet and stood inches from Darius' face. The rage in Darius' eyes was enough to make the largest of men back down. Kuro, however, stood tall and smiled.

"I knew I could get a rise out of you, my friend," he whispered. "I won't hurt her, I promise."

Darius lifted Kuro by his coat and shoved him backward. Kuro stumbled a few feet before regaining his balance, and raised a fist at the lord. But Darius moved fast and grabbed Kuro's fist with his gloved hand.

Kuro stared hard at the handsome lord, whose face came within inches of his own. He hated the man for taking Tara, and despised him even more for somehow managing to bring her back. He wouldn't let the hatred show. First he had to win the Test of Wills, only then would he put Lord of Gothman in his place.

"Fight her like a man," Lord Darius snarled, undaunted by the chivalrous smile. "She'll take you down like one."

"Trust me, my lord. I know exactly what she's capable of doing." Kuro's eyes gleamed. He yanked his hand free from Darius' and straightened his clothing. He slowly walked away from the outraged lord.

Patha announced the fights would continue, and the crowd pressed, again, against the arena. As Tara re-entered the arena and the crowd volume noticeably increased. Gothman and Runners pounded their boots on the wooden seats and hollered and yelled.

Tara stood in the center of the ring, calm and unharmed from the previous fights, letting the crowd show their respect. These people would follow her unconditionally. Kuro would have to kill her.

The next contestant entered the arena and Tara watched him, searching for any weaknesses he might possess as a warrior. He was a large man, standing head and shoulders over Tara. She recognized him as the one who had checked in when she had. He turned and held his hands over his head, causing the crowd to make even more noise.

Tara realized he was drunk. With his back turned, she jumped in the air and kicked him hard in the small of his back.

The crowd roared as he stumbled but did not fall.

He turned and howled at her. "Why you little bitch!"

Tara wasn't able to move fast before the man lunged forward, grabbed her, and threw her as if she weighed nothing. The ropes stopped her from falling, but she found her torso twisted in them and took a second to gather her bearings and balance. Hands were all over her, and Tara got the sensation that part of the crowd tried pushing her in, while others tried pulling her out of the arena.

Tara's clothes were twisted, and she felt groped as she finally faced her aggressor. A true warrior didn't always get to fight in the best of conditions.

"You're going to lose this one, little bitch," Bordo sneered and lunged at her again.

"And you're going to learn some manners," Tara hissed. She gathered her strength and jumped. Her legs went up, this time kicking him in the face. The heel of her boot hit him in the nose and blood splattered everywhere. It didn't stop the brute. This time when he picked her up, he slammed her to the ground.

Tara lay without moving. The large man stood over her breathing loudly, but she didn't move. The crowd yelled for her to get up and finish him off, but still she just lay there.

Reena's hands went to her face, and she started to cry.

"Don't worry, woman. I taught her this," Patha whispered.

Reena slowly spread her fingers and peeked between them, unable to stop watching her daughter in action. The large man approached Tara slowly. The noise from the crowd was deafening. Patha glanced around. Most didn't know the Runner who was undefeated and facing a giant. Already his daughter had their loyalty. He beamed with pride, although he was also pissed. Once Tara survived her way through this, and he had a feeling she would, she would go a couple rounds with him. Patha watched the giant Runner finally stick a foot under Tara to turn her over. Patha would wait out the Test of Wills, his people were too wound up to stop the event now. But when it was over, Tara would face his wrath! She already had the title she was out there fighting to win.

Tara moved so fast, most onlookers wailed their dismay when they missed what happened. She grabbed his foot, jumped up with lightning speed, and raised it high into the air, causing the man to fall on his back. Before he could move, she was on him.

After several punches to his face, she wrapped her hands around his neck and twisted his head within fractions of the breaking point. Then she sat on him and waited. Each time he tried to move, she turned his head just a little farther.

At last, the giant sobered enough to see his life was in her hands. He reached for the white cloth on his arm and threw it to the ground.

She jumped off, and the crowd sounded ready to riot.

The contestants that followed were all huge men. They hovered over her, and she made it look like a struggle to defeat each one of them. Each time, they lost, bloody and mad as hell. Tara remained unharmed.

At last the moment she dreaded arrived. Kuro entered the ring.

A hush fell around the arena as they saw the man predicted to win the Test of Wills stand before the undefeated woman.

Unlike the other warriors, Kuro stood facing Tara and bowed.

She stood undaunted and bowed in return. Then, to her surprise, he assumed the position of the ancient warriors: bent knees, straight back, arms bent with hands opened. He held the position until Tara matched the pose.

The crowd grew silent. No one moved. Everyone sat on the edges of their seats.

The Gothman were not familiar with this method of fighting, and most Runners had not studied it. Patha had taught Tara and Kuro the ancient fight when they were teenagers.

Kuro knew this would be the final proof he needed to convince himself that this Runner indeed the first, and in fact, only love of his life. Love as he understood it, of course. Tara was worth the fight, because with her came the rule of all Runner clans. When he'd lost the first battle for her love, he'd spent winters plotting and scheming. It was round two with Tara. This time he'd win.

Kuro began moving slowly around the arena, stepping lightly, and keeping his knees bent. He watched as the woman in front of him matched him move for move and not a peep came from the hundreds of onlookers. With speed quicker than the eye, Kuro darted toward her and chopped with his hand.

She blocked the chop with her arm, spun and kicked him while jumping into the air. He took the blow and returned one of his own. They continued to match each other, blow for blow. The crowd cheered, then grew silent after each attack.

Thirty minutes passed, and Tara had had enough of Kuro's style. He was mocking her and the ancient method of fighting. She unleashed her power, raging at him with blow after blow, not allowing him a warrior's courtesy of returning each blow.

Kuro went on the defensive, eager to find an opportunity to return to the offensive. The fear of defeat rose inside him, and not ready to accept it, he lunged and wrapped his arms around her.

She twisted, kicking and punching as he lifted her from the ground. She elbowed him hard in the ribs, causing instant pain throughout his body. He couldn't breathe. She damaged his insides but Kuro wasn't giving up. He knew how to defeat Tara.

As he let her go, he ripped her headscarf from her face. Both Gothman and Runner alike howled as their suspicions were confirmed, or realization hit them. As suddenly as they had gasped their amazement, the masses quieted, wondering how a dead woman was standing before them.

"What is this Test of Wills that you would have me fight a ghost?" Kuro turned and yelled to Patha. "No wonder she can defeat each warrior entering this arena. Will we let ourselves be ruled by a dead woman?"

The crowd stirred, murmuring as unrest created an unsettling feeling in the air.

Patha looked across the arena to Darius who returned his gaze. Neither wanted a riot to break out.

Tara glanced from Patha to Darius and guessed their thoughts. It would take little to stir the crowd. She glared at Kuro who had turned away as he uttered his disrespectful outcries to Patha. She jumped up and kicked him hard in the square of the back.

"Does that feel like the blow of a dead woman?" she screamed. The crowd roared with laughter as Kuro stumbled forward.

Tara showed no mercy and kicked him again, and he fell. Once on the ground, she hit him so hard in the side, he was unable to rise. She jumped on him and pulled his head back by his hair.

"Which part of me do you think is dead?" she said as she punched him on the side of the head. She threw his head to the ground and leaped to stand on his back. She jumped, landing on him so hard not an inch of breath was left in his lungs.

"I'm not dead and have returned to the land and people I love." She shook her head enjoying the cold breeze on her sweat-soaked face.

The crowd cheered and slowly began to chant her name. "Tara! Tara!" The sound grew louder and louder. Gothman and Runner jumped to their feet and roared. "Tara! Tara!"

Kuro appeared lifeless at her feet, and for a moment she wondered if he were dead. A doctor was escorted into the arena and soon called for a stretcher. With relief, Tara watched Kuro carried through the crowd.

She now stood alone in the arena as the crowd continued to chant. She turned to Patha, who looked at her with a hardened look she knew well. He wasn't happy to have been left in the dark. She clasped her hands in front of her and bowed low in respect.

Patha stood and was assisted down the stairs by several attendants.

Tara noticed how slowly he moved and hurried toward him as he entered the arena. He waved away the attendants and took Tara's hand as she helped him move to the center of the arena.

The crowd slowly sat and waited for the ruler of all clans to speak. Patha bent over and picked up her headscarf. As he reached to place it back on her head, she stopped his hand.

"No," she said loudly enough for all to hear. "I wear the clothes of the Runner to show the pride I have in my people. But, from this day forward, I will not cover my head so that I may honor my mama's people, the Gothman."

The crowd gasped as they heard about her mixed heritage for the first time. "I stand before you as rightful heir and future leader of all Runner clans. I also stand before you as Lord Darius' claim, the leader of Gothman."

Patha turned to Darius and raised his hand to salute and show respect to the Lord of Gothman.

Escorted by his guards, Darius led a small procession into the arena.

Patha took his hand and placed it in the hand of his daughter. He then turned and faced the crowd. "This day will be remembered for many winters to come. All of you have witnessed a great event in our history. We can tell our children and our grandchildren that we were present the day Runners and Gothman were truly united as one nation with two races that will never be defeated."

At this, the crowd stood and cheered loudly.

Darius turned to Tara and pulled her close. "You were incredible," he whispered.

She smiled up at him. "Crator told me I'd be victorious."

CHAPTER TWENTY-THREE

THE GUARDS encountered a major challenge creating a path through the crowds for Patha, Tara, and Darius. The leaders' motorcycles were brought to them, and once they were on them and surrounded by even more guards, they were able to move through the crowd with more ease. They rode slowly down the main street toward their home. A lot of the crowd followed, cheering their allegiance.

The party would continue into the night. Tara and Darius planned on joining them after a private family reunion.

Tara entered the house through the front door this time. She was nearly attacked by Reena and Hilda. Syra and Torgo were not too far behind. Hugs and kisses and tears followed. Then, of course, there were the twins.

Tara collapsed to the floor and gathered her children into her arms. She felt immediate panic and dismay when the two did not respond as eagerly and, in fact, pulled away.

"Don't worry, child." Reena patted her shoulder. "You did the same thing to me when I had an opportunity to see you at times when you were young. They'll learn who you are once again. It won't take you long to gain their love. Syra, be a good lass now and take them upstairs. Tara can come see them privately in a short while."

Syra reluctantly led the two toddlers by their hands and slowly climbed the stairs. "I miss out on everything," she mumbled.

"I can't believe you're alive!" Torgo exclaimed, and unceremoniously gave her a hug.

He had grown a lot taller than Tara in the past six cycles. He was as skinny as he was tall, but his muscle structure indicated he would soon look just like his brother.

"I couldn't believe I was dead." Tara laughed, feeling happier at that moment than she had in a long time.

The boy stood next to his brother. "You were incredible today. I've never seen anyone fight like that before."

"It *was* an incredible show," Darius added.

"More like unbelievable." Tara faced her family, beaming from ear to ear.

"Unbelievable is right." Patha entered the room. "Leave us everyone. I wish to talk with Darius and Tara alone." The tone in his voice was enough to clear the room.

Patha stood in front of his daughter with his hands on his hips. "Absolutely unbelievable!" Patha walked to the other end of the room before turning and glaring at his daughter.

She looked at him blankly, her smile fading. She glanced at Darius and then at her papa. "I can't take all the credit, Papa."

Patha walked quickly to his daughter and slapped her across the face with his glove.

She stood frozen; not able to remember the last time Patha had struck her.

Darius' muscles tightened, but he didn't allow his facial expression to change. Gothman were taught as children to respect their parents and their rulers. He remained silent.

"That was an incredibly stupid stunt you pulled. You almost started a riot. And why? Your pride and that damn ego of yours. What were you trying to prove out there?" Patha snapped. Then he turned to Darius. "And you? You knew she was here. You probably thought this was all rather amusing. You two are pathetic!"

Patha turned and paced across the room again. He walked back and forth as the two stood there, motionless and expressionless, like two children waiting for punishment. Patha stared out the window, down at the town, which was lit up for the celebration. "How long have you been here?"

"I arrived yesterday, Patha. But I didn't do any of this out of pride or ego."

"Enough. You're my heir. The Test of Wills did not need to happen. Why didn't you contact me and let me know you were alive?"

"I didn't have a landlink. After crossing the border I came across a clan, and they took care of me. Patha, all their stories were about the Test of Wills—the glory it would bring them, the triumphs they would have. If I announced that I was alive, Runners would have been in an uproar. All those who entered the Test of Wills had attracted followers, individuals who believed, for whatever reason, that their applicant would be the best ruler for the Runners. I saw such turmoil in this one clan. All the other clans would be in a similar state."

"And you wanted all Runners and Gothman to follow you unconditionally. Well, Tara-girl, you have that. They will! But you could have sacrificed everything if you'd lost. Those were not good odds. It was foolish." Patha was still in a rage. He turned on Darius, "You went out to see if the written test came from Tara and came back and lied." He glared with unleashed fury. "If you were my son, I'd flog you for that. As my daughter's claim, I believe I still have that right."

Patha stared at one and then the other. After a moment of silence he spoke, his tone quieter. "I'm very happy that you're alive, Tara-girl. I simply will not tolerate being lied to ever! Is that understood?"

Both of them nodded silently.

"I fear your thinking is still too reckless to rule two nations," Patha continued and at this both Tara and Darius stirred.

"That's not true—" Darius began but didn't finish when Patha raised his hand.

"It is true. What would you have done if someone had started to win over her? Would you have shot them? That would have started a war. And a bloody one at that."

"Patha, I knew I wouldn't lose."

"And how did you know that? Are you returned from the dead? Can you no longer be killed?"

"No, that's not it. It's Crator. He told me I would win, if I had faith."

"Crator? Is that what you said? And what do you know about Crator?"

"Do you know about Him?"

Patha didn't answer. Instead, he moved over to the couch and took his time sitting. He looked up at his daughter with raised eyebrows, and Tara saw how he'd aged in six cycles. "So has the dog-woman come to you?"

Tara gasped, but then sat across from Patha and smiled. Patha always knew everything. She shouldn't be surprised. "Yes, she's come to me. I'd never have made it home without her."

"And now you believe? You have faith?"

"Yes, I do." She looked up and reached for Darius' hand, and he moved to her side. "Darius has seen her in his dreams, too."

Patha looked up at Darius. "I've also seen her in my dreams," he told both of them.

"So Crator has spoken to all of us," Darius said. "We now have an entity guiding us and protecting us. Tara, we can claim all of Nuworld!"

"I think Crator has always been guiding and protecting us. We're just now figuring out He exists." Tara looked first at Patha, then at Darius. "If we plan to claim every nation, I fear we'll work very hard to do so."

"But it will be possible." Darius grinned at the thought, completely putting the reprimand out of his head. "Look at what happened in that arena today."

"Are you saying I couldn't fight like that on my own?"

"According to you, you've never fought on your own. Crator has always helped you."

"It was an incredible fight, wasn't it?" Tara grinned.

"I don't think this Crator would have stopped you from making a fool of yourself, though." Patha still scolded. "You need to start acting like a ruler, Tara-girl."

"I can rule." Tara felt challenged.

"Then no more running away from your problems!"

Tara was taken aback by this.

Darius shifted his weight and looked awkward.

"You will prepare a report for me outlining everything you know about the Neurians." Patha slowly stood. "In six cycles, both of you will perform the Runner wedding ceremony. In front of all Runners and Gothman, you will take your vows to rule these two nations, remain with each other 'til death, and be loyal to each other from this day forward!" He looked at them fiercely, then walked to the kitchen door. "Now, prepare yourselves for the celebration."

Tara hurried to the nursery after she'd showered and changed. The twins delighted in the attention, although Tara was no more than a friendly face to them. She sat on the floor and let them show her their favorite toys and bring books to her. But if one of them got hurt or wanted a toy the other had, they ran to Syra, and then to Darius, when he entered the room. They did not honor Tara with this attention.

"They don't remember me at all." She was overwhelmed with sadness as she stroked the soft curls falling past Ana's shoulders.

"Give them time." Reena had stuck her head in behind Darius, and now entered. "They'll be demanding all your attention before you know it, Tara-girl. You'll see."

Tara didn't want to leave them but affectionately hugged and kissed each child before she finally did. They were absolutely beautiful children, and she vowed that she would focus all her time on them starting tomorrow. They had a mama who loved them, and she wanted them to know it.

It was bitterly cold when Tara and Darius left the house. There were more people on the streets of Bryton than had been there earlier that day. They cheered and waved as the two drove by. A few children who had been allowed to stay up late chased after them as they rode their bikes slowly into town.

The valley at the end of town was consumed by activity. Hundreds of Gothman and Runners flooded the area. Three huge fires were obvious from the distance. The closest one appeared to be a good fifteen feet up into the air and was eight to ten feet in diameter. A small crowd, all in black or dark brown leather, stood around the massive fire, laughing and talking loudly.

The crowd parted to allow Darius and Tara close to the fire. Tara accepted a mug of ale and soon lost sight of Darius as she mingled with the crowd, moving from conversation to conversation.

Several drunken Gothman standing nearby were loudly making jokes about the female Runner who defeated all rivals in battle that day. Their comments insulted her gender, but she knew she would have to let the two races work out their differences. If she'd ordered their silence at that moment, they wouldn't be any closer to accepting the equality of men and women.

She watched with interest as several Runner women approached the men and began challenging their accusations. The Gothman humbly begged forgiveness but continued to insult the women with their suggestive lewd comments.

"I must say I like the way these Runner women look in all their leather." A large, drunk Gothman grabbed one of the Runner women.

"I wish I could say the same about you." The Runner woman smiled as the Gothman grabbed her then sent a hard blow straight to his stomach.

The two other Gothman burst into laughter and slapped their legs as the first Gothman stumbled backwards and slid on the packed snow. "Looks like someone needs to teach you some manners," he said, working to gain his balance on the frozen ground.

The Runner knocked the man back to the ground before he could stand. She lunged at the other two Gothman but they backed up. "We don't want to hurt you. We're just having a little fun."

"Oh, please, hurt me." The Runner woman mocked the men as she followed them, grabbing the back of their pants. "You're too cute to leave alone."

Disgusted, the men walked away.

The Runner laughed as she turned to face Tara. "Not bad, huh, sis?"

"Tasha, is that you?" Tara stared dumbfounded.

"Don't tell me you've forgotten your own sister? Although I guess I'm not as exciting as you are with all your adventures. Who would have thought you'd show up for the Test of Wills?"

Tara noted disappointment in her sister's words. "I take it you were cheering for someone else?"

"Well, Kuro, of course. He's wanted to lead the clan for so many winters. If you hadn't broken his heart the way you did, he'd be heir to lead."

"I think he wanted to lead the clans more than he wanted me, Tasha."

"It sounds like you just don't know how to keep your men happy."

Tara didn't like the tone in her sister's voice.

"It's a shame, that's all," Tasha continued. "Kuro had everything worked out so well. Considering how intelligent the Neurians are, who would have thought they'd turn out to be so superstitious."

"What did you say?"

Tasha hesitated for a second, then smiled again. "You should congratulate me, you know." She'd quickly changed the subject.

Tara was processing her sister's words about Kuro and didn't respond to her last statement.

"Fine, don't congratulate me. You're not the only one who can provide grandchildren, though. I'm pregnant!" she said triumphantly.

"Congratulations," Tara said simply. "Do you know who the papa is?"

"Of course I do. I won't upset you with the details though. I just hope it grows up to look and act just like its papa." Tasha smiled. "I'm sure we'll see each other again soon."

Tasha walked away, leaving Tara repeating Tasha's words in her head. What did she mean by her comments on the Neurians? And when had her sister become so loyal to Kuro?

Snow started to fall, and slowly the crowd thinned. Tara found herself near the makeshift hospital that had been set up for the wounded of the Test of Wills. She didn't feel obligated to see each and every contestant she'd injured. That would insult their honor. However, she wanted to see how Kuro was doing.

After politely listening to the opinions of several older Runners on how navigational training should be taught to the next generation, Tara excused herself and entered the large tent.

"Now don't tell me you've discovered an injury." Dr. Digo smiled as she entered the sanitized environment.

"I'm sure I'll be sore in the morning." She smiled back and rubbed her arms.

"I'd be surprised if you're not. So, Tara, what can I do for you?"

"I thought I'd see how Kuro is doing."

"Oh?" The tone in the doctor's voice told Tara he remembered their steamy teenage romance.

"Yes, is that okay?"

"I don't see why not. He's behind the first curtain." The doctor hesitated. "Tara, you should know, he's seriously injured. If we get him through the night, he may survive."

Tara nodded but didn't respond. She didn't regret their fight.

The large tent had cubicles with walls made from animal hide. The thickness of the hides added to the warmth in each room. However, machines rumbled inside the tent to force heat into the pseudo-hospital.

Kuro lay on an elevated, thin metal bed. It was collapsible, and therefore could easily be set up, torn down and moved, as needed. He had a bandage wrapped around his head with visible red stains on it. His chest was bare, thickly wrapped with more white bandages. Tara glanced at them, wondering how coherent he would be.

"Hey, beautiful." Kuro opened his eyes and smiled at Tara. "We put on quite a show out there, didn't we?"

"I got a serious reprimand for it." Tara smiled back at Kuro. "How're you feeling?"

"It's not as bad as it looks. How're you feeling?"

"My bruises are well covered," Tara lied.

"I'd love to rub salve on them." He smiled wickedly and then winced as he shifted position in the bed. "So, how did you like the Neurians?" Kuro struggled with a short chuckle. His eyes were glazed from the drugs the doctor had probably given him.

"They weren't that friendly." Tara moved closer to the bed. "Have you been down that way?"

"Ah, now, aren't you the tricky one?" He waved a finger at her. "You already know everything, don't you? I never doubted you were the best leader. I knew I would work at your side better than Lord Darius would have. He's so jealous. You two would do nothing but try to control each other. It would be such a distraction for you. You and I would have ruled as a team, though, just the way we planned it when we were kids."

"But we're not kids anymore, Kuro. Why don't you tell me exactly what you were doing in Southland?"

"Exploring, just like you were." Kuro got a faraway look in his eyes. "If they weren't so superstitious, everything would have worked out just fine."

"What would have worked out, Kuro?"

"You were supposed to return after I was ruler. Then we would fall back in love, and you would rule with me. It was planned so carefully." Kuro shrugged. "They needed to reestablish trade. No one wants that opium of theirs. Although I hear it makes sex fantastic."

"And you pointed out trade could be established with their oil."

"Yes, once I was leader."

Tara looked at Kuro in disbelief. "And so you devised the plan for me to be drugged?" Rage ran through her body. She looked at him coldly, her fists clenched. "How did you convince the Neurians to put me to sleep for six cycles?"

A gurgling sound came up from his throat when Kuro made another attempt at a chuckle. He grasped his bandaged side. "Six cycles? Gowsky was supposed to kill you. I had a backup plan in case he couldn't. I know what kind of effect you have on men, sweetheart. I worried he wouldn't be able to do it. It made him crazy not to go help you in that burning building. I knew that."

He looked at her, smiling. "I told him once I ruled the clans, the Runners would negotiate a contract to buy their oil. I told him it would never work with the current leaders of the Runners and Gothman. Gowsky trusted me. But he trusts that Crator-god of theirs more," he said with disgust.

Tara pulled her laser and aimed it. "Your lack of faith in Crator has resulted in your own demise."

"You are so beautiful when you're angry."

A long time ago she would have melted in his arms if he'd smiled as he was now.

"You won't shoot me. I know you still love me. I can see it in your eyes."

Tara aimed her weapon straight at his face.

Laser fire whistled through the air. Kuro died instantly.

Tara gasped in surprise. She hadn't shot him! Who had? She spun around and watched as Darius lowered his laser and returned it to his pocket.

Instead of looking at her, he turned and disappeared. She looked back at Kuro, lowered her head and stood with respect for the dead warrior for a long moment. Kuro hadn't died an honourable death, though. It had been his own choices that brought his dishonor. Then, slowly, she walked out of the makeshift room and left the large tent.

The snow and wind had stopped. A heavy, gray sky showed patches of deep, rich black where the clouds had pulled away. Most of the celebration had disappeared into the Runners' trailers or Gothman taverns when the snow had resumed falling. Light from remaining fires lit her path as she followed Darius, who walked in front of her, heading for their bikes.

"I would have killed him," she said as she straddled her bike.

"I felt I deserved the honor."

Tara looked up at the sky. The moon appeared through a black tear in thick gray clouds. She studied it for a minute, remembering the lady in the burning building who had talked about the Lunians colonizing the moon.

"Do you think there are people living up there?" She turned and looked at the rugged features of Darius' strong face.

"I don't know."

"I was told there's a colony living up there."

Darius looked surprised. He stared at the moon for a moment. "I'm sure if there are people up there, you'll see to it that they follow you unconditionally, my lady."

He started his bike and headed across the packed snow toward the house.

Tara took one last look at the moon and followed him.

ABOUT THE AUTHOR

Laurie Fitzgerald lives in Kansas with her three sons, four very vocal cats, and her Boston Terrier and Beagle. She spends her days writing, pruning her many rose bushes, and painting while listening to audio books.

Creating worlds has always been Laurie's favorite pass time. This book, and the rest of the Nuworld series, originated from a dream. Although inspired in many different ways over the years, the exciting part for Laurie is taking that glimpse into a new world and exploring it while getting to know the people who live there. You can explore these different worlds she's created as well. Visit www.lauriefitzgerald.net or www.lorieoclare.com (Laurie also writes as Lorie O'Clare) to learn more about her books, read excerpts, and find out what book Laurie is working on now.

Coming in February 2014 ~ **Nuworld: Tara's Revenge, book 2**

Keep reading for a glimpse at
Tara's Revenge.

EXCERPT FROM
NUWORLD: TARA'S REVENGE
BOOK 2

The Blood Circle Clan buzzed with activity, and Tara used caution as she steered her bike through the densely packed parked trailers and motorcycles. She looked for Tasha, which wasn't an easy task since she had no idea what kind of trailer her half-sister might have or what kind of bike she rode.

Tara moved through the camp, greeting people the way she'd originally planned. Her comm beeped.

"Tara?" Darius' baritone almost growled.

"Yes?"

"What are you doing?"

"I'm greeting my clan members."

"Your papa told you to do that tonight."

"Darius, I've got to do this." She cut communication at that point, not wishing to hear any lectures on obedience. Spotting Balbo walking alongside several trailers, Tara pulled up next to him.

"Tara, now this is a welcome sight." Balbo opened his arms.

Tara jumped off her bike to run into them. Her older step-brother had always been there for her as she grew up. She longed to unload on him the insults Tasha had spoken. As a child, he'd often comforted her after she and her sister fought. Tara understood why Tasha was jealous. After all, Tasha's mama had taken Tara in as her own and helped raise her. Tara had shown the qualities of a leader, not Tasha. But Tara wasn't a child anymore, and her half-brother didn't need the burden of her problems, so Tara held her tongue.

Balbo was a jovial man, in spite of having a daughter he was raising alone, and who was already starting to run wild. Tara never wanted to change that trait in him. She would set Tasha straight once she found her.

"It's so good to see you." Tara smiled and let go of Balbo. "I think someone else might be anxious to see you as well, not that she'd admit it."

"Has she behaved herself?" Balbo seemed prepared to hear the worse.

"She's been a great help." Tara avoided the answer she knew Balbo dreaded hearing.

Over Balbo's shoulder, a familiar figure approached. Tara stiffened. Her heart started thumping as adrenaline pumped into her system. Balbo turned to see what had caught her attention. The figure disappeared between two trailers, and Tara looked back at Balbo.

"What was it?"

"Nothing. I'll talk with you soon." She gave him a quick hug and hurried to where she'd just seen her sister.

As Tara walked between the two trailers, the sun disappeared behind one of them. Goose bumps travelled over her flesh. Children played at the other end of the trailers. A sight pleasant enough, but for some reason an ominous sensation trickled through her.

Tara remembered the excitement of settling in and having an area to call her own for a while. She reached down to help steady a toddler that had taken off too fast and started between the trailers. Several feet away, an infant sat on the ground holding steadfast to the long hair of an older child who wailed profusely in protest.

When she reached the end of the two trailers, the sun that hit her didn't warm her. Instead it seemed oddly cold for such a bright day. Tara gently released the child's hair from the infant's grasp. The child cried miserably and ran in the apparent direction of her mama.

"Well now, is this fun?" Tara smiled and reached down to scoop up the infant. The child reached for Tara's necklace, a teardrop-shaped ruby with a silver circle around it. The symbol of the Blood Circle Clan. A gift from Darius. "No, no," she said gently and held the child's hand.

The baby boy looked up into her face, and Tara froze. He had blond curls and the darkest gray eyes. She stared at the child in disbelief. He looked like Andru had at that age.

Two hands roughly ripped away the infant from her. "What are you doing?"

"I was…" Tara started, surprised, realizing the child had distracted her to the point of not recognizing the voice. She stood up straight and the amiability left her as she stared at her sister.

Tasha held the child close to her chest and cuddled him, smiling wickedly.

Tara was dumbfounded.

The little boy looked at Tasha, then at Tara. His chubby hand reached for Tara.

Tasha pulled it back, snuggling it with her own hand. "This is your Aunt Tara," she whispered to the baby although loud enough for Tara to hear. "You two have a lot in common." Again the wicked smile.

Look For NUWORLD: TARA'S REVENGE in February 2014

www.ingramcontent.com/pod-product-compliance
Lightning Source LLC
Chambersburg PA
CBHW020237200626
46816CB00001BA/17